A.H.M. SCHOLTZ

A Place Called Vatmaar

*A living story of a time
that is no more*

Translated by Chris van Wyk

KWELA BOOKS

First published in 1995 as
Vatmaar – 'n Lewendagge verhaal van 'n tyd wat nie meer is nie
Translated from the Afrikaans by Chris van Wyk

Copyright text © 2000 Kwela Books
28 Wale Street, Cape Town 8001
P.O. Box 6525, Roggebaai 8012
Copyright cover picture © Duggan-Cronin Collection,
McGregor Museum, Kimberley

Cover design and typography by Nazli Jacobs
Set in Plantin
Printed and bound by NBP, Drukkery Street
Goodwood, Western Cape
First edition, first printing 2000

ISBN 0-7957-0104-7

Contents

Dear Reader

I am going to tell a story of the coloured people of South Africa. They did not come from the North and also not from overseas. They originated here, true South Africans, who may one day be called Azanians.

Vatmaar's people were poor, simple, unpolished and tender. If one understands them as they are, one starts loving them. Ugly faces there were none, and they always treated a stranger with respect.

I will remember them.

The people of Vatmaar thank the typist, Philomena Baker, with gratitude for her selfless and humble labour.

A.H.M. Scholtz, Mafikeng.

Harry Lewis
The Mall

Rudolf Kamies
Happy Dreams

Koen La...
Klein Me...

Graveyard

du Toits pan
(Dam)

Nellie's Ouma
Mohameds
Ma Khumalo
Nellie Naleidie
Mr. May
Motta
Stoffel Jones
Cloeters

Old du Toits pan

Harry Look

Con. Ch.
Shop
Wing new

D.R.C.
Rectory

Cath Ch.

A.G.S.

Brd. ho

MAS. Ten

Shop
Bosmans

Mine Co
Lawyer   Council
Kosters

School
Shop

NEW TOWN

Court
C.O.E.
Lawyer   Police   BANK

HOTEL

Road

Gaol

Platsfield
Sports field

Square

□ Stoffel Jones
Cape cart

Du Toits
STATION

National Road to Cape Town

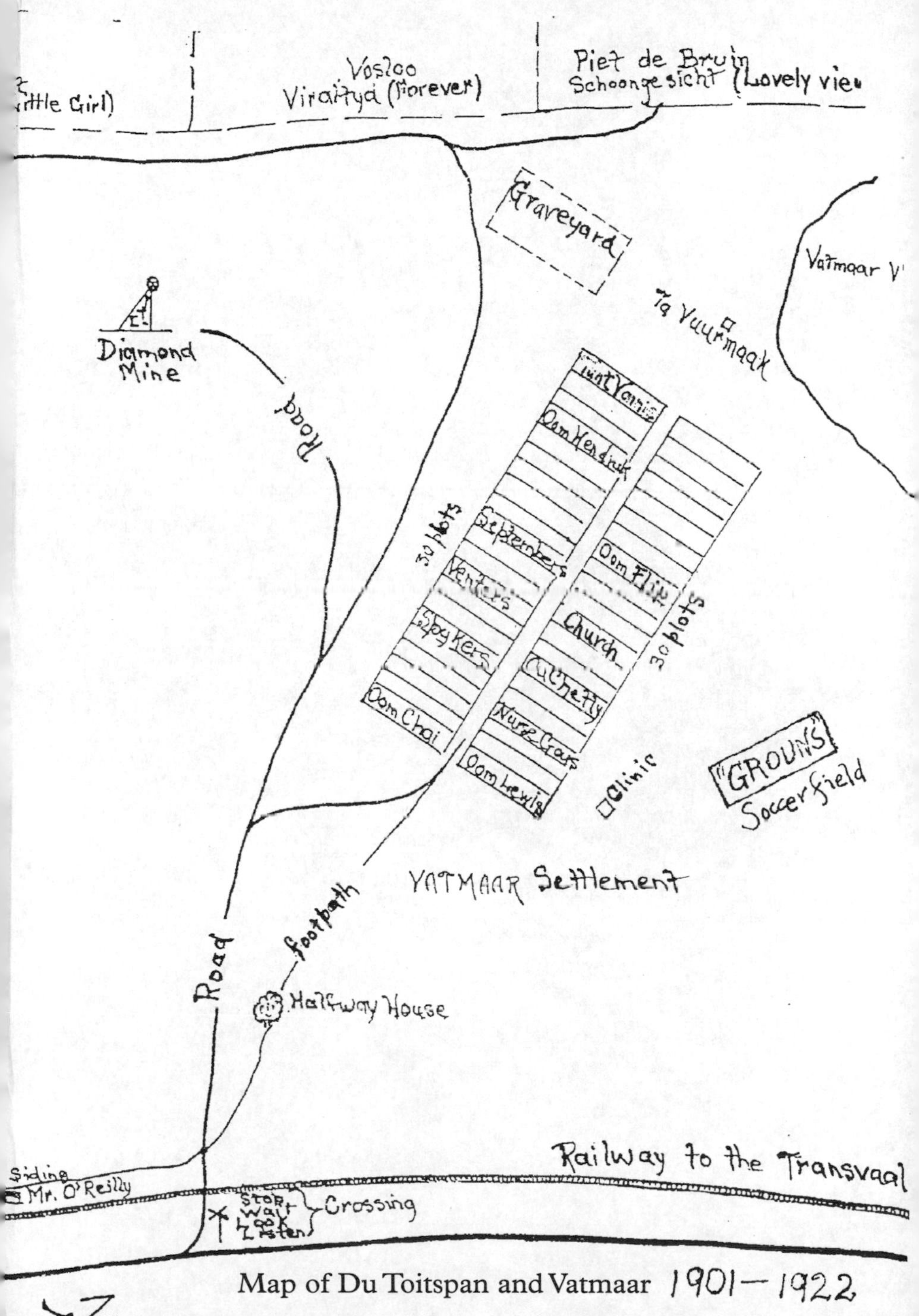

Map of Du Toitspan and Vatmaar 1901–1922

Vatmaar

Our home was a tiny settlement called Vatmaar, about four miles from Du Toitspan, a town with water taps in the houses and lights which you could put on by pressing on a button. There were high poles in Du Toitspan with thin wires tied to crosspieces of wood which our cleverer friends called telephone wires. None of us in Vatmaar had ever seen a telephone before. Our average age was about twelve years.

In Vatmaar we had to light candles in the evenings which you could buy for one a penny at our Coolie shop and two for a penny in Du Toitspan. Our water came from wells. The water was close to the surface if you had to dig a well, and as far as the oupas and oumas could remember, never dried up.

In Vatmaar we could keep our own animals for slaughter and make our own vegetable gardens.

A plot of two morgen cost fifteen shillings – one week's wages for most working folks. This was just for the corner pegs which the town council surveyor came to show you, because only the corner pegs were yours, not the plot. There were no wire fences, just the corner pegs.

The plots ran along one hundred yards of the street. There were sixty such plots – thirty on each side of the street which Ta Vuurmaak had scraped open before we were born, when he dragged his train water tank with his four oxen to the vlei.

The people of Vatmaar had to pay five shillings yearly to the Du Toitspan Town Council. For this they also got grazing rights on the Du Toitspan common. So, for the ownership of a plot, a new resident had to put down one pound – fifteen shillings for the corner pegs and five shillings for the yearly fee.

But first he had to go to the town council office and stand in front of a plan of Vatmaar. And to the question: Where? he had to say:

Near so and so. In those days almost no resident could read and write so the new resident just got the number of the plot on the receipt paper, and his name was written on the Vatmaar Settlement Plan. He then had to make sure he was in Vatmaar at nine o'clock the following Saturday morning to wait for the Cape-boy to come and show him the plot.

Saturday at sunrise, the new resident, and maybe also his family and friends, were already sitting and waiting for the Cape-boy who came to check if he had taken the right plot. When the man came past the halfway-house (a big camel thorn tree on the short cut to Du Toitspan) they clapped and shouted: There he is! There he is! And then they began to argue over who had seen him first.

It was always an old man on a bicycle, not at all a "boy", with a piece of rolled up paper in his hand and a wide smile on his face. Between the handlebars of his bicycle was a board with the words: *Du Toitspan Town Council.*

His first words were usually: Where is so and so?

At this point the new resident took off his hat and said, Here he is, Oom.

As soon as the corner pegs were shown, the onlookers brought stones and packed them around the pegs. The new resident's wife, and sometimes even the man himself, then kissed the ground and said, Thank you, Lord.

Then it was time for the luck – a paraffin tin full of khadie or Kaffirbeer, and a tot of sherry for the grown ups. Every drinker saved a bit of the drink and threw it on the ground with the words: That is the piss.

A young Griqua and his wife from Daniëlskuil also bought a plot. And after being shown the pegs, his wife said to him: Petrus, do what our forefathers did. He then walked around the plot and peed on all four pegs with the pee from one bladder.

Wild lions also mark their places like that with their pee, someone said.

Sometimes, but almost never, a prayer was said.

After the luck Oom Chai usually took the spade and said to the new resident: Now for the water. When they agreed on the spot, Oom Chai said: Thank you, Lord, for giving me the honour to take out the first spadeful of soil. Then all Vatmaar's people, young and old, helped to dig. And before the sun went down, Vatmaar had one more well.

There was no such thing as throwing rubbish about. Each one of us had a refuse hole on a corner of his plot and all rubbish was thrown in there, with the ash of the day's fire on top.

There was then still no church or police station to put fear into our hearts. No football team or dance hall to distract us. No doctors and lawyers to depend on. There were just footpaths in the veld with holes that closed on their own when it rained. And there were short cuts everywhere.

Vatmaar was poor, and yet we did not know poverty. I can't remember ever seeing a pregnant, unmarried woman. There were more children than grown ups. Oupas always said: I can still do that little job.

Deaths were wide apart but every now and then a baby was born. Nobody died of cancer because that was a rich man's sickness, but against diphtheria children never had a chance. And there were two kinds of TB: the fat one and the thin one.

Our children fought more than enough, but when our parents had an argument they said to each other: Be careful, the neighbours can hear you.

Vatmaar's children never knew about the Eighth Commandment, the one about Thou shalt not steal. We could never resist taking a spin with another man's bicycle. And we enjoyed running around with an old bicycle wheel without spokes or tube with a stick in the groove.

Toothache scared us more than anything else, because the victim had to walk to Du Toitspan with a rag around his mouth to keep out the wind. You had to go and pay a shilling at the hospital's Out Patients and then wait your turn outside with the other patients because the doctor didn't want the patients who were waiting to hear the screaming. Sometimes you tried to wait the pain away and then you got the feeling to run away. But the receipt paper for the shilling which you had already paid, kept you in the queue. The tooth was sommer pulled out alive. Only those who could afford it, paid extra for chloroform.

There was another thing we were scared of – that the doctor would break your tooth off. Some used to say: I should rather have used cloves and snuff. And when the doctor was finished with one person, then those who were still waiting outside wanted to know: How does he pull?

Most of the time we were in the hands of a horse doctor who used to say: Thank God it's out!

According to the white elite of Du Toitspan all the people of Vatmaar were the same, but we had our own I'm-better-than-you types. These were usually the English speakers.

Long hair, blue eyes and a light skin also caused jealousy.

The people had different words to describe their countrymen. In those days these names were totally suitable and acceptable, even those words which sound offensive today and which are not used any more.

The white people who fought against the English were called Boers (before they became Afrikaners) and the English were Rednecks. "British subject" were words which the Boers hated. All adults who were not from overseas and who were not white were called "boys" and "girls". The English called brown people "Capeboys" and sometimes "coloureds" – to the Boers they were Basters or Hotnots. A black man from Africa was a Kaffir and an Indian was a Coolie. Sometimes these words were used on purpose just to hurt a person's feelings, but most of the time neither the one who used the word nor the one who was so called, knew any better.

It was the custom to call an Englishman Mister and his wife Madam, a Boer was called Baas or Meneer and his wife Miesies when people spoke among themselves. Posh brown people were Mister and Missus. We called the grown ups Oupa and Ouma and Oom and Tante and they called each other Sis and Sissie and Cousin.

When I tell the story of Vatmaar I use all these words as they were used in those days – with the greatest love and respect and without wanting to hurt anyone.

Some people said that Vatmaar got its name from Ta Vuurmaak. He lived in a huge train water tank. It was covered on top with branches and grass to stop the iron from getting too hot in summer and too cold in winter.

The tank was near the vlei, not in the settlement, so Ta Vuurmaak did not pay a yearly fee. He made Kimberley bricks out of clay and driftsand which he collected with his wheelbarrow. A brick was twelve inches by nine inches by four inches and he sold them at two pennies each. All Vatmaar's houses were built with Ta Vuurmaak's Kimberleys.

Oom Flip carted the bricks with his trolley and for this he was paid in Kimberleys whether it was a load of twenty or fifty bricks. This did not include labour – you had to pack and offload the bricks yourself.

Ta Vuurmaak was the oldest oupa in Vatmaar and he always said the other oupas are young enough to be his children. Vatmaar called him Ta – father – Vuurmaak.

He wasn't a big man but he looked big. He always wore long pants with the legs cut off. He had bandy legs and people said: He can't catch a pig. His body was full of long, ugly scars, each one with its own story. He wore sandals made from riempies which he bought from Tant Vonnie.

He once said that by the time of the Rinderpest (1896), he had already sent his second wife back to her mama because she could not give him children. What he could not understand, he always said with a laugh, is that both women took other men and gave them children.

Ta Vuurmaak always wore a cap. When he took it off you saw

the nicest bald head you could ever imagine. With his toothless mouth he could eat the toughest meat. His eyes were always half closed. They were just two slits and you could never see the colour. His face, neck, hands and knees were all a bundle of bunched up wrinkles which made one believe he was well over a hundred.

He never forgets what he's seen, people said.

Ta Vuurmaak tells about the Queen's Cape-boys

On the Sunday after the day when the old people got their pension, we young ones always went to visit Ta Vuurmaak at his "cabin". That's what Tommy Lewis used to call the train water tank and everyone started using the name. Then Ta Vuurmaak used to tell us old stories of Vatmaar. He always had a bottle of sherry stored away for the occasion.

I could never understand why white people kill each other, Ta Vuurmaak said. A long time ago the English used to say they would give their lives for an old woman they called Queen and even though they didn't really fight seriously, the Boers, who had done nothing wrong, mowed down these Queen's people like wild animals.

I was sitting there on the square at the station where everybody who was looking for work came to sit, and where people came if they needed workers. Then along came this man called Chai to hire five Cape-boys to work for the Queen. There were just three of us and I don't know where he got the other two.

He then took us to an Englishman who told us he was Lance-Corporal Lewis. They would pay us sixpence a day plus rations – a tin of bully-beef and biscuits. We had to take our orders from this boy – and he pointed to Chai.

In those days there was no other work, just war work. The Rednecks called him Corporal because he wore one stripe on his arm. He and a company of four other men were on horseback. And we five boys and the rations were on a wagon with eight oxen.

We didn't know what our work was and we were scared of the Boers because they never missed with those Mausers of theirs. On the second day Chai told us that we were now in the Transvaal and that we should sleep lightly.

Shortly after that we found out what we were supposed to do.

Two of us had to watch the farm house. In the meantime the wagon with the Queen's men waited where they could not be seen. We had to look to see if there weren't any men around, so usually we went to the house and asked if we could have water from the well. But we had to be very careful of the Boer woman. Nothing scared her. See this scar here?

Ta Vuurmaak pointed to a long mark on his calf.

An old ouma who was watching us is responsible for this.

If we didn't spot any men we went to say so. Then the four men and the Corporal surrounded the farm house and the others brought the wagon nearer. It was then our job to see that the household's food and other things were loaded onto the wagon. Then one of us boys and one of the Queen's men had to take them to the concentration camp. That was what they called a jail for women and children. And before the wagon left, we, the boys, had to set fire to the farm house. This was so that the Boers could see what happens to those who want to fight the Queen.

Tell us more, Oupa, we urged him on.

One day this Kapenaar and I were walking past this vegetable garden when we saw these delicious big carrots. It was very quiet, not a dog barking. I got onto the stone wall that was built around the garden and I was just about to jump off and pull out a few carrots when – boom! It felt like something had knocked against my knee. I jumped off and ran. While running I thought: Vuurmaak, you can't be dead because I can feel you running.

When I got to the Queen's wagon, the Kapenaar was already there waiting for me. His name was Gamat. He looked at me with unbelieving eyes.

Gamat, I said to him, did you fly then?

Nay, Oom, he said, Oom know they don' shoot miss.

The Corporal said it was just a flesh wound.

My children, Ta Vuurmaak said to us, I'm not stupid. Long after the wound had healed I was still wearing the bandages on my leg. Whenever we had to do something that I didn't want to do, I made as if I couldn't walk on this leg. And I felt so good whenever Chai said: Leave the cripple-arse alone.

While he stroked the old scar, he said with his toothless smile: This is my very own truth.

We all looked at Ta Vuurmaak while each thought his own thoughts.

At the first farm house there was only an old ouma, a pregnant woman and two little girls, Ta Vuurmaak said. None of them ever cried or begged for mercy. Then the ouma remembered that the Bible was still in the kitchen. She turned back and walked through the flames.

I'm telling you what I saw, my children, Ta Vuurmaak said in a broken voice as he looked at us one by one. She came out of the house, her clothes in flames, but with the Book high above her head. The young woman ran and took the Book out of her hands.

Then what happened, Ta Vuurmaak? one of us wanted to know.

Then the ouma turned into one huge flame, her dress was burnt out, and her bonnet was the last to catch fire, and we looked at that old face. Not a tear came out of those eyes or a sound from her mouth. To this day, my children, I see that face as if everything happened yesterday.

Everything happened so fast. Suddenly the ouma was lying on the ground – just a black heap that smelt of burnt meat. We all went to her, but it was too late. She had blown out her last breath. And just then the fire let the roof fall in and everything went quiet.

Then Chai told us boys to fetch the spades and picks and to dig a grave right there next to the corpse. He said to the young woman, who was still not crying: Miesies, it is Miesies's honour to put the ouma in the grave.

She rolled the old woman into the grave and said the Our Father. Chai said it with her. With the Bible held tight against her chest she said: Father forgive them for they know not what they do.

She turned around to face the Queen's men on their horses and spat at them.

We filled the grave. The young woman took a piece of wood and scratched out a kettle from the glowing ash of the kitchen, filled it with sand and placed it at the head of the grave.

She just looked at the men who were still on their horses. They looked away, they could not look her in the eye because she wasn't scared of them. All this happened without the Queen's men lifting a finger. All I heard was Corporal Lewis saying: We must obey orders.

After this there were still four farm houses to burn down. This time Chai had other plans. After all, he knew how to use a white man.

But this is where Ta Vuurmaak got sleepy and said: I've already spoken too much truth. (He called his history "truth".) You naughty boys will have to wait for the other four houses. Go home now and do your work, I want to sleep.

It was a long wait for the Sunday after the next pension day. Ta Vuurmaak had a wine glass that he had taken out of one of the farm houses and he said this was his most prized possession. Only he was allowed to touch it. He called it his war memento. He filled it with sherry and said it should be drunk like Holy Communion, and then he drank the wine as slowly as possible.

After the first glass of wine, we nudged the biggest boy among us and said: Ask him.

Ta Vuurmaak, said the boy, tell us about the other four farm houses.

Oh, yes, the old man said. The first one was burnt down to the ground, like the orders of the Queen had said. It was Queen Victoria. I don't know when Chai and the Corporal had decided to change the Queen's orders to suit themselves. We, the spies, kept on doing the same thing. A Queen's man on horseback and one of the Queen's boys with the wagon and oxen had to ride with all the Boer women and their food to the concentration camp. That's what happened up to the fifth farm house. You all still remember how the first one was burnt to the ground, Ta Vuurmaak said.

Ja, ja, we remember, we chorused.

When the wagonload of Boers and their things left the fifth farm house, Chai said to me: Stick with us and keep your mouth shut.

He put his finger on his lips. Chai had three farmworkers with him, who the Corporal had also made boys of the Queen, also for sixpence a day plus rations. They had to help me take the iron sheeting off the roofs and to remove the best wood, windows and doors and to pick out the best household goods, pots and pans. Chai called it all "vatmaar" stuff, meaning stuff you can just take because it's there for the taking.

The best stuff was loaded onto the Queen's wagon until there was room for nothing more.

Then we made our way back choosing a shorter route which, it seemed to me, Chai knew very well. Our water tank was empty but Chai said to the Corporal if we ride right through the night, the next morning we'll have all the water we want, plus more.

Just as he said, we stopped by that big tree. It's dead now. Do you see the one?

Ta Vuurmaak pointed with a finger to the tree stump and we again chorused: We do.

Everything was very carefully unloaded and covered up with the iron sheeting. We packed stones on top so that the wind wouldn't blow it away. They gave me just about all the food and they said: Stay here until we come back.

I asked Chai where I should sleep. I couldn't, like a mouse, sleep between those things because the snakes always come for the mice.

Children, Ta Vuurmaak said, Chai is a clever skelm that one. He said to me: D'you remember that big water tank by one of the sidings here on the railway line, the one the Boers shot full of holes?

Ja, I said.

It will never hold water again, he said. So take four oxen and stuff to pull with and fetch it for yourself because it will make a really nice sleeping place for you.

That night I went with four oxen down to the train water tank. It began to rain where Vatmaar begins and the tank made the ditch which these days you call the Vatmaar Road.

Then one day, Chai returned with enough food for a month. He said: Just stay here, everything's over, they're busy at Vereeniging. We must get ready for peace.

Then he stayed away again for quite a long time. One morning he came with the Corporal (without uniform) to see if everything was still in order. They came with a little cart with two horses in front and with mealie-meal, coffee and sugar. Then I heard the Corporal say to Chai: You know, Chai, we were fools not to take sheep and cattle too.

Oom Chai tells Ta Vuurmaak about Oupa Lewis's love

Not long after that people came and began knocking iron pegs into the ground and marking it on a piece of paper. And amongst them I saw Chai. I went to see what's going on. When the Corporal and Chai began walking amongst the pegs and talking, I tried to understand what they were saying, but I could not. That's how I saw Vatmaar being put on paper.

We children were about to go home, but Ta Vuurmaak said he might as well tell the rest of the truth. By now the bottle of sherry was almost empty.

Chai had had a little too much to drink, Ta Vuurmaak said. One Christmas afternoon he brought a can of khadie. He said he had decided to pay me a visit because we went back a long way.

I was quite stunned to hear what was coming out of this man's mouth. He said the Corporal never spoke to the other Rednecks. He felt he was better than them. So every evening he would talk to this Chai. When they were alone.

Then Ta Vuurmaak told us what Oom Chai had told him.

The Corporal said that he had met a girl in Vryburg. Her name was Ruth. I didn't want to ask him if she was white or not white. I asked instead what's her surname. He said he didn't think she had a surname. Then I knew she must be black.

How old is this girl? I asked.

He said about seventeen.

Do her parents know about you, Corporal? I asked.

Yes, they all like me but the old auntie said: If you really want her, you must give bogadi (lobola) as you soldiers just make children by our women and then forget them. And another thing is you white-face people's children are not our own as you make them coloureds and help them turn against us.

Charlie, the Corporal said to me, it is now four months since we were in Vryburg and I cannot get her out of my mind.

I really felt sorry for this Corporal Lewis because he spoke from the heart. Do you remember the first house that was burnt down, Ta Vuurmaak?

Ja, I remember, Chai.

Well, I thought I can't stand it any more seeing the Boers suffer for nothing and seeing their wives and children being taken out of their homes and seeing everything they own being set on fire on orders from the Queen. I realised that we Cape-boys had to do the dirty work while the Queen's men stood and watched how we did it. I don't know what they would've done if we had refused. Maybe they would've handcuffed us and sent us to jail for, as they say, not obeying orders. Because we were not the Queen's Cape-boys, we were the Queen's men.

Do you remember the night we stopped near the second farm

house? That night we slept behind that blue stone koppie. It was there where Corporal Lewis said to me: Let's take a walk.

It was dark. We climbed right up to the top of the koppie and went to sit on two flat rocks. For a long time we sat there quietly. Because I had nothing to say, I kept quiet. I could hear his heart beating because the night was very quiet.

My Ruth, by God, I really love you. God, please do not let anybody raise a hand to her. I love you Ruth, Ruth, Ruth, the Corporal said suddenly. His eyes were closed and he opened them. It seemed to me he had forgotten I was there.

We again sat quietly. Then he put his hand on my knee and said: Charlie, you are the only friend I have.

Again we sat quietly for a long time. Then I thought, if I can find this man's weak spot I can use him. I thought about the next farm house that we Cape-boys had to set on fire tomorrow while he and his men sat and watched.

I said to him: Corporal, what would you have done if we Cape-boys were sitting on the horses and you and your men were burning down your Ruth's house?

He didn't answer, just sat still. Then he said in his surly army-voice: You, Charlie, must never think like that.

I said I was sorry but I was very glad to be his friend and friends forgive each other.

I stood up to go and piss thinking that he would also get up and that we would go and sleep. But he remained seated, with his elbows on his knees and his face in his hands and saying over and over: Ruth, my Ruth.

He had started calling me Charlie when he adopted me as his friend. Charlie, he then said, I don't see her blackness, you know.

Oh, I thought, then I was right about her being a black girl.

When we are together alone, she sits on my knee, with her hand in my hand. And we are one – I am not me and she is not she. Our heartbeat is one beat, and we take breath in between beats together. There is no time for thinking, for time stands still.

It is love, true love, Charlie. Our souls are united with God. How could I ever forget it? I say, thank you, God.

He got up and went to piss.

I went and sat on the rock again and thought about a way out of burning that farm house nearby. A house that also had love within its walls. The Boers also say: We thank you, Lord. The place seemed so innocent and homely.

The Corporal came back and sat down again on his stone. Thank God, he said, that I have not taken advantage of her. Which I could have and sometimes wish I had.

Corporal, I said, now that I think I know what's going on in your heart, I'll tell you what's on my mind.

Vuurmaak, Oom Chai said, you know what happened at the other four farm houses and how you landed up here with your stolen train water tank. So I won't repeat it. But I'll tell you what happened after Vereeniging.

Oom Chai tells how they got work after Vereeniging

I didn't want to go back to our home in the Free State, Chai said, because I had heard that Steven, my elder brother, was fighting for General Joubert and that the citizens there all had good things to say about him. And then there was you, Vuurmaak, with our stuff here near the vlei. And this Englishman who said I was his friend, I also couldn't get rid of him.

Then when we got to the place they call the Military Head-quarters, the Cape-boys were paid out and all our names and addresses were taken down so that they could send us our war medals. We all gave our addresses as C/o Du Toitspan Post Office. I gave your name too because I thought maybe you also have "next of kin", which is what they call your family. I also signed for your pay, Vuurmaak. I said you were dead and that I knew your family.

Can we see Oupa's war medal? we children asked Ta Vuurmaak one Sunday after pension day. One of us wanted to know: How many Boers did Oupa shoot dead?

The old man just laughed without opening his mouth. Chai brought me my money. The medal I swopped for a bottle of sherry, he said.

The Corporal, Oom Chai went on telling Ta Vuurmaak, saw to it that I got paid for three months more than I worked because I was his only friend. The Corporal also resigned from the army because he said he was now used to the sun and that he wouldn't fit in any more where he came from. The army captain said: Corporal, you have fought for the Queen and South Africa is now part of the British Empire.

The Corporal didn't get money like us but what he called a Barclay cheque book.

Now, he said to me, not a day longer. And away we went, on the train, to his Ruth.

As we were walking from the station with our hold-alls with all our belongings in them, this Ruth saw George coming – on the train he had asked me to call him George Lewis, no longer Corporal.

He started running away from me and I saw someone running towards him. He caught this running thing, threw it in the air and caught it again. Then he stood still and held it close like a mother holds a new-born baby. I went closer, but he didn't notice me, so I just walked past.

I went to sit under a tree and watched him carry this Ruth of his to where a lot of people stood clapping hands and singing ululu. And I heard an old man say: He is one of us.

He put her down. From where I was sitting she looked just like any other black girl who works in white homes. When I went nearer I saw that she was barefoot with just a thin clean white dress. It was a cold day but she did not feel the cold. George, as Corporal Lewis asked me to call him, introduced me to all the people as his friend Charlie.

Now I could have a good look at Ruth. Her swaying walk was more lively than that of an ordinary woman: she gave more one-for-you-and-one-for-me. Her breasts were full and made two points under her dress. Her neck was long and thin. Her face was of Africa – perfect teeth and clean, white eyeballs. And she also had something of her own, something beyond beauty.

They gave us a clean hut with a basin, a jug of water and two grass mats. And they said: It is yours as long as you stay with us.

The people were poor because they had lost a lot during the war. Brit *and* Boer had taken their cattle. Most of them had useless receipt papers for cattle and sheep stolen from them in the name of the Queen. The Boers just took what they wanted, saying: You Kaffirs are lucky we didn't shoot you first.

Next we went to the nkosi, the headman. George had brought a bottle of brandy for the men in Ruth's family, but he had to share it with the headman, which turned out to be a good thing because it put us in his good books. He told us everything we wanted to know about his people's marriage customs. He was one of the few who could speak English. He told us he would send someone to us the next morning to arrange the marriage and to point out a piece of land to George where he could build his hut and for grazing and ploughing. Of course after he'd paid the bogadi.

After an hour or so of "e Rra, e Rra" (yes, Sir, yes, Sir) we said goodbye to the headman. But first George wanted to go and say good night to Ruth.

The next day an old woman and young man came to see us. The headman had sent them to organise the wedding. The man came to interpret. The old woman said Ruth should have nothing to do with the arrangements.

George made a list of everything that was needed. Then he wrote down in his pocket book all the things he needed for the bogadi. Among the things Ruth's people wanted were an extra three-legged pot, brandy and tobacco. The young man then gave George the price of everything.

I don't remember exactly now, but it came to well over a hundred pounds. He had to draw it the next morning at the bank in Vryburg. After visiting Ruth the night before, he came to say she would ask one of her rra mogolo, elder uncles, to come with us and the two wedding organisers to the nkosi to hand over the money.

The following morning we were in Vryburg, sitting and waiting for the doors of the Barclays Bank to open. The doors had just opened when someone shouted: Hey, Corporal Lewis, I want to see you!

George jumped to attention and said: At your service, Sir. Then he walked to this man in expensive clothes. I heard George say: I will be glad, Sir.

The man took out a pocket-book, wrote down something, tore out the page and gave it to George.

He didn't tell me what this was about, but I could see that he was deep in thought. He withdrew the money from the bank.

That afternoon the five of us made our way to the nkosi to hand over the money. We again took a bottle of brandy to the nkosi which we had brought from Vryburg, and it wasn't long before we all felt good. And they never stopped saying what a lucky girl Ruth was.

Ruth's people said it would take at least one more full moon before the two could marry. George said it didn't matter, just as long as he could be near his natsi, his beloved Ruth.

Only after Ruth brought us our lunch the following day did George remember about the piece of paper. He said it was from his company commander Captain John Walker. He was now the director of a diamond company and he would like people like George to come and work for him. He wanted people from "home" which is what they called England. The captain was also a town councillor in a place called Du Toitspan. If George wanted work he should come and see him as soon as possible.

Holding the piece of paper up to the light George said: Here is the address of his office.

Then let us clean up and go and see your army captain, I said. We must have work because we have to live.

That afternoon we knocked on a door which just had *J. Walker* on it. They shook hands and both smiled. George introduced me as one of the Queen's faithful Cape-boys, whereupon the captain said: War brothers.

George jumped to attention and said: Yes, Sir.

Then the captain said: We will have no more of that, Mister Lewis. Remember, we're civilians now. I am Du Toitspan's personnel councillor.

It was his job to check that the workers were treated well and that they did their work properly. It was Friday and he told us to come and see him again on Tuesday. By then I'll know where to push you two in.

George again jumped to attention and said: Thank you, Sir.

I also knocked my heels together and said: Thank you, Sir.

The captain laughed. We quickly made for the nearest bar for a thank-you-God drink.

Tuesday morning found us waiting for the Du Toitspan Council offices to open. When the captain came he said: Good day, you two, come in.

There were two chairs facing his desk and he invited us to sit. I was the first to sit because George felt it was not good manners to sit down in the company of his regimental officer. The captain had to repeat: Sit, George. I'll start with your friend. Name? he said.

Charles Terreblanche, I answered, and he wrote it down in a big book.

Your work will be with the town surveyor. He has been complaining that his boy was off work a few days every month. Always after pay-day. Drunk, drunk, you know.

My starting pay was to be seven pounds two shillings a month.

There would be six working days a week with Saturdays a half day. With a pay rise every year and fourteen days' leave for every year of service.

Again I clicked my heels together and said: Thank you, my captain of the Queen.

You fool, he said, do you not know that the Queen is no more and that we now have a King?

So I just said: Thank you, Sir.

He wrote two letters, put them into envelopes, and said: You start on Thursday, the first of the month. Take this letter to the paymaster. You'll find him at the bottom of the passage, the door with the board, Paymaster. And take this letter to Mister Keely – the surveyor next to the fire buckets.

Mr Keely said to me: Hope you can work when you are drunk, for you are all the same. Be here on Thursday at eight o'clock sharp – and he pointed to the floor.

We would get our first month's pay just before the period which is called the Easter Weekend. Good Friday, Saturday, Easter Sunday and Easter Monday – four days in which to celebrate the marriage of George and Ruth.

George had a whole month to prepare things, but it wasn't enough time. I once said to him: George, why not take her and live together like man and wife?

He could, he said. But I don't want to. If I love Ruth as I think I do, I must also respect her and her family.

Well, then I just told him that we had to have our measurements taken the following day at the tailor, Moosa Keppie, and should also just check whether the black material for our suits had come yet.

Everything worked out and the suits were ready a few days before the wedding.

Ruth's parents were very poor. So I called aside one of her aunts and told her I would give her money to buy Ruth's wedding clothes. The next day she went to Bergers, the shop in Vryburg which sells dresses and things, to find out about prices and told me the next time she saw me. I gave her the money and told her not to tell George. She could tell Ruth though.

Ouma Lewis and Oupa Lewis are growing old together, but he still doesn't know where his wife's wedding clothes came from, Oom Chai said years later.

The wedding of Oupa Lewis and Ouma Ruth

Lance-Corporal George Lewis took things as they came. He was now Rra George Lewis, but he remained a true Englishman with only one thing at a time on his army-brain. He was always smoothly shaved with yellow hair cut short, yellow eyebrows above his blue eyes, a straight nose with thin lips and a square jaw which stood out. He smoked a pipe and walked like a soldier.

He was a happy man when he climbed off the two-horse cart the weekend before the wedding with the extra-large three-legged pot and two twenty-gallon drums for the pap. The brandy he took to our ntlo, hut, and locked it up with a hasp and staple which he had brought along.

The big problem was how he could get to the magistrate's office on the Thursday before the Easter Weekend since Friday was a holiday. He had already planned to get married by a special licence. Then I had a plan. George, I asked him, what does an Englishman love the most.

Wine, woman and song, he answered.

And whisky, I added. You buy two bottles of whisky. You give one to your Mister Richman and the other to my Mister Keely, both on Wednesday. And tell them the truth. All they can do is say yes or no.

Oh no! said George.

We do what that Englishman said about God, I said. Ask and it shall be given unto you.

Our two bosses were flat broke and only too happy to give us the day off.

George hired two Cape carts on Vryburg's square and told the drivers to wait at the big tree in the village – Thursday morning eight o'clock. He told them he would pay them the next time he saw them.

That Thursday morning George and Ruth and I and an oupa who told us he was her oldest oom, went off to the magistrate's office to pay the five pounds for the special marriage licence. The clerk filled in the papers. The magistrate came and asked George and Ruth if they took each other as man and wife. Both said: I do – as George had told Ruth to say the previous night. George and I signed the papers and Ruth and her oom each made a cross.

After this I had to ride with Ruth's oom in the Cape cart at the back while Ruth and George rode in the one in front. When we turned off the road into the stat, the people were standing on both sides of the path leading to the marriage hut screaming, clapping and singing ululu.

The nkosi and the oupas were sitting on chairs under a lean-to made of iron sheeting. There were also two chairs for me and George. I had to fetch the case of brandy and pour for the VIPs.

The quicker we get them drunk the better for us, George whispered to me.

I started with the headman and poured his cup up to the brim because he never told me when to stop. He drank immediately. There was no talk about a toast. I filled up all the cups to the brim, and some of the men had mugs which I also poured to the brim. Then the meat was brought. Big chunks, piled onto a plate of pap. There weren't enough plates and the young girls had to run to their huts for more.

After the gorging was finished some of the young women

brought tin mugs and buckets of bojalwa, beer. The headman had to drink first. He then passed on his cup to George, who, after a few mouthfuls, passed it on to me. And so it was passed on and on. The girl waited until the bucket was empty so that she could go and fill it up again. But behind her, in the meantime, another girl stood waiting with another full bucket or jug of beer.

After a while the men got up one by one and disappeared behind a huge rock. This was called the piss rock – only for the grown up men. Then they did what all drunk men do, it doesn't matter where, they all began to talk at the same time.

George indicated to me with his eyes to pour another round of brandy. I did the same as the first time, until there was no brandy left over. The nkosi could no longer get words out of his mouth and he and some of his people went off to their hut. Some of the guests just fell asleep in their seats.

Our arrangement with the headman and oupas was that George would take his new wife, before sunset, in the Cape cart, to a room in Du Toitspan which he had hired. I stayed over at the Cloete family who I had known since before the Boer war. All Ruth's possessions were in a mealie-meal bag. Getting through the greetings was not an easy thing because all the guests were in good spirits and it was "Dumela, dumela", on and on and on.

After the marriage George and Ruth visited her people often, but after a few months, only when a family member died. Her people said she no longer belonged to them. She became more George than Ruth.

After their sixth month of marriage they came to live in Vatmaar.

Ta Vuurmaak tells how it all began

The Sunday after pension day we were back at Ta Vuurmaak's cabin and he told us more of his truth about Vatmaar:

While I was in the Pan, as Du Toitspan was called, to buy tobacco, matches and other things, Ta Vuurmaak said, I bumped into one of our boys who belonged to the Queen. He told me that Chai had a white man's job. Then I went to the Town Council offices until it was time for Chai to chaila.

When he saw me he gave me two pounds to buy whatever I needed and to go back and go on looking after our worldly possessions.

That Saturday afternoon Chai came to visit me at my kaya. He brought along a bottle of sherry and told me how he came on the plan for Vatmaar. Vatmaar was the name that I gave to his and Corporal Lewis's stolen stuff. Now he just went and gave the place the same name too.

Apparently Chai was lying awake one night when he thought up the plan for what the English call a settlement. In his thoughts he saw the place near the vlei.

I spoke to George about it, Chai said, and he said he would like to live on his own with Ruth, away from his and her people. Because she was going to have a baby. Again George went to talk to his army-captain. The two understood each other well. The captain promised to put the matter on the agenda of the next meeting of the mine company and the town council.

At both meetings it was agreed that a settlement could be built on the mine property – five miles out of Du Toitspan, near the vlei which falls inside the Du Toitspan suburb. It would be an outer ward of Du Toitspan for the poor Cape-boys who fought for the Queen, and for others who would also like to live there.

Ta Vuurmaak said: Chai held the bottle upside down, took my hand and said: I haven't had such a good chat in a long time. Then he got on his bicycle and went off.

My tail of the story is, Ta Vuurmaak said, that Chai and his George came with four people and made two bundles of the Vatmaar stuff. Then Chai took half a crown and said to his George friend: Heads or tails? Chai could choose first. Then they took their stuff to where they had their plots.

You, Vuurmaak, the Englishman said to me, are well looked after. Take this brick mould and start your own business. People will

33

soon need bricks to build their houses. Only the three of us know how you got the tank, and with your monthly pension you can live like a king.

I took a few of the men who did not have work or who had been dismissed, and got them to make bricks. Of every three that were made, two belonged to the maker and one was mine.

After the winter Chai and George's rooms were ready for them to move in – the very rooms which they use these days as storerooms. They moved in. Chai on his own and Oupa Lewis with his young wife and one of her old aunts.

Every morning the two men got onto their brand new bicycles and went to work in the Pan.

Old Chetty's shop

The owner of the shop, Old Chetty, told us that he was from Natal but was born in India. He told us where India is but nobody believed him because he was after all one of us and he did live in Vatmaar. He was a thin man with a scattering of white in his short-snipped dark beard. He was light-black, not brown, with a thin half-moon nose and no front teeth.

We called Old Chetty the Coolie, and his two rooms, one for living in and the other for doing business, were the Coolie shop. He had everything that the people of Vatmaar needed, but more expensive than in the Pan.

The shop was in front and the living room at the back, with a double door in between. A sash window with wire netting prevented naughty boys from passing things outside. The shop was eighteen by eighteen feet and the backroom eighteen by sixteen feet. There was also a window in the backroom. The flat roof extended from the back to the front and over the front wall so that there was a verandah in the front of the shop. The verandah rested on four wooden pillars and a cross beam. Old Chetty had bought the iron sheeting from Oom Chai and Oupa Lewis. They said it was rubbish from the war. Nailed on the two middle verandah pillars was a plank with the words *General Dealer* on it.

Old Chetty closed shop whenever he went with his bicycle-cart with the big basket in front or with Oom Flip to the Pan to buy stock. Oom Flip had a cart and a one-eyed horse called Old Swing. This was his second horse. His first horse, he said, just went and died suddenly one day. This was before Devi, Chetty's daughter, could give the right change in the shop.

Her mother, Freeda, had left her stat in the time of the great drought. She was an orphan and stayed with people who made her work on the land. When she became a woman these people began making arrangements to marry her off for a good bride price.

Food was scarce and she was given a beating for something she did not do – the blue whip marks could still be seen the night she walked into Old Chetty's shop.

She later told how, on a dark night, she filled a calabash with water and set off on the path which the old people said crossed the tracks of the iron horse and went on into a big city.

She walked until the sun went down a second time. Then she came to the two tracks of the iron horse. She was tired and hungry and thirsty when she climbed through the wire. She made sure not to step onto the tracks.

Then there were no more paths, but she kept on walking. She asked Modimo, God, to take her hand. Eventually she found herself standing in front of a kind of house which she never knew existed and a man with a heart and a face which she never knew lived in this world. He opened the door and looked at her. Her dress was a mealie bag with holes for her head and arms. It was cold because it was winter.

The man looked at me and with his hands he said: Come. I went into the house because I was more dead than alive, she told. He gave me a mug of hot coffee, the first coffee I ever drank in my life. I went to sit on the floor with my back against the wall and I soon fell asleep.

Old Chetty's wife, Freeda, was short and looked like Ouma Lewis. The people of Vatmaar used to say she loves her husband with the love that is in the Bible.

Devi was their beloved only daughter. Like her mother she was short, soft from all the pampering, but she was built like her father. She had both her mother's and her father's face but she had small Morolong ears.

Devi was the only clever child in our school at Vatmaar. Teacher Elsa often allowed her to stay out for the day to go with Oom Flip and the pensioners to the Pan to fetch their pension money. Then she sommer took the money they owed her father, which was written down in an exercise book. The book was kept in a bag together with the money. The old folks never argued with her because they could not get anything from the shop until Devi came home from school. Then she wrote down everything they bought on tick, showed it to them and said: Sign. Which they did with a cross.

Her mother's actual name was Matemba but Old Chetty called her Freeda. With affection we called her Ma Coolie. She died during the Big Flu and after that Old Chetty was never the same again.

If anyone was in need, he always helped and he did many good things for the people of Vatmaar. When they thanked him, he lifted his finger and said: No thank me, thank Freeda's Modimo. His love for Ma Coolie never grew old and Vatmaar knew this.

It was Old Chetty who gave Vatmaar its first soccer ball.

Oom Chai tells where the mission church came from

Oom Chai enjoyed his work at the Du Toitspan Town Council's land survey very much because it was not as dangerous as his trade of farrier which he learned when he was a boy. The wages were low but he was sure of getting it every month. He had to look after the work's bicycle.

On a happy day, as he himself said, Mr Keely, the land surveyor, instructed him to take the instruments in the special bicycle with the big basket in front to a certain empty plot in the newly developed section of town.

While waiting there for Mr Keely he saw a young man in a black coat who also seemed to be waiting for someone. He could see by the way the man was dressed that he was a Dutch Reformed dominee, Oom Chai said. He took no notice of the man because he had learned long ago that if you work for the Town Council it was best to stay in your place and mind your own business.

After a while the well-dressed young man came over to Oom Chai who was sitting on a rock.

I got up, took off my cap and said: Good morning, Meneer, Oom Chai said.

He gave me his hand and said: Dominee Louis Pienaar.

I said: Charlie, Chai for short.

He laughed. Then he pointed to the instruments and said: Land surveyor?

Yes, Dominee, I said.

The first thing these dominees ask someone they meet for the first time is: Which church do you belong to?

Oom Chai had been waiting for this. He said: The mission church.

The dominee was so surprised that he shook Oom Chai's hand a second time and said: We're brothers, that's our sister church.

Then he asked where Oom Chai's mission church was because all the churches he knew here in Du Toitspan used English, whether the people understand it or not.

It is since 1857 that our Dutch Reformed church began having separate services for brown and black people, the dominee said.

Oom Chai nodded.

Then the dominee got a second surprise. Oom Chai said: In the Free State, Dominee. But I now live in Vatmaar. Dominee, Oom Chai said, we in Vatmaar need a mission church. I work with people who all belong to the English churches.

37

And the dominee said: Everything's going to work out fine, Chai.

Oom Chai began to think: Perhaps God has sent this dominee so that I can ask him for a mission church for Vatmaar.

Dominee, Oom Chai said, we in Vatmaar truly do need a mission church because there're babies and young children who have not been baptised.

Then Mr Keely arrived with a rolled up plan on his bicycle. Good morning, Father, he said.

Good day to you, Brother, replied the dominee. They began to speak about the plot and Mr Keely said the church is lucky to get the last corner stand. The dominee looked at the plan and said the church will take the two adjoining plots too, seeing that the corner stand was meant for a house. The rectory must be next to the church.

I suppose it will be all right. We don't want to have a town council sitting for every small thing, Mr Keely said.

Good, said the dominee. Then I shall write down their numbers and go and pay for them at the town clerk's office.

Mr Keely smiled and said: As you wish, Father.

Then I thank you, the dominee said. He quickly looked at the instrument box with the name *N. Keely* on it, and added: Mister Keely. And then shook his hand.

Charlie, Mr Keely shouted suddenly, take these things back to the office!

I was standing close to him and I wondered why he was always shouting at me when there were other white people around, Oom Chai said.

The dominee said: Wait, Charlie. He took out his pocket-book and wrote down his name and address and gave it to me. Come and see me. I'll see what I can do, he said.

Oom Chai was a brown man with a light brown face and hands. But when he took off his shirt to wash, his upper body was the colour of a well-washed khaki shirt. He was the only brown man with a handlebar moustache I ever knew. He was forever twisting the ends of the moustache, especially when he was thinking. His hair was pitch black and straight, the kind which we in Vatmaar called wet hair. His nose was not flat and his hair stopped at his ears where he began to shave his beard.

People said: He is too lazy to open his eyes.

He was a big man. To be in charge was something which always fell on him without him wanting it. He respected women and the men said they know why – a mad horse kicked him between the legs. Others added that it was a horse which he was too stupid to shoe. The kick gave him a strange way of walking.

The night after meeting the dominee, Oom Chai could not sleep because he lay awake thinking what to say and how to approach the man. And in the early hours of the morning he said to himself: I shall go and see him Saturday afternoon because we knock off at twelve. Saturday I'll go to work in my best clothes.

When Mr Keely saw Oom Chai in the suit which he had made for Oupa Lewis's wedding and which he wore only for special occasions, he said: Charlie, you may have the day off seeing that you are all dressed up. I don't know why, but people will think that I am the boy. Off you go, my boy.

Oom Chai thought to himself that surprises always came to him in pairs so he'd just go straight to the dominee. He looked at the piece of paper to make sure of the address.

When he got there, he saw that there was a front gate, a back gate and a side gate because it was on a street corner. Through the side gate he could see the front stoep and an open door. The gate was made of flat iron strips and fastened with a piece of wire.

While he was still looking around a tall black woman came to ask him if he had come to see the dominee. She could see this by his neat clothing and she looked him up and down from head to toe.

Yes, Oom Chai said. Then it was his turn to look at her from head to toe. She wore a Voortrekker bonnet of which the front had been cut away. Her dress covered her down to her ankles, only the toes of her bare feet stuck out. She wore a big safety-pin under her chin and her hands were the only other parts of her body that could be seen. It was summer and very hot.

Walk ahead of me, Baas, she said.

When Oom Chai walked through the front gate, the dominee appeared at the front door. While he too inspected Oom Chai from head to toe, he took his hand and said: Come in, Charlie.

The dominee was of average height, not thin, also not fat. He had a head covered with thin black hair and light-brown eyes. A thick, heavy, broad moustache hung from underneath his nose. He was dark, like most devoted Afrikaners, people who were proud to have Africa as their home.

The only disappointment is that they want our fatherland all to themselves, Oom Chai said.

While they were sitting in the study, the same servant brought two cups of coffee on a tray.

Thank you, Aia, the dominee said.

Then he said that he had thought about the matter: I believe we can help the poor people of Vatmaar. Only last night I had it on the agenda of the church council and everyone agreed that you people of Vatmaar could have our old hall. We don't use it any more as the bats think it's theirs.

Oom Chai stood up and took the dominee's hand in both his own hands and said: Dominee, the Lord has answered our prayers in Vatmaar.

It was these words that caused the breakthrough, Oom Chai thought to himself. As George Lewis would've said: If God is for us, who can be against us?

When the dominee again referred to him as Charlie, Oom Chai said: Just say Chai, Dominee, it sounds more like me.

Good, the dominee said, the church council has drawn up a list with conditions.

40

After looking around a bit, he found the piece of paper and began to read:

One, the building remains the property of the church.

Two, the people of Vatmaar must break down the building and cart it to Vatmaar themselves.

Three, the people of Vatmaar must not be under the influence of liquor when working on the building.

Four, one of our church's elders will be asked to meet you, Chai, and through you, the people of Vatmaar.

Five, you, Chai, will be the elder of the church and see to it that everything is done in a Christian manner.

Six, if there is not an elder available then you must see to the service, Chai.

Seven, the people of Vatmaar can rely on the charity of the mother church.

That is all, the dominee said.

Searching for appropriate words, Oom Chai said: Mother church, what a beautiful name . . .

The dominee wrote everything down on another piece of paper, put it in an envelope, and said: Chai, get the permission of Vatmaar's people, and the church council will find a willing elder to be of service to the mission congregation of Vatmaar.

Then he stood up and said: Chai, I am thankful to you for giving me the opportunity to help poor Vatmaar.

Oom Chai shook his hand and said: I cannot believe my ears.

Both smiled. When Oom Chai got onto his bicycle, he almost fell, black suit and all.

Now, to explain it all to the people of Vatmaar, he mumbled to himself on his way back, feeling if the envelope was still in his pocket.

Tomorrow morning I'll go to each house one by one and tell them to come to my house when the ten o'clock whistle blows, he thought to himself later while resting on the path, one foot on a high stone. Every house must send one representative – father, mother or any child over fourteen.

While resting like this, he wondered who he could ask to read the letter to the people. Old George Lewis can't read Afrikaans. His daughter can, but she is at school in Kimberley. Who could I ask? he said to himself. Then suddenly he remembered Cousin Cloete's son Paul. He turned around right there and rode to the older section of the Pan.

Oom Chai came upon Paul just as he was turning to go into his parents' house. Good day, Paul, Oom Chai said.

Good afternoon, Oom, the young man answered.

You're just the man I'm looking for. Is your father at home?

Ma's sleeping because she's not well. I'd rather not wake her, Oom. And there's my father coming right now down the path there – and he pointed with his hand.

Then we'll wait right here for him so that the three of us can talk business, Oom Chai said.

Good day, Stephen! How are you doing? Oom Chai said, getting off his bicycle to give Stephen Cloete his hand.

Good, Chai. And you?

Couldn't be better, Oom Chai said. Let me not beat about the bush, Cousin. I've come to ask Paul, and of course to ask you too, if tomorrow he can read a letter for me to the Vatmaar people.

Any time, Stephen Cloete said, I don't think Paul would mind.

Paul gave a little laugh, which Oom Chai took to mean yes. And then, while he looked at him, because Paul was thin, he said: I'll give you a lift on my bicycle. You don't have to take anything with you, your clothes are clean and good enough for a Sunday at Vatmaar. Stephen, Oom Chai said, then we'll be on our way! My regards to Molly. Paul says she's not feeling well.

Thank you, Chai.

Come, jump! Oom Chai said. And when Paul was on the bar, he called out: Thank you and goodbye, Cousin!

And the two of them pulled off.

On Sunday, just after the ten o'clock whistle, every household in Vatmaar turned up at Oom Chai's house – men, women and children. The lounge was too small and everyone had to go and stand under the big pepper tree.

Oom Chai took the hardcover book out of his pocket and gave it to Paul. Then he said: People of Vatmaar, this here is Paul Cloete from the Pan, a learned boy who has offered to read and write for us. First, we will take down the names of the residents who are here. We'll start with the greybeards, then the women, the working men, and lastly the children.

When all the names were written up in the hard-cover book, Oom Chai said: Let the children stand in front so that they can go and tell their shy parents what's going on.

Then he explained what happened and how it came about that he had the letter. He held the envelope in the air: Here are the conditions.

Then he handed it to Paul, who tore it open and began to read out loud.

Paul had to read it over and over because some people could not understand while others wanted to hear the good news more than once. A few said: Now our children can be baptised and get their names.

When Oom Chai asked: Who is against this? everybody kept quiet.

Oom Flip, who was still new in Vatmaar at the time, said suddenly, out of the blue: People, I, my trolley and Old Swing will bring the Lord's house to Vatmaar.

The women clapped their hands and somebody said: The Lord will bless you, Flip.

Oom Chai then divided the able-bodied men into three work teams and said to them: You are not volunteers. We will all be working together and if any family needs something, let them come to me. God will provide.

Then something happened which had never happened in Vatmaar before. Oom Chai said: Close your eyes.

He first looked around to see if everyone's eyes were closed and then he began: Our Father, who art in Heaven …

Very few people knew the Our Father, but everyone said Amen together. Oupa Lewis said his Our Father softly to himself in English.

After the meeting Oupa Lewis and Oom Chai walked off together. Well done, George Lewis said and slapped Oom Chai on the shoulder. I was thinking, where do you intend erecting the church hall?

I haven't thought about it yet, George. Where do you think we should put it?

The two walked on without saying a word. Then Oupa Lewis said: First, if you agree with me, we'll go and see Mister Walker.

Ja, Oom Chai said. Listen, you have to tell him that it was you who got this church hall for Vatmaar. And after a while: You know, George, Vatmaar doesn't have a plot that's been set aside for a church building. So now I'm asking you to go and talk nicely with that company-commander of yours. You speak better English than me and I'm sure he'll regard it as his duty to help a fellow soldier from the army – especially one who fought with him for the Queen.

Oupa Lewis didn't say yes or no. But his parting words were: Tomorrow after the tea break we'll ask for permission to see Mister Walker.

Okay, George, Oom Chai said, and smiled.

Mr Walker was not there on Monday, but when they walked into his office on Tuesday morning, he was very happy to see Oupa Lewis. Long time no see, he said, shaking his hand.

Oupa Lewis stood to attention and Mr Walker said: I told you before, I don't want any of that any more. Now you two sit down for there are chairs which are meant to be sat on.

Oom Chai looked at Oupa Lewis who winked at him, something which Oom Chai could not do so he just pinched both eyes closed.

44

Sir, Oupa Lewis began, and told Mr Walker how Charlie got the church hall and the conditions attached to it: And now a place to erect the hall.

Very good, Mr Walker said. I'll put it on the agenda of the next council meeting. And he wrote it in a book with a page for every day.

On the Friday afternoon Oupa Lewis received a letter from Mr Walker's office, delivered by his office boy, an old man with a dirty beard. Oupa Lewis decided that he wouldn't open it. He and Chai would open it together so that they could get the good news together.

That afternoon, at knock-off time, Oupa Lewis was waiting for Oom Chai where they left their bicycles. Because they always rode together back to Vatmaar.

Here it is, he said to Oom Chai, and showed him the letter.

Oom Chai smiled: I knew they'd give the church a piece of holy ground.

Oupa Lewis read the letter quickly and then handed it to Oom Chai. No, he said to Oupa Lewis, you read it out. I want to hear the good news from your mouth.

Then he read: The Town Council of Du Toitspan has made no provision for a church stand. Vatmaar is a settlement adjoining Du Toitspan town, where all the churches are situated. Signed: David Levin, Town Clerk.

Oupa Lewis read the letter again and then he wanted to tear it up. But Oom Chai said: No, George, give it to me. He put the letter in his pocket. The two got onto their bicycles and rode home without another word.

That was the Friday. On Saturday afternoon Oom Chai again went from door to door. He again asked them to send a representative or, if they liked, to bring the whole family to the meeting under the pepper tree when the ten o'clock whistle blows.

Some people mumbled: What is it now again? And others: I don't know, do you?

45

Sunday, just after ten, Oupa Lewis and Oom Chai headed for the tree, Oom Chai with the letter in his hands for all to see. They greeted the people with the words: We are happy to be together again.

Then Oom Chai told them in detail what had taken place in Mr Walker's office and how they got the letter. He held the letter high up in the air and said: Now our respected George Lewis will read the letter out for us.

Everyone was quiet, something unusual for the people of Vatmaar who liked to show that they were still alive.

Oupa Lewis finished reading and everyone was quiet for a while. Then Oom Flip said: May I ask a question?

Yes! Oom Chai said.

I didn't understand what our white brother was reading. Can you, Chai, not explain it in our language?

Oom Chai then translated the letter into the language of Vatmaar, Afrikaans.

Now we understand, everybody said as one man.

There was a long silence. Then a lovely woman with light hair said: It's better like this. We can't expect to get the church hall and its plot for free. We are not used to getting things for free. We've always had to work for what we wanted.

Vonnie, Oom Chai said, now you've said it. And to the others: Let us listen to this mother of Vatmaar. Come and stand over here with us.

Tant Vonnie detached herself from her two daughters and came to stand with the two men. Then, with a smile, she said to the people: We are going to buy our own church plot. She pointed to the first plot she set eyes on and said: Over there, that one with the stones on it that nobody wants.

She kept quiet, thinking. Then she said: After the meeting a boy and a girl will go and get an empty tobacco bag from Oupa Lewis. (Oupa Lewis was smoking his pipe.) She pointed to the two children: Go to each family and ask them to put something in the bag. Folks, give with a good heart, she said. It doesn't matter how little it is. And remember, my children – and she looked at the boy and girl – if there's a family that doesn't have anything to put in the bag, ask the oom or tante just to touch the bag so that we can have their blessing.

Oom Chai and Oupa Lewis thanked her as if with one voice. Again she smiled, and everyone thought, what a beautiful woman. Then she went back to stand with her two daughters among the people.

Close your eyes and say Our Father who art in heaven, Oom Chai appealed in a loud voice.

Oupa Lewis said his Our Father in his thoughts.

Then the meeting was over. Oom Chai and Oupa Lewis went to their houses, by this time no longer a single room, but a proper four-roomed dwelling. They were letting the old one-room dwellings to people as backyard rooms.

The boy and girl were waiting at Oupa Lewis's home for the tobacco bag. After making sure there was no more tobacco in the bag, he said: Let me put my blessing in the bag – and he took half a crown out of his wallet and put it in the bag.

When they came to Oom Chai, he saw the half-crown and said: I might as well follow suit.

Ta Vuurmaak also put half a crown in saying: Let me pay for my journey to heaven.

It wasn't long before the boy and girl were back at Oupa Lewis's house. Because it was his bag they reckoned that the collection should come to him.

You just sit there and keep that bag, he said and showed the girl a chair. And to the boy: You, go and call Oom Chai.

Oom Chai came and said: George, this was Vonnie's idea. Let the boy go and call her too.

Tant Vonnie came and the three of them counted the money while the boy and girl stood by. It came to one pound, two shillings and one penny.

There we have it! Oom Chai said. George, tomorrow you and

I are going to buy that plot with the stones on it for the people. The two shillings and one penny we'll keep as yeast in the bag. You look after the tobacco bag, George.

Ouma Lewis brought three cups of tea and gave the boy and girl a vetkoek each with the words: Thank you, my children.

The following Saturday afternoon Oom Chai again went to see the dominee, this time in his working clothes. Oupa Lewis went straight home because, he said, he could never get on with a Dutch dominee.

The dominee was pleased to hear that the folks of Vatmaar had agreed to the conditions of the mother church. Then Oom Chai told him about the town council not wanting to give the church a piece of ground and showed him the letter.

The dominee looked at it and said: Don't you know why they do not want to measure out land for the church hall?

No, Dominee, answered Oom Chai.

It is because it is an Afrikaans church. And they'll never know any better either.

He looked very disappointed. Then Oom Chai took out the deed of sale, showed it to the dominee and told him how the plot was bought. His face brightened up and the two shook hands.

Thank you, Aia, the dominee said to the black woman who brought in the coffee, this time in a just as long but different colour dress. I have good news for you too, he told Oom Chai. There is a Meneer, Oom Hans du Plooy. (He said Meneer because he expected the people of Vatmaar to say either Meneer or Baas.) He knows the birthplace of the brown man, he comes from Stellenbosch. He knows your people and he has asked the church council if he could be the mother church's elder in the mission church. Because there is no payment for this, everyone agreed, grateful for his generosity.

The following Saturday it rained. Vatmaar's people never worked in rain because, they said: Who will pay the doctor? Oom Chai again

48

made for the dominee's home to ask if he could meet Meneer Hans du Plooy.

I shall take you to him, the dominee promised. And from now on he will be my representative, do you understand? – as if Oom Chai was a nuisance.

Yes, Dominee, Oom Chai said.

Oubaas Hans du Plooy and his wife lived in the elite part of the Pan. The dominee introduced his elder to Oom Chai, who had never been scared of a white man: This is the man who has been proposed by our church council to be at the disposal of the people of the settlement. On the stoep were a table and chairs and the dominee said: Let us sit ourselves down right here.

Miesies Du Plooy brought two cups of tea on a tray and a servant carried a mug of tea in her hand. Miesies du Plooy greeted the dominee with a handshake and to Oom Chai, who was still standing, she gave a nod. (Oom Chai was wearing his working clothes.)

He is the man I've been telling you about, Gertie, Meneer du Plooy said to his wife. She looked at Oom Chai and pulled her face into what was supposed to be a smile. Oom Chai knew immediately where he stood with her.

Charlie, the dominee said, you and Oom Hans will be working together and at the next church council meeting we will note down your name as elder of the mission church in Vatmaar.

Thank you, Dominee, Oom Chai said.

The dominee then got up and left.

Hans du Plooy and his wife came from Stellenbosch where he had speculated with houses, the people said. Over the years he bought houses at a cheap price, fixed them up and sold them at a profit. Some he kept and rented out again at a considerable amount. His only daughter stayed on in Stellenbosch. He could have been in his sixties, a thin man with hollow cheeks and a cough – actually three coughs: Hoo, hay, hay! He rode a bicycle to keep fit and always said: The car's in the garage. He came to Du Toitspan on doctor's orders because he suffered from asthma and needed to live in a dry climate. He used snuff and offered the tin to whoever was standing nearest to him and he loved to see how they coughed and sneezed while the tears streamed from their eyes. He was a good man, the very opposite of his wife, and because they didn't have a better word the people of Vatmaar said of him: He is a darling. He taught Vatmaar the Our Father and Nearer my God to Thee.

After that Oom Chai said: That's enough now, we only need one hymn and one prayer.

The people of Vatmaar worked as a team on their mission church. The demolishers went to the church hall in the Pan every Saturday straight after work.

Oom Flip and Old Swing carted the building material to the stony plot. He usually made three trips on a Saturday afternoon – two to cart the material, and one to take home the men who were tired and who had been working until it was nearly dark.

Suddenly we children looked forward to Saturday afternoons, even if it meant giving a hand with the whole of Vatmaar. We used to listen to the grown ups gossiping about what happened this week again at their work in the Pan. Sometimes one winked to the other to show that this was something we should not hear. We made as if we were not listening and were not interested in what they were saying, but we were all ears, ready to repeat it all later when we children walked home. We were very proud to be able to say: Did you hear?

All the people of Vatmaar helped to unload building material and put up the hall. Meneer du Plooy showed us how to mark the wood and the planks with numbers before taking it apart. It was then very easy to put it all back together again afterwards. We didn't have artisans from the building trade, only their labourers, but these people knew what to do. And with Meneer Du Plooy's experience with the fixing up of houses nobody could've done a better job. The floor was made of Vatmaar slate. The building had a pitched roof, and there were four windows on each side.

When the building was complete there were painted numbers all over, and we children, and even some grown ups too, walked around going: One-one, two-two, three-three and so on, going around reading what was on the walls. Meneer du Plooy said: No, you are working on my nerves! – and asked Oom Flip to go and buy a few tins of red paint for the roof, green for the outside walls and white for the doors and windows. There was no ceiling or inside finishing and Meneer Du Plooy said there were no dirty number marks on the inside; the Vatmaar people can paint it themselves. So we bought paint ourselves for the inside and painted the walls white to door-height.

When the painting was finished we, the people of Vatmaar, looked upon our church hall with pride and in our hearts it was a flower that had just opened up. Then we began to prepare for the consecration.

Meneer du Plooy donated ten chairs for the VIPs of the community and also the table and tablecloth for the Bible, and a glass and a jug for water. But the community bought an expensive bowl for the baptism water which the dominee would bless.

That Saturday everybody helped clean the church yard, as the stony plot was now called. We took the stones and carried them away. Finally Oom Chai said: People, tomorrow, immediately after the eight o'clock whistle you must all be here, the grown ups with their chairs and benches.

The consecration of our mission church

Soon after the eight o'clock whistle the following day, the people began to arrive with their chairs and their benches, everyone in their best clothes. The children were scrubbed clean. There were only a few men and boys whose clothes were not patched. Patched but clean, they said proudly. The older women wore their Sunday dresses. Most had only two dresses – a Sunday dress and a house dress.

When Oom Chai was sure everyone was there, he opened the two doors, a whole four-foot wide. The children all had to come and sit in front, and if a child had a chair or a bench he had to give it to a grown up. Behind the children the grown ups sat on the chairs and benches, and those boys and grown ups who had nothing to sit on, stood behind them. Satisfied with this arrangement, Oom Chai said: Remember your places. Now we're going out to form two rows at the door. First the children, then the bench people and then the others. Then we come in again.

At the head of the two rows stood Oom Flip and Oom Chai, who was twisting the two points of his moustache between two fingers of each hand. A heavy railway grid lay ready on four stones. The witgat wood was ready to be lit when Oom Chai gave the sign, as soon as the bigshots appeared in the gate opening.

There were three trestle tables (which used to belong to the army) covered with handmade tablecloths. On one of them was the meat, neatly cut and salted. The liver was on another table in a dish together with the best pieces of the young ox which Meneer Piet de Bruin of the farm adjoining Vatmaar had donated. There were ten glasses of different shapes and sizes on a tray, and a jug of home-made ginger-beer, also an empty tray for the roosterkoek. The dough for the roosterkoek stood ready on the third table. And there stood the three grand old ladies of Vatmaar, Ouma Lewis, Sis Bet and Tant Vonnie, with their best aprons on and their best scarves on.

Meneer de Bruin and Miesies de Bruin came riding along in their Ford and waited near the church for the dominee and the elders who would be coming from the Pan. They arrived – four men and four women, the men wore black suits and the women their best hats. When they climbed out of their two cars, Meneer de Bruin went to greet them with a handshake. They stood still and exchanged a few words. Then the dominee walked out ahead of them to where Oom Chai and Oom Flip stood waiting for them, Oom Chai with his family Bible (which he said was older even than he himself and written in the first Afrikaans – by which he meant High Dutch) in a silk bag.

The buzzing of the people stopped.

The dominee greeted Oom Chai and Oom Flip and shook their hands. He said a few words and then walked further. The other guests came afterwards and greeted the two big men. At this point Oom Chai lifted his hand as a sign that the fire could be lit.

In front of the closed church door the dominee received the key from a young girl. There were two young girls, both barefoot and in white dresses. With his arms outstretched, the dominee prayed out loud, blessing our church, and unlocked the door. The young girl, holding a bunch of asters in a vase, was the first to go in because Oom Chai had said she must put the first foot over the threshold, she, the purest and most beautiful of Vatmaar. The girl put the vase on the table where the dominee would put down his Bible. She put her two hands together as one does when praying, curtsied, and turned around to sit on the floor with her friends.

George Lewis stood next to a chair under Oom Chai's pepper tree and watched the goings-on through British army binoculars. He helped put up the church and was very proud to be part of it, but as he said to Oom Chai: You know as well as I do that I cannot get on with a Dutchman. They have no flag, and now they rally behind their taal.

Oom Chai had forgotten to bring along a chair for himself, so he had to stand next to the seated bigshots. Some people felt sorry for him, others thought it was right like this and others felt it was his just desserts.

The dominee said: I am so thankful that God has given me the opportunity to welcome the beautiful and healthy people of Vatmaar into the bosom of the mother church seeing that Afrikaans is their home language.

There we go again, Oom Chai thought. It's our home language but their mother tongue.

This mission church, the dominee said, this building, was the first

Dutch Reformed church in Du Toitspan. When we built a bigger church, it became the church hall. And so it is that our first mother church has now become your first mission church.

Hereafter he read a chapter out of the Bible, the part that says you must build your church on a rock. It made the people of Vatmaar feel better about all the stones on the plot.

Then the dominee gave the congregation the number of the hymn. The ten guests opened their hymnbooks (because each one had such a book and a Bible with them) and sang: Holy is the house of the Lord …

It was only they who sang and the congregation enjoyed it. After his sermon, in which he said the servant is not greater than his master, the dominee blessed the water in the bowl.

Oom Chai got all the mothers and their babies and young children to stand in a row to be baptised. He took a new black hardcover book out of his silk bag in which he kept his Bible and handed it to Meneer du Plooy so that the names, surnames and dates of birth of the baptised (if they could remember it) could be written down in it. The Juffrou, Dominee Pienaar's wife (the wife of a dominee was always called Juffrou – "Miss" – as a sign of respect), took out of her handbag a packet of cards. These were baptism cards on which she copied the particulars from the hardcover book before handing it to the parents of the baptised child. Another hymn was sung when the baptising was over.

The dominee was the first to leave the church, and the other guests followed. Oom Chai led them to the table that was meant for the honoured guests and handed each guest a knife and fork on a tray. He then took the liver off the fire, put it on a plate, and said: Guests of Vatmaar, help yourselves.

He did the same with the meat. Then Sis Bet cut open the warm roosterkoek, and placed it, with a big chunk of butter, on the table. She moved mugs of ginger-beer nearer to the guests and said: Drink! don't be shy, it's Vatmaar's special. Then: Wait, she said, you people can't stand and eat. She called a few boys and said: Go and fetch chairs for our dominee and our church people.

Oom Chai took a mug of ginger-beer, roosterkoek and meat to his friend George under the pepper tree. When everyone was sitting and eating he said to the dominee: We did not give thanks before we started eating!

Good, Chai, the dominee said, we will not forget to say Thank You Lord when we have done with the consecration of the church.

Then, in a loud voice, the dominee said: Close your eyes everyone.

The whole of Vatmaar stood still while the dominee conveyed our thanks to God.

One of the honoured guests from the Pan enjoyed the roosterkoek so much that she told Sis Bet it was the best she had ever tasted.

Oh yes! Sis Bet said, it's an old Voortrekker recipe.

Then there were handshakes and more handshakes and still more handshakes.

After the guests had left, the Vatmaar people tried to eat everything that was left over. Nobody had cooked on that first Sunday in October.

The elder, Meneer du Plooy, always preached on the first three Sundays of the month, and Oom Chai on the last one. By now the people had learnt the words of Our Father, and also, as they called it, Oom Chai's song, Nearer my God to Thee.

When the white elder conducted the service, the church was usually full, but when Oom Chai preached, something which he took very seriously in the beginning, only a few people came. He could not understand this because he didn't know it was because they then had to sing Nearer my God to Thee as slowly as he did.

Oupa Lewis only came to church when Oom Chai preached. He came with his wife who never missed a Sunday service. When Oom Chai announced the book and chapter in the Afrikaans Bible which he had got specially, then Oupa Lewis opened his English Bible and read softly to himself. Even when a prayer was being said he would mutter the words to himself. He said he enjoyed the churchgoing. His two children, Elsa, the girl, and Tommy, the boy, were sent to an English boarding school in Kimberley where they became Roman Catholics.

The first funeral

Ouma Lewis was the first to be buried from the church. After the coffin was brought in and placed onto two small benches, Oom Chai walked up to Oupa Lewis. Without a word he took George Lewis's English Bible and put down his own Dutch Bible down on the table. He opened the English Bible and read: In my Father's house are many mansions, if it were not so I would have told you so.

The church was packed to capacity because the people of Vatmaar had been a part of Ouma Lewis. And it was a Sunday.

There was no preaching, and Nearer my God to Thee was not sung. There was only a long moment of silence.

Then this white man held the hands of his two coloured children and went to stand at the head of the coffin. He looked into the dark face of his beloved Ruth and in a beautiful, rich voice sang: Rock of Ages, cleft for me, Let me hide myself in Thee … all four verses.

The coffin was closed and placed onto Oom Flip's trolley and Old Swing knew she should not be in a hurry, the whole of Vatmaar was walking behind her.

By the graveside Chai began to sing in a broken voice Nearer my God to Thee. Vatmaar knew the words and sang it as if it came out of one heart and as if they were talking to the Heavenly Father. After this the coffin was lowered. Oom Chai threw a few handfuls of earth into the grave and said in English: Dust to dust, ashes to ashes – out of respect for his friend's language.

While the grave was being filled in, Oom Chai looked into Oupa Lewis's face, took his hand and led him away. They embraced each other as only twins can. Both began to cry. The tears dripped onto the shoulders of the two greybeards as they stood there. Everyone grew quiet. Then the two old friends dropped their arms and without thinking about it each took out his khaki hanky and wiped the face of the other. The people stood dead still. And watching this, slowly shaking his head, Oom Flip said: Love knows no borders.

Oom Flip tells about his transport riding

Oom Flip said that his people lived in Basotholand, a land which he had left as a piccanin.

A transport wagon came past their stat. When nobody was looking, he jumped on to see what it felt like to ride on a wagon. He never thought that if he rode away he would never come back.

I was enjoying my first ride on a wagon and soon I was fast asleep. Just before sundown I was woken by the agterloper, the man who walks behind the wagon. He called a man with a beard and spoke a language to him which I did not know yet. They were happy to have me because, as they said, I had come willingly. The agterloper asked me my name in Basotho and I said: Pelo.

Baas, he says his name is Pelo, the agterloper said.

The man with the beard looked at me. No, his name is Philipus, his name must come from the Bible, he said. This is what the agterloper told me afterwards in Basotho, but the baas almost never called me this.

Early in the mornings and in the evenings just before dark the baas looked into a stiff, thick, black book. On Sundays we outspanned and rested. At the outspans there were always other people about and the baas spoke to them and I could see they were talking out of this big black book which they called a Bible. Long after that I asked this agterloper what exactly was this Bible. He told me but I did not understand. By this time I was calling the agterloper by the name the baas called him – Neels – but he told me he is Oom Neels. There was another man, Saul, the front runner, but the baas called him Paul because, he said, the names in the Bible have also been changed like this. Oom Neels explained this to me too.

That first night away from my Rra and Mme I ate my first roosterkoek. We had a wagonload of flour that, as they said, had to go to the Free State. With the forefinger the men bored a hole in the sacks and let the flour run out and every time they filled a cup until there was enough in the dish. They laughed as they did this. I didn't know why they laughed but I laughed too. They liked it when I laughed.

That first night I cried and cried because it was cold underneath the wagon. All I had on was my loincloth. They shouted: Shut up, little Kaffir, shut up, little Kaffir! I didn't know what Kaffir meant. Later they heard my shivering and my crying because I could not keep my teeth still. Just before sunrise Oom Neels pulled out an empty sack from underneath him and threw it to me.

The further we rode, the more I longed for my father and my mother and my sister, Roba, and I dreamt about them. The only thing that took my mind off my home was sleep and work and Oom Neels saw to it that I got enough of that. Then there were also those strange words I had to learn.

The first words I had to learn were: Wash the dishes. After that they taught me: Make coffee. I liked to steal sugar. I usually got the leftovers. All the time I wanted my Rra and my Mme. But one thing at least, my stomach was never empty.

At that time I was very young, actually just a piccanin. My first life's lesson was that sleep can take away the longing for your mother and father. Throughout that winter I woke up regularly at night and cried until I fell asleep again. Most nights I couldn't get my Rra, Mme and Roba in my dreams. Oom Neels slept through everything until daybreak.

One outspan was near a dam. The wind blew over the dam and it was very cold. Oom Neels, the one who told me what to do because he spoke my Rra's language, later told me to creep in behind his back. The next morning he told me that I was his mosimane, his son. After that I didn't feel so alone any more.

There was always something that had to be washed and watercans that had to be filled. They made sure I was busy whenever we outspanned. They knew I wouldn't be so stupid as to try and find my way back home alone. The baas said: The little Kaffir will stay because he came of his own free will.

I couldn't wait until we inspanned again because then I could jump onto the wagon and creep into the sack and catch up on the sleep that I had lost during the night.

One day we outspanned near the place where the flour had to be unloaded. Just as it began to get light we saw springbok grazing near the wagon. Saul, the front runner, crept to the baas because we slept under the small wheels. The baas slept at the back under the big wheels, with all sorts of things between him and us.

Oom Paul pointed out the springbok to the baas. He got up with a rifle which he kept by his side in a bag. And kwa! kwa! there were two springbok on the ground. I saw it all because it was now my new job to collect firewood early in the morning before anything else. It was still cold but Oom Neels had given me a heavily patched shirt which covered me right down to my feet.

Nobody will understand how grateful and proud I was of that shirt, Oom Flip said, my first possession in the world.

The baas said: You fetch the buck and skin them. I'll clean the Martini. From that day on I called all guns Martinis.

I have never eaten so much meat in my life as I ate that morning and it was the first time I ate liver because at our home liver was grown ups' food.

There was always something to keep my mind busy, always something new to learn. At first I could not understand why the front wheels stayed in front and why the big wheels did not overtake them. Or why the Martini made such a loud noise. Or why so many white people had the name Baas.

One day the baas called me. He called me Philipus. I did not hear because until that day he always shouted Little Kaffir. Suddenly he got up and it was the first time in my life that I saw a big man angry. I looked at him and jumped up and ran around the wagon because I was scared. He got up from his folding riempie chair, picked up a piece of firewood, caught me and lifted up the back of my shirt. He gave me such a sound thrashing that I remember it to this day and will never forget.

That was my first hiding, Oom Flip said.

Eventually we came to an iron house with a roof on poles in front. We unloaded the bags of flour. Then we loaded onto the wagon all the hides and skins we could put on and tied them down with riempies. We also had to make place for a few wooden boxes which we had to put down very slowly because there was something inside that could break.

The baas called the place the Jew's Shop. He told Oom Neels and Oom Paul: I'm going to have a bath now. Pull the oxen forward. Then come here for your money. The Jew's Kaffir will look after the wagon. And Neels, tell him to keep his eyes open and watch the Jew's Kaffir – and he pointed to me.

Of course I did as I was told as I did not want another beating.

At the next outspan the baas said to Oom Neels: Bring me one of those boxes.

He was sitting on his riempie chair.

And you, Paul, bring the claw hammer, he added.

Then he opened the box very carefully and took out a bottle of yellow water. Oom Neels told me later it was called brandy. Very slowly the baas took out the cork. I couldn't understand why he was being so careful. When he had taken the cork out he laughed and said: Bring your mugs, thieves first.

We drank half the bottle and put the rest back in the box for the next outspan.

At the next outspan there was a friend of the baas. He took out the bottle but didn't give Oom Neels and Oom Paul any and they grumbled all night. When the bottle was empty and his friend was gone the baas took the hammer and broke the bottle. He put the broken pieces back in the wooden box and nailed it closed.

Only years later I realised that they had stolen the flour and the brandy, Oom Flip said.

The Jew called the baas Meester Swartz. Now you can see where I got my name from. I am Philipus Swartz through and through.

Oom Flip had a potbelly. He was shortish, but not very, with a round rear end that moved when he walked. He had a bald patch right at the back of his head. The grown ups called it a runaway blow. They said he had run away from a fight and then he was hit by a stone from behind and that made the mark. He had a round face, always clean shaven with, as he said, his own German razor. When he laughed you could see a gap in his front teeth.

Oom Flip was our only transport between Vatmaar and Du Toitspan. His trolley was always loaded, whether he was going or had come back. He never asked directly for payment for a passenger or a load. All he did was point to his licence plate which was nailed to the side of his bench and say: You see, my transport licence is two shillings a year. I have to pay it on time. I can't go and show the empty palms of my hands in the office in Du Toitspan like you do with me.

He usually said this when the people were already on the cart. And before he started out he said: It isn't fair to Old Swing. She always looks to see if I haven't overloaded.

Oom Flip always said he had bought Old Swing, his one-eyed mare, because nobody else would have her and that she knew it. Nobody ever heard Oom Flip say a harsh word to Old Swing and he also never kept a whip. She is part of the family, my eldest daughter, he used to say when he had nothing else to say.

Old Swing used to turn her head just before she pulled away.

People said she had to turn her head because it was the only way she could see the other side with her one eye.

Oom Flip said that he never got money from his baas Meneer Swartz on the transport road or on the diggings. All he gave him sometimes was a few pennies saying: This is your pocket money, you are my volunteer Kaffir.

He was already a full-bearded man and began to have feelings for a woman when Meneer Swartz sold everything he had, Oom Flip said. He loaded his own belongings onto the wagon, together with his wife, the Ounooi, and his two daughters, Grieta and Mollie. By this time Oom Neels and Oom Paul were both gone. They went to stay with their wives on Baas Delport's farm near Klerksdorp. The two new workers were very lazy and made as if he, Flip, was very stupid. To keep the peace Oom Flip just did most of the work.

The Oubaas, as they had begun to call him, said he was moving to the diggings near Lichtenburg.

When we got to Bakerville, we had to build a shack for the white people. Philipus Swartz had to sleep under the wagon, Oom Flip said. It was my job to fetch water in a scotchcart and to sell it to the diggers at sixpence a four-gallon paraffin tin. It was then that I met a very nice girl. I'll tell you later what her name was.

Sis Bet

In Vatmaar, Sis Bet was known as a Griqua woman. In the sunlight her skin was light-brown and in the shade it became dull yellow. She was quite a bit taller than her husband, Oom Flip, with a straight back and two generous buttocks. She had high cheekbones and a sharp chin and her eyes were never completely open but just two straight slits. Her dresses were cut straight and hand sewn. On Sundays you knew her by her dress, a Sunday dress with big yellow flowers on a blue background. She was one of the luckier women who besides her Sunday dress also had a weekly dress and a house dress. Most women only had two dresses. She always wore a scarf and on Sundays it was a yellow one, a Christmas box from Oom Flip.

Sis Bet was much younger than her husband. He called her Buck and she called him: My old man. Whenever they spoke to someone else about each other it was: my Bet, and: my Flip. Her only child, Little-Neels, was the spitting image of herself and she always used to say: He's more ma than pa.

Sis Bet and Oom Flip were among the prominent people of Vatmaar, he with his transport business and she with her khadie – a drink which made you nice and drunk – of honey and a veld root which only she knew where to dig for and which she always went to fetch all alone. She sold the liquor at sixpence a canfruit tin. This tin was called the "scale". When the khadie was strong the grown ups said: It's nice today. And then again: It's weak today. All Sis Bet usually said was: Take it or leave it. And it was always sold out before the sun went down

They were very proud of Little-Neels. Why? Because he had a date of birth. Neither Oom Flip nor Sis Bet knew their own birthdate. So they celebrated all their birthdays on Little-Neels's. Something which they did so thoroughly that the whole of Vatmaar was always asking them: So when is the big day again?

In church both always made sure that they each had a tickey for the collection plate. After church Sis Bet took off her shoes as soon as she got to the path and carried them home in her hands.

Buck! Oom Flip said once after a service when they were walking in the path. Did you hear what the preacher said about give and you shall receive?

When they got close to home, Little-Neels suddenly called out: Ma, look!

Where? his father asked and picked up a stone because he thought it was a snake.

At the bushes, Pa – and Little-Neels pointed with his finger.

My child! his mother said, and gave him a hug and lifted him clean off the ground. It's our two tickeys that we put in the collection plate and which Our Lord has given back to us double!

I count twelve chickens, Oom Flip said.

Oom Flip couldn't always count. When he began selling water at the diggings, it was the first time that he worked with money. Sometimes he gave too much change and sometimes too little. But he learnt quickly because Meneer Swartz instructed his daughter Mollie to ride with him and to work with the money until he could count money. Oom Flip was well known among the diggers and they liked him because he often gave a free can of water away here and there.

Mollie Swartz was young and like all young girls also pretty, no matter how dirty she was out there in the diggers' camp. She soon had a boyfriend, Philemon, the son of Meneer Steenkamp at whose claim the watercart stood most of the time.

And as Oom Flip always said, God works in twos. Baas Steenkamp had a servant girl who came to him regularly with her bucket and said to him: Ta, these people don't give me water to wash myself. They say it is too expensive to give away. They tell me to wait until it rains and then I can wash my dirty arse.

And so, whenever Mies Mollie and Baas Philemon disappeared behind the shack (because the shade was at the back and it was very hot) he filled her bucket. Sometimes Oom Flip left Mies Mollie behind at the Steenkamp's shack and then this girl asked Mies Mollie if she can ride with him when he goes to fill the cans, because her work was done.

Mies Mollie then said: If your baas is satisfied.

Baas Steenkamp always said: All right, go.

The white people called the girl Bet and very soon he was calling her that too. But he said it shyly and from the heart. (Buck only came later.)

It wasn't long before he was taking whatever money was in the money bag and giving it to Bet, because to him all money was the same. She then bought them brown sugar, and sometimes a tin of condensed milk in which they made little holes and then each sucked out half.

It was Bet who said: We must steal in such a way that they don't notice. And the white people never did notice. Sometimes Mies Mollie gave Oom Flip a tickey and said: Go and buy yourself something.

One day Mies Mollie again stayed behind at the Steenkamps. Bet got onto the cart without asking if she could come along. She held her hand against her ear. When he asked what's wrong she wouldn't say. When Oom Flip took her hand away he saw that her ear was swollen.

Did the wasp sting you? he asked.

Yes, she said.

Bana! Men! Oom Flip said, pulled her hand from her ear and held it gently, because it felt like something else which he had once held in his hand. Then he remembered – the Ounooi's silk handkerchief which he had to chase once because the wind had blown it away.

This was the first time that he had come so close to Bet.

The next time, when she again climbed onto the cart, when he had to go and fill the cans, her lips were swollen and she could hardly talk. He asked her what happened.

I fell, was all she said, not where and how, and he asked no more about it. Later, when he dropped her off at the Steenkamps' shack, she walked around to his side of the cart. She put her hand in his and looked into his face, her eyes shiny with tears. Then she turned around and walked away.

That straight back stuck in his mind until the next time he saw her.

Friday was washing day. The day on which the diggers washed their gravel. Oom Flip had to see to it that those diggers who had bought their water from him had enough to last until Monday because on Friday he had to turn the handle of the pan himself and see that the gravel comes to the sorting table, which was in fact the kitchen table. Only the most trustworthy workers were allowed to wash gravel. Most diggers did it themselves.

Oom Flip did not cart water on weekends, but the straight back remained before his eyes. On Sunday afternoon he decided to walk past the Steenkamps' shack. Just to see her would be enough for him. He still longed for his Rra and Mme and his sister Roba, but since setting eyes on Bet that straight back had taken their place.

The Lord's work is wonderful, Oom Flip said. The Lord knows what is good and nice for us, when our time is ripe. There I saw her, sitting under a thorn tree on a rock. I recognised her by the colour of her dress. As I came closer I could see that the dress had been washed, because it was the only dress I had ever seen her wear since I met her.

He walked around the bush and made as if he had not seen her. So she picked up a stone and threw it at him to catch his attention and to make sure that he'd look in her direction.

He walked straight to the bush and gave her his best smile because he saw how Philemon Steenkamp smiled whenever he saw Mies Mollie.

Bet stood up from the rock and said: You sit, Philipus. She went to sit opposite him and folded her arms around her knees.

Bana! Oom Flip said. Do you know something? This woman wanted to know everything about my life. From how I became Philipus Swartz to how I put the diamond gravel on the sorting table. And I, Philipus Swartz, had never said so many words in such a short time. Some things I had to say over and she laughed and I liked it when she said: How's that?

Then he would say it over, just to hear her laugh, not loud, just for his ears. He noticed that, whenever she was thinking, she would tilt her head backwards. And she liked it when he said that he had never in his life had a woman. This was after she had asked: Where is Philipus's wife?

It was getting dark and he said: Bet, we have to go to bed because I've got a lot of work to do tomorrow. Tomorrow is Monday. You know most of the diggers are without water.

This Oom Flip was the best worker that any boss could hope to have. He was more like a trained horse than a man.

Bet said: I'm scared. When he asked why, she said: The Oubaas has stayed behind. He knows what he wants to do. The others have all gone to Lichtenburg.

He asked again: What is making you scared?

The Oubaas is drunk, she said. Let me go and have a peep and see what he's doing.

Good night, Bet, Oom Flip said, because to him Bet was now lovey, sugar, condensed milk, holy and everything that's nice. Since he had met her his life was no longer the same. He felt as if he belonged to her. God, he said, as he walked away praying, is she not beautiful? Because God, Oom Flip thought, is the only one I can talk to about her and who will understand.

The next day Mies Mollie got off the cart at the Steenkamps' shack and Oom Flip waited for his Bet, as he had begun to call her in his thoughts. Just to see that straight back again, he said to himself.

Drive! he heard Mies Mollie scream. It's Monday. The people don't have water. Don't stand and die there!

By now he was able to count the proper change.

Later when he fetched Mies Mollie from the Steenkamps, on the way back to the Swartz shack, he asked her: Mies, where is the servant girl? I didn't see her.

She said she didn't know, but that the Ounooi had asked her (Mies Mollie) to help them clean up the place. And as if she was proud of it, she said: It seems the girl is sick. My Philemon says the sjambok did a good job, he says the Oubaas asked her to make him coffee, but then she told him to make it himself. Philemon says they got home in time otherwise the Oubaas would've killed her.

No knife could ever have stabbed deeper into my heart than those words, Oom Flip said. And that she had said it as if Bet were a horse that had to be broken in. As he looked at her he thought: I know you white people. I know you better than my own people.

All week Oom Flip did not see his Bet. Sunday, he decided, he would go straight to the tree and go and sit on their rock. When he got nearer he saw that she was already there and he walked faster.

Good morning Bet and what happened? he asked in one breath.

She wanted to get up from the rock but he said: Today you sit on the rock and tell me your story.

He could see she was sick. Her voice was crackly like that of one who feels sorry for herself and he wondered why she should suffer so. Her body trembled and he draped his jacket around her shoulders. He could see that she had not washed her dress this week.

She closed her face with her hands and cried and cried and cried. The more she cried the more Oom Flip said to her: Cry, Bet, let it all come out. Then you'll begin to feel better.

Later she stopped crying and Oom Flip took the hem of her dress and wiped the tears from her face and hands. There was a long silence. Then he said: Bet, now I know you when you laugh and when you cry. And in a heartsore voice he said: Bet, I will never let you cry.

And then he kissed her, his very first kiss, to seal his words.

After a while Bet said: One day, when God allows us to be alone, I'll tell you everything, Flip. But I promise you it will be before I tell you that you can have me. Because then, Flip, you will have the right to say you do not want me. And I'll ask you then to kick me under my arse like a horse that has not yet been broken in – and she gently stroked his chin.

Oom Flip did not want to hear such words, but he also could not forget them now.

Slowly he shook his head and quietened her with the words: I will never do it, Bet.

Sis Bet tells about the diggings

Sis Bet said that she had grown up in Daniëlskuil and that Captain Waterboer was her oom, the youngest of her father's brothers.

Philipus, I won't tell you about our Griqua way of life because you did not tell me about your Basotho way of life, she said. You said that you ran away from your kraal when you were still a boy. Now, Flip, let me tell you about myself.

I was in my becoming-a-woman years when my father's brother ... But let me first say: My father was dead and his eldest brother was the head of our home. He took care of my mother and us children.

This oom of ours was very good to me. He always gave me something nice and a smack on my buttocks. Because it was our job as girls to collect firewood, we had to go deep into the veld to collect firewood. I was alone because Kiewiet, my eldest sister, had walked ahead of me. Suddenly my oom called to me. He was sitting under a tree. I went nearer and asked: Oom Baaitjie, what can I do for Oom? I really liked him very much because he loved me, just like a father.

Then he grabbed me like an animal and threw me down on the ground.

She got a big fright because he was on top of her.

Philipus, she said, God gave animals horns with which to defend themselves, but all a woman has is her mouth. I screamed as hard as I could: Kiewiet! Kiewiet! He tried to close my mouth with his hand. I screamed: Kiewiet, he's killing me!

I'm coming! Kiewiet shouted back.

When Kiewiet came running, that old man who I loved as a father, ran away. Kiewiet never saw him sitting or running.

I was shivering with fright and I was full of dust. When Kiewiet asked me what happened I told her, because she was a woman who had a husband. But she said she didn't believe me. At the hut I put down the firewood, I went to fetch water at the well and washed myself. I thought that if Kiewiet did not believe me, then no one would. So I kept quiet.

But Kiewiet could not keep her mouth shut because it was first-class news. Not one of the family believed what I'd told Kiewiet. My mother said: Bet, my child, how can you tell such lies? Your father's brother is a respectable man from a family of captains.

Flip, that oom of mine could never look me in the eyes again and he stopped giving me something nice to eat. People began calling me that mad girl and my mother said she should've choked me early on.

So, when these people – and she pointed to the shack of the Steenkamps – passed through Daniëlskuil after visiting family of theirs and talking to my mother, my mother said to them: Take her and make her a human being.

The white people said they were from the diggings in Barkly-West but that they were on their way to the Bakerville diggings near Lichtenburg. They were looking for a housemaid. They gave my mother ten shillings, all they ever paid for my work.

That was three years ago, Philipus. Sis Bet looked out ahead of her, but her eyes were not seeing. Her mind was empty. The emptiness became too much for her and she began to cry again. Then she stopped and said to herself: I must be strong, I am alone.

You are not alone, Oom Flip said. There are the two of us and the Lord.

Do you see this dress, Philipus. This is my third dress, she said and pulled at the print dress. The first one my oom's daughter threw at me before I left there with these white people – and she again pointed to the Steenkamps' shack. She said: Here, you witch, take and cover your arse.

When I left nobody even said go well, Philipus. My whole family just stood there and greeted the white people as if they knew them. At me they looked as if I was one of a litter of pups that was being given to a new master. I didn't even have my own little bundle, Philipus, only the dress with the hatred of my family on it.

She wiped away her tears. Oom Flip put his hand on her thigh. I'm working for nothing and you're working for nothing. Our food is what falls from the master's table, he said to her with shining eyes.

Philipus, Sis Bet said, and stuck her finger in her mouth and pulled it out so that it made a sucking sound as her people do when they make a vow: The two of us, we will make it right.

Without another word she stood up and walked away.

The following Sunday took a long time to come because both their hearts, the hearts of the humblest of servants yet capable of the deepest love, were under that tree.

But in the end Sunday afternoon did come and the one was as eager as the other to come to the tree as soon as their work was finished. This time Sis Bet was the one to find Oom Flip under the tree. Afternoon, Bet, he said, stood up and pointed to the rock: Sit.

Her only dress was washed, he noticed, and it was the first time he had seen her wear a scarf. You look pretty in the scarf, he said.

Sissie Lena gave it to me.

Who is Sissie Lena? Oom Flip wanted to know.

She is one of our people but from Postmasburg. She works for Mister Goodall, an Englishman, the claim nearest to the road. She came to see me when I was sick and she went to fetch medicine that helped me. She said to me: This place where they are looking for things which they don't even know where it is, is godforsaken. There is not a herb bush to be found here. Sissie Lena brought the medicine wrapped in the scarf and when she left she said I could keep the medicine and the scarf. So now I can cover my head like a woman.

Philipus, Sissie Lena is the only friend in the world that I have – and Sis Bet looked down to the ground. Before you had come here to Bakerville, I always used to go to her. It's Sissie Lena who taught me what a Griqua woman should know. She told me what to do when a child is born and when the life has departed from a body. She taught me how to make khadie and where to look for the root. She is the one who told me: That is the secret, that root, and: If you can make khadie you'll never be without tickeys.

Sissie Lena told me everything about herbs, what they look like and what they can be used for. She said I'll know them when I see them because all Griqua women have that gift. That and a lot of other things she taught me. Sissie Lena, Philipus, is my mother who was sent by God.

I also want to call her Sissie Lena, Oom Flip said softly and with a bit of jealousy, because he also wanted to be one of them.

Sis Bet then told about how Sissie Lena wanted to know about the sjambok marks. I tried hiding them away but Sissie Lena is a big woman and she said: And now these marks, my child? So I just told her.

And what did Sissie Lena say then?

She said: It's better like this, my child. It's good that you didn't give in to that Steenkamp, the filthy swine. Every dog gets its day.

Sissie Lena's son also works for Mister Goodall. His name is Janman and he's about your age. His wife and children are in Postmasburg. I told Sissie Lena about you and she said that you once gave her water and change without her even paying you. Bet laughed.

She will never again pay for water, Oom Flip said. Not when I'm alone on that cart.

Philipus, Sissie Lena asked me to tell her about you.

What was it Sissie Lena wanted to know about me?

Nothing. She just asked me to tell her again what you said about your work with the diamond gravel. Then she said: We are going to use him to get out of here – and she put her finger on her lips to show that it was a secret. Then Sissie whispered in my ear: Keep your mouth shut. First I have to speak to Janman. Then she turned around and said: Good night, my child.

Sissie Lena's plan with the shiny stones

So Sissie did speak with Janman and he said they had to be very careful, they shouldn't be seen in the company of this man Philipus.

If the Boers have an honest Kaffir, especially one who grew up with them and who they could trust, they always watched to see that he had nothing to do with us clever Hotnots. And they see that he doesn't realise that to those whites a Kaffir will always be just a Kaffir, Janman said to her.

By now Sissie Lena knew about Sis Bet and Oom Flip's courting spot under the thorn tree. The people also knew that Mies Mollie was going to be the Steenkamps' daughter-in-law and that her father's Kaffir visits the Steenkamps' servant girl.

Tomorrow, Monday, Sissie Lena decided, I'll take something to Bet and ask her to go with me back to Goodall's shack.

Janman said to her: Ma, the main thing is for Bet to ask him if he's ever seen diamonds lying around on the sorting table and whether he tells his master if he sees them, and also where is his master when he throws the diamond gravel on the table. We will have to move inch by inch, Ma. It's very dangerous. We really must do our best to pay them back. These white people care more about their dogs than about us.

Sunday came and Oom Flip was under the tree long before Sis Bet. What's taking her so long? he sat and wondered. It was the first time in his life that time began to matter to him. Then Bet came, and he usually got off the rock so that she could sit.

But this time he took off his jacket and threw it over the rock. She liked this because it made her feel nice, just like a white woman, she thought. She let Oom Flip speak. Most of his words went through one ear and came out the other.

Finally she said: Philipus, let me hear how you put the diamond gravel on the table?

He told her that he was the one who takes the kitchen table

and puts it down next to the machine. If he turns the machine and there is enough gravel in it, then he shovels it into the kitchen bucket and spreads it out on the table. Then, if the baas is not there, I look to see if there aren't any stones lying on top, Oom Flip said.

How do you know when it's the right stone, Philipus?

The baas taught me and sometimes after he has looked he says to me: You look, my Kaffir. I've have found stones because he's old and he can't see as well as me.

And the other two workers? Sis Bet wanted to know.

Oh them. The baas told me to watch them and not talk to them and not to let them come near the gravel. It seems they don't like me. They say I want to be white.

Everyone on the diggings knew that Meneer Swartz doesn't tell when he has found a good stone. His diamond claim was one of the richest in Bakerville, the diggers whispered amongst themselves.

I heard the baas say things are not going very well for the Steenkamps, Oom Flip told Sis Bet. The baas said he knew Mies Mollie gives them water for free and that she can't keep away from their son. It would be a good thing, the baas told the ounooi, if they got married, then Philemon can sort the diamonds because our Kaffir has also now found himself a girl. Just like that, Bet.

Your girl, that's all I am, Sis Bet heard herself say, got up and said: Good night, Philipus.

He took her hand as if he was walking with her out of their lounge. He liked it. Good night, Bet, he said, and walked away as if he was stepping on air.

Sissie Lena went to visit Sis Bet one evening in the week. Next to the shack Mies Mollie, Philemon and Baas Steenkamp were standing together. As she passed them she said: Good evening, Baas, Kleinbaas and Kleinnooi. May I go and visit one of my Griqua family? Because if I do, tomorrow I will feel that the loneliness has gone, my Baas.

74

Yes, go ahead, old girl, Baas Steenkamp said.

When she got to Bet she kissed her and said: How are you, my child?

It was the first time that Sissie Lena had kissed her and that evening Sissie Lena was doing all the talking, all about Griquas and about Postmasburg. She spoke as if someone was standing outside listening. Later she took Sis Bet by the hand and said: Walk with me because there is no moon tonight. Your eyes are better than mine and the puff-adders love the path after a hot day.

A good thing too, Bet thought when she walked through her doorway, because there's Steenkamp and his wife, standing and listening to what's being said inside her living quarters. They disappeared quickly, so fast that the white woman actually jingled.

When they were a distance from the Steenkamps' shack, the two women stood for a while. The older took the hand of the younger and whispered: Don't speak loud. Did you speak to him?

Yes, Bet said.

Tell me everything.

Bet told Sissie Lena everything and Sissie Lena wanted to hear it a second time.

So Sissie Lena said: Treasure him like gold. I'm going to talk to Janman. I'll see you next week. She put her finger on her lips. Keep your mouth shut, we'll be leaving here, you'll see.

They said good night and while she was walking back, Sis Bet thought to herself: Leave here? Who wants to leave here? Not leave my Philipus! But I will wait and see and do what Sissie Lena says because she knows best.

The following weekend while Sis Bet and Oom Flip were sitting under their tree (because they now called it "our tree") trying to make the time move slowly by not speaking and not falling asleep, Sissie Lena was waiting for Janman. When he came they also went to sit under a thorn tree so that they could see if anyone was coming. After she had told him what her neef, her cousin, had told her, Janman said: Say it again, my Mother, I just cannot believe it, but then again I do believe it. Sometimes a white man really picks a cane for his own arse! What do we do now?

Janman, his mother said, we don't have much time because time and luck don't often work together. I'm going to tell Bet to ask this man of hers to bring one of those stones. But she has to tell him how dangerous it is, because if he gets caught, he'll go and die in jail.

Ja, she has to first give him a good fright, said Janman.

So, after they had thought out their plan very carefully, Sissie Lena said: You know, my child, we must be honest with this man because I know all the people that have been caught tried to cheat each other. So the most important thing is to be honest with each other. There are four of us in this thing.

They had been under the tree almost all morning when Sissie Lena said: You're right, Bet will first have to talk some real fear into him.

Who knows, said Janman, I don't think he can be that stupid, because first he gave the people too much change when they paid for water. But now he won't give you a penny more or less. And the funny thing is, if he feels like it then he doesn't even take your money.

Sissie Lena's plan was that Bet should first make sure that Philipus does not take any chances. Then she had to ask her if she really loves him. If he said yes he did, then she had to put her arms around his neck and give him a long kiss. She should wait awhile and ask him again: Do you really love me? Will you do something for me? Say he says he'll do anything for her, then she should say: Bring me some of those shiny stones.

I'm sure God is on our side, Sissie Lena told Janman, because don't you think God can see how these people are treating us? For a free person to have to live like a slave is worse than being a slave that has been bought. The bonds are all the same.

It was getting late and Sissie Lena got up. I have to go and do my kitchen work.

Good night, my Mother.

Good night, my child.

Both walked back thinking and thinking and thinking, mother and son, both each their own thoughts on their different paths. We should rather let their love grow than break it, Sissie Lena thought, because I have never before seen Bet in such a good mood.

She again went to visit Bet on a weekday evening. This time she said to herself: I'll be more careful because after all I know they eavesdrop.

The life of a diamond digger is hard. All the time he hopes that he'll find a stone that will make him rich. If he doesn't strike it lucky then his family and his workers suffer with him. But his workers always suffer the most because even if he does get a good stone he still treats them as if he's having a bad time.

Among the diggers there were a few who bought diamonds from the workers of other diggers for next to nothing. Everybody knew about it. Diggers are friends because they know the same sort of life. But despite this there was a deep mistrust among them and at Bakerville they were always trying to find out things about each other.

Sissie Lena was one of the lucky housemaids. Because they were English, the Goodalls allowed her to eat in the kitchen of their shack. Even her clothes she got from them, including a headscarf to show that she was a servant who worked indoors. When she drank tea she put her mug on a saucer. She also got a piece of yellow soap every Saturday. The piece that was left over from the week before she usually gave to Janman. But this week, she decided, she would give the leftover piece to Bet because she had not given Bet a piece of soap for quite a while.

When she pulled the piece of iron away from her doorway she saw Bet lying on her bedding. Bet, she said, I've brought you a piece of soap, my child.

Bet opened her eyes because she wasn't sleeping. It was just getting dark and she didn't have a candle because the Steenkamps were not doing well. Since digging on their new claim, they had found not even one diamond. A candle for a maid is a waste of money, they said.

Sissie Lena again started with her stories, this time stories about her childhood. Then she said it was time to go.

Wait, I'll walk with you because I heard they killed a puff-adder in the path last night, said Bet. When the two had walked a good distance and made sure there was nobody nearby, Sissie Lena didn't ask Bet if she wanted to do it, she sommer told her what she had to do. And while she was laying out her plan she said over and over again how dangerous it was and that Bet should give Philipus a good kiss and then come with the if-you-love-me bit.

The whole plan remained stuck word for word in Bet's head. They said goodbye and when she walked away, Sissie Lena said to herself: Some people have all the luck but they are usually stupid. No, not even that, they are real apes.

That Sunday Sis Bet was the first at the tree. When Oom Flip saw her, he began to walk faster. At the tree he greeted her with a handshake and she took his hand and pulled herself off the rock. Then he let go of her hand, took off his jacket and folded it into a pillow and put it on the stone for her.

Did you even wash your jacket, Philipus?

Yes, he said, I don't want you sitting on a dirty cushion.

They sat and they sat and drank in the being together. Then Sis Bet came out with it. She did exactly what Sissie Lena had told her to do. When Philipus told her that he really loved her, she put her arms around him and kissed him and, without thinking, he put his arms around her and held her tight. She loosened her arms from around his neck, but he kept holding her tight. He went down on his knees and remained like that.

I'll only do it for you, Bet, he said slowly. Then he kissed *her*, still on his knees. Later it got late and they both got up. Oom Flip took her hand and led her away from the thorn tree. They said good night to each other and went home.

It was the longest week in Bet's life. It seemed to her that Sunday would never come. And Sissie Lena didn't come and visit to break the week. But when they sat next to each other on Sunday with not much to say to each other, Bet thought what a good man her Philipus was because he had done what she asked him to do and the waiting was nothing.

It's my lobola, she told him with a laugh.

The diggers' workers who did the actual digging, knew that diamonds were selling at unbelievable prices, but they never knew the right price. Nor did Oom Flip know and he didn't know what the stones in his inside pocket were worth.

Would you mind if I first tell you how I came by that sore ear, that swollen mouth and the sjambok marks, Philipus?

He said nothing and she told him everything. He sat very still, like someone who was being beaten up while his hands were tied behind his back.

I believe you, Bet, he said after a while. My baas did the same to their young maid, Flossie, but she ran away and I never saw her again. The Ounooi just said the Oubaas would never have done such a thing.

Again there was a long silence.

Then Bet told Philipus to put the stone that he had brought her in her hand. There were two. One was as big as a thumbnail and yellow. The other one was halfway as big and white. Oom Flip lifted up their sitting rock and she hid the two sparkling stones underneath. Then she said: Only you and I know.

The begetting of Little-Neels was out of wedlock, yes, but completely among the angels of love. This one-dress Griqua girl had nothing to give the older man. But he wanted nothing from her because he was used to being the least.

When the fire of love was burning at its highest, she touched him in a place where he had never been touched before. He sat motionless and breathed through his mouth as if he needed to cool off his heartbeat. Hereafter there is no recollection. No pause, no rest. He just kept going. Very few young bulls could keep up with this young old man. And when his body could no longer keep up, he rolled over and lay beside her on the grass, blowing out his breath through his mouth. Phew, he thought, heaven cannot be better.

Bet wanted some more.

Then, like all engines that are hot, they cooled off on their own. It had been their first time and there would never again be a first time.

After that he was a man and thought like a man. Now he knew what was yes and when to say no. They sat next to each other without being ashamed that they had done what nobody had ever taught them to do. And satisfied that they could do it. Because now we have eaten grown ups' food, thought Bet.

Buck, he said, now we are man and wife. As if it was an order. She believed him.

She got up, took the jacket and held it so that he could stick his arms in. He took her hand and led her out from under the tree. They did not say good night to each other, just nodded their heads, which meant much more.

It was winter and a cold wind howled over the diggings. Bet took Mies Mollie and Philemon their tea on a tray.

Maybe there is compassion in the world after all. Mies Mollie had on a thick jersey and long socks while Bet could not drape a blanket over her shoulders when she served the tea, standing shivering on her bare, burst feet.

Come, Bet, Mies Mollie said, come ride on the watercart tonight so that I can give you a jersey.

That afternoon when Oom Flip came to fetch Mies Mollie, Sis Bet also climbed onto the cart. Oom Flip looked to one side, but when he rode away asked himself: What's going on now?

At the Swartzes' shack Mollie said: Wait here. She came back with a red jersey with long sleeves that was worth more to Bet than the two diamonds under the rock.

In the meantime Bet had been thinking and thinking where she should hide the stones because the fear that she had to plant in her Philipus now had her in its grip. But she was not without a plan.

Mollie was of the same height and build as Bet and Bet said to her: My Mies, I am asking for some of Mies's old bloomers please.

Mollie went into the shack and was back with the piece of underwear and said: Take it, but don't ask me for anything else because you people are never satisfied.

Thank you very much, Bet said, clapping her hands together and not forgetting to add My Mies.

This was just what Bet wanted – heavy black bloomers with elastic in the legs. She walked away very thankfully, put on the jersey as she walked and the bloomers behind a bush.

The next day she asked her mies if she could go to Sissie Lena when her work was finished as she would like to show off her new jersey. Go, my girl, she said.

At the Goodalls' shack, which looked better than those of most of the other diggers, because even if they were rich most diggers chose to live as if they were poor, Bet greeted Mrs Goodall: Morning, Merrem. My work is finished and so my mies said I could come and say hello to my sissie.

She is just round the corner doing the washing.

Thank you, Merrem, Bet said.

The two Griqua women greeted each other with a kiss. Sissie Lena winked and asked: Did you come right?

Bet knew the danger of talking about such things and winked back. All that she said was: Under our tree. Both laughed. She went to help her sissie at the washtub. They didn't speak much because both knew if their own people found out someone had a diamond, then they would want half the money: Or I tell the police.

Sis Bet knew many stories of people who were cheated, robbed or had spent many years locked up in jail and she was very careful and thought hard. They are not going to catch my Philipus, she decided.

When the washing was done, Sissie Lena made two mugs of coffee, a privilege which Bet did not have at the Steenkamps. Then Sissie Lena said to her madam she was going for a walk with her grandchild.

Let us go, the older woman said.

Bring some needle and cotton, Bet said softly.

Without asking why, Sissie Lena obeyed.

That morning Bet made sure she was alone when she tidied the baas's bedroom. She opened the wardrobe and took the red silk handkerchief out of the top pocket of the baas's jacket. Her dress did not have pockets and she hid it in the safest place – in the leg of the bloomers. Now I know where to put the stones, she thought.

Without saying a word, she and Sissie took the path that led away from the Steenkamps' shack, which brought them to the other side of the tree.

They are my stones, Bet thought. And I won't let them leave my hands before the money is in my hands. Under the tree she went and sat on the rock and smiled and looked at the grass because she remembered about the previous Sunday.

Come over here and lift the rock up, she asked Sissie Lena.

Bet took out the two diamonds. Her sissie put the rock back in its place and Bet went to sit on it. First she showed the small diamond and then the other one.

Bet, Bet, Bet, my child, we did it! Let me keep them. I'll give them to Janman to sell.

Just as I thought, Bet said to herself. I've been with her all afternoon and not once has she asked about my Philipus, the man who has done what I asked him to. It's the first time that I've asked a man to do something for me, and he did it. And to think it's so dangerous, if they had caught him they would've locked him up forever. I can win or lose, but it will be with the diamonds in my hands.

Bet took the needle, with the cotton already threaded through the eye, from the reel and bit off a length of thread. She made a knot and stuck the needle into her dress. The dress, patched here and there, once had a colour but now it was just a dirty white.

Her sissie sat on the ground in front of her like an old woman: on her side with her legs stretched out sideways. Bet lifted up her dress and took out the silk handkerchief.

Where she got that silk hanky I wouldn't know, thought Sissie.

Bet took the two diamonds and put them in the silk handkerchief and folded it into a square one and a half inches by one and a half inches and sewed it up. Then she asked Sissie Lena to lift the stone again. She closed her hand around the red parcel so that her sissie could see it clearly and then shoved the hand underneath the stone. Then she pulled her hand back and opened it so that Sissie Lena could see that she left it under the stone. But in the meantime she had the red parcel in her other hand.

They both laughed and Sissie Lena said: Let's go, we don't want them to see us here.

Without another word they were gone. Where the path forked and they had to part, they came to a stop and Bet said: Only Sissie and I know.

You're a good child, Sissie Lena said.

The next day after work she went to visit Janman. We did it! she told him.

How big and what do they look like?

Like this – and she showed him her thumbnail. And like this – and she showed him half of her nail. A yellow one and a white one.

Show me again, my Mother, he said. Then I'll have to believe you.

She put her forefinger in her mouth and pulled it out so that it made a sucking noise. It's true, she said, swearing in the Griqua way and crossing her two fingers, which meant: We never lie.

We have a lot of thinking to do, my child, she said. But we'll leave it for Sunday. You know where.

Tell me, my Mother. Where are the stones? Does Mother have them?

She did not answer. She just put her hand on his shoulder and said: Good night, Janman.

That week Oom Flip saw a few diamonds lying on the gravel. He went and gave them to the baas. But they were tiny little diamonds.

You are the best Kaffir in the land, Oubaas Swartz said.

I could've taken them too, Oom Flip thought to himself, but my Bet told me I shouldn't do it again.

That Sunday afternoon Bet was again with Oom Flip under the tree. She was surprised to see that somebody had turned the stone around and had forgotten to put it back in place.

I know who it is. From now on I'll be even more careful with her, she said to herself.

Oom Flip came and the shadows were full of their togetherness. They said very little and spoke only about what had happened to them in their own lives – not about diamonds because they knew very little about diamonds, just that they were dangerous things. And we don't want the danger to scare us, Sis Bet said.

They had both come here from other places and they knew there were better places than the diamond diggings. Places where you can plant a little food and harvest it, where you can put something in the ground and be sure what will come up there.

They spoke a lot about going away from this godforsaken place and its people. Since he had met his Bet, Oom Flip had learnt another kind of life and now he wanted to be free to work for himself. But how and where to go they did not know, which is why they just sat and held hands until it was time to go. It gave at least some comfort.

Neither of the two was schooled in matters of religion and their God was not the same in their thoughts. Each had their own picture of a Great Giver of that which was good, but their prayers were the same: Help me, Father. And most of the time their Father did help them.

Without greeting but with his hand held tight in hers, Philipus said: We are going to ask the Lord.

84

He left her hand and walked away.

Under the other tree sat a mother and her son. The son was very excited because he had met one of their people who was from Du Toitspan. The man worked at the Barkly-West diggings and there, he said, is a diamond buyer who had twice bought diamonds from him. With the money from the last diamond he had gone back to Du Toitspan to get a house because he had a wife and two children. He could buy everything they needed plus a lot of goats and a milk cow to keep them going. Now he was back again. Stones, he said, are very scarce at Barkly-West. That is why he was here in Bakerville to look for work.

What is his name? asked Sissie Lena.

Jakob Kierie.

I don't know that name, she said.

Sissie Lena was quiet and very worried because she had only one thought: Where is that red bag? She left all the talking to Janman. Then she asked him: Did he give you the name of the diamond buyer?

Yes, my Mother. Mister Hall-Stone.

Yes, she said. I once heard Mister Goodall tell his wife Hall-Stone in Barkly-West pays better for diamonds than these velskoen diamond buyers of Bakerville.

Now we have the buyer but not a diamond, Sissie Lena thought with a sigh.

I hope Jakob Kierie finds work. I told him Mother is also here on the diggings. He said he would like to meet Mother.

Suddenly Janman got up and said: Ma, I'm leaving now.

Sissie Lena remained seated on the stone until it was almost dark. She said to herself: The thought is eating me up. I must go and see Bet tomorrow.

Monday afternoon Sissie Lena took Bet an old towel. She carried it loose so that everybody could see there was nothing in it. Bet was busy shaking out blankets with her ounooi because the September wind blew so much dust into the shack.

Afternoon, Ounooi, the dust is finishing us, my Ounooi, Sissie Lena said.

Yes, my girl. It's the last blanket, then you and Bet can sit and cackle.

Sissie Lena and Bet laughed.

I brought you a towel, my child, Sissie Lena said. It's old, but a person can still use it.

She went to put it in Bet's little shanty and used the opportunity to look around quickly. There wasn't much. She lifted up the old sheepskin off the floor and the blanket off the bed and scratched in the ground with her fingernails, but it was too hard. She was just about to shake out the blanket when Bet looked in at the opening.

Oh yes? she laughed.

Sissie Lena got such a big fright that she couldn't get a word out.

Bet waited outside for her sissie to come out. The older woman crawled out on all fours because the door was about as high as a table. Bet took her hand and helped her up. When she was standing upright her sissie said: What a horrible sleeping place. But you don't know any better.

But one day I will, Bet said. My work's done. Let's go to your place where we can walk through the door.

Sissie Lena took Bet's hand as if it was a child's. Come, my child, she said. And Bet looked at her with eyes that said: I don't trust you.

They walked slowly, both deep in thought.

Do you still have the red bag?

Yes, Bet said, Sunday when I got to our tree the rock was thrown over and there was the bag in the grass. Maybe a cow had tramped it over.

Her sissie threw her arms around her. How lucky we are my child! she said.

Bet could feel her sissie's heart beating. You're a wide awake old girl, she thought.

86

Without words they walked on. The one did not trust the other, yet they were people of the same kind.

Tell me, my child, did you put the stones back under the rock? Sissie Lena asked later.

No, no, my Sissie. In another safe place.

Lena sighed but said nothing. Thank you, Lord, was all she thought. Then she told Bet about Janman's new friend and that Janman wanted to bring him to meet her under the tree. She told Bet everything that Janman had said about the man.

Good, then I'll bring Philipus with me to your tree on Sunday.

Good, Sissie Lena said. I'll see if I can get a jug of Kaffir beer.

Good, then I'll be on my way, Sissie.

Sunday afternoon the four Griquas and the Basotho sat under the tree and passed around the beer so that everyone could get a few mouthfuls. In this way the liquor lasted longer.

When the jug was empty, Sissie Lena said: Well now, Jakob Kierie, tell us about the place you come from. What do they call it?

Du Toitspan, he said, and the white people speak mostly English. But there's a new place not far from the town where you can buy a plot for fifteen shillings and five shillings a year. There's lots of water. And I spoke to one of our people there, his name is Ta Vuurmaak. He says people buy bricks from him and he doesn't have to work because he gets an old-age pension.

What kind of a thing is a pension? Oom Flip wanted to know.

They laughed and then Sissie Lena told him. Which was a good thing because Sis Bet didn't know either.

Oom Flip asked lots of questions. They couldn't understand why he asked such stupid questions.

Then Jakob Kierie said: The people in that place struggle a lot because they don't have transport and the transport in the Pan is expensive.

This news set Oom Flip's head spinning. He sat dreaming of his own oxen and wagon. No, he thought, not oxen, a horse and cart or maybe mules. He gave a little laugh from his heart because now he knew his own desire.

Sissie Lena did not say that they had diamonds.

What if we get hold of a stone ...? is all she asked Jakob Kierie.

Then you must give it to me so that I can sell it and give you the money like I also did for Mister Goolam who has a groceries shop in Barkly.

They didn't say yes or no. Every one of them got a faraway look in the eye but saw and said nothing.

Then Sissie Lena said: The main thing is to get away from here. We mustn't run away if we move because they'll have their suspicions. And it will be: They've stolen a stone.

Let them say what they like, Jakob Kierie said. I go where I please. I am after all a free Hotnot.

We'll leave it there then, Sissie Lena said and took the jug. Let's meet again Sunday, again here – and she pointed to the tree. Everyone went his own way, deep in thought.

Old Man, Bet whispered in his ear, tell them all you want to marry me then watch their faces and tell me Sunday. We must let the diamond buy our horse and cart – because she saw how his face lit up when he heard about the transport problem. By now she knew her Flip's moods as if she had known him all her life.

I'm going to tell my ounooi that I'm going to get myself a wife and that it is you, Buck. And then I'll see what they say.

They held hands and looked into each other's eyes. Then Oom Flip smiled and said: Then I'll be on my way.

The following Sunday Oom Flip took a walk to Sis Bet's shanty. He stood outside. Bet, are you there? he asked, and he thought to himself: I am not scared of anybody any more because she is my woman. Only yesterday Mies Mollie wanted to know why he gave that maid two canned-fruit tins of water – one is mos enough to wash her dirty face, she had said. He did not like the way she said it, so he replied in a loud voice: She is my wife.

Neither Oom Flip nor anyone else knew why Sis Bet wanted the extra tin of water. But at night she covered the water with the towel which Sissie had given her for a cushion. In the tin she hid the "red danger", as she called the parcel, and in the mornings, took it out, squeezed out the water, and put it in its place between her legs.

You must not stink, she kept thinking when she put it where it belonged.

When Bet told Ounooi Steenkamp that Philipus wanted her for his wife, she said: I don't want another Kaffir and maid on the claim. One Kaffir and maid is more than enough. So if he wants you he must take you with him. He's getting too big for his boots and the sjambok hasn't had work in a long time. Maids are everywhere. I give you a kick under your arse and immediately someone else is there to take your place.

That is what her ounooi said, Bet told her Flip. And since then the Steenkamps began giving her less and less food. She went to bed hungry and got up hungry.

Every evening that week Philipus brought her half a loaf because he was no longer scared of her white people.

But one night Philemon asked him: What's that you have there, Kaffir?

My wife's bread.

You forgot to say Baas, my Kaffir, Philemon said.

Philipus just looked at him.

Buck, he said later, when I told them I'm going to marry you the whole Swartz family laughed. You're not a man yet, my Kaffir, the oubaas said – who had known him since he was a piccanin in a loincloth. Have you tasted? Is it nice? Now you want to throw away your good oubaas for pussy.

Oom Flip did not say a word. He just looked at his oubaas because with those words he had just stamped into the ground the respect he had felt for him.

Mies Mollie immediately said: Keep him away from the gravel. My Philemon said he'd do the sorting any time. Pa just has to ask.

Buck, Philipus told her, the Ounooi then said: He's no longer our Kaffir, he's a strange Kaffir. Keep him in his place.

Oom Flip was sad and Sis Bet felt sorry for him because she knew that she was the cause.

That Sunday the five people under Sissie Lena's tree were deep in thought after the jug of Kaffir beer was empty. When Bet told them what her ounooi had said, Sissie Lena said: It's just what we wanted, it's in our favour that she said so.

Then Philipus told his story and they all laughed over his oubaas's words that he was not a man yet and whether he's tasted already because to these people words were words, each one with its meaning, whether they were good or bad words.

Sissie Lena said her madam understood immediately when she said she had to fetch her inheritance otherwise her brothers would leave nothing for her. The madam must've taken it that Jakob Kierie had brought this news because she saw him with me last Sunday and she said I could take all my stuff and that she'll give me my pay as long as I just get her another maid, one she can trust as much as she trusts me.

Madam, Sissie Lena said, Madam is a very good madam. I say thank you to Madam for treating me like a human being. I am leaving with a happy heart and I leave Madam behind with a good heart.

I told her that I already found someone for her and then the madam said I must just tell her when I want to leave.

It all sounds very good, Jakob Kierie said, but where's the stone? I can't think before I've seen the stone.

The stone's time is coming, Sissie Lena said with a wave of her arm.

Good, Janman said, that's that then. I'll go and fetch my wages on Saturday and Bet also has to ask her ounooi for her money. Philipus will also ask for his money and on Sunday we all meet here again ready to leave on Monday. It's summer and it's better to travel in summer than in winter.

Where is the stone? Jakob Kierie again wanted to know.

Don't worry, you just find us a buyer, Sissie Lena said. Right? See you on Sunday because on Monday we're leaving.

The following Sunday morning Sissie Lena found Philipus and Bet at the tree. And now? she asked.

Bet was the first to tell what her ounooi said when she asked for her wages: We've already paid your mother, and you're lucky to get a stupid Kaffir for a husband. Take your things and go to him!

So I rolled up my things in the blanket, left the sheepskin and the other rubbish and came to sit here and wait for you.

Philipus said that he first put away the watercart and took care of the horse before going to tell the oubaas that his work was finished.

Then you should go and wash and wait for your food as always.

No, my Oubaas, I'm leaving, I said. Please give me my money I've been working for all these years.

Then Oom Flip kept quiet, deep in thought but without thinking.

What did your oubaas say? Bet wanted to know. The tears began to drip out of his eyes.

He said: Go away, you bad Kaffir! And he chased me away as if I was the neighbour's dog.

Bet wiped his tears with the towel and said: His day will come, Old Man.

My madam even gave me food for the road, Sissie Lena boasted. She also had two heavy trunks with her. She had come here with one of them and the other her madam gave her when she saw that her stuff was too much for the one suitcase.

Janman arrived with all his belongings rolled up in his blanket. And so did Jakob Kierie. Oom Flip had two blankets and a knapsack of rawhide with a strap to carry it over his shoulder. It was a fairly big bag and he always kept the strap over his shoulders. This made Jakob Kierie believe the stones were in the bag.

Oom Neels gave me this bag when he left the oubaas, Oom Flip said knocking on it with his hands.

Then Sissie Lena said to Bet: Let us women go and throw away some water. They went to squat behind a bush. When they came back, Sissie said: Bet, let me hold the stones.

But Bet replied: Sissie, I'll hand them over when we sell them in Barkly-West. When only the four of us are together.

Oom Flip and Sis Bet find Vatmaar

It took the five of them nearly two weeks to get to the Windsorton railway station. There they slept in the waiting-room.

Jakob Kierie wanted the diamonds because, he said, he had come such a long way with them and still they did not trust him. How could he sell the stones without having them in his hands?

Everyone kept quiet because they knew Bet had them, or maybe they were in Flip's bag with the brown goathair. But Sissie Lena was not sure.

They agreed that Janman and Jakob Kierie should go to Barkly to see if they could get to see Mr Hall-Stone. They found him in his office, but he said all his money has been paid out, they must come back on Wednesday. As they walked away Janman learned his motor-car number off by heart: CC 14.

On the Wednesday all five of them went back to the diamond buyer's office, but the old man who looked after the small wood and iron building said: I got a message that Mister Hall-Stone is not coming in today.

You go so long, I'll come later, Jakob Kierie said.

The four walked back to the waiting-room at Windsorton and gave the station boy two shillings for having looked after their stuff. Oom Flip naturally had not left his bag there.

Come with me, Philipus, I'm rotting already, Bet said to Philipus when the others went to sit and rest. You keep a lookout while I wash.

She squeezed the red bag into the water until the smell was out and put it back again where it belonged. Philipus saw nothing.

Sissie Lena and Janman's money grew less and less and they knew Bet and Philipus had no money left and that they would only have some again when they sold the stones. Jakob Kierie had long ago said straight out: I have no money and I am the seller so you have to look after me.

Sissie Lena could not take it in any longer. When Bet came back she said: Give me the stones. I've been looking after you and Philipus since we left Bakerville. My money's almost finished and it's only fair that I keep the stones.

Yes, Bet, Janman said. Do as my mother says.

Bet made as if she had not heard a thing. Then Philipus took a tobacco bag full of sixpences and shillings out of his knapsack. This was money which Bet had told him to steal from his oubaas, with the warning: Be careful they don't find you out. And the Swartzes never did find him out.

He threw the money out onto the bench and without counting made four stacks. He pushed one stack forward and said: Here, my Sissie, then pushed the other stack forward and said: Here, Cousin. Then he said: Bet, I carry the money, you work with it.

What a man, Sissie Lena thought, and yet so simple.

They bought a watermelon and kept a piece for Jakob Kierie. They were just about to sleep, when he arrived. They could see that he was drunk. With him were a white policeman and a well-dressed coloured man.

There they are, my Baas, he said.

They had to take all their stuff and carry it out in front of two men on bicycles. Jakob Kierie walked behind with the white policeman. At the police station the sergeant asked: What is the charge?

Let us search them first, the policeman said in English. One of their sort says that they have a diamond to sell.

Sissie Lena understood this, but all Bet and Philipus knew was the word "diamond".

They were searched over and over and over. Jakob Kierie was

very sure that they had diamonds on them and he kept saying: Baas, I saw the diamonds.

No, Sissie Lena said, Sir, we just came to take the train to Kimberley and from there to Postmasburg.

When they found nothing, the sergeant called his wife because he was sure that the diamonds were sewn into the ugly patches on Lena's dress.

Come! the sergeant's wife said and closed the door. She felt all over the patches. Then she opened the door and called: Manuel!

The coloured man came to the door and she said: You look.

She gave him the dress and again closed the door. He felt and looked and made sure there was nothing there. All the time Jakob Kierie watched the detective's hands without blinking an eye, because he was tipsy.

After Sissie Lena had been searched, the sergeant's wife said to her: You go. She got Bet to take off her dress. It was very dirty so she threw it on the floor and said: Sit on the bench. (Before the white woman had said she could go, Sissie Lena also had to sit on the bench.)

Bet knew what to expect. She stood up and said: Miesies, I have my monthly illness. Then she slapped her hands together as if in prayer and said again: Miesies. And then cried: I've got my monthly illness.

The sergeant's wife could see that Sissie Lena understood English and she said: Let the other woman come here. What does she say? she asked Lena.

Madam, she say she have her monthly periods.

But to make sure, the sergeant's wife pressed Bet down on the bench and said: Open up. Bet did not understand the words but she knew what they meant. She opened up as she was told to do.

Sis! shouted the sergeant's wife, pulled a face and went to the window to clear her throat and for some fresh air. Then she went out of the room and said: Darling, the poor women have nothing on them.

94

Bet came out with tears on her cheeks. Touching her shoulder, the white woman said: Sorry, my girl. The sergeant said you may go.

Lena understood this and said: Come, you.

On the way to the door they heard Jakob Kierie mumbling: The white woman has the stone.

Since he has given us such a lot of unnecessary work, lock him up, Manuel. He is drunk and will be charged for being drunk and disorderly. Take him away! the sergeant ordered.

Because it was late afternoon, Janman said: What's the point of going back to the waiting-room. The train will only get to Kimberley tomorrow afternoon. We might as well sleep here.

His voice sounded sad because he thought the diamonds were gone and that he would have to go home to his wife and children after coming so far for nothing.

Sissie Lena was once again the same as always because she knew where the diamonds were, because only the red parcel could give off such a bad smell from Bet. And yet she wasn't sure. The young girls of today aren't as clean as we older women, she thought, specially if they didn't work for a madam. I'll take one last chance, it's either the stones or a dirty arse.

Right opposite the small iron office they came across a pepper tree with branches that hung low. We'll sleep here tonight, Sissie Lena said, and tomorrow we sell the stones – and she looked directly at Bet nodding her head slightly.

Janman was very surprised. One sometimes has to dig in surprising and deep places for a diamond, he said. He was now a new person and he added: I'm going to buy us some bread – and he took an empty bottle to fill with water. We don't know what lies ahead, he said.

Philipus sat motionless thinking that Jakob Kierie was just as bad as Bet's baas and his own oubaas – their jackets were made from the same cloth and cotton. He thought about what had happened to them, and how they wanted to know where he had got his German razor. He had kept quiet because he was in another world. His lessons in life as a man without a baas had begun. He was now on his own and had to stand on his own two feet, and Bet was his responsibility.

Old Man, he heard Bet say, look after our stuff. Me and my Sissie are going to wash at the tap as soon as it's dark – and she pointed to the bush behind the little office.

The sun was already high in the sky when the diamond buyer arrived in his Buick motor-car with the CC14 numberplate. Sissie Lena said immediately: Give the stone.

No, Bet said, we're all going together.

That morning Bet had got up early and had a good wash. She had squeezed the red bag until she knew it couldn't smell any more. Philipus stood nearby to keep watch over her, and because he had his knapsack with him, she stuck her hand into it and pressed the red danger into it as deeply as she could.

Together they all walked to the buyer's office, Philipus with the bag over his shoulder, because they knew he wouldn't leave it behind.

Morning, Master, Sissie Lena said and then softly: Diamonds.

You four together?

Yes, Master.

Then close the door.

Take out the stone, my child, Sissie Lena ordered Bet.

Bet stuck her hand deep into the knapsack, which was sewn together not with cotton but with sinews. She took out the red bag and the razor with the same hand.

Take the knife, she told Philipus and put the red bag down on the table. Cut it open, Old Man.

When he did this the most beautiful diamond the buyer had ever seen fell onto the table. He said so himself. Flawless and clean. The white diamond had a flaw.

Did you put it in cleaning acid?

No, Master, Sissie Lena said.

Bet smiled and thought: If he only knew how it was rotting.

The diamonds were worth much more than this Mr Hall-Stone was prepared to pay. He then asked Sissie Lena: Where's your diamond digger's licence?

But she knew how to work with an Englishman because she knew them better than she knew the Boers. Master, she said, give us what Master think is a honest price. We know Master will help us poor people, for it is our luck.

Fuck your luck, he thought with a smile. It's my luck too, I'll give you a quarter of what it's worth.

Then he took his magnifying glass and looked carefully at the white diamond. I'll give them a third, he then decided. Eight hundred pounds! he said.

Make four, Sis Bet said. For poor people to survive they had to know counting and numbers. Reading and writing was for their more privileged brothers and sisters.

The buyer made four stacks of two hundred pounds each. Each one took their stack. Bet put her and Flip's money in his knapsack. You keep the money, I work with it, she said.

Mr Hall-Stone was very happy to have struck such a bargain. And on top of it, they did not even ask what he would give for the white diamond. He decided to be kind to them. Where are you going? he asked.

Kimberley, Sissie Lena said.

I'll give you a lift there when I am finished with those people outside, he offered.

When he was finished he locked the door and shouted: Where are you?

Here, Master, Sissie Lena said.

Oh no, not with all those things! The trunks I will not take.

Then they arranged that Bet and Philipus would ride with Mr Hall-Stone. Sissie Lena and Janman would walk back to Windsorton and take the train to Kimberley from there. That was how they separated in twos. When they said goodbye the four said to

97

each other: God was with us. And in their hearts they said: Thank you, Lord.

Bet and Philipus were alone in a strange world.

Years later, when Oom Flip and Tant Bet were well established in Vatmaar and Little-Neels a sturdy youngster, Oom Flip bumped into Jakob Kierie in the Pan. He had just been released from prison after three years for having uncut diamonds. He said that Oubaas Swartz in Bakerville had died a poor man like most of the other diggers. His daughter Mollie had got married to Philemon. Their only child was dead. Oubaas Steenkamp had taken his own life. Both old men had said if they only knew they would never have allowed those two creatures to leave because they were the last of their kind left in the world. They had taken their luck away with them leaving behind only grief for the whites. This is apparently what the witchdoctor had told them.

This, Jakob Kierie said, is what the white people in Bakerville told each other.

In the motor-car to Kimberley not a word was said. Mr Hall-Stone pulled up at the station without asking. What a contrast, he said, looking at the two getting out.

Thank you, Master, they said and waited for the motor-car to pull off.

The waiting-room, Bet said, because she got to know the waiting-room at Windsorton station.

From this station here, Oom Flip said, we are going to do all our business.

While looking for someone to look after their blankets, they found out that they could leave them in the parcel-office at six-pence a bundle. Away from the diggings Bet begin to feel out of place in her ugly dress. Let's go and see where we can get food and where the shops are, she said.

When they got to Bergers and saw all the beautiful clothes for

98

men and women in the window, they stepped inside. After they had paid, the man behind the counter said they were the best customers he'd had in years – it was usually only diggers who bought like this when they had found a diamond.

They chose everything they needed, and bought two trunks.

It was a happy Bet and Philipus who slept that night in the waiting-room on Kimberley station.

When Bet dressed herself up the following morning as Philipus had always seen Mies Mollie do, he took a hairbrush from his suitcase.

For us both to use, he said.

Bet wrapped up the old dress in a piece of brown paper and said: You I will not throw away.

They left Kimberley by train for Du Toitspan, another unforgettable experience for them. There they again went to book in their stuff at the parcel-office. Then Oom Flip said: Now for a horse and cart.

No, Bet said. Now for Vatmaar.

Outside the station they saw the Pan's Cape cart. Good morning, Oom Flip and Bet said, and when they saw that it was a coloured man and not a white man, they added: Meneer.

Good morning, you, replied Stoffel Jones. When he saw that they had no luggage with them, only the big, hairy knapsack, he said: What can I do for you?

It's a lovely Cape cart and a well-looked-after horse, Philipus said – because the first thing he ever loved was a horse called Cat. That's the kind of horse I'm going to buy, he told Bet.

Stoffel Jones heard this. I know where you can get a good horse, he said. He was thinking about the commission that he could earn because he and the Boer Koen Lambrecht got on well together. And what about a trolley?

I have a trolley to sell, the kind with narrow wheels. It's been standing for over three years. He was quiet for a while, then he said: By the way, my name is Stoffel Jones.

Philipus Swartz and my wife Bet Swartz, Oom Flip said, taking his hand.

Like I said, Stoffel Jones said, if you're interested I'll get the wagon builder to fix it up and paint it. Just tell me what colour you prefer.

Green with yellow stripes, Oom Flip said.

By the way, where do you two friendly people come from?

From Daniëlskuil, Bet said, and Oom, my Philipus doesn't have much money. But if your price is reasonable and we can afford it then maybe we can do business.

I know, Stoffel Jones said. Money is very scarce these days.

At that moment, a man came closer cupping his hands.

What do you want? Stoffel Jones asked him.

I'm looking for work, my Baas, any kind of work, even if it's just for food. I haven't eaten in three days. Please, my Baas, just a tickey for bread. I'll clean the cart and the horses for a piece of bread, my Baas.

Go, go away, go, go away, you rubbish! the Cape cart driver shouted suddenly. Go to the white people, or to your church! – and he waved his arms like one chasing away a dog.

The man was now so nice to us, now he's in one proper rage, red in the face and shaking all over, Bet stood thinking. He's coloured, I wonder, did he inherit his short temper from a white parent?

She nodded to Oom Flip to come and listen, turning him around so that Stoffel Jones could not see the knapsack, she said: Give me five pounds, Old Man.

She folded up the five pounds as small as she could and walked after the man because he walked away when Stoffel Jones took out his horsewhip.

Oom, Oom! Bet called after him.

The man turned around, standing with eyes full of tears. Bet took his hand, put the piece of paper in it and folded his fingers around it. When she got back to Philipus, he whispered to her, also with watery eyes: Thank you, Bet. You work with the money, I look after it.

The man unfolded the piece of paper. Then he turned around as if he didn't want anyone else to see. Then he turned around again and looked at Bet with disbelief in his eyes and quivering lips. Then he pressed the fist with the five-pound note tight against his heart and walked away hurriedly, because he thought that maybe she had made a mistake.

Sis Bet and Oom Flip never knew and will also never know what that worthless piece of paper, which nevertheless did have value because its value was written in indelible ink, did in their lives. It opened up for them the Heavenly door of luck which so few people enter and which so many wish to enter. That hungry man was surely sent as a bringer of luck for the one who wanted to accept it. Because is it not written: Give and you shall receive?

Somebody came to hire the Cape cart. And Stoffel Jones said: Don't go away, you two. See you again later.

We'll wait, Oom Flip said.

Bet and Philipus went to buy some food and went to eat it in the waiting-room.

Transport we now know where to find, Oom Flip said, but first we have to get a roof over our heads. We must find out about this place called Vatmaar.

When they walked out of the waiting-room, they again saw Stoffel Jones.

Oh there you are! he called as if he was glad to see them. He opened the door of the Cape cart and said: Get in Miesies Swartz.

Bet winked to her Old Man, which he liked.

We'll buy the transport, Bet said, but first we want to find out about Vatmaar.

Wanting to impress, Stoffel Jones said: I know the man who's the headman. As soon as he has his lunch-break, we can go and see him.

That is how they met Oom Chai.

Oom Chai said: You are the kind of people we want in Vatmaar. But you must first go to Vatmaar to see which plot you want.

No, Oom, Bet said, beggars can't be choosers.

Just give us one with a seven, Philipus said.

After lunch the clerk-of-works was also back in his office. Oom Chai said to him: Sir, people for a plot in Vatmaar.

Which number? he asked.

Philipus put his finger on the number 17.

All right, said the clerk-of-works, it will be one pound. He took out the receipt book and Bet took a pound note out of the knapsack.

Tomorrow at nine o'clock my boy will show you number 17.

Thank you, Sir, Baas, the two heard themselves say.

Saturday morning Stoffel Jones took them together with all their belongings to Vatmaar. But before they left Stoffel Jones said: The people of Vatmaar are waiting for the luck. For them this is a big day – and without another word, he stopped at the Off Sales.

Sis Bet, who as a Griqua had the right to buy liquor, bought three cans of sherry at six shillings and sixpence a gallon, and even a bottle of brandy.

The man from the Du Toitspan Town Council showed Oom Flip and Sis Bet plot 17 shortly after their arrival in Vatmaar.

Thank you, Lord, they said and kissed the ground.

The well was dug. As was the custom, the first mug of water from the well was passed around so that everyone could take a sip to be part of the well. After everyone had drunk of the first water, Sis Bet and Oom Flip took a bucket of water and walked off to where they were alone. Each one tasted a few sips.

Our water, Sis Bet said.

The Lord's water, Oom Flip said.

The sun had just gone down. They knelt down facing each other, holding hands, looking into each other's eyes and could not find the words to say. Tears of joy flowed. Love they knew and had, but to be accepted as fellow human beings, this touched their hearts deeply.

Father, was the word which came from Oom Flip's mouth like a deep sigh. Father, they said together and cried. They had no more words because the feeling was in their hearts. Time stood still. Then Bet cupped her hands and Oom Flip threw water into it. She washed her face and then she washed his. Then she took the hem of her dress and dried both their faces.

It was then that she felt the first kick of the child that she was carrying. Father, she said again and squeezed Oom Flip's hand. Her cup of joy ran over. Hand in hand they walked back.

This was Sis Bet and Oom Flip's first day at Vatmaar, the 27th November, a Saturday, which they always remembered as the day of the Lord.

Broer, Ta Vuurmaak's shepherd-owner

Ta Vuurmaak was a very old man. How old, nobody knew. His age could only be estimated by the stories about his childhood. He was a true Griqua, he said with pride.

With his brick mould he had made his contribution, but soon he was even too old to fetch his monthly pension. He gave Sis Bet the job of drawing his money and looking after him. He did not need much and Sis Bet gave him the best his pension could buy.

To me, it is an honour and a privilege to do this, she always said.

There were Griqua children who Sis Bet wanted to hear and re-member the stories of their origins. They were her own son Little-Neels, and the two neefs Roman and Nicholas Klipsteek.

Sis Bet always bought the monthly groceries: a bottle of sher-ry, a pot of honey and a packet of dry prunes, and sheep liver. Sis Bet then also filled the bread bin, which Ta Vuurmaak had made out of two paraffin tins, with boer biscuits. She had learnt to bake while she was working for the Steenkamps on the Bakerville diggings.

The sherry Ta Vuurmaak drank only on Sundays, out of his goblet, calling it his Holy Communion. The honey he ate with a tea-spoon, any time he felt like having some. The prunes were to loosen his tummy, he said. Sis Bet got half of the sheep liver. The boer biscuit he soaked in sugar water. And whenever Sis Bet brought his things he always said: Bet, I give thanks to the Big Man of the Heaven and Earth. I am content, my child.

Once a week, the oupa used to spend one whole day visiting someone in Vatmaar, so that he could know what was happening and what the gossip was. But the time had come when he could no longer walk the distance from his train water tank. And one Saturday Sis Bet found him struggling to get up out of his bed. She always went on Saturdays to clean up his cabin and to wash his clothes. He had asked his womanchild, as he called her, to do this for him so that he could have a clean Sunday for his Holy Communion.

From the time that Ta Vuurmaak could no longer come to Vatmaar, the children started visiting him at his cabin.

Sis Bet bought him a kaross from the people who made them in Bechuanaland and he was very pleased with it.

The children enjoyed Ta Vuurmaak's company very much and made him feel like one of them. And, he said to Sis Bet, let any child come to the cabin, not only the ones who look like our people.

Of milk there was plenty, because Ta Vuurmaak had years ago bought two Swiss milk goats from the Cape and they bred into a fair sized herd. Some were stolen, others he sold. The goat kraal was near a camel thorn tree. He did not build the kraal under the tree because a tree attracts lightning. That's what the oupa said when one of the boys asked him why the kraal was empty and the goats were lying under the tree ruminating.

His shepherd-owner, as Ta Vuurmaak called him, was a man who learnt rather slowly. But once he knew something, he never forgot it again. He also did not know what it meant to be lazy and he also did not know what it meant to be scared. He was the descendant of Cape slaves and his name was Broer. Our boys thought him simple. But Ta Vuurmaak said the goats would belong to Broer when Ta Vuurmaak himself died. Everyone knew this.

This Broer was not fond of chatting to people, as if he knew what they thought of him. And when women spoke to him, he just smiled as if he had not heard them. Like everyone who was looked down upon by his fellow man, Broer would go and seek comfort in the veld and chose the company of the goats. He used to sell goat milk, but now with all the boys at the cabin, he enjoyed giving them the bucket of milk free.

Thank you, Broer, we used to say, and Broer just gave a nod.

Sis Bet bought cheese cloth and showed Broer how to make cheese with the leftover milk. There was also always thick milk and Ta Vuurmaak often said to a boy who was on his way home: Take some of this food with you, we have more than enough.

All the boys were good catty shots, and there were plenty of doves. Sis Bet showed us how to make soup from the bird meat, and she regularly allowed Little-Neels to bring along vegetables from their garden.

Our parents always went to tell Broer when a boy did not want to do his chores at home. This Broer would then take a stick and mark a line about twenty paces from the cabin and the boy could then not put a foot over that line until his mother said that he was now back to doing his work again.

Sis Bet also taught Broer how to make mageu out of mealie-meal.

The boys enjoyed being at the cabin. Sis Bet had only one condition – that we listen to Ta Vuurmaak's stories and make his last days peaceful ones.

Ta Vuurmaak tells about the Griqua culture

Nothing! nothing! my children, said the oupa one afternoon after a long silence just before we were supposed to go home. In this life, one of the finest virtues is to share. Share with your brother who is in need. It will come back multiplied.

The front section of the water tank had been removed even before any of us boys had been born. The rivets had been neatly knocked off with a chisel and hammer. The top and sides had since that time been covered with old and new branches. People who went out gathering firewood and who had a green branch, would pass by the cabin, take a dry branch from the cabin and leave the green one in its place.

Between the green branches there lived all sorts of creeping things, especially lizards and chameleons. Ta Vuurmaak said that, from the time that he had dragged the tank here with the oxen, he had never seen a snake near the cabin. But there were green and brown praying mantises of different sizes which we were not allowed to kill. The oupa told many stories about the mantises and we children liked that. He said that the mantis and the chameleon were made by different Creators. We Griqua people can understand what the mantis is saying just by looking at the movements of his head and forelegs, and we are never wrong.

The chameleon is just like everyman's friend, he said. Put him amongst robbers, and he will become a robber, and so with everything. He always has the colour of where he is. Just like us people, the oupa said. But the mantis and the chameleon are both the people's friend because they keep his place clean of insects, some of which we cannot even see.

Ta Vuurmaak, Roman asked, did Ta play football when Ta was a boy?

No, my child, the oupa said, but we children had other things to play with, like the claystick and the small bow and arrow that our fathers made for us, and when a boy was old enough, they showed him the poison beetle. We were also expert at throwing stones at birds in trees. And on some of our tournament days the young men played a game with us which we called head knocking. They had to knock each other's heads without using their hands. The winning blow always knocked out the opponent.

The oupa gave one of his cheerful chuckles: It was not fighting, the girls enjoyed it. The tournament was usually held during the goats' mating season.

Our Great Man of God, Heitsi Eibib, the Messenger of Tsui, God of All Things, Ta Vuurmaak said on another day, told us many winters before the white man came, that people would come who were the direct opposite of us in the way they looked and lived. And we did not believe Him. He said people would come from the big water, in a house that the wind would move across the water.

In every respect they would be different to us, only the wind which we breathe through our noses and the water which we drink will be the same. Neither we nor they will be able to live without it. Cohabiting, birth and death will also be the same for the newcomers and ourselves. But their food will not be like ours, and their bodies will be covered in a skin different to ours to keep out the cold. Their shoes will be closed and no wind will enter them. Our faces are yellow-white, theirs will be reddish white. Their noses will be long and their lips thin – not as fat as ours. Their hair will be long and covering their necks, and yellow like the sun, and any other colour, even red. Their eyes will have the colour of the heavens, and all the other colours which we see in the eyes of the birds. They will ride on an animal that is much faster than our cattle and which does not give milk.

They will carry things in their pockets which light fires for cooking without you seeing how. A person would not be able to run away from the long iron thing in their hands which makes fire, because that fire will catch up with him and kill him. And they will take what is ours through the blood of our bodies.

Are you listening, my children? Ta Vuurmaak asked.

Yes, our Ta, we replied. Because the oupa had painted a picture with words which we saw before our eyes and which came from his soul and his heart. Before each sentence he first thought carefully to make sure that what he was going to say, that the words were what he had listened to by the fire under the night sky when he too was a boy.

Our people did not believe the words of Our Great Man of God. But some of our people who walked for countless winters on the sand beside the Big Waters, they saw it.

They had already been there for such a long time that they began to speak and live differently to us Griqua people. Yet they were of our blood. It was they who saw the horses coming over the Great Waters. It was they whom the white man called the Strandlopers.

Our Great Man of God walked on the Earth many times. And every time, whenever his body got too old, he left it behind for a new life which he received with the birth of a new person.

Ta Vuurmaak, one of the boys asked. Was our Heitsi Eibib just as old as Ta Vuurmaak?

My child, Ta Vuurmaak said. I am a person. Not a man of the Heavens and the Earth at the same time. And then he said: You must never just walk past a place where stones have been thrown onto a heap. Pick up a stone yourself and throw it onto the heap, even if you have to go and fetch it from far away. Everyone with Bushman and Griqua blood in his body must do it, even if his blood has been mixed with other blood. Because who on this Earth can choose his blood? That piece of Griqua in you will feel that here is a part of me under these stones.

Ta Vuurmaak had respect for the Sun and the Moon and he dropped his voice whenever he spoke about them.

Heitsi Eibib, he went on to say, had three servants. These Elders washed before the Sun came up and again when it was halfway. And again before it went down to sleep. They were Suneaters. They took in its strength from the moment that it pushed itself through the Earth and stopped just before the Sun changed its colour. And then again at the end of its day's journey. They took the strength of the Sun between their eyes into their bodies, which made them different to us people. Eating they did only once a day – just before the Sun took its downward path.

It was their work to look after the needs of Heitsi Eibib and the people brought them honey, ostrich eggs and that which grew in the earth. As well as liver, but hunted and slaughtered from living animals only, never from an animal which had died on its own. They themselves did not eat meat, only fish. As soon as they had served Our Great Man of God, each one of them went to sit under his own tree.

The first people cut meat into strips when it was in abundance, and sprinkled it with salt and sometimes also with the ash of a certain tree and herbs. Then they hung it up to dry, in the shade, not in the sun. To be eaten without ever having put it on a fire. We called it biltong. At first the white man would not eat it, but now they say it is their invention – like everything of ours that is good. They always take the best for themselves.

People came from near and far to the three Elders to be healed. Whether the sickness was in the head or in the body, they cured it by placing their hands on the head of the sufferer. Then they spoke with Heitsi Eibib to change the colour that beamed from the head from sick to well.

It has been said that the Elders' spirits leave their bodies when they are sleeping and that they could then fly in their spirits wherever they wished to go.

What is a spirit, Ta Vuurmaak? one of the boys wanted to know.

It is that part of us which leaves the body when we die. It cannot die because it belongs to Tsui-Goab. He is the Creator of everything. The other side of the Heavens, the Sun, Moon and Stars, the Earth and the Waters and everything in it, below and above. He is the Creator of the white man and of the Griqua. And, my children, said Ta Vuurmaak softly, we are both afraid of Him and we love Him. Some people can see a spirit, usually those who have been born with a caul.

What is a caul, Ta? one asked.

It is the membrane or film that covers the baby's face at birth. People keep it and dry it out because it's a big protector against the evil forces in life. People who are born with the caul are those who can talk with those who have died.

How do I know if I am a spirit, Ta Vuurmaak?

When you dream, my children, you are in the land of the spirits. A spirit is not something to be fooled around with.

Why, Ta?

Because there are spirits and there are spirits. The good spirits belong to our Great God Tsui-Goab and the evil spirits to Guanab. It is they who bring sickness and ill luck. The witchdoctor uses spirits to heal or to hurt people.

But why would they want to hurt people?

Because it is their work, my child. Everyone on this Earth has a job to do, whether it is good or bad. The difference lies in the reward. Good brings forth good and bad brings bad.

How does a witchdoctor catch a spirit?

Like I said, my child, there are spirits and there are spirits – countless. Some witchdoctors, usually women, will dance until they are in the land of the spirits. We call it the livingdead. It is these spirits which harm people. The spirits which heal the sick we find in those bushes which are called herbs. The big thing is to use the right herbs for the right sicknesses. Some herbs can be eaten and with the root of the mor plant you make khadie. And you all know what morogo tastes like. The herbs are gathered with the help of the moon. The Full Moon and the New Moon, but the strongest herbs are harvested when the Moon makes water. This is always after a drought. And, my children, if you have a tickey and it is New Moon, look at the Moon, turn the tickey over and put it back in your pocket. The tickey will grow and money will come your way unexpectedly. But only once.

What about the flowers, Ta Vuurmaak?

They are herbs too, my child. And the flower is actually what you can call the climax as when people have sex. First there is the flower and then the seed. Take dagga. If you look at it like that in your hand you would never think that the smoke of those green leaves could take you away to another world. Whether it is good or evil. Do you children see what I mean?

Yes, Ta Vuurmaak, we all said.

Then the oupa ended with: The world is more spirit than earth.

It was for over a month that the children had been going to Ta Vuurmaak's cabin every day for the storytelling and to clean up the place. Every night two different boys slept there — after their parents had said they could. Sis Bet called in a doctor to come and check Ta Vuurmaak so that he could write out a death certificate for when Ta Vuurmaak leaves us. It will be death from old age, the doctor said, making a note.

Oom Chai kept the o.h.m.s. Ledger Register. It was given to him by the Office of Births and Deaths in the Pan. He signed when he was given the book because he had to record Vatmaar's births and deaths.

Sis Bet wanted to bury the corpse before it got stiff so that Ta Vuurmaak could be the last to have a Griqua burial. Because Ta Vuurmaak could never understand the Christian faith.

He said that when he was a boy oupas used to sit around the fire and tell their children stories about the white man, stories which they in turn heard when they were boys. They told about the time when the white man first came, how some of the strangers bartered things we did not know for our cattle and sheep. And as with all nations, some were good and some were bad. The bad ones rode deep into the veld and just took what they liked without giving anything in return. And sometimes they killed our people and took their things so that these things could remain theirs.

Our ancestors never had a word for steal before the white man came.

They told about how the white people also had a habit of sparing a boy's life so that he could look after his father's stolen cattle and sheep for them. And a young girl's life would be spared so that she could work in the kitchen.

These boys and girls were treated worse than dogs, but they had to sleep amongst the dogs until they, as they put it, became human.

They also told about how they had been given new names, Dutch names, if they survived the hard new life. Because they were given the sjambok for the slightest transgression against this new kind of life. The sjambok always hung within reach behind the kitchen door.

When the first white man came he had never before seen an ostrich and so many kinds of game. Then he began taking the best grazing land and said that it was his.

It is they who taught us about stealing, the oupas told Ta Vuurmaak during those evenings when he was a child. The white people said we are wild, but in our wildness we were prepared to share what we had. We never thought the world was ours only. But these new kinds of people did not know this.

One of the oldest oupas sat by the fire on a winter's night and told how he had run away from the white people. Even though he was grey from old age the sjambok marks could still be seen on his back. His thumbnail had been burnt with a red-hot iron so that his baas could identify him. And there was told of a kitchen girl whose stomach began to swell. Her miesies knew it was her own husband who was the father. She had the woman tied to a tree with a strap and gave her the sjambok just whenever she felt like it. When the woman died, the white woman's husband put the dead woman on a horse and went to throw her away in the veld.

We, the Griquas and the Bushmen, are not people, the white people said. And they hunted us down like animals and stormed into our homes and killed us as if we were a danger to them. They loved their dogs more than us, the people whom they hated.

In the old days we had our big days of feasting, Ta Vuurmaak said. The biggest day was when the rain came after a long drought. Then we gave thanks to Tsui-Goab. After a big drought there was never much to eat but we could let our hearts and spirits be happy. Even though our stomachs were not full.

There was also the day on which the Sun cast its own shadow. We knew it was the Sun which made the grass and the herbs grow, the trees and all the food that comes from the earth. And we honoured the Sun. We also had many celebrations for the Moon. And we celebrated the first two teeth of a child – and when a girl became a young woman. We also celebrated marriages and gave the last respects to someone who was dying.

So, my children, you can see that we had many happy days. But what does it help if I, your Ta, tell you what my oupas had told me about our celebrations. You are Christians now and you will never understand it.

Then the boy who was called Roman said: Ta Vuurmaak, we learn in church that God is Love.

That's just it, my child. The Great God Tsui-Goab is Love, but not the love of the people on this earth.

On another day Ta Vuurmaak said: The first white people in our land lived without those who should see that they live like whites. As I've told you, my children, our ancestors had their days of celebration. We had respect for our women and never took a woman against her will. She had to be taken through a celebration. We never stole the fruits of a woman. As I have told you, before the white men came we did not even have a word for stealing. These people came and taught us even another word: rape, and brought sicknesses of the sexes which our herbs could not cure.

The oupa wiped the tears from his cheeks.

These first white people had nobody to keep them in check. Their stubbornness was horrifying. They were called the trekboers and it was they who opened the way for the Voortrekkers. Another word for them was the frontiersmen.

So, Ta Vuurmaak, these people knew where the waterholes were? asked Roman.

Yes, replied the oupa. They killed us to get the watering places. They didn't know we would share the water. They didn't know we believe that we belong to the water and not the water to us. Now take the Karoo. If you do not know where the water is, you will die. And no person will be so stupid as to just load his family onto an oxwagon and ride into the unknown, whether it be Griqua, Englishman or Boer.

The white men who are called Englishmen were not so bad because they were well controlled by their captains. But the Englishmen were very cunning, my children. They sent what they called men of God – their missionaries – to get us to leave our God. Our God, who looked after us, His people, long before they had ships to sail across the Big Waters. These Englishmen taught us to cover ourselves and not to go about like Adam and Eve who were their first people. Then they taught us that we should not steal – after they had first taught us about stealing. Then they brought people to look after us, to see that we did what they had taught us to do – the police.

You see, my children, they took, but when we take they call it stealing. Then they built what they call jails. To put us in them for what in their eyes is wrong. To be locked away is the harshest punishment you can give a free Griqua because we are used to the wide open spaces.

Ta Vuurmaak shook his head very slowly.

After many droughts our Big Brother, who had been given the new name of Captain, had become a Christian together with all his people. Then he became a lover of brandy and that which his own people had given him to look after for them he sold for next to nothing. Then they built a church and said that it was the house of their God.

My children, the old man said, there is nevertheless a lot of good in these Christian teachers. They have helped us in many ways. And one must never bite the hand that feeds you. It's just that we have lost and they've won.

Ta Vuurmaak, Roman said, what were the names of our forefathers' captains?

My child, said the old man, the Big Brothers of our forefathers, their names have been washed away by time. But the new names of the captains, the oppressors and the sell-outs, are Andries le Fleur, Andries Waterboer, Adam Kok, Pieter Davids, and there are others too.

The blood of our forefathers can be seen in many people in the land. The white people did not come from their homes across the sea with narrow slitted eyes. And these with the fleshy arms and fleshy thighs, they belong to the Griqua nation. When a white man and a Griqua get married, their children's skin remains white. Not like when a white person and a black person get married, because then there will be dark patches to be seen around the fingernails and toenails.

Another feature of our forefathers is frizzy red hair and round buttocks – white people have straight hair and hanging buttocks. The Bechuanas with their light skin, high cheekbones and straight slit eyes are all part of our Griqua nation. On all the other, whether they are Nama, coloured or something else, our forefathers left their mark. Our forefathers lost everything, except their blood.

Now I have spoken enough, the old man said. I am tired.

He turned around and fell fast asleep, without a care in the world. Like a true Griqua.

Ta Vuurmaak dies and is buried

Roman took the kaross and covered Ta Vuurmaak as softly as he could. Because the boys had begun to love the old man with a deep respect. The sun had still not gone down and the boys ran to their homes to go and finish their little chores. Only Roman and Little-Neels had the privilege that night to sleep in the cabin.

Soon after daybreak, Broer, as usual, brought the old man his half mug of goat's milk, still warm from the udder. As usual he touched the old man, who always then woke quite easily. But this morning the old man did not stir. And, as simple people always have a sixth sense, Broer said to Little-Neels: Wake our Ta.

Little-Neels tried. Then he rolled the oupa over so that he faced him. His eyes were wide open and so was his mouth. Little-Neels got such a big fright that he swung around and ran out. Roman also ran out and went to stand with Little-Neels. Broer remained in the cabin and again tried, as gently as possible, to shake the old man awake. Tears fell from his eyes onto the kaross.

Without further thought, the two boys ran off – Little-Neels to go and tell his mother and Roman to tell his mother that the old man could not wake up.

Sis Bet came as fast as she could and said to Little-Neels: Go and tell Oom Chai.

And Oom Chai in turn said to him: Go and tell Vatmaar.

Roman also walked by each plot saying: Ta can't wake up.

It was the time of day when the people of Vatmaar set off for Du Toitspan to go and work. But everyone stood still because the Groot Ta of Vatmaar was no longer there.

Oom Chai told Sis Bet that he would ask a few men to bring picks and spades and to dig the grave. Because he had the death certificate, which the doctor had already signed, with him, he only had to fill in the date. Sis Bet then told Oom Chai how the grave should be made.

It was then that Broer began to cry so bitterly. He pointed to the two boys who were also crying and holding each other around the neck. Roman was saying over and over: I didn't do it on purpose.

Sis Bet, hearing what they were saying, decided: I'll wait until they have finished crying and then ask Little-Neels what's going on. She cleaned the cabin and took out all the things. The old man was rolled into the kaross and they sat the body, with his knees under his chin, under the tree.

Little-Neels, come here, his mother said and walked with him to where the others could not hear. My child, she said, tell your mother what you mean by: I did not do it on purpose.

Mama, he said, Roman tramped on the very big mantis. Mama knows how they walk about just as they like. Roman tramped on him and so he died. Ta saw what happened and went to put the dead mantis on a branch outside the cabin and said: Just like the mantis breathed out its last wind, so too will a Griqua breath his last wind tonight.

The big men cleaned out the cabin some more, splashed water onto the walls, the roof and the floor and then swept it out. Actually, Sis Bet said, the home should be cleaned with fire but the iron tank would not burn. The iron bed and the bench were then carried out together with the goblet and thrown onto the heap of dry branches on top of the train water tank. All the Ta's clothes were also packed onto the tank, because, Sis Bet said, nobody had the right to wear our Ta's clothes. Then they threw the blanket and the skins which were on the floor on top of everything and sprinkled the paraffin from the lamp on the heap and called Broer and handed him a box of matches.

Then, in front of all the onlookers, Sis Bet said: Broer, everything of our Ta that remains after the fire belongs to you.

All Vatmaar said like a choir: It is so.

Broer could barely light the match, but only he could carry out this last rite.

Everybody stood around the fire waiting for the smoke to go where all smoke goes.

Then Oom Chai came and said: Bet, I've done what you've said.

Thank you, Chai, she said, turned to the people and spoke to them, because some asked: Who is going to bury him? while others wanted to know: When is the dominee coming?

People, Sis Bet said: When our Ta was still strong he asked me to bury him like a Griqua. I didn't know how until Ta himself told me what to do. Now I'm seeing to it that his respected wish is carried out. As you know, everything that remains belongs to Broer. He had the honour of burning out that which will never be used again. Now he will have the honour to carry our Ta to his last earthly resting place.

Ta Vuurmaak was a short little man and because he had reached such an advanced age, he was very light. Broer carried him, crouched and rolled into his kaross. At the grave he handed the corpse to Oom Chai to hold. He went to light the fire packed with buchu, khakibos and wynruit branches.

The Ta had told Sis Bet that it had to be the holy nkha bush and buchu branches, but if she could not get the nkha bush, which she had not seen in many years, she could use the khaki bush and wyn-ruit, which came later.

When the lovely smell of the three herbs and the smoke drifted from the fire, Sis Bet made sure that the corpse of the Ta was on its haunches, facing to where the sun comes up. In a loud voice she said: TSUI-GOAB – and lifted her arms high up and looked in the direction of the sun and said again: TSUI-GOAB, take that which belongs to TSUI-GOAB.

The smoke which smelled so lovely made thin curls in the air and then swirled like a whirlwind until all the smoke was gone and only the grey coals remained.

Broer was still standing in the grave. Then he began taking a spadeful of sand from everyone to show that they were also from the earth. Then, softly, without throwing it, he began to sprinkle the sand onto the kaross with the body inside it. After everybody had given their spadeful of sand, the stones were packed. And af-ter all the stones had been packed, a small headstone was placed into the furthest corner of the grave. Because Ta Vuurmaak had said to Sis Bet: Do not ever let my earthly resting place be between those of Christians because they will call me a heathen, a man with-out God.

There will be no meat feast today, Sis Bet said to the people. Ta Vuurmaak has not left us a descendant.

The people of Vatmaar who had witnessed it all, spoke about the burial many years thereafter in soft, reverent voices.

Our school

We attended school in the church building until the day when the bigshots of Du Toitspan were ready to build us a school. There are not enough children to warrant a school building, they had said.

Mistress Elsa Lewis was a qualified teacher who taught at the Du Toitspan Undenominational School. When our school came Oom Chai recommended her. He had a list of names of people who had asked the Du Toitspan Town Council to make her our teacher because she lived in Vatmaar. Her father, George Lewis the Corporal, who helped shoot people for the Queen in the war, was also nearing the end of his life and Oupa Lewis, as we called him, would be glad if his daughter was near him if he needed her, Oom Chai said.

Everyone at Vatmaar who had a roof over their heads was on the list. Oom Chai, the elder of our mission church, said the only payment that the congregation wanted for the church building was that the school children should clean where they have messed.

One day two white men arrived in a Cape cart, the one which always stands at the Pan's station. Oom Chai had been told beforehand of their coming. He had to make sure that the grown ups who were not in work in Du Toitspan were "spick-and-span" – as he said with the few English words which he always used.

These two men from the Pan were very neatly dressed. Oupa Lewis called it London-wear.

They looked at the church building and at the little troop of us children, and said: Good, we'll put in a good recommendation.

Oom Chai unlocked the church for them but they did not go in.

Afterwards Oom Chai said: They think they're too good to go into a poor house of God.

At the end of the month Oom Chai received a letter. On the envelope was written *Vatmaar Community*. The letter said that from the first of the coming month Mistress Elsa Lewis would be our teacher. School would be held in our mission church. And: Miss E. Lewis will be on the payroll of the Du Toitspan Town Council. Medium of teaching: English only.

Oupa Lewis was asked to write a letter to the town council on behalf of Vatmaar because they always listen to a white man. Just let us be grateful, said Vatmaar, English is better than nothing.

We soon found out that Teacher Lewis wanted to be more English than the English themselves and looked down on us because we spoke Afrikaans.

Teacher Elsa, as we called her, was called the Mistress by Oom Chai and the other grown ups.

She was neither short nor tall and had much the same complexion as Sis Bet. She was nice and round and the people used to say that she walked to her church in the Pan on Sundays to shake some fat off, but as soon as she got home again she made up double for the loss by eating twice as much. Her hair was very coarse but well brushed – and even when she bent down it stayed in its place. She had a resemblance to Oupa Lewis, who was also fat with a pot belly. Because she had a double chin she usually left the top button of her blouse undone. She wore glasses which made her look different to all the other women of Vatmaar. She changed her earrings whenever she pleased and we who went to her school knew in what mood she was by looking at her earrings.

Teacher Elsa had a bicycle which she used to ride to her school in the Pan. Her brother Tommy always rode along with her on his own bicycle. Because she was the oldest she was always bossing him around and used to say to him: On Sundays we walk, you know how much I enjoy walking to church on a Sunday.

But it was for another reason. Everyone at Vatmaar took the

short cut to the Pan, nobody walked to the crossing where the built road crossed the railway line, we stuck to the short cut past the siding.

Near the path lived a young man. This young man was Irish and he lived with his parents at the siding. His wife had died while giving birth to their child in Belmont and his parents said he could stay with them for as long as it took to get over his loss. He was also Catholic and, like Elsa and Tommy, he took the same path to church. Elsa and Tommy would fetch him from his parents' home so that the three of them could walk together.

Oupa Lewis said: Elsa, there is nothing wrong with your bicycle, but you walk to church on Sundays. And you always take something with you for this young man. What happened to that coloured man who was with you at the teachers' college in Kimberley? I notice that you don't get any letters from him any more. What happened?

Dad, she said, I prefer a white man to a coloured man. I want somebody like you, Dad.

My child, the oupa said, my child, a decent coloured man who you can call your husband and who can call me Dad, is all I want. This whatever you call him – Irishman, has not the guts to come and meet me. But let it be, Oupa Lewis said and walked away.

The gossip-path from the mission church to the khadie pot knew about this Irishman and Teacher Elsa. Some said: He's just flirting with her, and others: She's encouraging him.

To us school children she was the prettiest woman we had ever seen. Mostly we were astonished by her clothes and her earrings.

Once, when one or other important person came from the Pan, Oom Chai had to wait for him to show him the children in the school. That Friday Teacher Elsa put red paint on her lips and powder with a sweet smell on her face. She wore high-heeled shoes, just like the women from the Pan. And good gracious, did she look pretty!

The man from the Town Council paid more attention to her

than to us. Later the two went to whisper outside. Then Oom Chai walked over to the man from the Town Council and greeted him with a handshake. The man had hardly left when Oom Chai stormed into the church, chased us out and locked the door.

We could hear him gasping for breath and we wondered what's going on. We heard how he was talking and we knew if he gets so excited he speaks so that his stomach shakes. Not here! we heard him say. Not here. This is the house of God! Go and wash your face. Wash that mess off. Then you can get back to your work. Go! Wash off that mess and come and teach the children. To think that that Redneck was getting randy here. You're lucky I was here. You coloured women just don't say no to a white man. Go, wash your face!

We will never know if our teacher cried or ran away, because when the twelve o'clock whistle blew, which meant the end of the schoolday, Oom Chai opened the door, looked at us and said: Go home.

The next day began as if nothing had happened. On Saturdays we only went to school to say the Onse Vader, Our Father, because, Oom Chai said, it was in our mother tongue: Afrikaans, our home language, the language of my mother and father, created by the slaves and poor Flemish soldiers.

The old man never tired of reminding us about this.

After the prayer all of us children then cleaned the church together. If Oom Chai was satisfied, he just walked to the door and held it open. Then we knew our work was done, and we walked out.

Then we had to go and do what our parents wanted. Because I was the oldest among us children, Little-Neels and I had the same house chores. We each had a special bucket, the dung bucket. We had to fill it with cowdung, moist cowdung if possible, with which our mothers then smeared the floors.

At school our blackboard was a table which was stood on its side on top of another table. It was not a good substitute for a blackboard and one day when Oom Chai was finished with all his business in the Pan, he thought about our blackboard and said to himself: Today I'm going begging for a blackboard.

He went to see one of the Town Council members, who sent him to a white school with an envelope on which was written: *On His Majesty's Service – O.H.M.S.*

The man at the white school took the letter and read it and took Oom Chai to what he called the storeroom. Inside he said to Oom Chai: Take one, they are all broken, but take the best.

Oom Chai took the best blackboard and easel and asked for a few broken pieces of chalk for our children to write on the blackboard.

We all had slates which cost sixpence together with the slate pencil. Teacher Elsa had to buy her own chalk.

We did not have playtime at the school as we heard the children in the Pan had. We had to work full steam from the eight o'clock whistle right up to the twelve o'clock whistle. Sometimes we couldn't hear the whistle, but then we looked to see if we couldn't see the train's smoke. Our stomachs were also good time keepers. Teacher Lewis always said we are so stupid that the extra learning time is a favour. It was just Devi, shopkeeper Chetty's daughter, who she said had brains: You others are all empty barrels.

We school children all went barefoot. Those who did have shoes only wore them on Sundays. Our clothes were neatly patched by our mothers, with all the patches a different colour and size. Our parents chose a jacket or pants one or two sizes bigger so that we could grow into them.

Sums were not so bad because we all knew how to count. But about the English words we knew only the sounds, not the meanings. We usually said things like: Ek gaan nou home toe. Or: Kam for come; wat for what. Things like that, just to help us remember what we had learnt, because Teacher Elsa said: To use it is not to forget it.

We learnt the English language with what they called a coloured-mind and thought of Afrikaans as our own language. Afrikaans they did not need to teach us.

Oupa Lewis's burial and the feast

Tommy Lewis and his sister Elsa said they are Catholic and it wouldn't be right if they came to our mission church. I couldn't understand it, but my Da said: Number one, they speak English and number two, they think they're better than us.

What is wrong with our mission church? You answer me that, my mother said. Tommy still has to take his hat off in church and show his curly head. And he's so proud of that parting that he's cut through it with the scissors. Karel, did you see the big new photo of his father that's been hung in such a way that you can't miss it when you go into their house? she asked.

Yes, I've seen it, Lucy, my Da said to my mother. I forgot to tell you – I saw it last Monday when I went to pay the ten shillings rental for our house, or should I say our stable! Oupa Lewis looks like the lid of a chocolate box with its overdone colours. I think he would've looked better in plain black and white. But why is there not a photo of their mother too? She was such a nice old lady, Ouma Lewis. There is enough space to hang her too.

No, instead they've got that old calendar of 1919 hanging next to the old man. You see, Karel, my mother said, Oupa Lewis was a white man. Straight from the home as he used to call his country whenever he introduced himself to a stranger or when he had too much to drink. They are proud of this old man, and it's only because he's a white man that they want to remember him. But not Ouma Ruth – only because she was a Tswana from Vryburg.

Lucy, d'you know something? These coloured and black women take good care of their white husbands, they treat them like lords.

True, my mother said. And they think they're better than us who have coloured husbands. She put her arm around my father.

What difference does it make now? Tommy is the spitting image of his mother, just a little lighter. And Elsa looks like her father, only she's got curly hair.

It's funny how people forget. Oupa Lewis had died just the previous November. Meneer de Bruin had taken Tommy in his Ford lorry to his father's brother at The Mall on the other side of the Pan to go and give him the sad news.

Tommy never told us himself about the reception that he had got there. Meneer de Bruin also wanted to say nothing at first. But on the day of the funeral he cut off a piece of chewing tobacco and put it in his mouth, chewed a few times and spat as if he wanted to spit at something. Then he laughed as if it was no longer a secret.

They had sent Tommy around to the back door, he said. And this after bragging to me all the time on our way to his oom's farm about how proud he was to have a white father, a real Englishman, who fought for the Queen. Imagine. This half-breed telling me this.

Meneer de Bruin put his hands on his hips. I am in the first place an Afrikaner with an Afrikaner Bible and then I am a British subject. My people sit in government and one day, the dominee said, we will be the government itself.

He was a respected man, this Meneer Piet de Bruin. Tall, thin, with a yellow and white beard. Always in corduroy or khaki trousers, except on Sundays. He was the only white man at Oupa Lewis's funeral. He had on his Sunday clothes, a jacket with two wings which they called a tailcoat. Miesies de Bruin, who was affectionately called Ounooi, was short and looked much older than her husband. She had lost all her family in the Anglo-Boer War in the concentration camp at Mafeking. She had on a long black dress and a hat. Pieter, their only child, was also there.

We of Vatmaar were used to them and it seemed as if they knew all our shortcomings and our needs. But they also always knew where to get someone to help them with their farm work.

Oupa Lewis had died towards evening and Mr Tommy wanted

the corpse buried as soon as possible because it was summer and the days were hot. The carpenter, Mr May, who was known for his exceptional coffins, brought the coffin from the Pan.

A coffin should match the person who is going to be buried in it, he always said. And he wanted the money in his hands before the dead was placed in the coffin. The price was ten pounds, on delivery.

That's the price of two bicycles, my Da said.

They bury the coffin and not the person, somebody else said.

Mr May made sure that Oupa Lewis fitted into the coffin and then said: My work is done, you don't need me any more, thank you. He shook hands and left.

The Catholic priest and two nuns arrived soon afterwards. The nuns were beautiful – it was the first time that I'd seen a real white skin, unblemished by the sun.

The Du Toitspan Catholic Church had their own transport – a two-seater coach with blankets on the wooden seats. It didn't have a door, just a footrest, which was also used as a step. The coach was pulled by a mule which looked just like a Catholic, as Sister Klompie always said.

The priest wore a long, black dress. I could not understand why a man had to wear a dress to ask God to take the man in the beautiful coffin, which will be covered with dirty sand and stones, to heaven.

My mother said the two nuns were from Ireland, a country not far from the land where Oupa Lewis grew up. They were married to the church. I couldn't understand that either but I asked no more questions because I knew marriage is grown ups' business and my mother's eyes would just say: You're too big for your boots.

The coffin was placed on two chairs facing each other. The wreath which Mr May had brought with him was hung on a nail just above Oupa Lewis's photo, forming a nice circle around it. The front door and kitchen door were left open so that people could walk through after looking at Oupa Lewis.

It was the first dead person I had ever seen. He looked so alive and so worthless with his face which just looked in one direction.

When everybody had seen what they had come to see, the priest in the dress (I heard Teacher Elsa calling him Father) touched the necklace with the cross on it around his neck. The two nuns and the brother and sister also touched their necklaces with crosses. Everyone closed their eyes but only the five of them played with their strings of beads, one by one, until after Amen was said. Then someone touched the lid of the coffin, but Oom Chai (whom the Father called Charlie) immediately showed him not to touch it yet.

Oom Chai said a prayer in which he said how good Oupa Lewis had been and that the angels in heaven were waiting for him. He prayed in Afrikaans, the language of Vatmaar. And I thought to myself: So Oupa Lewis has not left us yet then.

After the Amen we all sang as slowly as we could the hymn we sang every Sunday in church: Nearer my God to Thee. Then there was a long, drawn out A-m-e-n and after that it was time for the poor man's prayer – the Onse Vader, the only prayer we all knew off by heart.

Oom Chai motioned to the coffin's lid and I could not believe my eyes – they had used nails which had to be screwed in! When the last one was tightened, the coffin was ready to be put on Oom Flip's trolley. With the one-eyed Old Swing up in front.

The previous day Oom Flip took the wheels halfway off and greased them together with the spare wheel so that there would be no unwelcome noises, he said.

The cemetery was just outside Vatmaar and only one path led to it. Nobody dared to go in that direction after dark. We all fell in behind the trolley and Old Swing just walked as slowly as she could. It was hot and everyone tried to look sad.

At the grave, Meneer de Bruin, the Ounooi and Little-Piet stood waiting near their Ford lorry. Our cemetery was not fenced off and nor was there a gate. The graves were not in straight rows because they were dug where people decided the earth was softest. The graves were not numbered and nor was a record being kept. There was just at every head end some object from the household to identify the grave, most of the time a teapot or a vase.

At Oupa Lewis's grave the priest took out a bottle of water and sprinkled three times.

In the name of the Father, the Son and the Holy Ghost, I heard him say. Then he blessed the grave.

The coffin was lowered into the grave with two ropes. Somebody took a spade but Oom Chai lifted up his hand and said: Wait.

While turning the tips of his moustache with his right hand, because he was holding his Bible in his left hand, he said: I ... Then he again twisted his moustache as if he could not think without twisting it. And then he said Mr Tommy Lewis and Mistress Elsa had asked him to say a few words.

This old man knew how to make a short story a long one and to speak without thinking. He gave the Bible to Mr Tommy Lewis next to him and began twisting his moustache with both hands. I am a man with many friends, he said, but that man who is no longer with us ... He first looked at the coffin for a long time and then he went on: I am grateful to say that I was his only friend. It is he who put Vatmaar on paper. It is he who spoke to his army captain, Mister John Walker. It's a pity that George first had to die before we knew that he was a Catholic. Of all the coffins that I have ever seen – and he pointed to the coffin – I must say that this one is good enough for King George.

Tommy Lewis pulled at the sleeve of Oom Chai's jacket and said: Finish off now, Oom.

He looked at Tommy thoughtfully and then again began twisting his moustache.

Some people began saying: Te-te-te, while others said: A-aa-aaa.

The priest smiled as if he understood what Oom Chai was saying, but one of the nuns came straight out and asked Teacher Elsa what he was saying. She just gave the nun a look and the other nun leaned over so that she could also hear.

People, Oom Chai said, we all have to die, whether you are white or black. Amen.

Then the grown up men took turns to fill up the grave. And Oom Chai began singing, as slowly as he could, Nearer my God to Thee. Everyone joined in because we knew the words and we wanted to show each other that we knew them. While again twisting his moustache, Oom Chai took his Bible from Tommy Lewis. Then he took his Zobo pocket watch out of his waistcoat pocket, nodded, put it back, and made sure the chain hung properly. Then he said: The family has invited everyone to their home for a meat braai.

He walked away, the people following him. Only the humblest among us stayed behind to fill the grave.

Meneer de Bruin waited for someone to crank up his lorry, something we all knew had to be done without being told. When it started, Meneer de Bruin lifted his arm in greeting and was off.

The orphaned brother and sister had two sheep and a goat slaughtered. Meneer de Bruin, on his way back from his oom's farm, had apparently said to Mr Tommy Lewis: Buy two sheep and I'll give you a goat for free, they were herded in just yesterday by the farm workers.

My Da had also gone over to the Lewises' house opposite our house. They lived in the big house while we lived in the old stable where Oupa Lewis had kept his two horses when he was much younger. My Da called the old stable the-roof-over-our-heads and my mother turned it into a home. And I was very proud to be able to say: I'm going home.

Da told about how he had stood waiting in the shade for Tommy Lewis to ask if there was something that he could do for him when Meneer de Bruin arrived. He greeted: Good day, Meneer de Bruin, good day, Tommy.

Meneer de Bruin liked the people of Vatmaar calling him Baas, but my Da, a farrier, regularly helped him shoe his horses. When talking to my mother, my Da spoke of de Bruin, but to his face he called him Meneer.

I give you this castrated goat as a gift from one white man to another white man, Meneer de Bruin said to Tommy. He pointed first to the goat and then to the scar from the Boer War on his left arm. He was not my friend because he was an Englishman. But a white man, our dominee said, should look after another white man, even though we Afrikaners had to pay so dearly for our Fatherland.

Oom Chai came around the corner of the house just as Meneer de Bruin turned to leave. He did not see Oom Chai, but Oom Chai had heard what he said. Yes, Karel, he said to my Da, twisting his moustache with his thumb and forefinger and with a lifeless look on his face. A white man will always love his white enemy but hate his black friend. Thank God George Lewis was more black than white.

The sun hung over the railway crossing, baking it with its heat. The crossing was almost halfway to the Pan. There was no gate in front of the crossing, just a board with a crooked cross on it and the words: Stop. Wait. Look. Listen. We couldn't see the train from Vatmaar, but we could see its smoke and could hear its whistle.

It was the whistle which was important to us at Vatmaar. It told us when to get up and when to go to bed. In the mornings the four o'clock whistle woke up those who had to walk to work in Du Toitspan. The six o'clock whistle was for those who had bicycles to ride to work. And school started just after the eight o'clock whistle. On Sundays church began as the ten o'clock whistle sounded. We never knew whether the train was early or late, we just spoke about the first whistle, the second whistle, the school whistle and the church whistle. Every Sunday Oom Chai set his Zobo pocket watch to ten o'clock when he heard the church whistle.

It was the first time I had seen so much meat being eaten at one time. That morning Old Swing had brought the witgat tree stumps before she was groomed and the trolley cleaned. There was a dish of salt and a small tin that looked like a Christmas box. They said it was pepper. An old railway sieve, an iron sheet with round holes in it, was placed on four big stones and levelled out with smaller stones.

The dominee with the dress sprinkled water from his bottle and said: In the name of the Father, the Son and the Holy Ghost. All the meat was under the pepper tree, some pieces hanging from the tree and some pieces on the kitchen table. Teacher Elsa did not like the idea of using the dining-room table.

Ma brought her bedsheet to be used as a tablecloth, a lot of patched together sugarbags which Dad had bought at two pennies each. They had been sewn together by hand and washed until it was as white as it could get. The Father, as everyone now called the dominee, blessed the meat and we had to close our eyes. Some of the grown ups cut the meat into smaller pieces and handed it out saying: Sprinkle salt on to your taste.

The fire burned and everyone was happy because we people of Vatmaar were meat lovers. Most of us would give away our sweets for a piece of meat.

The Father and his two nuns who were married to the church, were the first to eat their meat. The people of Vatmaar had been told to bring along their own plates and knives. The Father then looked at his pocket watch and said to Mr Tommy Lewis: It's getting late, Tom, we have to go. He took him aside and said to him: You know, Tom, we must take something with us for the church and pointed to a leg of mutton.

Yes, yes, Father, Tommy Lewis said and unhooked the meat from the wire where it had been hanging on a branch. The leg was put into a bag – after the bag had quickly been shaken out.

The two nuns sat on one bench of the cab and the Father, with the leg next to him, sat on the other bench. After a few Bless You's they were on their way. Their driver was a young man from the Cape, a real Cape Coloured. We didn't like him because he just wanted to be among the bigshots all the time. But Teacher Elsa was very proud of him. She said he played the organ in their church. We children had never seen or heard an organ being played.

Everyone remained until most of the meat had been eaten up or secretly sneaked away. The evening's ten o'clock whistle had long ago been blown. It was a real grand feast, with only meat. Some grown ups actually said: It's a pity there's nothing to drink here. Afterwards even the full moon itself was praised because every now and then someone would say: And we give thanks for the full moon.

Teacher Elsa and her brother looked happy that their duties had been done. They were cheerful with the guests. They just had to be anyway because how could the people of Vatmaar mourn on full stomachs.

Sis Bet was the first to dance a few steps. Holding her dress with one hand and taking a few steps which kept to the rhythm, she began to sing: If you want me, you can have me. Where is he? Where is he?

Everyone joined in the dancing. Oom Chai and the other old men danced their steps under the pepper tree because they did not want the others to see them.

We did not have any musical instruments at Vatmaar then and those who were not dancing clapped their hands keeping the rhythm for those who were.

Then the bragging started. Some said they had danced the ma-bok – a dance in which you had to swing the hands – before they had come to this lifeless place. The oumas with the huge back-sides showed that they knew just how to throw them about – to the delight of the grown up men. Not to be outdone, Teacher Elsa said: Where are my school children? Come here, all of you.

Everyone was quiet. We were put in a row – twenty-one of us. Teacher Elsa lifted up her hands like she does at school and dropped them again and we began to sing the only song we had learnt at school: Three blind mice, three blind mice, see how they run ...

We had to put up three fingers and close our eyes with our hands to show that we were blind. When it came to "see how they run", we had to turn around and make as if we were running on one spot. Then Teacher Elsa turned around, and to the surprise of the parents she smiled.

One mother said: I've got the tree but where does the nice come in?

People began getting up from the ground where most had been sitting. Everyone wanted to give Mr Tommy and Mistress Elsa a handshake and say: We feel for you, thank you, Tommy, and thank you, Mistress.

My Da sent me and another boy to fetch water to throw on the hot coals, because, he said: One never knows what could happen.

Later, walking home with Da, he asked: Son, what's this nice that you're learning about at school?

He held my hand and I could feel his fatherly pride flow into my hand.

Tant Vonnie and her daughter Suzan

They sat chatting on two riempie chairs outside Oom Chai's house, when Suzan, Tant Vonnie's youngest daughter, put down a tray in front of them with two glasses of thick milk. She said: Good day, Mister May and Good day, Oom Chai.

Mr May smiled, stood up, gave her hand a squeeze and went to sit again with sparkling eyes.

Suzan was in her becoming-a-woman years and in those years girls were always in demand. Oom Chai, who knew Mr May could not be trusted with young girls, said: My child, take what you need and go home and come back again tomorrow. Thank you.

Of all the older women and young girls, the threesome, Tant Vonnie and her two daughters, were the prettiest in Vatmaar. They were German Basters and beauty, then as now, was measured in European features, hair and complexion.

Tant Vonnie and her daughter owned nothing, or let us say, very little. They lived at the mercy of others in an outside room which had once upon a time belonged to them because Tant Vonnie was one of Vatmaar's first inhabitants. The one-room had been built with Ta Vuurmaak's Kimberley bricks. It had a window and a door which could open. The hinges were two pieces of leather and the latch was a stick on a riempie. The corrugated iron roof was held down with stones and the walls and the floor were regularly smeared with cow dung which gave the room a nice smell.

Later her husband, like Oom Chai and Oupa Lewis, also built a bigger house on the same plot. But when she and Kaaitjie came back from Sannah Vosloo's funeral, Tant Vonnie had to sell the house to Mr Wingrove. She just kept the outside room and said one room is better than nothing.

The two women slept on animal skins on the floor. Every day the skins were rolled up together with the blankets and cushions. A slab of slate about one yard by one yard rested on four poles planted into the ground. On top of it stood three plates and three cups and underneath the stone table there was a paraffin tin to draw water from the well. Tant Vonnie's husband had dug the well with Vatmaar's people. Now it belonged to their neighbour, Dirk Twala. He had paid for it with a cow and a calf.

Two years before the cow died in the big drought, and the calf which had grown into a young bull, was slaughtered.

Then most of the wells dried up, just like the catchment dam on the other side of the cemetery. But Tant Vonnie's well and a few others always had water and everyone could come and get water there. Nobody was sent away because Dirk Twala had said, even though the well was his, bought with a living thing, the water would always belong to Tant Vonnie. She could give it away as she pleased.

And as it goes with people who are poor, the water and most of the bullock's meat was shared with the people.

The fireplace was outside the one-room. Three big pieces of slate were stuck into the ground in three sides. The fourth side was open. On a stone stood a three-legged pot and an old dish to wash in. On the side wall were a few slate stones packed onto smaller stones as benches. Just outside the door was a patch of green plants – the wild garlic which Tant Vonnie's husband had planted the day before he went to war and which made the best cures for winter colds and for chest ailments.

She always let the wild garlic draw in castor oil in the blue bottle and placed it so that the sun shone on it. One tea-spoonful and people never came back for more. Tant Vonnie never wanted to say how much the medicine cost, even if they asked her straight out. She just said: Give whatever you can.

Few people came empty-handed, even if it was just with a little salt. But in Vatmaar salt was never given away after sunset because the people used to say: You're giving your luck away.

In the one-room a riempie was spanned from corner to corner and on it hung all the clothes and wash rags.

Tant Vonnie and Suzan got along well. She also got on well with her elder daughter Kaaitjie, but Kaaitjie worked for Mevrou Bosman in the Pan and only came to visit onc Sunday every month. Tant Vonnie and Suzan sometimes sat together for hours without saying a word. In the mornings, before rolling up their blankets, the two went down on their knees and thanked God for the new day. They usually ate only once a day, and then the two stood together, held hands, closed their eyes and said: Thank you, Lord, for whatever was in the three-legged pot. Then every night, after rolling open their blankets, it was: Thank you, Lord, for the health which we enjoyed today.

Without thinking what tomorrow would bring, they would lie awake on their earth beds, without desires and without hope, as happy and contented as only a well-fed baby could be.

They could not read and also did not own a Bible. Once upon a time Tant Vonnie had her Heinrich's father's Bible, but it had disappeared together with all her other stuff while she had been taking care of Sannah Vosloo. But Tant Vonnie was hungry for the word of God. She believed it as she heard it and never asked any questions.

She did not know when her own birthday was and she could not remember her daughters' birthdays. She just always used to say: Kaaitjie was born in winter and Suzan in spring.

Suzan greeted everyone with a smile, which said more than words. It was the smile of a grown child. If anyone wanted something done, it was always said: Go and ask Suzan. Even if it was something which their own children could do just as well.

Like her mother, Suzan was almost never paid in cash for her help.

Tant Vonnie was the washerwoman and especially people with a dark complexion liked having her work for them. Most of the time it was in exchange for something to eat and Tant Vonnie used to say with pride: We have never gone to bed hungry.

Out of jealousy ugly things were said about Tant Vonnie. She was never in a hurry because her day began at sunrise and ended at sunset. She walked slowly and with small steps. She was an older woman but one of the Cape Coloured women said: It's because of breeding that she walks like that, from bringing six children into the world for nothing. Another said: She never knew her father, God is punishing her. It's her lot.

Suzan was a strong girl because she had to do work which was normally meant for boys. And she was well built, strong, and pretty, with very light grey eyes, natural red cheeks and lips and two long plaits which hung over her young breasts. The two golden plaits with the yellow stripes in them were tied up at the tips with ribbons torn from rags.

She was known for her bright and hearty laugh.

Suzan was her mother's breadwinner. She regularly tidied up

Oom Chai's house but early in the mornings she first went over to the Venters to milk their little herd of Swiss and other goats. She always took along with her an empty wine bottle for the milk which Tant Venter paid her for the milking.

The big milking bucket and a smaller bucket waited for her on a sawn off branch. She would ask Tant Venter to put it there the previous day so that she wouldn't have to wake them up so early in the morning. But there was another reason.

The Venters had two sons who slept until the ten o'clock whistle. They were forever trying to touch her, on her cheeks and on her hair. Why? she wondered.

One day she asked her mother.

Suzan, her mother said, you are now in your becoming-a-woman years and I'm going to tell you what my mother told me when I was as old as you. Men, she said, will do anything to get a girl like you into their hands, especially older men. They prefer to sleep with younger women because, they say, it makes them feel younger. You know what I mean by sleep?

Yes, Mama, she said, I think I know.

So you've tried it before?

No, no, Mama. But one of Tant Venter's sons has tried. One morning he suddenly threw me on my back and I felt his thing against my leg, warm and stiff. But he's not strong so I pushed him away. That's why I go and milk the goats before they get up. And Meneer Venter once said he would give me one and six if I slept with him. He said he'll tell me where I should wait for him. That's why I say I know what it means, Mama.

After she had milked the goats, Suzan always had to wait for Mevrou Venter to open the kitchen door for her. Then she said: Good morning, Tante, and put the big bucket on the kitchen table.

Mevrou Venter did not want Suzan to put her own bottle on the table. Suzan could not understand why.

Mevrou Venter always just said: Go and fetch your bottle, and then she poured the milk in at the kitchen door, the bottle usually half full but most of the time less. Take! she would say, pushing the bottle towards Suzan.

Whenever they drank tea or coffee, Suzan and her mother would add the milk to it. If not, they would fill the bottle with water so that each could have a full mug. They used to pick a herb in the veld called mashoekashanie, with which they made tea together with the milk.

Not long ago Suzan's mother had lengthened her dress so that it could cover her calves. She was not used to it yet, but it felt nice because the long dress kept out the cold better.

Gabriel Venter was the older of the two boys. His father regularly caught birds in a trap but he only kept the ones with black heads because he could sell them for a shilling a pair in the Pan. People liked these black-headed birds because they sang like canaries. All the other birds he left to fly away.

It was Gabriel's job to go to the traps after school and to take out the blackhead birds and to let the other birds fly away. But before he let them go he would first take a white thorn from the mimosa tree and prick their eyes, sometimes one eye, sometimes both. We school children would shudder at this and we called him Old Dead Eye.

Years later, when Suzan left Vatmaar with that man and his child, Gabriel Venter returned from Kimberley where he had worked as a male nurse. We heard that he was on holiday with his wife, Lettie, and their two children. And do you know what, Reader? Both the children had been born blind. We of Vatmaar knew why, but afterwards I always wondered if this was really deserved.

Suzan tells her mother what Nellie Ndola told her about Tommy Lewis

Mama, does Mama know Nellie? That black woman from the Pan who always visited Mr Tommy Lewis?

Yes, Tant Vonnie said, but I haven't seen her in ages.

138

Mama, Nellie Ndola says she has already tasted.

And then Suzan told her mother how Nellie always came to visit Mr Tommy Lewis on holidays when the shop where he worked was closed for the day. She also came to visit on some Sundays and then he would give her a red book to take with her when he gave her a lift on his bicycle back to Du Toitspan.

Suzan told her mother how Nellie would come and talk to her whenever she sat under Oom Chai's pepper tree while waiting for him to come and tell her what she should do. She could see Nellie was very proud that she knew Mr Tommy Lewis.

Mama, mama knows how these people carry on when they think they are better than us. Some time ago I walked past Teacher Elsa and them's house. Then I heard Teacher Elsa shouting at Tommy: That black Kaffir bitch thinks that she is my equal, and you telling me to call her by her name! She is becoming too friendly with you, the black Kaffir bitch!

I couldn't understand why she was saying such things about Nellie, Mama, Suzan said. But two Sundays ago Nellie asked me to walk with her to the halfway-house.

The halfway-house is a very big camel thorn tree. They say that when the first people came to Vatmaar it was just as big as it is now. From that time it has never changed. If you sit under it you can feel its heartbeat.

But after sunset nobody sits under it because they say that during the Freedom War the Rednecks hanged a burger from one of its branches – they said he was a spy. To this day people point out the branch, which is always dripping with red sap. Nobody ever takes the gum, although they will take gum from any other thorn tree. This, the people say, shows you that the man was innocent when hanged. The corpse too was never cut loose, they left him hanging from the rope for the vultures to come and finish him off. This innocent man is now the guardian of the tree and he stands upside down with his hands on the branch from which he had been hanged – that's what the people say who were born with the caul.

When we came close to the halfway-house I said to her: Nellie, you must be very clever.

What do you mean? she asked.

Well, you read all those big books which Mister Tommy Lewis gives you.

Bah, she said, I wonder what my mother will say.

She put her hand on her heart and after a few steps she went on talking: Suzan, I don't read that book. I can't even read. My Rra works with him at the Du Toitspan General Dealer. Tommy does all the paper work and my Rra is the shop boy that delivers all the stuff and must see that the shop is clean. My Rra thinks he's a very good man because he gave him a raise. He now gets three shillings a day. He also told the baas how hard my Rra works.

The book I always had to take to the shop and give to Tommy, but I wasn't supposed to let my Rra see it. If there was somebody nearby I had to say that Mistress Elsa has sent me to give it to him. Then he used to give me a packet of sweets and other nice things. He also gave me these shoes and this scarf. But I always had to make sure my Rra was not in the shop. Sometimes he used to take the book back with him after the halfway-house. And there weren't any other books, Suzan, it was just that one with the red on the outside.

What do you mean by after the halfway-house, Nellie?

Mama, Nellie looked at me, stood still, and gave a little chuckle that bubbled out of her mouth. At the halfway-house he was a wonderful person, she said. There he said I belonged to him and that he could do with me just what he liked, he doesn't need my permission. People who love each other are one, he said, not two people. Then he kisses me and has a good look at my breasts and at the bottom, you know what I mean, don't you, Suzan?

I nodded.

Then he starts with his rubbing and his feeling. I must tell you Suzan, it was very nice and I looked forward to it. Then, after he had had his four times, as he called it, he became another person. Now I can see what a fool I've been, and how stupid I've been.

Nellie shook her head slowly from side to side.

Then he said he is now so tired after doing his best to give me pleasure, after giving me his love, he's sure I won't mind walking alone to the Pan. Then he kissed me and said: Goodbye, darling. And rode away. I believed him and walked home – very happy. Walking and thinking how nice it was to be a darling, the road was never long. But today he called me a low-caste and his sister chased me out of the house and called me a forward Kaffir bitch.

That's after Sunday before last when he had given me the book with the red outside to take with me – after we had first drunk milk and eaten scones at his house. Then he fetched his bicycle and let me sit behind. At the halfway-house he again began calling me darling and again did what he always did. But before he had had his four, I said: Tommy, you know what?

What, darling? he asked.

I told him that it was now more than three times since I last saw my monthly sickness. I thought he would understand seeing that he was a grown man and so educated. And as he said, because we loved each other we are one, not two people. But that Sunday his voice got hard like someone who is scared and cross at the same time. Let us finish, he said.

When he was busy with his fourth time, he again said he will never leave me and that I was his forever and that he'll see to it that my Rra gets another raise. But when he was finished he sat for a long time with his elbows on his knees and his head in his hands. When I put my hands on his shoulders, he pushed them away. When I tried to say something, he said: Shut your mouth – just like that. Then suddenly he said he's got a plan.

You know Lukas, your neef, the one that gets called to off-load the supplies when we are in a hurry, he said. You know, Nellie, I can give him a permanent job with us. If you love me, you'll do what I tell you to do. Now try and fix Lukas up with something. He pushed his hands in between my legs. Then you can say that he did it to you. He touched my stomach. People won't be cross with you, they'll feel sorry for you. I can tell your father what a pity it is that Lukas has taken advantage of you. You two seem to understand each other. I'll say to your father it will be best to give Lukas a job so that he can marry you – the shop can help him with the lobola, which can be taken off his wages every week. If you love me, you will do what I tell you to do, Nellie.

Then he kissed me and rode away on his bicycle.

I took a long time walking home. The road was never before so long. His words kept ringing in my ears: If you love me. I kept saying to myself: I love you, Tommy, my Tommy. Didn't he say we are one? He knows what's best because, like he said, it's the best for both of us. It must be, I thought, because we love each other. It was the Sunday before last. A few days later I got hold of Lukas. He and his girlfriend, Nono, just like always, were sitting on a broken wagon near his Rra's house. I went up to them and said: Dumela. They both smiled at me. Nono said she wished she had a pair of shoes like mine and pointed to my feet.

A person doesn't desire something you have, I told her. I also got onto the wagon and went to sit next to her.

Lukas gave Nono a nudge with his elbow and told me they wanted to get married and told me he worked one day a week, two days if he's lucky, with my Rra at the General Dealer's. He got two shillings a day, and if he could just get a permanent job, even if it was just for one and six a day, he'd be happy. He'd look after his job and do exactly what his boss told him to do. His Rra told him he'll help him with part of the lobola so that he doesn't have to take Nono with empty hands. And Nono's Rra said he can leave the rest till after the first child, but then he and Nono's mother want to raise the child.

Nono said she prays every night to Modimo to give Lukas a job, and Lukas looked at Nono and said they must ask Modimo for any kind of work so that they can become husband and wife.

Nellie told word for word everything else they had talked about.

It's nice of you to come and sit by us, Nellie. One day when we've got our own hut you must come and visit us, Lukas said. I'll serve you a cup of tea on a tray.

Nono laughed and jumped off the wagon. I must go, she said, I have got my monthly sickness.

Lukas walked with her to her Rra's home. I remained seated on the wagon thinking about what Tommy had told me to do.

Mama, Nellie stood and put her arms around my shoulders. Suzan, she said and looked at me with eyes which saw nothing, it feels to me as if all this has happened so quickly, that it's not true. You are the first and only person I've told this to. Nobody else knows, perhaps only God

She pushed up her shoulders as if she wanted to reach her ear. When I looked at her like this, Mama, I thought: This Nellie is not ugly like people are always saying about black people. I looked at her flat nose with the big nostrils. Her lips were full and her ears very small. Her skin was black, but also not that black. Her teeth were clean and nice like a row of mealie kernels. The browns of her eyes were small in big white pools. Tears ran out of them. I thought to myself: Where have I seen you before?

When she took her hands off my shoulders, I remembered: She looks just like Ouma Lewis and I was fond of her because she was the same kind of person as Ouma Lewis.

Nellie had stopped talking and I thought: Why do they say she's a Kaffir? Nobody ever said such ugly things to Ouma Lewis.

Nellie thought for a long time before she spoke again. Lukas came back after taking Nono to her hut. He said to me: Still sitting here?

Ja, Cousie, I said, and patted the place next to me with my hand. He knew what I meant and climbed onto the wagon next to me.

You must be careful you don't do this to Nono, I said and made a hump on my tummy with my hand.

No, Ousie, I won't. I'm too scared her mother will chase her away and that will hurt me a lot.

Cousie, I said, putting my hand on his thigh, but you have tasted somewhere else?

Never, he said. Nono and I are talking about marriage, not about such things. There are too many other things to talk about.

I moved my hand further up until almost between his legs. He didn't move at all. His one foot was still in the bush next to the wagon. I thought to myself: All men are the same, I'll kiss him, then I'll open his fly just like my Tommy taught me.

Nellie told me word for word, Mama.

He still sat dead-still and said: Ousie, what are you doing? – and laughed softly. I stuck my hand in and grabbed it. It was just busy rising and getting warm.

Do you know Lukas, Suzan? she asked.

No, Nellie, I haven't seen him yet, I don't know him, I said.

Well, she said, he is two years younger than me and much shorter. He is my Rra's sister's child. I had my hand on this thing of his and it rose even higher by itself. When I gave it a few squeezes it jumped out of his pants. I would never have thought this small Lukas could carry such a big thing. I then did what Tommy had taught me to do, I pushed it backwards and forwards.

She showed me with her hand how she did it, Mama.

I could hear his heart beating faster. Then it was that thing – the cream shot out.

The two girls lived close to nature and for them things were words and words were things and they said a thing like it was.

Suzan began to think about going home and she was tired of hearing Nellie talking about things which did not affect her.

She said: I'm going now, Nellie.

No, no, Nellie said and again put her hands on Suzan's shoulders. Not so soon. I'm already feeling better and the sickness in my heart is getting lighter because you're listening to me, Suzan. Suzan, let me face the Pan because that is where my future lies – and she looked towards the Pan. Under that red roof there on the other side – she pointed with her finger – is where Tommy lives with his sister who thinks I am a low-caste Kaffir. And on that stone there – she pointed under the tree – lie my thoughts about love, and here I carry the burden.

And then Nellie went on with the story where she had stopped.

Lukas was very surprised and said: I never knew.

I asked him: Was it nice?

He nodded and put his thing back in his pants, leaned backwards and lay flat on his back and said: Now I'm tired. I never knew it could be done like that.

I left him there on that broken wagon and went home to sleep. The following night I again found the two of them on the old wagon.

Dumela, Cousie Lukas, I said.

Dumela, Ousie, they both said.

Mind if I sit?

Nono patted the place next to her: Sit here.

She said that many men are going to the mines for work.

I want to go too, Lukas said. Rra Ronnie's son left last month. But now the other day Rra Ronnie received a telegram that he should come and bury his son Moetsi in Johannesburg. He had to let the mining company know as soon as possible because they can't keep the body forever. He had to say whether the company should send the coffin on the train. The telegram ended with: Reply as soon as possible. Rra Ronnie got the packet with poor Moetsi's belongings this very day, as well as the wages for the time that he had worked, together with five pounds accident insurance.

It's lucky the train comes through Du Toitspan, Nono said, because now they can send the corpse. Otherwise, they say, convicts bury the dead miners. The priest gets paid for his work and then all he does is send the grave's number with a few nice words for the family of the dead.

Tomorrow we're going to the station to fetch the coffin with poor Moetsi, Lukas said. To think he had gone to the mine to go and earn his lobola. Poor Mieta, she can't stop crying, she says she should've taken him without the lobola or made a baby with him so that she had something to remind her of him.

Nono, I said, all we can do is feel sorry for each other, what else can we do?

I'll never leave my Rra's house, Lukas said suddenly. I'm happy here, work or no work. And he gave each of us girls a little nudge with his elbows.

Good night, Nellie, Nono said, jumping off the wagon.

Good night, I said.

Lukas held Nono's hand as they walked away.

Soon after Lukas came running back out of breath.

I came back quickly so that I could get you here, he said. I didn't want you to go and I couldn't ask you to stay in front of Nono. She's very jealous.

I said: It's still early and I thought I would sit a while longer. He again got onto the wagon. For a while we sat quietly without saying too much, each one with their own thoughts. Then he started with it by putting his hand on my thigh.

How did Moetsi die? I asked him.

We don't know, he said.

But they say there's usually a piece of paper nailed to the coffin saying it shouldn't be opened. It gives the miner's address and number. Isn't it possible that they could put somebody in the wrong coffin? I asked.

Yes, Nellie, they can. White people don't know we have feelings too. They hurt us and we just have to say: Ja, baas. Even their children are beginning to say: Kaffirs aren't people.

146

The death seemed to have cooled off his randiness. Then I put my hand on his. He immediately started talking about something else. I'll never forget what happened last night, he said.

You mean you've never done it before?

Legoka, he said, the other boys call it pulling wire.

Was it nice?

You mean that thing?

Then I put his hand under my dress between my legs.

Nellie stopped talking and thought about what to say next. Then she said: You know, Suzan, we only wear bloomers when we have our monthly sickness. She again thought about everything so that she wouldn't leave out anything. He started feeling and feeling and said: It's a brush, just like mine.

Now let me feel your brush, I said. I loosened his pants and his big thing came out by itself. Its blue head shone in the moonlight. I didn't touch it because I remembered what happened before when I touched it.

Suzan, she said, d'you know what? I didn't think about Tommy Lewis any more. I lifted my legs onto the old wagon and went to lie on my back and waited. He, as the man, knew what to do. Nobody is taught these things, you know, Suzan? I wondered: When is he going to stop pushing it in? He was slow, not as hasty as Tommy. I loved him right there for this thing that he carried around. Lukas was much better than Mister Tommy Lewis. If it happens, the world stands still, your ears hear nothing, it just goes zing, z-i-n-g.

Then I heard Naleidi, Lukas's sister, shout: It's Lukas!

No, it can't be! Nono screamed.

In the moonlight Naleidi began picking up stones to throw at Lukas. But he jumped off the other side of the wagon and ran away. Then they threw stones at my head.

She lifted her doek to show Suzan.

They tore my dress and called me a mosadi oa dikgora and said they would bewitch me. Then suddenly there were lots of

147

people. I don't know where they came from. They wanted to know what happened. Naleidi was screaming and doing all the talking.

You can see by her shoes that she's a bad person! she screamed. I'm going to bewitch her!

Nono held her hands against her ears as if she did not believe what she saw. And she cried as if she had just lost her baby.

Then I ran away. But my head was still dizzy from the knocks. I ran to my ouma's house in the old section of Du Toitspan. I told her that I was sitting with Neef Lukas when Naleidi and Nono came to hit me because I was sitting with Nono's natsi.

They're wrong, my ouma said, Lukas is your neef and you can sit with him wherever you like. That Nono is jealous, I've been watching that one and I don't like her. Imagine, two bullies beating you up for nothing. Let us go to the police station and tell them what happened.

No, leave them, Ouma, I said. Modimo will punish them.

That takes time, Ouma said. The police will punish no later than tomorrow.

Ouma rubbed a little paraffin on my bumps where the stones had hit me. Then she gave me tea with some wilde-als in it.

The next morning I didn't want to go home, so my ouma went with me. My Rra had already gone to work when we got there. My mother cried and put her arms around me and said: I don't believe them, my child. I don't believe them, my child.

I'll stay here for the day to see that your father doesn't hit you, my ouma said, because he's always believing what other people say. Then my ouma asked my mother: And so what did they say happened, the liars?

They say Naleidi's husband came home from work with a terrible headache. They gave him some aloe sap in water to drink, and Naleidi wanted to put some castor oil leaves on his head to break the fever. So she asked Nono to go with her to Miesies February to ask for some. It was when they walked past the old wagon that they saw what Lukas was doing. He didn't even hear them coming, my mother said.

Most of the people didn't believe them because Lukas is my neef, Suzan. Some even said: Nono's jealousy cost her a good man. That afternoon when my Rra came home from work, he immediately said: Where is she?

Not she, say where is your daughter! Ouma shouted. Look how they threw stones at the poor girl and tore her dress, all for nothing!

She asked me to forget it because the Good Lord will see that they are punished.

What more do you want? my ouma asked. She is still so young but she always forgives others, just like her father. Leave the child alone now and come and walk with me to my house.

When my Rra came back my mother put three plates of pap and magoepelas on the table.

Suzan, said Nellie again, I don't know why I'm telling you all this, but I'm really beginning to feel much better.

We have an old Bible, they say it's a Dutch Bible, that my Rra got from Enoch, my eldest sister's husband, because my Rra asked for a Bible together with the lobola. My Rra said that because he doesn't smoke he doesn't need a pipe and tobacco. My Rra believes that only a girl who hasn't yet been with a man could touch the Bible. And before we would start eating I would always wait for my Rra to say: Go and fetch the Bible. Then I would fetch it from the cupboard and put it down next to him, behind his plate of food. My Rra then put his washed hand on the Bible and said Amen, because he couldn't read. But we took it as the Word of God. My Rra says so and we believe him even though I don't understand it. But that night, for the first time my Rra didn't ask me to fetch the Bible. We just closed our eyes, he put his hands together and said Amen and the tears dripped from his eyes.

Suzan, Nellie said, and began to cry herself. It hurt me more than Tommy Lewis's words or Naleidi's stones could ever do.

Today I came to tell Tommy Lewis that I did what he asked me to do and he and his sister chased me away like a dog. Voetsek! he said.

I put my arms around Nellie and held her tight, Mama. Then she squeezed me. We dropped our arms and walked away from each other without saying a word. Then, as she walked she turned around and shouted: Lukas will never chase me away!

Tant Vonnie's predicament

One cold winter morning Tant Vonnie was washing clothes for a black coloured woman – the kind that hates white-skinned coloureds. While Tant Vonnie was busy at the washtub, she brought her a mug of hot coffee. While Tant Vonnie was still wiping the foam off her hands to take the coffee, the woman, Mevrou September, threw the coffee on the ground and shouted: Finish washing my husband's white shirt, then it's you and me!

I just have to rinse it, then I'll be finished, Tant Vonnie said.

What finish! the woman shouted, pulling the shirt out of Tant Vonnie's hand and pushing her against the tub. The tub fell off the bench and Tant Vonnie fell into the spilled water.

Mevrou September began screaming and swearing hysterically: You're a thief! You stole my ring!

Tant Vonnie stood up very slowly, her dress and hands all muddy. Mevrou September again pushed her into the mud and kept on screaming: You're a thief! You white Baster!

Neighbours came out to see what the terrible noise was all about because Vatmaar was not used to such things.

Tant Vonnie was an elderly woman and she again got up very slowly. It was then that the mounted policeman who patrolled Vatmaar once a week for complaints, galloped up.

What's going on here? he asked when he came to a standstill.

Baas, this woman, Mevrou September said, pointing to Tant Vonnie, stole my wedding ring. My husband's father had it made from a sovereign for his wife. His wife died and when his son, my husband, married me he gave his son the ring to put on my finger. So you see, my Baas, the ring's got sentimental value.

So you want to lay a charge?

Yes, my Baas.

He took a writing pad and a pencil out of his pocket.

Full name?

Mevrou Martha September.

Address?

Vatmaar.

The charge? This woman stole your wedding ring that was made from a sovereign?

Yes, my Baas.

And you, thief, what's your name?

Yvonne Müller, Tant Vonnie said. She showed her hands and said: I've never had a ring on my fingers, Meneer, not since I know myself.

And you are from Vatmaar? he asked, without taking notice of what Tant Vonnie was saying.

Yes, Meneer.

Tant Vonnie turned to the people who had come nearer to make sure they miss nothing.

I had a man for whom I brought eight children into the world. He never gave me a ring to put on my finger, she said, showing her hands. There was a ring but it was around our hearts, we could never lose it, not even in death. My fingers are made for work.

Then, as it was told later, a tear came from her left eye, the one which she couldn't see with because a hornet had stung her there years ago.

They stood dead still and looked at her, the people for whom she had worked for whatever they wanted to give her and to whom she never said it's not enough. Some deliberately took advantage of her kind-heartedness and would say: Come tomorrow. Tant Vonnie never went back the next day and just said to her daughters: We're not beggars. She was of a higher stature than them and knew earthly poverty. She had no fear and to live a clean life was her first priority.

Eyes downcast, her neighbours walked over to Mevrou September. Settie, they said, to comfort her, to think we always trusted her. What a big blow for you. But at least the law is there for people like her.

They helped her pick up the shirt and washtub.

The policeman who wore a white helmet heard what they had said. He put his book and pencil in his top pocket and said: You are right, I am the upholder of the law, I will have her charged – and looked at Tant Vonnie. And you, Martha September, see that you are at the charge-office tomorrow morning at nine o'clock.

Tant Vonnie, who looked like a scarecrow, with heartache and a hard life written all over her face, had a heart of pure gold. She was fearless in her love of others. She was the victim of circumstances and the price she now had to pay was because she was different to those around her.

The policeman climbed off his horse and handcuffed her hands in front of her. Then he said to her: Walk out in front of the horse, a prisoner never rides with the law.

Tant Vonnie searched for her other sandal. Whenever she had no other work she made sandals in her room. She used rawhide, with the animal's hair still on the outside. Around her now stood women with sandals on their feet which she had made for them and most of the time had given away for nothing, and not one of them looked to see if they could find her other sandal.

The policeman was back on his horse and wouldn't wait any longer. Come, he said. Walk! Take the road to the Pan. Let's go!

Tant Vonnie began walking with her short steps, but now faster than usual. Out of their houses along the way, mostly only half-built, grown ups and children came.

Come and look at this, they said, laughing. And from house to house it was said again and again: She's a thief! She's a thief!

Tant Vonnie lifted her head and looked at them because they did not scare her. She knew them better than they knew themselves. She began to pray and whenever the foot without a sandal picked up a thorn she would wipe it against the ground to remove the thorn. Then she thought to herself: How far away is Du Toitspan where I haven't been in years? God, help me. God, help me.

Over and over she said this in her mind as she walked. And then she began to say: Lord, You must help me – until she grew tired of saying it.

The right side of her dress was one muddy rag which had begun to dry in the cold wind. She wasn't cold, in fact she was sweating, because that morning she had put on two dresses for the cold. She then began saying the Our Father and begin thinking about a great man in heaven who was looking down on earth and seeing what His creatures were up to.

Our Father, she said again and thought, He is also the Father of Mevrou September and the people of Vatmaar who had laughed at her and called her a thief. Then she again said to herself: Will I ever make the crossing? It's funny, when I think about church things it takes my thoughts from my feet and they just keep on walking, thorns or no thorns.

Then she started thinking about sayings that she had heard, things from the Bible. Things like: God is a jealous God. She had never understood it and she didn't understand it now. Lord, help me please, she heard herself say.

It was easier than the Our Father who is everyone's Father. My God, she said, and thought about Him as only her God. My God, please help me.

When Mevrou Venter's neighbour came running with did-you-hear? she spoke to Mevrou Venter but looked at Suzan and said: The mounted policeman caught a thief.

Suzan remembered how, when she was still a child, she saw how a thief who had stolen a sheep – one of those Persian sheep with the black heads – had to walk out in front of the policeman with the sheep. The sheep's legs were tied together and he had to carry it on his shoulders.

This was the picture which she thought she would now see again. So when she came around the corner of their house, she could not believe her eyes. The bottle of milk slipped out of her hands. She bent to pick it up because it had fallen in soft sand, but no matter how she looked, it was true. It was her beloved Mama, hands cuffed and with a grey mud patch on one side of her dress, walking as fast as she could with her tiny steps.

Suzan threw away the bottle of milk and stormed down on her mother. Mama, Mama, what have they done to Mama? she called holding her mother around the neck.

They stood still. Suzan kissed the eye which could not see but which was not dead.

Go back home now, my child, Tant Vonnie said.

No, no, Mama, I can't, I can't, Suzan cried.

Love would not obey love.

The policeman brought his horse to a halt. But then he remembered again in his one-track mind: I am the upholder of the law, and he commanded: Leave the prisoner alone or I'll arrest you!

Suzan took her hands off her mother, stepped away from her and looked him straight in the eye. Do what you like with me, she said. I said: Do what you like with me!

Go away! he said, the prisoner has to walk.

He turned his attention away from her because no man has words to calm a fearless virgin. She turned around, took her mother's elbow and walked even more slowly.

They walked without saying a word. Only after a while Tant Vonnie said what she always said when her prayers lost all hope that they would be answered. The Lord knows best, my child, she said, because she had to put something in the place of hope.

We'll see, Mama, Suzan said softly.

When they got to the halfway-house, the policeman ordered: Sit there – and he pointed to the stones under the big old camel thorn. I'm coming back now.

He galloped to a thicket of thorn trees, dismounted and felt in his pockets for newspaper which he always carried with him. When he found nothing, he looked around for a smooth stone to use in place of the paper. He relieved himself, used the stone and threw it away. When he came back he said: Hurry up, get going!

As they reached the main road by the footpath which goes over the railway crossing onto the main road, Tant Vonnie and Suzan began to pray together: Our Father, who art in heaven ... Over and over.

When she thought about what had happened that morning, Suzan stopped praying. It was so unbelievable and yet it was true. We are surely the victims. A few paces further on, while looking at the scene around her, she glanced at her mother.

It's not a dream, and then again it could be a dream, but from my Mama's side I will not budge, she thought. And she walked on still as if in a dream, seeing nothing, hearing nothing, just holding onto the sleeve of her mother's dress as tightly as she could.

Mother and daughter walked together like horses inspanned to a cart. Not once did they wish that they were dead.

In the silence of her thoughts Tant Vonnie thought about the postcard which she had received so long ago from her husband Heinrich. There was a shiny, bright picture of a harbour with boats and buildings on the beach and underneath was written – according to those who could read: ALEXANDRIA, EGYPT. Behind was his regiment number and next to it: Sergeant H. Müller. *My beloved*, was written there because in those days everyone wrote English: *Hoping this card finds you in the same emotional state as when we parted. I have touched this card with my hands. So you, Vonnie, if you touch this card with your hands, you are touching where I have touched. Let our fingers feel the heartbeat of our hearts. Remember, it is said God is within us at all times. The God that lives within us to Him we pray for our next meeting-together or death do us part.* It ended with: *Your loving husband Heinrich.*

It now felt as if she had the postcard in her hands and when she thought about the people of Vatmaar she thought: I do not want to be part of their God. They all say: Our Father, Our Father, while each one of them has his own thoughts and most of the time wanted something for nothing. Then it occurred to her, as if a voice was talking inside her: Seek first the kingdom of God inside you because I live inside you.

It was one of the few things she still remembered which Heinrich used to recite from the Bible. Father, she said aloud, respected Father in me – and after a while: Thy will be done.

It was then that they saw Meneer de Bruin in his black Ford lorry on the main road, driving slower and stopping near the crossing. He got out and waved his hands.

Good day, Neef, he called and waited for the policeman on horseback to come nearer.

Good day, Piet! the policeman said and got off, and the two walked with outstretched arms towards each other.

This policeman was one of the few public servants who could speak English and Afrikaans.

What have these two creatures done, Rigard? Meneer de Bruin asked, pointing to the two unlucky women.

Tant Vonnie opened her mouth to say: Good day, Meneer de Bruin, but no words came out.

I'll help you take them to town otherwise you'll knock off very late today, Meneer de Bruin said.

I'll be very grateful. One white man always helps another white man, the policeman said and shouted: Get on, you two! to make sure he was still in command.

Tant Vonnie could not get her leg over the side of the lorry. She lifted her dresses as high as she could, but she still could not do it. The two men stared at her ivory-coloured thighs, unspoiled by the sun. One looked to the other and smiled, as if wanting to make sure the one saw what the other saw.

Suzan stood helplessly on the lorry. She wanted to open the gate of the lorry but Meneer de Bruin noticed and said: Don't tamper with my things!

Let the thief get on herself, she's a prisoner, the constable said.

It was then that Onie-as, the Tswana man who always rode with Meneer de Bruin, went down on all fours and said: Step up, Ma Vonnie.

She climbed up and went to sit next to Suzan.

No, Meneer de Bruin said with a smile, rubbing softly under Suzan's chin, come and sit in front.

Piet! the constable half shouted, let the Kaffir sit in front, he is not allowed to sit with the prisoner. And don't drive away from me, drive slowly, old mate. And don't forget to stop in front of the charge-office.

As they drove off Tant Vonnie said with a sigh: I thank you, my Master. They have made of me a thief but I am no thief. My Master who lives inside me, I have found you. I am no longer a seeker. After all these years my Heinrich's body will have turned to dust, but his words on that postcard have come alive. To this God who lives within us, to Him we pray. And I feel the burden that I have carried, has disappeared. I feel light and above these earthly things.

On the lorry Tant Vonnie smiled and then giggled. She gave Suzan's hand a squeeze and said nothing, but her thoughts went to Schoongezicht where Piet de Bruin was the Baas and the law.

Tant Vonnie's memories of Schoongezicht

This Piet de Bruin, who is he after all? Now that I have found the Master, I may not besmirch His temple with bad thoughts, Tant Vonnie thought. But the time when she was taking care of Piet de Bruin's sister Sannah Vosloo, who had lost everything in the Freedom War, still came up clearly in her thoughts.

First this Sannah Vosloo's husband was killed at Paardeberg and then her two sons, who were not even men yet but who had gone on commando to take revenge. Her farm house was burned by the Tommies with everything in it and she was taken to a concentration camp with only what she had on her body. From sleeping on the wet ground, they said, she and her friends developed kidney trouble. She was much older than her brother and her husband's farm was next to his. Because she was sickly and without a soul in the world he asked her to come and live with him and his wife Anna.

Sannah Vosloo then said she could not accept charity with empty hands, he should join her farm to his. Because, she said, if a man ever again takes me, he will be wanting the farm and not me. You, Piet, are the only family I have left.

And Anna de Bruin said: I will take care of Sister for the rest of her life. Farm or no farm. I know a good coloured girl who can take care of Sister Sannah.

On the back of the lorry Tant Vonnie sat thinking about the times when she was in the company of Old Sannah, which is what she called her in her thoughts. At the end of her days she was just like a baby and had to be treated like one. She, Tant Vonnie, was her only friend, nurse and servant. The old lady called her Vonnie and she called her Sannah because she had asked her to use her name. Then it feels like we're friends, she had said.

Her kind are now all dead. Neatness was for her the principle thing, not like other Boerwomen who always think the Bible fixes everything and they must have a servant for everything, Tant Vonnie thought.

Ja, Old Sannah always said, there is no better place than the Bible to record the family's births, deaths and marriages. After Vereeniging I returned to the ashes of what my husband and I had built up. Our house, we both called it. There was nothing, Vonnie, nothing, just ash, she had said.

Old Sannah's thoughts always wandered deeply in those bygone years. My brother and I walked back to the donkey cart we had to ride in because the Tommies had taken all our horses and cattle. The donkeys we borrowed from Onie-as's father. Like a person who can't believe his eyes, I looked back and saw something shining in the rubble. I turned back and went to fetch it from the ash and rubbish. It was, believe it not, Vonnie, our little tin kist with its piece of wood which we used as a latch. I thought to myself: Funny, between the rubbish there is still value for the heart.

I held the kist in both hands, like one holds one's first-born. I put it on the donkey cart and opened it. There was my husband's Bible, still wrapped in his grandmother's Voortrekker bonnet. For me it was like finding gold. No, Vonnie, more than gold. It was our Bible with the High Dutch words. When we went to Du Toitspan for Holy Communion I took the Bible with me so that the dominee could write in my husband's and sons' dates of death.

About the suffering in the concentration camps Old Sannah could talk for hours. She always said it was such a waste of valuable time.

The Tommy, she said, no, actually his superiors, the officers, thought they were the only civilised people on earth. The poor Tommies had to do all the dirty work, like seeing that we stand in rows to be counted and to get what they called rations. The officers said we are uncivilised, but they tried everything in their power to humiliate us and break us down, all in the name of their Queen. And wherever the flag, the Union Jack, hangs, that is apparently where their Queen is.

I was fond of her, this Old Sannah, Tant Vonnie sat and thought, because she had known a few better days and more hard times. I used to give her tea made from peach leaves and used to put a buchu vinegar cloth on her kidneys. This gave her some relief. She used to say: I won't say thank you because you know I am grateful, my friend.

It was I who closed her eyes after the death rattle and washed her and laid her out for the funeral. After the funeral Piet de Bruin took me aside and said: Thank you for what you have done for my sister but I do not need you any more. Then he gave me the two half-crowns which I had placed on her eyes to keep them closed. Because she died with her eyes open.

No matter, there was a day when you did need me, Piet de

Bruin, I remembered as I walked back to Vatmaar after the funeral with my bundle and my little Suzan. When your wife Anna went to spend the weekend at her brother's in Du Toitspan. She would come back after Holy Communion.

That Saturday I almost gave in to him, Tant Vonnie sat thinking now. But thanks to my love for Heinrich, who was to me still alive even though he was dead, I could resist. He started it. He touched my behind and said: They're still healthy! After I served him coffee on the stoep, he asked for more coffee. Then he said: You're getting prettier by the day.

When I again walked past him he again tapped my behind, laughed and said: Call me Piet, it sounds better than Meneer. What do you say, old Vonnie? and he winked.

I took no notice of him. You have a wife! I told him and walked away. After lunch, while Old Sannah was having her afternoon nap, I went to sit on the verandah. He came to tell me: The Kaffir girl has gone to her hut to feed her baby and the others are in the field. And Onie-as has gone to fetch the cows for milking. It's only you and me, all alone. Sister Sannah's sleeping, we mustn't wake her. I really would like to put that bag of mealies on a slate.

That's funny, I thought, it's a hot day and there's not a cloud in the sky, why should the mealies be put on the stone as if a big rain was coming. But I'll go and help him anyway because his wounded arm is not very strong.

He let me walk out in front of him to the storeroom. When we were inside he kicked the door closed. Then he took a bag and covered Sannah Vosloo's coffin which stood ready, as if he didn't want the coffin to see what he was doing.

Because I did not know what to expect, I just stood still. I thought maybe there was a snake or a rat. Then suddenly he pushed me over a bag of mealies. I thought he was pushing me away from the snake. But then I saw him pull his braces off his shoulders. I deliberately asked loudly: What are you doing? He bent down and lifted up my dress with one hand while with the wounded arm he pressed me down, his hand on my forehead.

A woman's long dress is very cool in the summer and we never wore bloomers when it was so hot. We were used to walking about without them. When he felt that there was nothing under my dress he moved his hand from my forehead and I had to open my mouth wide because his hand was pressed up against my nose. His thumb got into my mouth and that's when I bit with all my might.

He tried to pull his thumb free and lifted my upper body on his thumb. But I kept on biting. He screamed as softly as he could: Let go of my thumb, please, let go, please, Vonnie, let's get done. Then he pulled me upright by his thumb in my mouth. I saw that the door was half open, spat out his thumb and ran out. Luckily he couldn't move very fast with his pants around his knees.

I was standing outside to get my breath back when he came out. He held his thumb to his lips and blew as if he wanted to cool it off.

You swine, you dirty swine! I said.

He put his hands against his ears to indicate that Old Sannah will hear me. Just then Suzan, who was still a little girl, returned from the ploughed land, walked past us and greeted: Mama, good day, Meneer.

I never said a word about this because, even if I had told his wife, she wouldn't have believed me. After all, their husbands would never do such a thing to a servant – even if they knew it was true they still would not believe it.

Piet de Bruin walked away like a wounded bull. And since that day he's been trying to pay me back.

It was the next Monday that Anna de Bruin told Tant Vonnie she was taking Kaaitjie with her to Du Toitspan.

After all, white people can simply not get by without a servant. When her sister-in-law, Mevrou Bosman, saw that Kaaitjie had different ways to the young girls in the Pan, she asked if she could keep her. She would give her ten shillings a month, food and place to sleep to look after her two children.

Kaaitjie said: I first have to ask my Mama if I can stay.

You stay here, I'll speak to Vonnie, Mevrou de Bruin said to her. That's how Kaaitjie began working for Mevrou Bosman.

Tant Vonnie was very upset when Anna de Bruin came back and told her what she had done and she said to her: Miesies de Bruin, you have no right to give my child to the Bosmans and to tell her what to do. You Boers think that if a person works for you then she and everything she possesses belong to you. I wonder when you Boers will start thinking differently. You still have slaves in your heads and as long as you treat people who work for you like this then a dead man is better off than your workers.

Piet de Bruin heard everything she said and she was just waiting for him to put his penny's worth in too, she was ready for him. But he said not a word to take his wife's part.

After Sannah Vosloo's funeral Tant Vonnie and Suzan went back to Vatmaar. During all the months that they were gone, there was no one to take care of their outside room. When they came to the room, the door was standing open. Everything inside had been plundered.

And that was part of the payment I got for looking after his Sister Sannah! Tant Vonnie thought.

She and Suzan began a new life in poverty, with only Kaaitjie's ten shillings a month which she earned at Mevrou Bosman's.

Tant Vonnie remembers Onie-as's punishment

After Old Sannah's funeral I thought: Now he is satisfied because he has told me to go without paying me. But today when he saw the cuffs around my wrists, I knew he was still not satisfied, Tant Vonnie sat thinking. But at least old Onie-as is here, the only gentleman among the three men. Because, no matter who they think they are, before God they are just men, nothing more.

Then she remembered:

One morning Onie-as was busy milking the cows. Just as he loosened the rope from the last cow's legs, she kicked over the bucket. As he made a grab for the bucket he scooped some manure into it.

Meneer de Bruin was livid, and when the baas was in a bad mood everyone left him to do what he thought was right. After all, in his family's eyes he was never wrong.

I'll teach the Kaffir a lesson so that he never does it again, he thought and shouted: Get to the storeroom!

Like a good servant Onie-as obeyed.

Meneer de Bruin followed him with the sjambok.

We could hear the lashes landing and heard Piet de Bruin scream: Stand still, don't run away!

Because the baas expected him to stand still like an animal and to absorb the anger that was in his heart.

Stand still, you Kaffir! we heard him shout before each lash and there were lots of stand-stills.

Please, my Baas, please, my Baas, I won't do it again. Hit me, my Baas, I am just your Kaffir.

There were many more sjambok blows.

Hit me, my Baas, hit your old boy.

Those were Onie-as's last words. After that we heard only the sjambok blows.

Maybe he grew tired of hitting Onie-as, or maybe he was satisfied, but suddenly everything was quiet and Piet de Bruin came into the house out of breath. He hung up the sjambok on the nail behind the door. His wife gave him a glass of water and said: Cool off, my love, he deserves it.

We didn't see Onie-as for a few days and heard from one of the other workers that he had run away. But then we saw him again because the baas said: He's my Kaffir, and went to fetch him.

I saw Onie-as again when he again brought in the milk the next day. He looked sick and I gave him some wynruit and wilde-als to make tea before bedtime. He had horrible cuts on his body and I sent Suzan to the veld to go and find some kopiefa leaves and to squeeze the sap onto the cuts. I also told her to pour fine sand onto the open cuts. There was such a deep cut on his neck that he could not turn his head.

Suzan said afterwards there were more blue marks than open cuts.

We all felt sorry for the poor Onie-as, all except the white people. Suzan said to me: Mama, I don't understand it.

Later, when Onie-as and I were alone and he was much better, he said to me: Ma Vonnie, do you think God saw how the baas hit me?

I said: Onie-as, God sees everything.

Then why did he let the wrong one get a hiding?

What do you mean?

It was after all the cow that knocked over the bucket, not me. Ma Vonnie, I won't bewitch him because I don't have money for the witchdoctor because the witchdoctor wants too much money to bewitch a white person.

But I'll fight him the Tswana way.

Sannah Vosloo tells true stories about her life

Tant Vonnie's mind went back even further:

One Sunday afternoon when Meneer de Bruin went with his family to Holy Communion, Suzan and I went to sit with Old Sannah. She was always keen to tell true stories about her life and she was happy when someone wanted to listen.

She always began with: You know Vonnie, we Boers got along well with the black people on the farms. We taught them to work and we taught them that they were lower than white people. And they were very obedient until the English came. The English wanted the whole country and all its people to be under their Queen and English to be the only language to be spoken.

But you know, Vonnie, there is no difference between a Boer and a Brit if they both stand naked and they shut their mouths. This young boy I'm going to tell you about, his mother and I grew up together, we were like two sisters. Since childhood. I wouldn't want to hurt her, even though she is no longer with us and she now lies in a concentration camp without a number or anything to mark her grave. Because we never knew which one of us would be the next to go.

I won't tell you what her name was, also not what her son's name was. He was born out of wedlock, like many of us in those years. I'm not telling his name because it wasn't his fault and these days he has a prominent job at the Du Toitspan Town Council. His only weakness, and I despise him for it, is that he was born one of us, a Boer, but now he thinks he is better than us just because he has taken an English wife who thinks a Boer woman is not her equal. And now he goes to the English church. The last time I saw him as a genuine young Boer was when he returned with my son, Kallie, from commando to come and look for provisions, rations.

Onie-as had a much older brother, Duma. His deep voice made him sound more manly than the other boys. But he had the intelligence of a child and did everything that Kallie told him to do.

This Duma was Kallie's mounted servant. When they came to the farm I gave them everything that I could spare. And at the very next skirmish after that Kallie was killed.

She wiped away her tears which always began to flow when she mentioned her husband's or her sons' names.

After Vereeniging we heard that this boy, whose mother was my friend, and who was a friend of my son, who did not even have a proper funeral, had become a handsupper. They say he wasn't even taken captive, he just rode over to the khakis and became a joiner.

Now this Duma got lost after Kallie was killed. Because he was black he was chased about by his own people because he couldn't speak English like some of the freedom fighters and so he went to find himself another baas. It was then that he saw this friend of Kallie ride over to become a joiner and it was from him that I heard about what happened:

It was winter and cold when Duma came upon a dead Englishman. He took off the man's coat. His pipe and tobacco was still in his coat's pocket. Then Duma rode to the laager where he was captured by us, his own people.

He was taken for a spy because was smoking the expensive pipe which only a commandant and field cornet could afford. He apparently laughed when they called him a spy. Then they took him to the commandant who did the sentencing for all who were accused of spying.

They say black spies were not shot but were castrated to frighten other black spies. Duma said that it took eight men to hold his arms and legs, but they cut them off, both his testicles, and, he said, it must have been with the bluntest knife in the camp. Afterwards someone threw salt on the place where the eggs were, like one throws sand on a fire to kill it. Then they left him lying there to die or to do whatever he liked.

Vonnie, Old Sannah said, if ever I have felt sorry for a man then it was for that Duma, not because he was a black man but because he was a man.

After that he got very fat and did not live long after the English burnt down my house. It was he, I later heard from the children, who found our kist under the washbasin and then buried it under the basin and covered it with some ash.

We, the Boers, Old Sannah said, made a big mistake. We lost just about all our worldly possessions and most of our people too. But the black people had just such heavy losses. If we had long ago taken the black people onto our side, which was then out of the question, we would've chased the Tommies into the sea.

This land was the black man's and the Boer's – Afrikaners, as we are called now – which the English took with their weapons.

Ag, said Old Sannah, it's all water under the bridge. Today the

English and the Afrikaners are one. But I want to tell you, Vonnie, we will not stop fighting until the land once again belongs to us.

But let me get back to that young man, the Boer who wanted to be an Englishman. When he was two weeks old, his mother's milk dried up. We gave him cow's milk mixed with water. The baby got very sick because he could not keep it in and he was dying. Then one of the maids gave birth, Duma's sister. Her mother, that is, the baby's granny, said: Go and call Thataro.

I'm mentioning her name because she died before Duma, Old Sannah said. I was holding my friend's baby in my arms when this maid walked in. She was very scared at having been called, and it was the first time that she had put her foot in a white man's house. The old woman said to her: Sit – and pointed to a goatskin on the floor.

She went to sit, shaking and very nervous. The old woman then told her in her own language that she should not be scared, we will not hurt her. It's just that our child's mother doesn't have milk.

The baby cried and cried without end, but its little voice was already beginning to fade. This Thataro, who was so named because she was her mother's sixth child, looked at the baby and nodded her head. She knew what she had to do.

The baby's mother first gave her a mug of coffee to calm her. After Thataro had drunk it, she gave her the half-dead child. She already had her breast out and my friend gave her a damp cloth to wipe it off.

You won't believe me, Vonnie, but the child took the breast after a few sucks, held it with both his little hands and drank himself to sleep. Later I took him and went to lay him down. He slept right through the night, the first night in a long time that the family really rested. Then the old woman said to the maid: Thank you, you must come again when the miesies calls for you.

Thataro stood up and my friend put her arms around the maid and said: Thank you, God.

Why not Thataro? I thought to myself. Did God not send her?

Thataro walked away and they didn't even give her a nod of the head. But from that day on I knew God's milk can be carried in a white or a black breast.

Thataro was very obedient and came whenever she was called, even in the middle of the night. They no longer washed her breast off with a damp cloth and most of the time she picked the baby up herself. He got used to the smell of the breast because he was always in a hurry to put it into his little mouth. After three weeks he was a strong little child.

You know, Vonnie, it's always the granny who looks after the illegitimate child. After a while he was weaned on thin porridge. He was a friendly child who was forever laughing. Thataro's son also grew into a healthy little boy and looked so sweet in his loincloth. Those two little boys were bosom friends and where the one was you would find the other.

And like it goes in life, Vonnie, the father never once came near this child of his. And when he heard that the child had drunk on a black woman, he cut all ties. That's why the child was given its mother's surname. Later she married another man who took her with the child and all. He said: I will take you with everything that you are and have.

It's a pity there are so few of these men. My friend never had another child.

Then Sister Sannah said: Now I am tired, Vonnie. Turn me around so that I can face the wall. I'll sleep quicker that way.

Tant Vonnie remembered more: It was while she and Suzan were still in the old woman's room that Onie-as came in with a bucket of water. It was his job to see that the nkgo, the claypot, was always full of water. The water in the nkgo was used only for drinking water because the claypot kept the water very cool, especially in summer.

Suzan saw Onie-as through the slit where the hinges of the door are, but because we were sitting behind the half-open door, he did not see us. Suzan took my hand and with her eyes she said: Look.

I was so shocked that my heart began to beat faster. With my fingers on my lips I showed Suzan that she should keep quiet. Luckily Sannah was fast asleep.

We saw Onie-as open his pants and pee in the water and then spit in it. Then he began whistling a tune and walked away with the half-empty bucket.

I don't know if it was the first time he had done it, but what I did know was that the water in the pot was for the white people only. Not even me and Suzan could use the mug which always stood next to the pot.

I told Suzan to keep absolutely quiet about what we had seen because it could mean the death of the poor Onie-as. Only then I remembered what Onie-as had said about his Tswana way of fighting.

Tant Vonnie wondered what he was thinking about now in the lorry sitting next to his baas. Piet de Bruin probably thought she had forgotten how he tried to rape her in his storeroom. She had not forgotten. Nor had she forgotten what Onie-as was doing to his baas's drinking water, something which neither Onie-as nor Piet de Bruin knows she knows.

What other secrets does Onie-as not carry in his head, Tant Vonnie wondered.

Tant Vonnie comes before the law

Piet de Bruin took the longest possible road through the Pan to the charge-office. The policeman on horseback started getting excited and showed him to stop, which he eventually did. Onie-as got out and dropped the lorry's gate before Piet de Bruin could stop him.

Tant Vonnie walked barefoot down the street because she had

kicked off the other sandal. But the handcuffs she could not hide away. The passers-by came to a standstill watching her and Suzan.

After giving her a look and a cunning smile, Meneer de Bruin rode away.

They walked to the charge-office with the policeman on horseback behind them. Some people shook their heads and others laughed. One elderly woman said: I wouldn't want to be in her shoes.

Another busybody asked: What has she done, Constable?

Oh, she is a thief, he said.

They had to wait for the policeman while he dismounted and tied the bridle to the iron pegs outside the charge-office. Then he shoved Tant Vonnie into the charge-office with the words: Move, you skelm!

A sergeant stood behind the counter. What have we here, Constable Prins? he asked.

She stole her madam's gold ring in Vatmaar, Sarge.

And did you tell her madam to be in court tomorrow?

Yes, I did, Sarge.

The sergeant dipped his pen in the inkwell and wrote: Theft of a golden wedding ring. Name of her madam?

The constable took out his pocket-book. Martha September, he said.

You from the Cape, Constable?

Yes, from Stellenbosch.

Have you noticed that all these mixed-blood people who are descended from slaves are either Afrika or one of the calendar months, from January to December?

Yes, Sarge, I have.

He stuck his pen in the inkwell and said: And the name of the culprit?

Yvonne Müller, address also Vatmaar, Sarge.

You are doing a fine job, Constable Prins, ridding this place Vatmaar of thieves. I'll put your name on the promotion list.

170

Thank you, Sarge, he said, I am only the upholder of the law, but Sarge is the law.

Anything to declare, or you will be searched, the sergeant warned Tant Vonnie. She loosened the safety-pin on her dress and the dress pocket fell onto the cement floor.

One dress pocket, Sarge, the constable said, and put a label on the bag.

Take the prisoner away, the sergeant said.

The constable, the upholder of the law, loosened the cuffs, and when she looked at his white forehead, because he had to take off his helmet, she thought: Not even you, Rigard Prins, are above the law.

A black constable called Petrus was called to take her away. He trotted nearer, stood to attention, and said: Yes, Sergeant. Then he took a big key from the wooden keyholder and said: Come.

Tears streamed out of Suzan's eyes, but she couldn't cry any more. She knew there would be no mercy for her mother. The noise of the keys and the iron gate brought a fear into her still childlike mind which she could not understand.

Then Constable Rigard Prins, the upholder of the law, said to her: My girl, you can come and sleep at my place tonight. My wife won't know because she's in bed with flu. You'll get a good plate of food and afterwards I'll come and see if you have everything you need.

The black constable came past with an tin plate of boiled yellow mealies. Again Suzan heard the keys. So that's my mama's food, she thought. She jumped up and ran out. She just ran and ran until she had to stop to catch her breath. Across the square at the station she saw the old Cape cart and the driver. She walked over to him.

My child, why are you running so? the man asked.

No words would come out of her mouth.

After the cell door was locked, Tant Vonnie unrolled the only blanket in the cell, went down on her knees and began to pray:

Father, my Master who lives within me, You who knows why I am here, if this is Your will, I thank you. You know what the best is for me. Master inside me, I thank you for the small price I have to pay today for the loss of my pride and for the big prize that I had won today, for now I know where to find you. My God, be with Suzan and Kaaitjie. That is all I ask of You. Father, I know you will find an unseen protector to guide my two daughters.

She got up, took a handful of mealies and tried to eat them. It is food after all, these yellow mealies, she said to herself.

She and Suzan had eaten nothing since the night before. She threw the mealies back into the tin plate. She shook her head and said: I can't eat alone.

A tear rolled out of the eye which couldn't see. Suzan, Suzan, where are you? she said out loud. Where are you, my child? Because she was absolutely alone, locked up. A woman who had lived close to nature was now a caged-in animal. The darkness of the night took away the walls and rescued her.

It had been a long, tiring day and now she cried herself to sleep. Early the next day she was woken by a dream: Somebody had shaken her awake under a bright white light. Yvonne, the voice had said, you have asked and you shall receive because I am at all times with you.

She sat up straight and folded her arms around her knees. What a relief, she thought. I feel light, as if the burden that I had to carry has disappeared. Then she thought suddenly that she could not speak in such a way with her Master and she again went down on her knees.

Master, she said from within her heart, thank You. I know where to find You.

It was then that she heard the sound of the keys. A tin plate of food was pushed under the cell door, with milk in another tin plate.

Bottles are not allowed in the cell, said a black policeman she had not seen before. Your child brought you this food last night.

She came with a friend of her sister's, she said. She's staying with her.

Thank you, Rra, she said.

Suzan sees Kaaitjie and meets Kenneth Kleinhans

When the driver of the Cape cart saw how Suzan was shivering with fright, he put his hand on her shoulder and said: Don't be afraid, girl. I am Stoffel Jones.

He gave her a mug of water from his waterbag and said: Drink this water, but first go and sit in the Cape cart so that your blood pressure can settle down.

He gave her a sidelong look and wondered where he had seen her before. She could not be from Du Toitspan, because here the girls her age, judging by her breasts, do not wear torn rags for ribbons. He left her alone and went back to stand by his horse.

After she had drunk a few mouthfuls of water, Stoffel Jones stepped nearer.

What happened, my child? he asked because he had a daughter her age and he thought what would happen to his Maureen in such circumstances. Where do you work? What is the name of your miesies?

When she still said nothing, he asked: Where do you come from?

Because he knew that the white people from the Pan prefer servants from the backward districts.

Vatmaar, Suzan said.

Yes, now it comes to me, you work for Miesies Bosman.

No, not me, Oom. My sister Kaaitjie.

There aren't any trains now and people don't use my Cape cart this time of the night. The sun's going down, I may just as well go home and eat something. My wife will be happy because she always says it's so nice if the whole family eats together. I have to go past the Bosmans' house. I'll drop you off there.

Thank you, Oom.

He gave her hand a fatherly squeeze.

Thank you, Oom, she said again.

When they stopped at the Bosmans' house, Stoffel Jones said: Go around the back. They're the kind of people who believe a coloured should know his place.

She jumped out of the cart and ran off like young people do. The back gate was open and there she saw Kaaitjie under the pepper tree, busy pushing one of the children on a swing.

Kaaitjie stood like someone who did not understand what was happening. Then she shouted: Suzan! – and ran towards her. They hugged each other and Suzan began to sob bitterly.

Stop now, my sister, there's no time to talk, Kaaitjie said. Sit here on this stone. I just have to go and wash the children quickly. There's my room – and she pointed to a whitewashed building. One half is a storeroom and I have to lock it when I go out. Now I carry the key on a piece of string around my neck because I'm scared I'll lose it. The miesies said if I lose this key – and she held up the keys in her hands – she'll take off the money for a new lock from my wages.

She opened the door for Suzan, and after washing the children, she came back to Suzan who had in the meantime eaten all the leftover food in the room. Just in time too, because she had begun to feel faint from hunger.

Now I have to wait to be called for my food, Kaaitjie said. I've already taken my mug and plate to the kitchen. I'm not allowed to leave it there and I have to wash it at the outside tap. I've asked the miesies if my sister can sleep here with me tonight.

Then Kaaitjie began to mimic her miesies: I've already given you permission to see that young Hotnot. I don't like him because he calls me Mevrou. I just hope this is the only sister you have, I don't want a new sister here every week. Understand?

Yes, Miesies, I answered, said Kaaitjie. But now I can't wait any longer. What happened, my sister?

One sister placed her hand on the other sister's and between sniffs and wiping away tears Suzan told her what had happened. Kaaitjie kept on interrupting her with: I don't believe it. It can't be true. But can the Lord not see what wrong these people are doing?

I don't know, Suzan said.

Come and get your food! Kaaitjie's miesies shouted from the kitchen.

When she gave her the plate of food and the mug of coffee, she said: I don't have food for your sister too.

Thank you, Miesies.

Kaaitjie put the plate in front of Suzan. You eat. I'll have the piece of bread, she said.

Suzan began to wonder if what had happened today was true and if it wasn't just her full stomach that was making her feel so strange. Then Kaaitjie said: I'm going to fill the half barrel with water so that we can have a bath. Then we'll feel much better and it is time I looked my best. Then she laughed.

Suzan laughed too and wondered: Who will say no to a bath?

Once washed the other's back and when they had finished bathing, they took the tub and threw out the water and took a grass broom and swept the dung floor and threw the buckskin over the wet patch. The wet floor gave the room a clean aroma. Then the girls combed their hair and both made two long golden plaits like their mother had taught them.

Like people who had grown up without watches and almost always knew what the time was, the two sisters were finished in time.

It is now his time to come, Kaaitjie said.

Who?

You'll see. She laughed and looked out the door towards the gate. Here he comes now! she stamped her feet excitedly on the floor.

He came to stand in the open door and asked: May I come in?

Kaaitjie stood still and without a word, opened her arms. He stepped over the threshold and they held each other tight.

Suzan could not believe her eyes. It seemed as if she had given her sister up to somebody else. She could hear both their quick breaths as they searched for air to feed the flame of their love. Together like this, the two changed the atmosphere in the bleak storeroom completely.

Suzan looked away when the young man kissed her sister and she wondered what their mother would say.

Eventually he looked over Kaaitjie's shoulder and said: This must be Suzan.

They dropped their arms and he gave her his hand. Take your Ouboet's hand, Suzan. I am the eldest, not so, Kaaitjie?

Yes, my love, she said and put her hand on her mouth as if to pull the words back.

I brought us a bottle of ginger-beer and a vetkoek. And a glass because one doesn't drink ginger-beer from a mug.

He opened the bottle and tipped some into the glass. He gave it to Suzan saying: Guests first, my sister-in-law.

Then he went to sit between the two girls and said: Phew, but I'm tired. What about you two?

They both gave a short laugh.

Now tell me what brings you here, Suzan?

Then Kaaitjie told the story her sister had told her, without taking out or adding words.

I don't believe it, I don't believe it, he kept saying.

This Kenneth Kleinhans was thirty-two years old and he was working on the new Masonic Temple of the Freemasons. He had been recommended for the job for two reasons: one, he was more a craftsman than a tradesman, and two, he was an initiated member of the coloured people's secret semi-religious lodge called the Free Gardeners.

Today he had finished the dome with its skylight and tomorrow he would be attaching the copper lightning conductor to the top of the dome.

He had completed a course as a carpenter and had his qualification papers. He did not want to be a doctor or a teacher as his parents had wanted.

He was tall and thin with real coloured features: very light-brown eyes and straight black hair, with a neat Clark Gable-moustache. And he was always clean shaven. On the building site he was a respected young man, hardworking and conscientious as his boss said. His salary was the same as a white craftsman's, something which caused a lot of jealousy.

In his short life there were many mothers who tried to push their daughters his way. But he had never felt anything for them, he told Kaaitjie whenever they were alone in the storeroom. He told her about his qualifications but she did not know what it meant. Then she asked him what matriculation meant and it took him almost all night to explain it to her.

She always asked him a string of questions, and Kenny, as she called him, had to explain every time until she understood. She also asked him about his work and what he would be doing the next morning, and he liked it that she was so interested in him and in what he did. She was proud of him and his voice alone could set her heart beating faster.

The Bosmans knew what specialist work he did. They greeted him with a: Good evening, Kleinhans. But behind his back he was: that Hotnot.

After Kaaitjie and Suzan had told him about their mother, he took his bicycle and said: I'm going to see what's going on there. What is your mother's first name?

Vonnie, they both said.

Vonnie Müller?

Yes, they again said together.

When he rode away, he said to himself: I can't go empty-handed. At the cafe he bought another vetkoek, a piece of sausage and a bottle of milk.

Kenneth Kleinhans remembers how he met Kaaitjie

Kaaitjie, my Kaaitjie, he said to himself. I can't believe there are people who would want to hurt you and your people. I love you, I love you so much. Your mother is my mother too, no matter who or what she is. I will accept her even if she is a thief.

He again recalled that Sunday morning when he saw her sitting on a stone outside the Dutch Reformed church. It was as if a magnet had drawn him to her. Never, never before in his life had he had such a feeling. Maybe it was this "love at first sight" he had heard people talk about.

He immediately said to himself: I'll push my bicycle – and walked over to where she was sitting. When he got to her he asked: Are you waiting for someone?

Ja, Meneer, she said, I'm waiting for my miesies. She is Miesies Bosman. I look after her two children.

Just then the church came out. He heard a woman with an expensive hat on say: There's my nursemaid. Come, Kaaitjie, take the children.

Kaaitjie gave him a smile which touched his whole being. This Kenneth Kleinhans was never the same again – it was only a part of him which got up from that stone next to the church. The next Sunday he was back there, even before the service had started. The same woman who had called the girl to fetch the children, but now in another outfit, arrived with the same two little girls and her husband.

He had to restrain himself from going over to this woman and asking her where her "maid" was. The next Sunday it rained, already since the Saturday, without end. Everything was under water. He thought to himself: They wouldn't let her sit on a wet stone so close to the house of God. And he'd be a fool to get himself splashed full of mud on a Sunday morning. He had not even opened yesterday's newspaper, he would read it and use the day to rest, he decided. He also wouldn't go to church. His church, the Wesleyan church, was just two blocks away, but the street was like a river. Then he thought about another excuse. His father always said: Too much church is not good for anyone – too much of anything is not good for anyone.

The next Sunday was his monthly long weekend and he took the three o'clock train to his parents in Graaff-Reinet. When he got back, he had half-forgotten the girl because his mind was preoccupied with the dome of the temple. The architect liked giving him sketches rather than scale drawings and he had to work out the details himself.

Then one Sunday afternoon he decided to go to the café to buy himself something nice. The food at the boarding house was the same from Monday to Monday and a hardworking man is always hungry. The Italian woman with her macaroni, her "special" as she called it, knew that they would just complain after they had eaten, and by now she always made sure she was far away.

Like most bicycle riders he took the back road next to the main road. When he rode past an open gate, he recognised the two children under the pepper tree. He got off and asked: Where's the maid?

It was then that Kaaitjie came out from behind the tree, and said with a laugh: That must be me, Meneer.

He stood there holding his bicycle while she came over to him. What can I do for Meneer? she asked.

He said to himself softly: It's her! The same girl with the same colour dress. But now he could see that the dress did not fit her. It must be second-hand. He stretched out his hand and said: My name is Kenny.

She laughed, and when he asked: And yours? she said: Kaaitjie.

He thought to himself: You are my Kaaitjie, too big dress or not.

Then he asked her where she had been the Sunday after their first meeting, and she said that it was her monthly Sunday off, when she got her wages and took it to her mama in Vatmaar.

179

I usually spend only five shillings on food, because if I buy too much it's too heavy to carry to Vatmaar.

And what do you do with the five shillings left over?

I give it to Mama, Meneer.

Fancy this, he thought. Still so childish, and simple, as we call it in Graaff-Reinet, and in her poverty her smile is so innocent and honest. So you get ten shillings a month? he said.

Ja, Meneer. Mama says we should be grateful for the little because one day when we have a lot we'll know how to appreciate it.

I would like to come and visit you. I promise you, Kaaitjie, I'll behave myself.

I first have to ask my miesies, she said. But to herself she thought it would be all right because she had once heard the miesies say: I hope she gets a boyfriend soon so that he (meaning her husband) can keep his eyes off her. Kaaitjie didn't laugh about this and with tears burning in her eyes wondered: But what does she think of me?

I will also behave myself, Meneer, she answered.

It was then that Mevrou Bosman came out of the kitchen door and shouted: Bring the children and come and wash them!

Ask her right now! Kenneth said.

It was to him like an eternity before she came out of the kitchen door, threw her hands in the air and shouted: Yes! Then she went back inside.

After another eternity she came out again. He said to himself that her way of walking and the sway of her body was as natural as that of a young lioness.

They stood there chatting, she with her hand on his bicycle handle as she laughed and looked him straight in the eye. She still called him Meneer and looked at his shoes and his clothes and spoke about Meneer's bicycle.

He asked her if she would like to go for a little ride with him on the bicycle.

Please, Meneer.

Then he heard: Come and get your food!

She left him standing right there and he watched as she took a tin plate and a mug from the windowsill, went into the kitchen and came out with the plate filled with food and a mug of coffee. She went to put it in a small outside room – after she first unlocked the padlock on the door. She came out, locked the door again, and ran back to him. He could see she was running to hide her shyness.

She put her hand on his hand on the handle, looked him in the eyes, tilted her head to one side, smiled and said: Good day, Meneer Kenny. Then she walked away.

He called after her: Kaaitjie, Kaaitjie, here, have this – and held out the packet of sweets to her. She turned around, smiled, and then shook her head.

After she had closed the door, he stood there waiting for a while. Old boy, you'd better be off, he told himself.

That is how he had met this girl he called his love. He smiled with a sigh.

Kenneth and Suzan's problem

The charge-office was a long way from the Bosmans' house. Kenneth parked his bicycle with one pedal on the edge of the pavement.

Good evening, he greeted the sergeant on night duty. I've brought something to eat – and he held up the paper bag – for a Mevrou Vonnie Müller.

Without greeting or looking up, the policeman said: Vonnie? He stared at the book in front of him. You said Vonnie, did you not?

Yes, Sergeant.

I'm sorry, my boy, nobody by that name here. He closed the book. Sorry, he said again.

Kenneth Kleinhans took the packet and tied it to the new carrier at the back of his bicycle. He had put on the carrier recently to go out riding with Kaaitjie on Sunday afternoons.

On his way back to the two girls he kept saying to himself: It can't be true. Kaaitjie, my Kaaitjie, God bless you. And you too, Suzan, who is so much like your sister.

He wondered what her parents would say if they met her, his Kaaitjie. To his father intelligence and education were everything. His favourite piece of wisdom for him, his only child, was: My son, intelligence never chooses its vehicle or appearance. And Kenneth always believed his father to mean that his wife should be of the same calibre as them, his parents. He, the principal of a prestigious high school and his mother, a sister at the hospital. Both were highly respected people who had a big house with running water and electricity and who even had their own Chevrolet car.

His mother was all for a girl with European features for him, and she had often tried to match him up with someone or other. It was hard for him to keep disappointing her. And here was his Kaaitjie – she was not educated like them, but she knows the world. And she is fearless and honest, even if she is simple. She told him that she had never before eaten with a knife and fork and that she could not read. But she knew her numbers. Up to now he had already taught her a few new words and their meanings.

She thought the lessons he had been giving her and the books, most of them magazines from which he read to her, more important than courting. Half of their time together was given to the explaining of words. She preferred Afrikaans and she loved to learn, which he knew was the surest way to success. And she said to him: If you ever want me for your wife, I will not say yes to it until I am on the same level as you, my husband. Then she laughed again: But now there is only one man for me, and there will always be only one, and his name is Kenny.

Some people in his home town called his parents hoity-toity. He had even wondered if it wouldn't be better to marry first and to face the consequences afterwards. Then on the other hand, he thought: No, she can stand on her own, my queen who was born into poverty. She had no choice and she doesn't want to be what she is not. My Kaaitjie.

When he turned into the path, he saw the two girls standing exactly where he had left them.

When he left, Kaaitjie went to show Suzan her slate and books and the Huisgenoot magazines he had given her and from which he was teaching her to read. Suzan told her that he teaches her in the evenings when he comes to visit. And in the day she then says and does what he had taught her, over and over so that she can remember it.

I don't want him to think I'm stupid, Suzan.

But why haven't you told Mama about Meneer Kenny, Kaaitjie? Mama knows what's good for you and for me and after all the three of us never kept secrets from each other. Then suddenly she said: But you're my older sister and I apologise for having said that.

Kaaitjie flung her arms around Suzan and said: Let's go and wait for him.

While they waited Suzan asked lots of questions because she wanted to know everything about her new-found Ouboet.

What does he talk about, Kaaitjie?

All sorts of things.

Does he talk about his work?

Yes, a lot. He says most of the time he has his lunch alone, but sometimes the white tradesmen come and sit with him at lunch time. Usually, he says, when they want him to help them with something. He says the brown and black workers sit under a big thorn tree. And the things they talk about! Then he always laughs and he doesn't want to tell me. But once he did tell me:

You know what, Kaaitjie, he said, these poor people earn just fifteen shillings a week. Today they were sitting and smoking a dagga-zol. The one coloured man then said they will always be in rags and take whatever the white man throws away because trousers cost ten shillings and they get only fifteen shillings a week.

But I understand, another said, one day when our wages go up we'll be able to buy more things.

You don't understand, the baas-boy replied, if the wages go up to one pound, the trousers will cost fifteen shillings.

If the white man could've made us, he would've, a black man said from the side.

The coloured baas-boy had something to say about this. The white man can make us, it's true, he said. But the one thing he can't make is the cock – that beats them.

Everyone laughed and some said: It's true, and others: I believe it.

Kaaitjie laughed too as she told the story and Suzan looked at her sister and thought that she had changed since the last time she had seen her.

Then they saw Kenny come around the corner.

They have nobody by this name at the police station, he said when he stopped.

I believe it and I don't believe it, said Kaaitjie.

Oom, Oom, my Oom Ouboet, Suzan stammered, in front of the police station there's a blue glass lamp with letters on it.

Yes, I know. It was shining and it says "Police". He took the brown paper bag from the carrier and said: You might as well have this.

No, Meneer, no, Suzan said, and began to walk quickly in the direction from which Kenny had just come.

Without another word, he turned his bicycle around and rode after her.

When he reached her, he said: Come, get on, I'll go and show you.

They rode in silence to the charge-office and got off.

This is the place, Meneer, said Suzan. She went in and said:

Good evening, Mister, Sir, this Oom and I have brought some food for Mama.

She remembered the tin plate of yellow mealies.

But I saw this man half an hour ago. There is no person here by that name. What is the name of your mother, young girl?

Vonnie Müller, Meneer, Sir.

The sergeant laid the book on the counter and opened it. He pressed his hand on each name. You said Vonnie. Here is no person by that name.

Look again Meneer, Sir. She did not want to say Baas in front of her new-found Ouboet even though she knew a white man was more approachable if you called him Baas.

No, the sergeant said. You better go home. Perhaps she is sleeping somewhere after having had too much to drink. Come again tomorrow.

Kenneth thought: I'm glad I've convinced her that her mother is not here.

He walked out and took his bicycle by its handlebars, ready to climb on. Suzan came out afterwards and went to stand near him. Then she turned around and went back into the office. This time she said: Baas, look for Yvonne, Yvonne Müller. Vonnie is what people call Mama.

Now the sergeant was really cross. It is the very last time! he shouted. Do you hear me?

He again let his finger slide down the names and then he said: Here it is, Yvonne Müller. Charge: theft of a wedding ring. She will appear in court tomorrow at 9 a.m. Did you hear me?

Suzan nodded because she knew only a few English words. Yes, I understand. Sergeant said tomorrow nain ay-em in the court.

Constable! he shouted and a black policeman appeared.

Sir, the man said, standing to attention.

Take this food to the cell of Yvonne Müller, it's number five. And don't give her the bottle of milk, pour it out into a tin dish before you push it under the grill gate.

Thank you, Sir, Kenny heard himself say.

What did he say, Oom?

He said your mother will appear in court at nine o'clock tomorrow morning.

She stood still, thinking. Before getting onto his bicycle, Kenneth also hesitated a moment before going back.

Any bail, Sergeant?

No, that is for the court to decide, it is out of my jurisdiction. Do you have the telephone number of a lawyer?

No, Sergeant.

Go to the post office. There's a telephone book in the booth.

Kenneth and Suzan rode to the post office. Three lawyers, together with their partners, were listed, but all opened only at eight the next day. Kenneth wrote down their numbers in his pocketbook.

When he came out of the telephone booth, Suzan said: This is a tellerfoan, isn't it, Ouboet?

Yes, he laughed and said he'd phone the lawyers the next morning at eight. We start work at seven o'clock. I'll tell my boss I've got urgent business and that I'd like to take the day off.

Suzan got on to the back of the bicycle and they rode back in silence. When they turned out of the main road into the footpath, they saw Kaaitjie still standing where they had left her. She ran to them.

Is Mama there?

Ja, said the two with one tongue.

Thank You, Lord.

Kenneth stopped for Suzan to get off, and sighed: Whew, now I'm tired.

Kaaitjie went to stand in front of him, put her hands on the bicycle handlebar and stared him in the eye. She closed her eyes and tilted her head back. Her young, firm nipples pressed against the thin cotton of her dress because she had not yet begun to wear a corset.

He knew what she wanted and kissed her full on the mouth, and kept on so that the kiss could sink in. Then he told her what he tells her every night, and that Suzan will tell her everything and that he will come pick her up the next morning before eight. Good night, you two, he said and rode off.

Good night, they called after him like a little choir.

Then they went to lie down. They did not sleep well but were up as usual before daybreak. Then they waited for Kenneth Kleinhans.

Tant Vonnie meets four other transgressors

The cell door was, as usual, opened at six o'clock. Tant Vonnie was told to go and hang the blanket and the mat outside. She also had to empty the slop bucket, throw water from another bucket onto the cement floor and sweep it clean. Then she had to wash her face at the outside tap.

She saw four other prisoners also coming out of their cells. Good morning, Miesies, they said one after the other as if they were all in one boat.

You are Hendruk, aren't you?

Yes, Miesies Mooller.

The other three said the tante won't know them because it's that first time they have seen the tante.

My name is Neels Vool, one of them said. How many bottles did the Old Miesies lose?

He thought that she had been caught for trading in liquor. At that time only white people could obtain a licence to sell liquor to "Non-Europeans" from a bottle store or bar. Neels was what they called a mailer, someone who bought liquor for a black man. Because black people then were not allowed to buy wine or "spirits" as it stated on the Right of Admission board. After he had bought a bottle of wine (the ordinary worker could not afford brandy) the mailer was allowed to drink the wine in the bottleneck.

Then he gave the rest of the bottle to the man who had given him the money to buy it.

This always took place in the back alleys and the mailers knew when the policeman on duty would come by, but sometimes the policeman appeared unexpectedly and it was then that somebody got caught, mostly on Fridays or Saturdays when black people got their pay packets.

This was how Neels Vool had been caught. He was a Griqua and proud of it, because the law said his race could buy white man's liquor and go about without a pass. Because his people were classified coloured, a mixed race.

Neels Vool earned his bread from selling liquor, and was known as an honest mailer because he always handed over the change. A bottle of sherry cost a shilling and workers were usually paid with a ten shilling note and two half-crowns.

Some mailers of course just walked past the bottle store and kept the black man's money for themselves. After waiting for a while, the black man would go and see what has happened to his mailer. If he didn't get him he would tell everyone he came across: I'm going to bewitch him.

The shebeen queen, as she was called, sold a bottle of sherry for two shillings.

Coloureds and blacks lived together in peace because they were more or less in the same boat. It was just that the black man was not legally allowed to drink, as the law called it, white men's liquor. The bottle store keeper had to keep a register of liquor that was sold to coloureds. He had to write down the name and address, because a coloured was allowed to buy only one gallon – six bottles – per day.

For each bottle of wine the mailer received a tickey from the shebeen owner, usually someone who didn't want to work and who sat where he couldn't be spotted easily, to look out and give the sign whenever he heard the noise of the Harley Davidson motorbike. This bike had a sidecar in which the white detective would put the transgressor if he could catch him. The detectives were called the raiders.

Neels Vool was sure his sentence would be the usual one pound fine or ten days hard labour. Hard labour meant that you got up at six in the morning, winter or summer, folded your blanket (because you had slept on the cement floor or on a grass mat), cleaned the cell and then ran straight under the cold shower in the yard while the warders laid into you with their batons. You each got a piece of rag for a towel.

The food was boiled yellow mealies and a boiled carrot or beetroot from the prison garden, depending on what was available. There were three menus: black, coloured and white. Indians and Chinese fell under coloured. A black convict had to walk barefoot, a coloured got shoes and a white convict got socks and long pants in winter. A white convict slept on a bed and he was not obliged to work outside the prison walls.

But let's get back to Tant Vonnie and the other four prisoners. The black policeman said: Come, you lot! – and tied the four men to each other with two handcuffs. Tant Vonnie's hands he tied behind her back. He got papers from the sergeant and said to them: Move!

The four men walked in front, Tant Vonnie at the back.

There was an assegai tied to the handlebar of the black policeman's bicycle and a knobkierie in a leather holder attached to his belt. (A black policeman was not allowed to carry a firearm or to arrest a white man. If he saw a white man breaking the law, he had to fetch a white policeman to arrest him.)

It was nearly eight o'clock and the townsfolk were on their way to work. Most were used to seeing handcuffed men on their way to court, but never a handcuffed woman without shoes. To them she looked dangerous and they quickly gave way in front of her.

The men walked as if they were in a hurry to get to the court cells. Tant Vonnie lagged behind. She could not keep up with the policeman on the bicycle. The policeman smiled at the people who stared open-mouthed at Tant Vonnie as if it was an honour to guard such an unusual creature.

Tant Vonnie's thoughts were busy with: Where can my child be? What could have become of her? She's not used to a big town. Who brought the food? So many questions without answers.

Then she prayed: I thank you, my Master-Lord. Thy will be done, anything, my Master. I will accept the good or the bad, even the worst. My God within me, Thy will be done. Father, you know my fate, you know that I did not steal that ring, but if this is the punishment for a sin, for having broken one of your laws, then I believe it can only be for the better, to teach me to love Thee. No one is stronger than death, but now that I have found Thee I am above death for I am soul.

She looked at the staring bystanders, some dead-still on bicycles with one foot on the pavement. To her it was as if they were all players in the same dream.

At the court their cuffs were taken off. Here were more cell doors with a space underneath for a tin plate to be pushed through. Each one was given a plate of mealie-meal porridge without salt because salt was a privilege only enjoyed on Sundays.

They waited in silence. Everyone was tired of thinking and wondering what to expect. Neels Vool asked the Chinaman next to him: What for?

Chan Look looked up. They knew each other well. You know what for, he replied.

Chan Look, the fahfee player

Chan Look was the son of a Chinaman who in 1905 had come to work on contract on the mines in Kimberley.

His father once told about how, after his contract was over, he had just bought a train ticket for half a crown and got off at its destination. All he had on him were his two blankets in which he had rolled his clothes and tied up with a rope, and his savings. This he hid in his secret flannel money belt which he tied around his body, fastened in front with a button.

On Du Toitspan station the conductor said: Ching Chong Chinaman, off you get, this is Du Toitspan.

That night, he said, he slept in the waiting-room because it was winter and very cold. The next morning he asked a man who said he worked at the railways if he could leave his blankets at the station because he wanted to go and have a look around the town.

Okay, the man said, it will cost you sixpence.

When he came back the man had gone with all his earthly possessions. He didn't like the place, but walked back to town, heartbroken about the loss of his stuff. He went to the new hotel, which had opened just that week, to look for work as a waiter or chefboy.

The manager said: You are completely different to these people. There's your room – and he pointed to the new servants' rooms. I'll pay you as much as I think you are worth, do you understand?

Yes, Meester Petersen, he said.

He had his own, brand new room, for the first time in his life.

The chef, Mr Pierre du Pont, drank a lot and Harry Look quickly learnt to cook just like him, wash the dishes and to be waiter too. One day Mr du Pont got sick. The manager was worried and said he didn't know where to find a cook to help out until Pierre got better. He never noticed that Harry was already doing most of the cooking.

Wait see tonight, Meester Petersen, Harry said.

Mr Petersen thought: Okay, then I'll wait until tonight.

That night was the same as usual. Some people even asked: Harry, tell me, did Pierre get better so quickly?

Harry just shrugged and said: Not know, ask boss, and went on with his work.

Pierre never got out of bed again. Harry tried to help him with his medicine and took him food in his room in the corner of the hotel. Eventually he died. The hotel staff buried him.

Then the hotel owner said to Harry: Harry, I see the work's too much for you. I'll get someone to help you with the serving.

No, Meester Petersen, just get someone for dishes.

Harry was thinking about the tips that he would lose if he lost his job as waiter. His tips were sometimes more than his wages.

Good, I'll see to it, Harry, Mr Petersen said.

The next day he said to Harry: I can't find a man to wash the dishes, but I've found a young girl, an orphan. She's eighteen and she says her name is Lisa. Shall we give her Pierre's room and nail the interleading door closed and just leave the outside door open for her?

Mr Petersen got used to Harry and began taking him into his confidence in matters regarding the running of the hotel. Eventually he put him in charge of the chambermaids and cleaners.

Harry received a good few increases, but he began to feel very lonely. The same routine every day and nobody to go to after work. He did not like strong drink and he also did not give money away. His money belt had begun to bulge from all the golden sovereigns – because it was still the time of golden sovereigns.

Harry and Lisa were soon getting along well and within two years Lisa gave birth to a baby boy. Harry named him Chan.

Mr George Petersen was a religious man and he said to Harry: I no longer want that girl here. I'll give her a month's notice and find somebody else to put in her place.

Meester Petersen, Harry said, not Lisa's fault, my fault. I old enough to be father of Lisa. Child, my child, look like me. Real Chinese.

Yes, Mr Petersen said, I know, and all your offspring will look like Chinamen because Chinese blood is very strong. But it's final, I've already given her a month's notice.

She nowhere to go, Meester Petersen. Hally go also. I also give one month notice.

Mr Petersen said: I am the boss here and I'm not in need of a Chinese Coolie.

I lesign, Meester Petersen, Harry said.

As waiter Harry used to listen to many secrets and gossip stories. He knew everything that went on in Du Toitspan. He heard that the Irishman Angus MacNamara wanted to sell his shop. It had only one backroom because Angus was a bachelor. Behind his back they said that he was fond of black women. He wanted to go to Johannesburg where there were better prospects. Nobody was interested in his tiny shop built of Kimberley bricks because it was in the poorer section of the town.

Is true you want to sell shop, Meester Angoos? Harry asked him.

Where do you get enough money to buy my shop, you Ching Chong? Angus MacNamara did not want to start haggling with somebody who did not have money. He walked away and called over his shoulder: Fifty pound and twenty-five pound for the stock. At my lawyer's office tomorrow at nine. Take it or leave it.

I'll take it, I'll take it, Meester Angoos, tomollow nine o'clock at Loland and Bouel.

The following morning before nine Harry was already waiting at Roland and Bouer. Angus MacNamara did not turn up. Harry waited until eleven o'clock.

He said to himself: Hally Look, you must have shop. God knows it's just what you need. Please, God, he said, You know Hally, You know Lisa, You know Chan and You saw shop. Please, God, put all these together. Hally ask it with heart and money belt.

Harry had never before taken money from his money belt. That night he counted it for the first time and he was just over halfway when he had counted seventy-five pounds. Satisfied, he put back the sovereigns.

The next day he went to Angus General Dealer Shop and said: Meester Angoos, I wait by Loland and Bouel. Whole morning. What happen?

I want a round figure, Harry.

Okay, Meester Angoos, Hally give lound figure. I give hundled pound, take it or leave it.

There were no customers and Angus MacNamara said: I'll lock up, let's go.

They settled everything at the lawyers – the rates and the title deeds – to put the building and its stock in Harry's name for one hundred pounds. Harry also had to pay the lawyer. Mr MacNamara signed all the papers and said: Harry will bring the money tomorrow and sign the documents and then everything will be his.

That night Harry could not sleep. Lisa was in his room with the baby. He said to her: No more loom-loom. Now just loom.

The whole night he practised signing *H. Look* until there was no place left on the piece of brown paper. Must make sure, Lisa, he said, and turned the paper around on the cardboard box and started all over again: *H. Look. H. Look. H. Look.*

In the early hours of the morning the two closed the door and locked it by turning the wooden latch. They hung a blanket over the window and by candlelight counted out a hundred pounds.

Next thing we buy, Lisa, he said, bicycle with flont callier and next we make vegetable garden. And we show people of Du Toitspan how to play fahfee.

And that's how fahfee-the-game-of-chance began in Du Toitspan. The game has thirty-six numbers and each number has a name. Most of the time numbers were sold to coloureds and to housewives by runners who went about selling them. The cheapest numbers cost a tickey. After selling the numbers, the runners all came together at a certain time, usually out of the sight of the law, and then the banker, as Harry Look was called, arrived with the winning number on a folded-up piece of paper in his pocket. He opened the paper and showed the winning number to the runners who then each handed him their lists with their numbers and the money. The banker then went through all the lists and gave them the money for each time the winning number appeared on their list.

It was an honest game because the players knew the runners, and the Chinaman, the banker, was well liked by everyone. He paid seven and six for each winning number, for which the runner received a shilling. Do-dai meant that the banker could not pull the same number twice.

On somebody's birthday his birth date was played – even a person's attitude to life and appearance was given a number. Dreams were also important, because if a housewife or her husband had a dream, they asked the runner to analyse the dream and to give it its appropriate number. He then gave them one or more numbers to play and many times the dream numbers won. The numbers were concocted by the players.

Then, after the banker had pulled, as it was called, the runners went back to the winners to give them their winnings. The players remained standing where they were when the runner passed, and the runner gave the sign of the winning number. The number was never shouted out and each number had its own sign.

Often the winner took the last tickey in the house, thought up a number, played, and won.

There were winners every day. The players were satisfied and the Chinaman was happy. The only problem was, it was against the law.

The fahfee numbers are: 1 – king; 2 – monkey; 3 – sea/water; 4 – dead man; 5 – tiger; 6 – ox; 7 – skelm; 8 – pig; 9 – moon; 10 – eggs; 11 – carriage; 12 – dead woman; 13 – big fish; 14 – old woman; 15 – bad woman; 16 – pigeons; 17 – diamond lady; 18 – small change; 19 – little girl; 20 – cat; 21 – ship; 22 – elephant; 23 – horse; 24 – mouth; 25 – jail/big house; 26 – bees; 27 – dog; 28 – herrings; 29 – small water; 30 – fowl; 31 – fire; 32 – gold/money; 33 – little boy; 34 – shit; 35 – pussy; 36 – lobster/penis.

Some names were in English and Afrikaans, others only in one language. English or Afrikaans, both were popular.

Harry and Lisa had only the one child, Chan. He looked like a true Chinaman, but in the narrow slits were his mother's blue eyes. Those blue eyes made Chan look shy, almost as if he wanted to say: But how is it possible?

Harry died when Chan was nineteen years old and the boy was

the only heir to Look General Dealer. Because his father had raised him like a Chinaman, he made a success of both the business and the fahfee game.

His mother Lisa was still alive and she wanted him to give up the fahfee business because it didn't have a licence like the shop. But every time Chan said to her: I'll just pay the fine and then I'll start again. It's the only way I can help our poor people. If they win I give them seven and six for their tickey. And these days lots of white people are playing too. I'm not scared, Ma. They can't send me back to China, we are both South Africans.

At the Du Toitspan magistrate's court, 21 June 1928

At the court cells the policeman looked in at the cell door and said: Neels Vool, get ready, you're appearing first.

Don't worry, Neels, Chan said, I'll pay your fine.

Thanks, old pal. I'll see what I can do for Tant Lisa in her garden.

Neels Vool was called and asked to plead: Guilty or not guilty?

He answered: Guilty, crown.

Ten days or one pound. Take him away, the magistrate said.

Then the prosecutor called: Bennie O'Grady

Bennie O'Grady, the stock thief

Bennie O'Grady was a true mixed white South African. His grandmother was orphaned at about the age of ten when her trekboer family was murdered by marauding raiders. And because nature preserves that which guarantees the balance and perpetuity of life, she was found hiding behind a shrub which hardly covered her, by a Griqua cattle herder near Philippolis.

She was pure white at birth, but accepted by Adam Kok's people and happy with them after she had got over her grief. Her name was Anna Swartz and she kept this name until the day she died. Jakob Bek made her his wife, but she called him Jakob Swartz.

196

Their only daughter, Grieta, was married to the son of a Dutch Reformed church dominee, Paul. They had two children, Paul and Benjamin. Paul died when he was still a child. Benjamin became Bennie.

He was a real South African, a real mixed-breed whose features, like so many other South Africans, can be seen in their descendants, just take a look at the fleshy thighs and upper arms on our rugby fields.

Bennie could not resist meat, on the hoof or slaughtered. One rainy day he stole yet another sheep from a farmer's kraal.

Hendruk January, he now told Hendruk, never make the mistake of saying you are guilty of committing a crime. Remember, now, always say you're innocent and do your best never to look guilty. (Bennie believed he was better than Hendruk because he could read and write.)

What about the so-help-me-God that they let us say, Meneer? Old Hendruk asked softly so that the policeman in the corridor couldn't hear them.

Hendruk, have you ever realised that a lie can set a prisoner free? Or as they say, pardon? What's easier? Many an innocent man has been found guilty by the magistrate simply because he has spoken the truth. So what difference does it make? You see, Hendruk, I always do my work on a rainy night. If the farmer hears a noise he thinks it's the thunder. The rain also helps wash away my footprints. And in the end the farmer is grateful for the rain, and I am grateful for the sheep. Before I used to go on foot, but now I borrow a bicycle, so that I can get to where I want to be faster, and further, not only on the farms here around the Pan. I always give a hind leg to the bicycle owner whenever I return the bicycle. This makes the owner happy and he'll always be ready to lend it back to me.

But then how do they know that Meneer stole the sheep? Old Hendruk wanted to know. Because Meneer is with us in jail now.

Bennie O'Grady laughed softly.

My job now is to use my mouth. You know mos there is no fine for stock theft, the least is eight years hard labour. The biggest problem is the witness. These days they mos mark their stock with special cuts on the ears or they brand marks onto their bodies, and if you bury the skin the dogs come and dig it up or the rain washes it out. But if you do what I do, Old Hendruk ...

What does Meneer do?

I burn the skin. I make the fire on top of it when I cook the meat and I make sure not a scrap of skin remains. That is the secret. You must try it out sometime, Hendruk.

Never, never, Meneer, I'll never be able to do it. If Meneer says Meneer is not guilty even though Meneer has stolen the sheep, then Meneer must be guilty.

In a manner of speaking, yes, Hendruk.

God saw Meneer steal the sheep.

True. And God will hear me when I say: Not guilty. And God even knows that I've burnt the evidence, which the magistrate doesn't know. So, I am not lying to God.

Next, the policeman called: Bennie O'Grady.

Yes, Sir! he said and stepped over to the barred door and went to stand in the dock.

The prosecutor read out the charge. The theft of a sheep, guilty or not guilty?

Bennie looked around him as if to make sure where he was and then he shook his head. Not guilty, Your Honour, he said in a soft voice.

The prosecutor took a Bible and said: Swear that you will tell the truth, the whole truth and nothing but the truth. Say: So help me God.

So help me God, Bennie said softly, shaking his head. Then he repeated, loudly: So help me God. The carcass that the policeman took is mine, Your Honour. It belongs to nobody else but me, Your Honour. How can anybody steal his own goat? How does Meneer Lambrecht know that the meat belongs to him, Your Honour, now that it's become rotten and stinking? – and he pointed to the witness.

Oh, now I see, said the magistrate, pinching his nose closed with his fingers. Take it away! he ordered the policeman. I have recorded it as evidence.

From whom did you buy the sheep? asked the prosecutor.

I did not buy the sheep, Meneer. I saw it come into this world from its mother who belonged to me. To think that I am being locked up for theft and my meat taken away from me to rot! And Bennie wiped his dry eyes as if tears were streaming from them.

Then the magistrate asked: Is there anyone who can vouch that the sheep belonged to you?

Yes, yes, Your Honour, you can see by the cut on the sheep's left ear, Your Honour.

Bring the evidence in again, the magistrate said to the police man.

No sheep ears, Your Honour, the prosecutor said, just meat.

The magistrate put his elbows on the bench and held his chin in his hands. Looking out in front of him, he said: So it is theft of meat, not theft of a sheep. He indicated to Bennie to come out of the dock and to stand to one side. He then asked the prosecutor: Where is the man who laid the charge of the theft of a sheep?

Meneer Lambrecht stood up and the magistrate indicated to him to go and stand in the witness stand. Your name?

Koen Lambrecht.

Where did you keep the meat so that the accused could steal it?

On and inside the sheep, Meneer, Your Honour.

Any questions? the magistrate asked, looking at Bennie.

Your Honour, that is goat's meat and can you please ask Meneer Lambrecht what is the difference between the smell of rotten goat's meat and rotten sheep's meat?

The bones are not the same and you, Bennie, are a smooth talker. And Meneer the magistrate – pointing to Bennie – he offered me two pounds if I did not come to court.

Your Honour, Bennie said looking squarely at the magistrate, I can buy two goats for two pounds and Meneer Lambrecht knows that, Your Honour. Old Koen, he said, and looked at Meneer Lambrecht as if he knew him very well, you know as well as I do that I don't eat mutton.

Case dismissed, said the magistrate, dipping his pen in the inkwell.

Bennie had won the case. Smiling, he said for all to hear: Justice has triumphed – and thought about the other five sheep that he had stolen from Meneer Lambrecht.

The magistrate gestured to the prosecutor who stood up and shouted: Order!

The entire court stood up while the magistrate left the hall through a side door. The people left through the public entrance. It was tea-time.

After tea-time the prosecutor caught sight of the magistrate at the side door. He stood up. Order! Silence in court! he shouted.

The magistrate came in and sat down.

Next, the policeman shouted, Chan Look!

The Chinaman stood up and went to stand at the cell door so that it could be opened. He went straight to the dock and waited for the charge.

Running an unlawful game of chance in which money was involved, guilty or not guilty?

Guilty, Your Honour.

Five pounds or thirty days. Take him away! said the magistrate without looking up.

Chan was taken back to the cell to wait for the money, which he knew his mother would send with the old black man who worked for her.

When he arrived with the five pounds, Chan sent the old Xhosa man back for another pound, for Neels Vool's fine, and to tell his mother that the money he had on him had been confiscated by the police.

Hendruk January and the shiny stone

Hendruk January came by ox-wagon from Wellington into the interior. But he walked most of the way. He took care of the oxen without payment and gave them water at the outspans. Only his little bundle was allowed to ride on the wagon. Now he was a confirmed bachelor in his fifties.

He had found work at the Du Toitspan Town Council. His job was to keep the gutters and rainwater furrows along the streets clean. With a spade he gathered together the driftsand, which came down with the rain, and loaded it onto a dump-cart. The dump-cart was driven by his friend, Old Vink, and pulled by a mule called Bluelips.

Oom Hendruk had a big head. His rough beard was cut in line with the bottom of his ears. He was broad-shouldered and when he sat down, he looked much bigger than he actually was. When he stood up straight, he was short with drooping shoulders and a bent back from earning his bread with a spade. His nose was broad but not actually flat, and he still had all his teeth. He always said: I don't know what toothache is.

Oom Hendruk was a member of the Congregational Church, a church which was founded by his own people, the coloureds. He was an elder and a highly respected man due to the way he conducted himself. He lived in an outside room in Vatmaar and washed his own clothes.

Children were always going to his room because he gave them old bread. The wagging tongues, as the gossips were called, said behind his back: He gives the children bread so that he can feel them, the swine. The old fart can't manage anything more now.

These same old women regularly borrowed money from him which they never gave back. Because, they said: Oom Hendruk is assured of his place in heaven – and then borrowed some more, just more than the first time. Or they used to say to him: Oom Hendruk, read me a chapter from the Bible, I feel so oppressed.

Then he went to sit on his little doorstep, opened the Bible anywhere and read: The Lord is my shepherd, I shall not want – exactly as it was in the Bible.

Before they got up to go they would say: Now I feel better, Oom Hendruk.

Yes, my child, the Bible fixes up everything.

'Strue, Oom Hendruk, how about a little something? – rubbing forefinger and thumb together.

Some borrowed money from him to, as they put it, make it grow a little at the fahfee. Others really did buy bread, because in those days there were no welfare organisations. Oom Hendruk could tell one from the other and he always said: Come again, I'm glad I could help you. To him fahfee and bread was one and the same thing. He knew that in either case he would not get his money back again.

Oom Hendruk was a kind-hearted man, but stupid he was not, because he always made sure he had enough for himself.

He was the elder who took up the collection at every church service. When he took it to the altar he would take a tickey from his waistcoat pocket and put it in the plate. Then he would hand it to the dominee to place it on the altar and bless it.

In those days poor people believed that tickeys were meant for collection plates in church.

At Communion Oom Hendruk was always the first to receive the Holy Blood. And even though he was a teetotaller, he always took a big gulp. The church people always said: That big gulp is enough to make any mailer drunk!

Now that Oom Hendruk was sitting in the biggest trouble of his life, everyone said what a big fool he had been, he should've brought the diamond to them to sell. The whole community and all his church friends were against him. They said: He'll never hit such luck again, not ever again in his whole life. And no matter what punishment the white people give him, it will be well deserved.

Next, the policeman called, Hendruk January.

Baas? Oom Hendruk said, walking to the cell door.

The policeman pointed to the dock.

Oom Hendruk looked around him and saw his whole congregation as well as other people also sitting there. By now the diamond, in the telling and retelling of the story, had grown to the size of a hen's egg.

The evidence, the diamond itself, was on an upturned cup on a desk near the magistrate's inkwell. Sparkling beams of light shone from it because it was spotlessly clean from all the sucking it had been through in Oom Hendruk's mouth, according to the people.

The prosecutor read out the charge: You, Hendruk January ...

Yes, my Baas, he replied, because there were times when a coloured thought he would get sympathy or compassion if he's humble.

You are charged with having been in possession of an uncut diamond which you tried to sell, guilty or not guilty?

Guilty and not guilty.

We will record it as not guilty, Your Honour, the prosecutor said.

That's right, said the magistrate. For in Roman-Dutch law a man is not guilty until found guilty. Carry on.

Thank you, Your Honour – and the prosecutor took the Bible and asked Oom Hendruk to place his hand on it.

The old man thought to himself: What a relief. Now that I've got the Bible on my side, I'll just tell the truth, just like it happened. Because who can be against me if I have the Bible on my side. I'll show Bennie O'Grady who is bigger, the lie or the Bible. (Oom Hendruk didn't know that Bennie's case had been thrown out.)

I.D.B. (Illegal Diamond Buying) as it was called, was a law against nature which had come from the time of Cecil John Rhodes, when it was made to keep the diamond monopoly in the hands of a few white people. Poor people who were lucky enough to lay their hands on a diamond, were most of the time given very heavy jail

203

sentences. And the stones which were picked up were usually of gem quality.

The diamond which Oom Hendruk was lucky or unlucky enough to get, was of such quality, almost five carats, blue and flawless, which gave it its value.

Where did you find the diamond? the prosecutor asked him.

In the driftsand, Baas.

How?

While I was throwing the sand from the spade onto a heap, I saw something shining, my Baas. So I picked it up. Because it was shining like that I thought it's probably one of those diamonds the people are always talking about.

How did you know it's a diamond if it was the first time you've ever seen a diamond?

Baas, the people always say if you put a diamond in your mouth, it's cold. I put the stone in my mouth and it was cold. So I said to myself: Hendruk, now you are rich.

Who did you show it to first?

First to my reverend and then to a few friends.

And what did they say?

They all said: Hendruk, now you're a rich man.

And what did your preacher say?

Baas, my dominee said we must ask God where to sell the stone. Then we can build a new rectory. So I asked him if we shouldn't go to a white man we can trust. Then the reverend said to me they're all the same, these whites, and that I can't trust them. So I said: Reverend, the only white who ever talks to me is my foreman, Mister Harry-John Welsh. He is the one who gives me my pay packet. But usually all he wants to know from me is where he can get hold of one of our young girls.

Then Oom Hendruk kept quiet to think a little. Then he said: I didn't tell my reverend that last thing, Baas.

He thought again and tried to tell the story as accurately as possible, keeping an eye on the Bible all the time:

The reverend then closed the door so that he and I could be alone in the room with God while we prayed. The reverend then asked God who he wanted to sell the diamond, the reverend himself or me, Hendruk.

So then the reverend said: Please excuse us, Lord, that we didn't first say thank you for the stone. Then he held his hand out to me for me to give him the stone. I didn't want to give it, and so I showed with my finger: No. Because my friend Vink who drives the scotch-cart told me that I shouldn't let it get out of my hands. Vink said: Hendruk, you take the money with one hand and you hand over the stone with the other. And try to get somebody who'll keep his mouth shut, like Bluelips, the mule. The reverend then asked God to help us find someone with a lot of money, someone who would by the diamond from His servants, Elias Cobb and Hendruk January. So then we both said Amen.

What did you do after the reverend had prayed?

Baas, Reverend Cobb took half a crown out of his purse and said it's the quickest answer you can get from God. Heads or tails, Brother? he asked. I said: Tails. The reverend threw the money up, opened his hand and it was tails.

Why did your reverend throw up the money? asked the prosecutor.

Baas, to see who God wanted to keep the diamond.

So you won and kept the diamond?

Yes, that's why I kept it and went to see my foreman the next day after work. Before leaving the rectory the reverend said we must throw the half a crown up again. With the coin in his hand he said: Tails and I keep the stone and heads, we leave it under the altar. But I said to him: No, Brother, and wagged my finger. God has already spoken. I gave him my hand, the one that didn't have the diamond in, and said to him: Good night, Reverend. The next day was a Thursday and during the breakfast break I went to my foreman's office. Mister Harry-John Welsh was glad to see me and I knew why he thought I had come to see him.

What did your foreman think you were coming to see him about? the prosecutor wanted to know.

Oom Hendruk first stood thinking with a finger on his lips and then answered: I think he thought there is a young girl who needs money and that I had come to tell him about it.

Did these girls give you some of the money that Mister Harry-John Welsh gave them?

No, Baas, but they always say they can trust him because he always pays after he has done the thing. So my foreman said to me: Hendry, do you want to borrow money? He knew that I never borrow money from him. I didn't say anything and Mister Harry said: How much? You can pay me back a little, each month a little as you receive your pay. And you can settle with someone like Molly.

Who is Molly?

A young girl, Baas. So I said: No, Mister Harry, I'm here about this thing. And so I showed him the stone. He almost lost his breath and he said: Let me see. And then he said: You and I are brothers, and he embraced me. Then I handed him the stone and he said he would give me five pounds for it. I said: No, it has to be worth more than five pounds. Then he said: Five pounds is worth more than this piece of glass. He took the stone and put it in his pocket and walked to the door. Then I said: Give my stone, Mister Harry, I don't want five pounds for it, I first want to go and see my reverend.

He said: It's a dangerous thing you're doing, Hendry. Tell your reverend you've lost it and tell me what he said tomorrow when you come back to fetch your five pounds. I'll give you the week off as a bonus.

Then I remembered what my friend Vink had said to me: Do not let the stone leave your hand. And here was Mister Harry telling me he will never trick me because five pounds is worth more than this piece of glass. He was almost out the door when I tripped him. He fell against the wall and I took the stone out of his pocket and helped him up. It was then that I saw his eye swelling right there before my eyes and I said: Sorry, Mister Harry, I didn't mean to hurt Mister Harry.

And then what happened? the prosecutor wanted to know.

The municipality's security guard walked past and asked: What's going on here? He looked at Mister Harry and said he had seen everything. He thought I had hit Mister Harry on the eye but he didn't know it was about that stone – and Oom Hendruk pointed to the diamond on the upturned cup. Mister Harry got a fright and said: This Hotnot wanted to sell a diamond to me and when I said I do not buy uncut diamonds he hit me. Look, there he still has the diamond in his hand. So the security guard said: Open your hand, Oom Hendruk. This security-guard knows me well. His name is Joseph April.

So what did the security guard say? the prosecutor wanted to know.

Baas, he said: Oom Hendruk, you blarry fool. Why didn't you come to me?

How long did you have this uncut diamond in your possession? the magistrate asked.

Three weeks, Baas.

And then what happened? the prosecutor wanted to know.

Joseph said I should give him the little old stone and I saw him winking at Mister Harry. I said no, I'll never give it to you. Then Mister Harry said: Joseph, let's rather take him to the charge-office before we lose our jobs. At the charge-office the sergeant said I should give him the diamond before he writes the charge in the book. I thought to myself: Hendruk, you blarry fool, why didn't you just take the five pounds.

What did the sergeant say when you gave him the diamond?

Baas, he said he heard that a person can pick them up in the streets but he never believed it and that I was the biggest fool he has ever come across. He asked my name and I said: Hendruk January. Then he said the charge is dealing in uncut diamonds without a licence and the possession of an uncut diamond. Then the sergeant called: Constable! and a black policeman came and the sergeant told him to search me and lock me up.

Then the magistrate cleared his throat and said: What has the accused to say before sentence is passed?

While giving the Bible a last look out of the corner of his eye, Oom Hendruk thought: Now that I've told the truth the truth shall set me free.

He thought for a while and then he said: I did not steal the stone, I picked it up. It belonged to the earth. Just like food can be taken out of the earth and sold for money, people should be allowed to sell these shiny stones too. The difference lies in the people.

The courtroom was packed with coloureds, his people. Quite a few mumbled: It's true.

Silence! the policeman shouted.

After a while the magistrate said: Ignorance of the law is no excuse, eight years hard labour. Take him away.

The policeman again had to shout: Order!

Everyone in the courtroom stood up. The magistrate stood up and walked out. It was lunch time.

When Reverend Cobb heard that Oom Hendruk had been sentenced to eight years hard labour, he rushed to the court's cells to see him, because the sentenced prisoners are taken straight to jail after the court proceedings.

Oom Hendruk, he told the congregation the following Sunday in church, was in a dream state. And I am sure the old man believes someone will come and wake him up and tell him it was all just a horrible dream. I asked Oom Hendruk for the keys to his room so that I can take his things to the rectory until we see each other again.

He said: Get the bicycle at Bluelips's stable. The key to the room is at the charge-office, but there is a spare key underneath one of the two sitting stones in front of the door. It's wrapped in a piece of rag.

Oom Hendruk didn't speak again, Reverend Cobb said. He just looked at me with unbelieving eyes. I held out my hand to greet him, but he just looked at it, turned around and went to stand in the corner where I could not see him. I said a quiet prayer and then left.

The next day Reverend Cobb went to fetch the bicycle at Old Vink's. Then he went with Cape cart driver Stoffel Jones to fetch Oom Hendruk's things in Vatmaar. He found the key underneath the stone and loaded everything just as it was onto the Cape cart. He said: I went and looked in at the house, when he gave the key to the owner of the room.

After a while Reverend Cobb wore Oom Hendruk's Sunday suit, which he first took to the tailor to have altered. The rest of the clothes he handed out to the poor because, he said, he was scared the mice would eat them up.

Reverend Cobb now had a bicycle with which to do house visits, and Oom Hendruk's Zobo pocket watch to show him the time so that he could leave before the women's husbands returned from work. He did well as reverend of the Congregational Church of Du Toitspan, one of the few coloureds who had been given the chance to improve his lot.

Oom Hendruk died during his first winter in prison. Nobody in Vatmaar knows where he was buried or how, and nobody cared. Only Reverend Cobb sometimes reminded the congregation about Oom Hendruk by saying: God knows what's best.

Yvonne Müller

After lunch the court resumed, with the magistrate at the bench.

Next, the policeman shouted: Yvonne Müller!

Tant Vonnie did not mind because she was not interested in the conversation in the cell. She was one of those few people who could

209

listen without hearing and without being deaf. She got up and walked to the cell door.

Tante, the policeman said softly, come. In the courtroom he showed her the steps to the dock.

When she placed her foot on the first step, in her thoughts she touched her heart. Master, she said, Master, Thy will ...

There were not many people left in the courtroom because people were only interested in the diamond case. Also Tant Vonnie was not known in Du Toitspan.

The prosecutor read out the case: Theft of a wedding ring, guilty or not guilty?

Not guilty.

Then the prosecutor handed the charge-sheet to the magistrate and the policeman took the Bible and said: Place your hand on the Bible and swear that you will tell the truth and nothing but the truth. Say: I do.

I do.

The plaintiff, Your Honour, said the prosecutor, Mevrou Martha September.

She walked over to the witness stand trying to look important.

Tell us in your own words, Mevrou September, how your ring was stolen.

Jes jor orner, jou know, she began and pointed to Tant Vonnie, she is my washerwoman. My farder-in-law he make dat ring from a old gold coin what dey call a sovereign, for my mudder-in-law when dey get married. My mudder-in-law died and when her son got married to me his farder said to me he take me as his own daughter and his son mus' put his mudder's ring on my finger. So, jor orner see der ring got sentimental value.

Thank you, said the magistrate, you may step down.

The plaintiff then said to Tant Vonnie: What do you have to say?

Meneer, she said, I have never in my life had a ring on my finger.

Have you ever been married?

Yes, Meneer.

Without a ring?

Yes, Meneer.

Can you explain why?

Mother was very old and sickly. When my Heinrich arrived from German West Africa, he had nowhere to sleep and he knew nobody else in Vatmaar. He asked if he could stay with us until he finds work – my mother had also come from German West Africa a long time ago and he could tell. Then he would pay us because he didn't have a penny. He got a job quite soon and the little wages he got he brought home just like that and gave it all to my mother because he didn't drink or smoke. Meneer, me and Heinrich quickly became like sister and brother. Soon thereafter my mother passed away. On her deathbed she took my hand and Heinrich's hand and put it together and told us it is her wish that we get married. The death rattle came and she breathed her last breath. We lived for a long time still as brother and sister. The people said: They sleep together, don't worry – which was not true. Heinrich had never been with a woman nor me with a man. Then, one winter's night, I threw my blanket over him and crept in under his blanket behind his back. The next morning he said: Now we are married, we have fulfilled our mother's wishes. That day I took his name.

The prosecutor stood up and said: That's got nothing to do with the theft of the ring, Your Honour.

Let the accused carry on, the magistrate said. It's very interesting – he looked at Tant Vonnie and nodded.

Meneer, she said, this is the first time I speak to somebody about my marriage.

Any children? the magistrate asked.

Yes, Meneer, eight, and Heinrich said when he returns from the war we will get married with a ring. But my Heinrich never came back from the war.

Then the court saw how a teardrop fell from the eye which was alive but which could not see.

That is why I have never in my life had a wedding ring, Meneer. And these days, Meneer, a slice of bread is much more valuable to me and my daughter than all the rings in the world.

You said, you and your daughter?

Yes, Meneer.

You also said you had eight children.

Yes, Meneer. I lost six in the Big Flu of 1918. They were all buried together in a trench without any of Vatmaar's funeral rites.

Do you not get a war-widow's pension? the magistrate asked.

No, Meneer.

They magistrate knew she would not qualify for a widow's pension without a marriage certificate. He looked at the diamond on the upturned cup from the previous case. He put his finger on the cup as if placing his hand on a ring. Then he asked: Who arrested this woman?

Constable Rigard Prins, Your Honour, replied the prosecutor.

Call him.

Are you Constable Rigard Prins?

Yes, Your Honour.

Did you arrest this woman?

Yes, Your Honour. She stole a wedding ring.

Did you find a wedding ring on this woman's person?

No, Your Honour. I thought she had it on her finger.

Did you see it on her finger?

No, Your Honour.

I order you, Constable Prins, to be in my office tomorrow morning at eight o'clock.

Then the magistrate turned to the prosecutor. See that this woman receives a new pair of shoes and a dress. Also transport back to her home, money for a day's wages, and food. Oh yes, and report to me within seven days if she has been granted a war-widow's pension. Case dismissed.

He looked at Tant Vonnie and said: You are free to go, Mrs Müller. Come to my office, the court will grant you your marriage certificate.

Tant Vonnie's inner being beamed out past her outer circumstances, earning the respect of everyone. The tattered dress, bare feet and unkempt hair with its silver sheen did not matter. The magistrate nodded to her. She looked back at him, full of gratitude.

It's all in a day's work, he thought. Sometimes the unexpected or the unusual happens, but never a dull moment – but Tant Vonnie was different to all the others.

Because it had been the last case of the day, the court adjourned.

The unexpected happens

Tant Vonnie was taken to the magistrate's office.

Oh yes, he said. Please sit.

He pulled out the chair for her. Then he went to sit behind his desk and took out a marriage certificate book. Maiden name? he asked.

Yvonne Schmidt.

Born?

Rehoboth.

Date?

Unknown.

Husband?

Heinrich Müller.

Born?

Windhoek.

Date?

Unknown.

He signed the certificate – *Steven Collins, Magistrate* – and stamped it. Tant Vonnie made her cross.

Congratulations, he smiled, Mrs Müller – and held out his hand to her. After giving her the sheet of paper, he looked into her face to see if there really was a tear. And there it was again, just the one drop.

213

She lowered her face so that the teardrop would not roll down her cheek. So very feminine, he thought. He lifted up her hand and kissed it.

The prosecutor, who had been waiting at the door, said: This way, Tante. Shall I lead the way?

Please, Tant Vonnie said.

In his office he said: Please sit – pointing to the chair. From his desk drawer he took out a "good for"-book and wrote: *One only ladies' dress, One only pair of ladies' shoes*, and tore out the page. On another page he wrote: *10/- worth of groceries*. Then he said: I've already phoned the dominee's wife. She'll be here at any minute.

Then he took three half-crowns out of the little box marked *Petty Cash*.

Tant Vonnie rose and, used to receiving the sour with the sweet, said softly: I am grateful, Meneer.

The prosecutor could feel that it came from her heart.

Just then the dominee's wife arrived and the prosecutor introduced them: Mevrou Pienaar, the dominee's spouse, and Yvonne Müller.

Pleased to meet you, they both said and shook hands.

Then the prosecutor explained the magistrate's wishes.

Juffrou must take these, said Tant Vonnie, and handed the papers to the dominee's wife with a smile.

The prosecutor explained to the dominee's wife all about the war-widow's pension and she said: All I need to fill in the form is the marriage certificate.

Is that all? Tant Vonnie said, holding out to her the *On His Majesty's Service* envelope.

Mevrou Pienaar opened the envelope. Yes, this you must keep safely, Yvonne, she said when she saw her name on the certificate. Let us fill in the application form immediately because I can see you're not from Du Toitspan.

Yes, Juffrou, Tant Vonnie said, Vatmaar.

The prosecutor took a form from a pigeonhole and handed it to the dominee's wife. She filled it in. Sign here, she said. Tant Vonnie made her cross. Then the prosecutor signed it and added his commissioner-of-oaths's stamp to it.

Do you know anybody here in Du Toitspan, Yvonne? asked the dominee's wife.

Yes, Juffrou, my eldest daughter, Kaaitjie. She works for Mevrou Bosman, but I don't know where it is.

What address should we use?

Vatmaar, Juffrou.

You said your husband was a sergeant in the army, killed at Square Hill?

Yes, that is what they said when I received a letter with this on top. Tant Vonnie pointed at the O.H.M.S. on the letter.

Come, Yvonne, the dominee's wife said, looking at the clock on the wall, it's almost half-past three and we still have a lot to do. First we'll get a few dresses and shoes on appro, as they say. To herself she said she wouldn't want to be seen in public with this old woman out of the sticks. I'll take her to the rectory and get her cleaned up first, she decided.

They got into her Plymouth car. Tant Vonnie held onto her knees because she had never before in her life ridden so fast.

What are you thinking about, Yvonne? the dominee's wife asked.

Tant Vonnie let her head rest against the soft upholstered seat. It's unbelievable, she said. They will never believe me in Vatmaar if I tell them, Juffrou. Now I am in another world.

When they stopped at a shop with big glass windows, Tant Vonnie said: Is Juffrou going inside?

What kind of shoe would you like? You do realise you can choose from the best?

A closed shoe with a very low heel, please.

And the size?

I've never in my life had a size.

The dominee's wife laughed and while looking at Tant Vonnie's unwashed feet she said: I'll take a seven and an eight. The dress should be my size because we're about the same height. Colour?

Yellow, my Heinrich always said yellow is his colour.

Mevrou Pienaar put her hand on Tant Vonnie's thigh and said: Sit, Yvonne.

After a while the shop boy came out with her with a few parcels. Put it on the back seat, the dominee's wife said, climbed in, inserted the key and turned. The engine sprang into action.

Oh yes, Tant Vonnie said with a laugh, it does work with a key.

The car turned in at the back gate of the rectory.

Get a clean towel, the dominee's wife said to a big black woman. And to Tant Vonnie she said: In here – pointing at the bathroom. Aia, said the dominee's wife, put paper in the geyser so that the miesies has warm water.

Tant Vonnie wanted to tell her that she was used to washing in cold water, but she thought: I must at least not show that I'm totally backward.

After the bath Tant Vonnie was shown the spare room. All the new dresses and shoes lay on a table. The yellow dress with the big flowers fitted perfectly. Then Tant Vonnie said: The thick petticoat will do.

Keep it on and put the dress over it, the dominee's wife said. The size seven shoe, does it fit comfortably?

Very, Tant Vonnie said.

I asked them to include a brush and a comb and to add it to the price of the dress. Here it is. It's yours to keep. She brought a hand mirror closer. Look in here.

The first thing Tant Vonnie said was: Is that me, do I look like that? And then she sat still, quietly looking at herself in the mirror before she began to brush and comb her hair.

The dominee's wife thought: A simple woman, I might as well give her the mirror too. She took a sheet of newspaper and wrapped the mirror in it. Aia, she called, bring a piece of string! – and tied it around the mirror. That's for you, she said to Tant Vonnie and also gave her a big brown cardboard box for her old dress and petticoat.

Tant Vonnie took her pocket, which had been pinned to her old dress, lifted up her new dress and pinned it to her new petticoat and said: I have to keep something of myself otherwise I'll be completely new.

They both laughed.

Then someone shouted: Bonnie, Bonnie, are you here?

Yes, the dominee's wife replied.

It was Oom Faan who had recently lost his wife in a motor accident, the third such accident in Du Toitspan's history. Because she thought that Tant Vonnie was not of the same class as her oom, the dominee's wife said: Come, Yvonne, it's getting late.

Yvonne, said the old man, what a beautiful French name – and holding her hand he thought to himself: She is the one, she looks just like the woman the fortune teller saw in the tea leaves.

I'm Faan, he introduced himself.

Vonnie, Tant Vonnie said.

They may not be from the same class, Mevrou Pienaar thought, but I can see that Yvonne Muller is afraid of no one, maybe just a little shy.

She placed her hand on Tant Vonnie's shoulder. Tante, she said, it's getting late.

Tant Vonnie took the brown paper bag and the dominee's wife carried the mirror. The groceries had been bought and were already in the car. They climbed into the Plymouth while Oom Faan still kept staring at Tant Vonnie, struggling to find something to say.

Goodbye, Oom, the dominee's wife said.

Goodbye, Bonnie and Yvonne.

She smiled at him, her shining silver-streaked hair made into a bun behind her head.

Mevrou Pienaar stopped at the Bosmans' house and said: Wait here. She knocked and the house-maid opened up. Is your miesies in? she asked.

No, Miesies.

Is there a Hotnot girl working here?

Yes, Miesies, she's at the back, Miesies, with the children. The Miesies does not want her in the house.

That's right, Mevrou Pienaar thought, you can't trust these Baster girls with our men. A real Afrikaner should keep them in their place.

I'll go around the back then, she said. She got back into her car and drove around the block to the back gate.

There they are. Thank you, Master! Tant Vonnie said aloud, her hand on her heart.

Kaaitjie and Suzan stood up and looked around. Who are these two wealthy white women and what are they doing here in the back alley? Kaaitjie said, and in the same breath: Where is my Kenny? I don't know why he hasn't arrived this morning.

It's Mama! Suzan shrieked running towards her.

At first Kaaitjie hesitated and then ran too: Mama, my Mama!

They both hugged their mother crying: Mama, Mama, my Mama, my Mama. What happened, why is Mama looking like this?

It's getting late, we still have to get the Cape cart, the dominee's wife said behind the steering wheel.

Not wanting to spoil a good ending and who also not wanting the juffrou to think she was ungrateful for everything she had done for her, Tant Vonnie said: Good, Juffrou, I'm coming. Suzan, get in, we have to go now. I'll tell you all about it at home. And you, Kaaitjie, in a few days you get off and then I'll tell you everything again.

Wait, Mama! Kaaitjie said, ran into her room and came back with a piece of bread wrapped up. It's all I have, Mama!

Mother and daughter hugged each other. Tant Vonnie could see something was wrong. It also felt to her as if her daughter belonged to someone else. Ag, she thought, maybe I'm wrong.

They kissed and Tant Vonnie got into the car.

A dumbfounded Kaaitjie was left behind. Could it be the work of Kenneth Kleinhans? she wondered. He's so clever, I wonder what happened. My day off is still so far away – a whole three days. But Kenny, where is he? He'll come, I know. And Mama has changed so. Kenny also came from nowhere. Is it all perhaps a dream? Mama riding in a car as if she was used to it. Suzan was real, but now she's gone. The dream is gone. And I, Kaaitjie, must wake up. If Kenny comes tonight I'll have a lot to talk about.

On the way to the Cape cart Bonnie Pienaar sat wondering: Two such lovely daughters, both untouched and pure. She gave Tant Vonnie a sideways look, thinking: And even though she's an old woman she's attractive enough to catch the eye of someone like Oom Faan, a man who can pick and choose from his own class and not be interested in them. She was tired of the widows and the spinsters in the congregation who kept asking her to put in a good word for them with Oom Faan.

Then she thought again: Maybe this old woman and her two daughters are poor whites living where they feel at home: among the allsorts. The Pan's Member of Parliament told our church elders there's a new plan being worked on to uplift the poor white Afrikaner. The railways and Public Works will be organised so that there'll be work for them. And those who are really backward – their children will be sent to boarding houses and will only be allowed to go home to their parents on certain days. The M.P. said it's a sure way of raising the Afrikaner above the Kaffir and the Hotnot and to restore their pride as Boers.

Bonnie Pienaar, wife of the dominee, was slim and on the tall side. She had thick black hair with round, slightly fat cheeks. There were fine downy hairs on her upper lip and her voice had a manly sound. She again looked at Tant Vonnie and thought to herself: My husband told me we should do our best to keep the almost-baas Hotnots in their place. Then she smiled and thought: You're one of them. Even my aia did not call you Miesies because these Du Toitspan maids know their community.

She stopped at the Cape cart. Old Jones, here's a job for you, she said. Take these two to Vatmaar. Here's the slip, I'll sign it and you can fetch the money tomorrow.

Thank you, Juffrou, he said, and took the "good for".

Stoffel Jones took the two packets of food and the brown paper bag. The dominee's wife stayed seated in the car and just said: All the best.

Stoffel Jones removed his cap and held it with both hands against his chest. Mother and daughter simply smiled because they could not get a thank you to pass their lips.

Then Stoffel Jones said to Suzan: But you're the one I took to your sister.

Yes, Oom.

And Mevrou must be Mevrou Mooller. He took off his cap again and stretched out a hand to Tant Vonnie. Miesies is really looking nice. Mevrou Mooller gets more beautiful each day.

Thank you. Meneer Jones is looking good too. How are the people at home?

Fine. No use complaining.

He walked around the horse and cart to make sure everything is in order.

We better be off then. I don't want to ride back in the dark because it's not a moonlight night.

Tant Vonnie said nothing because she was tired after the long day. Suzan too, had had a day of worry and anxiety. The rattling of the cart soon had them sound asleep. A jerk and a Ho-ho-ho! shook them out of their deep sleep.

The Cape cart had a little half door and when Tant Vonnie leaned over the open top half, she saw Johnny September standing almost in front of the horse. Please, please, Meneer Jones. Please, Meneer. Look, my wife can't walk any more, he pleaded.

Tant Vonnie pulled her head back to listen without being seen.

Her poor feet are full of blisters, Meneer, please have mercy. He held his hands in front of him like one who was praying. Please,

Meneer, I can walk, just take my Settie with you. She is an honest woman. The Lord will bless Meneer Jones.

Tant Vonnie saw that Johnny was standing so close to the horse that the animal could not move.

Just a moment ago I saw your wife walking as if there was nothing wrong with her feet. Then she must've heard the horse, because she looked around and then you looked around. And then I saw her take her shoes off and make as if her feet are sore. I know you very well, you've always got a clever story to sell. But I will load you up for two shillings, said Stoffel Jones.

I don't have a penny on me, Meneer Jones, Johnny answered. I'll pay Meneer when we get to Vatmaar.

No, never. I don't trust you. I'll make it one shilling, or otherwise I'll use my whip – first on you and then on the horse. And where's the money from selling that gold wedding ring you say you picked up?

It wasn't me, Meneer Jones, you're making a mistake. Meneer Jones is a grown man and I'm young enough to be your child.

Johnny don' know who steal my ring, Meneer Jones, Mevrou September spoke for the first time. I know who stole our ring but de magistrate let her go because he tink she is white. Mr Jones know, me and you we both got black skins and we get judge by our skins.

Tant Vonnie heard all this and thought: A person doesn't steal with the colour of your skin, but you forgive when you yourself want to be forgiven. So he is the thief who stole the ring and sold it. And his wife thinks he would never do such a thing. Stolen the ring which his mother wore on her finger? It just shows you, love can be good and love can be bad and both can be true love.

For the last time I say: One shilling or get out of the way!

Stoffel Jones shouted because now he was really angry. Then Tant Vonnie took a shilling from her dress pocket and gave it to him. Here is a shilling, Meneer Jones. Let them get on.

Stoffel Jones did not know that Tant Vonnie had appeared in

court that day, nor that Mevrou September had made a case against her. Get on, you crook, he said taking the shilling.

Settie September was shocked to see Tant Vonnie in the Cape cart wearing a new dress and shoes. She could not look her in the eye and Tant Vonnie thought: If she had had a tail it would've been between her legs.

Johnny September was just as surprised as his wife. Afternoon, Tante, he said.

She just looked at him and said nothing.

The cart pulled off: Clip-clop, clip-clop, clip-clop, their heads bobbing to the clip-clop, clip-clop.

Tant Vonnie sat there thinking: Suzan and I have both been judged, rejected and humiliated. My honour has been restored in the courthouse but not in Vatmaar. Nobody from Vatmaar was in court. I wonder which lies are going to be told and made up now. But tonight I'll open a tin of corned beef, slice up an onion, and add some bread. And, if Suzan wants to, she can have dried fruit and drink the ginger-beer.

Tant Vonnie was on the verge of falling asleep when Mevrou September showed her husband with her eyes the bottle of ginger-beer in the cardboard box.

Johnny September was skinny, built like a grown boy, but with the head and hands of an old man, more Indian than African. His wife Settie was twice his size. She imagined she was better than others because she spoke with a Cape accent, but she was more black than white. She and her husband were a better pair than a married couple.

You know, Johnny, I'm so thirsty, she said.

Tant, said Johnny, can my Settie have some ginger-beer? She is so terribly thirsty.

Give them the ginger-beer, Tant Vonnie told Suzan.

Settie took it without a thank you and drank. You know, Johnny, I so thirsty I can't drink fast.

Take it slow, darling.

222

She drank the bottle about halfway and passed it to him. He threw the rest down his throat in one huge gulp like a seasoned boozer. He held up the bottle to show his wife that it was empty. The two of them laughed.

Give the bottle to me, Tant Vonnie said, I need an empty bottle. Again he lifted the bottle. They laughed again and he hurled the bottle out of the Cape cart.

With her left hand Tant Vonnie pulled back the bolt of the half door. With her right hand she dragged Johnny September to the door, lifted her foot high and kicked him out with her foot against his back. Then she grabbed Settie by her woolly hair while holding onto to the side of the cart with her other hand.

But no matter how hard she pulled, the woman wouldn't budge because she gripped both sides of the cart with her hands with her legs tight against the opposite seat. Then suddenly Suzan grabbed Mevrou September's one shoe from the floor and hit her on her big toe with the heel.

Ouch, you bitch! Mevrou September screamed.

Suzan hit her even harder with the heel of the shoe.

Ouch, you bitch, I say! Then she let go with both hands and grabbed her toenails. Which gave mother and daughter a chance to push her out of the Cape cart.

Both Septembers made strange noises when they flew through the air. The two in the cart heard what they would rather not have heard said. Then Suzan threw Mevrou September's shoes out.

The horse found its load easier to pull now, and added to this it was now downhill all the way to the crossing. After a while Tant Vonnie started laughing and she said: Suzan, I don't know where I got the strength from, but no civilised person will first forgive someone and then let them think you're scared of them.

Eventually the cart reached their home and stopped at the well. Nobody took any notice of the Cape cart. Tant Vonnie didn't mind because she didn't want Stoffel Jones to see where she lived. Because she knew these well-off coloureds were also class conscious and judged others according to appearances.

May I please have some cold water to drink, he said, pointing to the empty canned fruit jar hanging upside down from a peg at the well.

Please sit down, Meneer Jones, Tant Vonnie said. I'll give Meneer Jones the water, accept it as a token of my thanks.

While lowering the bottle into the well, she said to Suzan: Just put our things down right here, Meneer Jones is in a hurry.

After he had drunk and given the empty jar back, he said to Tant Vonnie: Where are those two crooks? I don't trust them.

I threw them out, Tant Vonnie said.

I felt the cart getting lighter but I thought it was because of the downhill, Stoffel Jones lied, and he thought: I won't ask you now what's going on, but I'll find out soon enough.

He still hadn't heard about the court case and he could feel there was something he didn't know. Goodbye, Mevrou Mooller, he said. I'm in a hurry because there's no moonlight tonight. He lifted his cap. Sleep well.

They carried their parcels to their one-room with the thought: Aren't we lucky! It *is* all true. Thank you, Father.

Yvonne Müller found her house cleaned out by thieves when she came home after the death of Sannah Vosloo. From Sannah's brother, Piet de Bruin, she had received no sympathy or thanks. Among the Boers it was rumoured that her name appeared in the old woman's will which had been drawn up by the late Dominee Simons, but Meneer de Bruin carried the key to his sister Sannah's kist.

Tant Vonnie had hired out her four-roomed house to the Wingroves while she was away. But on her return she had to sell it to them because now she was worse off than before she had begun her charity work. She sold the house at a give-away price because in Vatmaar there were not many well-off people.

Fortunately Mr Erick Wingrove, who had bought her house,

used to be Mr James Pringle's father's garden-boy. Mr Pringle's son David grew up with Erick and when David Pringle became head of Du Toitspan's new Undenominational School, he appointed his father's garden-boy as his school's caretaker.

When the money from the sale of the house ran out, Tant Vonnie and Suzan had to go and work for people who were not much better off than them, most of the time just for a bit of food. In those days a widow was very lucky if she managed to get married again. Tant Vonnie received many requests and when she turned them down, these men would make her life unpleasant by spreading false bedroom stories. Which made her more determined to get on with her daily work without any bitterness. The people of Vatmaar, most of whom were unschooled, believed the gossip about her. Even her daughters, the belles of Vatmaar, had to taste the acid of these lashing tongues. But in their poverty they always lived a clean life and kept their pride – something which was rare among the poorest of the poor.

Tant Vonnie accepted many things as her lot – even the loss of her six children, her husband, and then her house she saw this way. She was kept going through the memories of her beloved Heinrich. She had never seen his corpse and when things were going very badly, he consoled her in her dreams, which were vivid. She then said to herself: How can I take another man and wipe out the picture of Heinrich? Not one of them is of the same calibre and stature as my Heinrich – even if he could not write his name and even if he worked for me with a spade. Then she would smile to herself and a tear of contentment would roll out of the eye which could not see.

Her daughters also knew what it was like to have without wanting more, because she told them about the days when life was easy, even though they were eight children. And one day, when these days of poverty and scorn are behind us, my children, she said, we will know how to appreciate the good times without forgetting the bad times. Because the wheel never stops turning. One day it's on top and the next it's bottom. And if it was at the bottom, the next day it's on top again. Because even kings have children with their slaves, remember that, my children.

After they had packed away everything that night after the court case, Tant Vonnie said: Now I'm tired. Suzan, bring the bedding. Take the grass broom and sweep out the room. Do you remember when we found a rolled-up snake among the blankets?

The room was swept, the bedding shaken out and spread out on the smeared floor, because they had no beds. They were too tired to prepare supper and just ate prunes – something which Tant Vonnie said she had already forgotten the taste of. They ate them outside on their stone chairs, each with a mug of drinking water. They ate without thinking about stopping. Only when the cardboard box was empty did they go back inside. They lit a candle and Suzan laughed, saying: I cannot remember us ever having a new candle. Most of the time we had to go to bed before dark.

They went on their knees to thank God for the day, ending with: Above all, we thank you, Lord, that we may witness the sunrise and the sunset.

Mother embraced daughter. Good night, my child, she said and Suzan replied: Good night, Mama.

Tant Vonnie blew out the candle thinking: What a lovely word Mama is. Long ago, she had had a mama, like everyone has or has had a mama. This is one of the few things in life which cannot be stolen.

In the middle of the night Suzan woke with stomach cramps. She jumped up and ran to the outhouse. Soon thereafter her mother had to run too. In the dark she first felt to see where Suzan was because she was so tired that she had not woken up when Suzan said: Mama, my stomach wants to work.

Suzan had to get off the longdrop and give her mother a turn, and that's how it went almost all night.

This gave Tant Vonnie a chance to think about the future. Before this day of the court case had come, she had taken life as it came. Now she thought: Now that we have food for almost a month, we can do something for ourselves. Kaaitjie will be here on Sunday, then we will tell her about our plans and our new life. Because there were prospects for a war-widow's pension. But don't let us warm ourselves with cold ash. In the meantime we will just count our blessings.

The next morning the two of them overslept, something they were not used to, and both got up with a headache. Tant Vonnie prepared some lukewarm water and added a pinch of salt. She drank some and gave some to Suzan saying: Drink as much as you can and let it work out well.

And work out it did because towards midday both were weak and faint and went to lie down, and slept all afternoon, something which they had never done before.

Tant Vonnie woke up when she heard Suzan scratching in a packet for food, Suzan, she said, let us eat the bread, it will bind the stomach.

Then we'll eat Kaaitjie's bread, Suzan said.

They went outside to sit on their stone chairs and when they had eaten, Tant Vonnie said: Now I am sober, my brain is clean enough to think about what lies ahead. Suzan, tidy up the room and let me be alone for a while.

When Suzan was finished, she came back. She and her mother sat quietly without saying a word. This they could do because they got on well together. When the stars began to come out Tant Vonnie said: Come, let us go to bed.

It's the first time I see so many stars, said Suzan.

They are always there, it's just that you've never taken notice of them before. A cloudy night can bring rain and food for all the inhabitants of the earth. But a star-filled night, that has a beauty of its own, her mother said.

They said their prayers as usual, blew out the candle and turned in. Tant Vonnie held her daughter's hand and said: I have decided that tomorrow we start doing something for ourselves.

The next day they rose at the usual time, just before daybreak. They took the food out of the two bags and the brown paper bag as if it were Father Christmas's stocking they were unpacking.

The cans we'll keep for last. And today, Suzan, you will not be milking goats. The Venters' lazy sons can do their own milking. See if the spade is still on the roof. That's all we need, together with a whole lot of energy to do something different.

What would you like for breakfast? Tant Vonnie asked in the same way she used to hear Mevrou de Bruin ask Little-Piet.

Mealie-pap, butter and sugar, Suzan replied without hesitation.

Yes, but you've forgotten the milk. Take this tickey – and she took one from her dress pocket – and go and buy us a bottle of milk from Oom Chai, his milk is the cleanest in Vatmaar.

After breakfast Tant Vonnie said: Let us preserve what we have received. Put the food back in the bags, and close them with something. I'll go to Oom Flip and ask him to go and buy us a hasp and staple, and he must not forget the screws. I hope he hasn't already left for the Pan.

When she came back, Suzan was sitting and waiting for her, because she had finished her work. The spade leaned against the wall.

Nobody had asked them yet what had happened two days ago, because the people who had seen Tant Vonnie being arrested could not believe their eyes now. Normally a whole lot of people would've appeared by now to ask for the services of mother and daughter, maybe in exchange for a plate of food, because money they almost never gave, but nobody had come yet.

Please don't allow anybody into our room because we'll be away all day, Tant Vonnie went to ask Mrs Marjorie Wingrove.

Remember my promise, Mrs Wingrove said to Tant Vonnie. If you have enough money one day you can buy your house back from us for the same price we paid for it. I really want to go back to Du Toitspan to be near my children.

Their children almost never came to visit, Mrs Wingrove always complained, because she and her husband's coffins had already been made and stood in the spare room. The old man liked showing his grandchildren the coffins and then he would lie in his to make sure it was still his size – and the children hated it.

All they wanted from Tant Vonnie, she said, is that she looks after their coffins until the day they needed them. They knew she wouldn't say no, and she didn't.

Of course I'll do it for you, she said without hesitation. But to herself she thought: They've got it back to front. A person dies first and then you get the coffin. Only some of my children were buried in blankets. The others were thrown in that trench and covered with sand so that the germ could die with them and be taken out of the air. At least that is what the people believed. There was no dominee, no prayer and no smart coffins.

My old man Erick says he will sell the house to nobody else but Mrs Mooller, said Marjorie Wingrove.

Thank you very much, Miesies Wingrove.

The Wingroves were the same age. She and her husband both drew old-age pensions. He regularly went to visit the children in Du Toitspan and sometimes slept over, leaving his wife all alone at home. And if she scolded him about it, he would say: But Old Vonnie is always there if you need her.

After a pause Tant Vonnie spoke again: One never knows what lies ahead, she said. We'll see.

Then mother and daughter made their way to the cemetery.

The cemetery was not fenced off and the graves were overgrown with grass and weeds.

Tant Vonnie said: You know, Suzan, I haven't been here in years. I remember there's a tent peg driven into Norman van der Westhuizen's grave.

Why a tent peg, Mama.

It's a long story which I'll tell you in a while.

They looked, but could not find the peg. And the trench with the dead could only be made out by the whitewashed stones packed in a long row.

Why such a long grave, Mama?

It's true, it is long, because black and white, any colour were simply just thrown in to kill the germ. Let's go and see where it ends.

This is where the white stones stop, Mama.

There are no more graves here, let's go back again, her mother said.

There, Mama! The peg.

Yes, you're right, my child.

Mama, tell me now why the ditch is so long. Did they fill it all up with dead people?

Suzan, don't talk about the "dead". It's not a nice word. Rather say "the departed". Remember there are two brothers between you and Kaaitjie who sleep here. Do you know why it's such a long grave, Suzan?

No, Mama, tell me.

Because a grave is usually six feet deep, but here they had to stop when the lime stone got too hard or the diggers got too tired. So they made it long but not deep. Let's get started, my child. We pack the stones which are inside outside and then we make two straight lines. We can talk while we work. There's no hurry.

Who dug the ditch and who brought the corpses here, Mama?

Suzan, it was Oom Flip and his wife and Oom Chai who did the work. And to this day none of us in Vatmaar has ever said thank you for what they did. Not even me, Suzan. If we finish here with what we want to do, nobody will know it was us. Then we'll get ourselves something to slaughter and have a braai to say thank you to Oom Flip, Oom Chai and Sis Bet. Oom Flip never wanted any money for the use of his horse and cart. What a man! What a Basotho! He really is one of us, a true Vatmaar.

Mama, why did we, me and Mama and Kaaitjie, why did we not get the flu? And how did this flu get to Vatmaar?

Suzan, the way it came, that's how it left us. On its own. But it is said the Cape Corps brought it with them in 1918. It was called the bubonic plague and it was Sis Bet who gave us wild garlic to drink, which helped us. Because those who did not drink it went to bed and never woke up again. To this day you'll see wild garlic growing at the homes of old Vatmaar people. It also keeps snakes and mice away. And while we're talking, Suzan, I want you to lift the stones because you're stronger than me, and I'll stand ready with the spade because there might be scorpions or snakes underneath, one never knows.

The walk to the Pan two days ago had taken its toll. After a while Tant Vonnie said to Suzan: Those five miles to the Pan have taken five years off my life. Now I can really say I am an old woman. I can feel the old age creeping up.

As they got closer to the peg, Suzan said: A person works faster if there's a nice story waiting. We're near the peg, Mama.

Ja, it's completely rusted. Maybe we can paint it, we'll see.

The story of Norman van der Westhuizen

Who was this Norman van der Westhuizen, Mama?

And then Tant Vonnie told the story: He was your father's friend, here in Vatmaar and on the battlefield. This man, Suzan, lost his father in the Boer War at Modder River. Now the Boers fought against the big and powerful British nation, but more like hunting game than making war. Because most of them had never gone to school, only knew very well how to handle a rifle. They were not drilled like soldiers, but they were very obedient to their elders. All that I can say is, the Boers gave the English hell. The Rednecks couldn't hold a candle to the Boers when it came to shooting. So the English went and burnt down the Boers' farms and shoved their wives and children in a jail of barbed wire which they called a concentration camp. These poor people died there like flies.

This man's father was from the poor class of Boers, because he was a sharecropper on a farm. It is said that it was he, Kerneels van der Westhuizen, who raised a stone here and there and spanned the barbed wire across the grass the night before the Scottish, with their little dresses, called kilts, and bayonets charged the Boers. The Boers were lying and waiting for them and, as they say, shot them down like rabbits. A ricochet bullet caught Kerneels van der Westhuizen. That means, Suzan, that the bullet bounced off something, a rifle or a stone, and bounced back to the side that it had come from. He lies buried on the spot where he died in the battle near Modder River.

In the concentration camp his son, Norman, who was actually Borman, lost his mother. He said he remembered how they put his mother into the grave with her bonnet on her head and how he had to jump in to pull the bonnet over her face so that the stones and the sand wouldn't fall on her face. He said that, as young as he was then, he always remembers that no one cried. A deep grief added a new fire to their hatred of the Tommies.

After Vereeniging nobody wanted him. By then he was about thirteen. He had to steal food to stay alive and his body was full of weals made by the whip, he said. He remembered his age because his mother had to tell it to the Tommies, who wrote it down next to his name Borman van der Westhuizen.

Then, in the heart of winter, he came to a place where a three-legged pot full of pap was cooking on an open fire. He decided to wait for it to cool off and then take the pot and run away.

He had just picked up a stick to lift the pot by its handle when a black woman said to him in his own language: No, don't do, ask you get.

He said to the black woman: I ask – and put his hand on his mouth.

She laughed, took the pot off the fire and said: Go fetch wood. You cold.

He went to fetch some wood nearby, put it on the fire and soon he was warm. He was barefoot, with just a khaki Tommie jacket which he had stolen, on. His feet were full of chilblains.

You know what this old lady did? Norman van der Westhuizen asked your father.

Heinrich, he said, she fetched two tin plates and a calabash of milk and dished us each a huge heap of pap. The first decent meal I had eaten since my father left on commando.

From his heart he called her Ma because he knew she had taken the place of his late mother. He loved this new, black mother from the every beginning because she was all he had on this earth. And, lucky for him, she had also lost all her children and her husband in a black concentration camp.

She then put a tin of water on the fire and said: Sores on your body very bad. Look after fire, I look for wild kopiefa leaves.

She came back and put the leaves on a table made of two army trestles and a loose plank.

Bring water, mosimane, she said.

He carried the water into the hut and saw the leaves and a clean rag on the table. She undressed him and said: Your ma where?

He pointed to the ground with his finger.

Pa?

Again he pointed to the ground.

Brother and sister?

He shook his head: Nothing.

You not lie?

He again shook his head.

Then she put her arms around him and said: Me nothing, you nothing – and again took her hands off him. He saw tears in her eyes. Where sleep? she said.

He shrugged his shoulders and the tears trickled out of his eye too, the first time since he had pulled the bonnet over his mother's face at her funeral.

Then she said: I believe – and bathed him with warm water and boersoap, the first bath in his life which he really could remember. I will never forget it, Norman van der Westhuizen said to your father.

After the bath she crushed the kopiefa leaves and rubbed the yellow juice onto his sores. As she rubbed the leaves over the sores she asked: What name?

Borman van der Westhuizen.

Her face brightened and she said: Norman, good name. Master Norman White, I his washwoman. The table and that iron. With her one hand on the table she pointed with the other to a flat-iron filled with dead coals. I pay Master Norman one shilling one week. Next week I finish pay.

From that moment he remained Norman. Borman belonged to the past. She gave him a blanket to wrap around him and said he should sit out of the draught. He went to sit in the corner because it was a four-cornered room. She said: You sit, Norman. I throw clothes outside in sun because lice climb off when sun gets hot.

His clothes were just the khaki Tommy uniform jacket which hung to his ankles, with brass buttons and cut off sleeves.

Now that I think of it, Heinrich, Norman said to your father, I can't remember how the sleeves were cut off or whether I got it like that without sleeves.

And then Tant Vonnie told Suzan what Norman van der Westhuizen told her man Heinrich:

I sat in the corner and thought with my childish understanding: She is black but her touch is white. And I had heard so many bad things about black people. I am going to stay here, even if I must also make myself black. My own people said to me: Be off, go away. As if I am a dog. But this black aia is a mother because I felt her breasts when she held me. She just said to me: Don't steal, ask, and don't lie.

With those thoughts still in my head I fell asleep. When I woke, I left my whole past along with the sleep. I was Norman and I

234

called her Ma. The sun was about to set when she again brought me a plate of porridge, this time with an egg and a jam tin full of water. She sat on a little box at the table and looked at me and said: You must not lie and if you want to go, you are free to leave. Your jacket is still wet but it will be dry tomorrow. I am going to bring it in otherwise the goats will eat it up tomorrow morning.

She crushed the left over kopiefa leaves and smeared the juice on my sores. I wrapped myself up in the blanket and she said: The candle is finished, we will not have light tonight.

She made a bed for her on the floor too, on an animal skin. Then she went onto her knees.

And do you know what happened next, Heinrich? She said the Our Father in English. I went to kneel next to her and put my hands together. I said Amen with her, because I knew at the end of every prayer there is always an amen. I could feel a motherly warmth flow from her. I went back to my corner with the blanket. I did not think but I also did not sleep. But early in the morning it got very cold. Then I threw the blanket on my new mother because in the moonlight I saw how she shivered under her one blanket, and I crept in behind her back.

I woke up the next morning with my arm around her neck. She turned around and her face was near mine. In my child's mind came the words: We are. There and then I began to love her, the bond between us was sealed. From then on we spoke Setswana most of the time. And she was proud when I spoke Setswana to her amongst other people. To me Kaffir language, as the coloureds and whites call it, was our language.

I also went with her when she took Master Norman White's washing back, but I had to wait outside in the street while she went into the house. I never knew why, until the day she got sick and struggled to walk. She asked me to put the clean washing, which she had already folded, into a clean flour bag in the sun on a paraffin tin to make sure there were no lice in the washing. Because the lice walk out in the sun.

When the time came for us to take the washing away, she could hardly walk again. She asked me to pick some leaves from the pepper tree to put on her head. I did what she asked and said to her: Ma, I will take the washing to Master Norman.

Take it, but please keep it clean, she said. And then she gave me a tobacco bag and said: Put the money in here.

Master Norman White was about to go out when I walked into his house. He said to me: Is that my washing?

I said: Ja, Oom, because I was used to calling a white man Oom. He looked at me, laughed and called: Lorna, come and have a look. Isn't he cute? Where is Khumalo?

Khumalo was my mother. I said: Sick, Oom.

A white woman walked in and said: I'll be damned. A real poor white boy.

A boy about my size came into the room. Mommy, he said, who is this dirty Boer? When he walked past me he trod on my bare foot with his shoe. You are now under the Queen, he said.

I kept quiet because I knew it was their washing which gave us food.

Bob, his mother said, have you any clothes which you would like to change for new ones?

Then I smiled at him because I knew it was better to make a friend of him than an enemy. Again he walked past me and this time he stamped his heel on my big toe. Ow! I said because it was sore.

His father had seen what happened and said: Bob, that's the last time that you ever do a thing like that.

Mrs Lorna White came back again, very angry. What happened? she asked. I told you before not to scold our son in front of his inferiors.

Lorna, Lorna, Master Norman said. Look, look, the boy's foot is bleeding.

Without looking at my foot she said: You give him the money and I'll give him some clothes.

I put the money in the tobacco bag and put the new washing, which had been washed just the week before, in the flour bag. Thank you very much, Oom, I said. I still had my Boer pride and I just could not say Baas.

I closed the wire-netting door of the verandah, put the washing on the stoep, and sprinkled some sand on the bleeding toe. I felt sorry for myself and began to cry, which always helps to relieve the pain. This Bob White then came out and said: Wait. He looked into the flour bag, went back into the house and came out with a good pair of boots, the first pair I ever owned.

I quickly wiped the tears away because I didn't want him to see I had been crying. He tied the boots' laces together and hung them over my shoulder and took my hand and walked with me to the back gate. Then he said good bye with the words: I am sorry. I'll never do it again.

I believed him.

At home I gave Ma the bag with the money in it and showed her the boots and the clothes. She gave me a few hugs. I liked it. Then she gave me some money to go and buy bread and a tin of jam. I also had to go to our neighbours – I don't remember their names any more, he told your father, but they were coloured people – for a twig or two of wilde-als.

It was after the New Year celebrations, I remember, when my mother said to me: This pocket is full – what she meant is the dress pocket is full of money. We're going to buy lots of hens and then they'll lay eggs for us. But remember, it will be your job to look after them, and we are going to make them a place to sleep.

You know, Heinrich, he said to your father, my mother took me to a school for coloureds and said to the teacher: He Norman white and me black, we make coloured.

But it was just the other way around – she thought she was white and I again thought I was black. So colour never came between us. (Coloured was the word they used for brown people who came from the Cape.)

Whenever I came from school, I took the washing to Master Norman White because Ma became too tired to walk up the hill to their house. Master White started treating me in a very friendly way because I discovered that I should make him think I was inferior to him. I began calling him Master Norman because my mother told me: Call an Englishman Master and a Boer man Baas and then you can twist them around your pinkie. Every time Master Norman called their housemaid and told her to give me a slice of bread and jam.

Our school only went to standard three. When I finished standard three Ma went to ask Master Norman White if he didn't have a job at the post office for me. She asked for work for Van der Westhuizen because he didn't like it that I was Norman. I got a job as a messenger, delivering telegrams with a red bicycle. I had to leave the bicycle at the post office after work.

Master Norman White died and his son Bob took over as postmaster. It was this Bob who put in a good word for me so that I became a postman. I was then given the mailbag and the red bicycle to look after. And so we built on two more rooms, bought furniture and put a wire fence around our yard. After that my mother stopped doing washing because I said: It's my turn now to look after the family.

She taught me not to lie and never to steal. I will never forget her words, and also not the first and last time Bob White stepped on my big toe.

Like I said, Suzan, Tant Vonnie said, he was your father's friend. Neither of the two ever smoked or drank or went to church.

When war broke out in 1914, it wasn't necessary for him to join because he had a good job at the post office. Work was very scarce and because your father was just a labourer, he had to join out of necessity.

Why, Mama?

Your father couldn't get work and there was a poster with a

soldier on it and the words *Fight for the King, God bless the King.*
So said those who could read. A soldier gets good food, good
clothes and a rifle. And we were assured of a monthly allowance,
as they called their wages. The soldiers quickly got leave to come
home from their camp in Kimberley.

What is leave, Mama?

It's a few days off from the camp, a kind of holiday. The unmarried ones could choose the best girls because in their eyes they
were heroes. And I was very proud of your father. He quickly became a sergeant – a soldier with three stripes, and the wages were
more every month, I mean now the allowance.

One weekend when your father was on leave, Norman came
from Du Toitspan to see him. You know, Suzan, they always sat
together without saying a word, as only bosom friends do. Then
your father told him about army life. It was much better and very
different to those days in the Boer War when they both suffered
without any compensation. But luckily the wounds had healed.

Your father's story went to Norman's head. That Monday morning he gave a week's notice at the post office. The postmaster said
he would have to finish off at the end of the month.

I can't remember the name of the new postmaster, Tant Vonnie told Suzan, because Bob White was also in uniform. But anyway, this Norman, who was your father's friend, was one of those
people who, if they've made up their mind about something, nobody can tell them otherwise. So the postmaster said to him: If I
accept your resignation you may leave immediately, but you're
going to lose all your pension money.

It doesn't matter. I'm on my way to the doctor for a check-up
and if he says I'm all right for the army nothing's going to keep
me here.

The doctor said he was fit and healthy and that same afternoon he was off to camp.

The next day his mother, we called her Ma Khumalo, came to
Vatmaar to come and ask me about the army. I told her what your

father told me. She could not understand it. Why? Why? she asked me. After suffering so much under these people as a child, he is now prepared to go and lay down his life for them.

I, Vonnie, Ma Khumalo said to me, I love him more than any King of England. And to think he gave up a good job just to hear he must give his life for King and Country. The king is very good to fill young men's heads with rubbish. Or maybe he's got a very good witchdoctor.

The next time I saw Ma Khumalo was at the city hall where we went to fetch our money every month. She told me he looked so brave and handsome in his uniform when he came home on leave. She wished his real mother and father were still alive to see him. Even the girls who never used to greet her, came to visit and asked when he would be on leave again. Then she gave them his letters to read and her photo of him to look at.

And do you know what one girl said who read his letters? Ma Khumalo asked me. She said: We've got no hope, he'll never leave this ouma alone.

We both laughed and felt proud of our two men, both with a bond which bound us without us being married to them or having given birth to them.

It just shows you, Suzan, neither King and Country nor anything else could keep them apart. They loved each other more than brothers, they got along very well and still there was a place for me and Ma Khumalo in their hearts.

Your father, as I said, was a sergeant, and Oom Norman a private. He always wrote your father's letters for him because your father couldn't write. And then one week they came here on what they called embarkation leave. Seven days, because after that they would depart by ship to a place near the battlefield.

After that your father's letters became very irregular. Oom Norman could, if he wanted to, join the European army, as it was called, because he was white. The pay was better, but he didn't join.

What does it sound like to you, Suzan? her mother asked. Both fighting and dying for King and Country, but the Cape Corps gets less for the same noble work. And after they had helped win the war, the coloured people were sent back, just like that, to their same old standard of living.

When I received the telegram that your father is dead, I went to the army's pay-office and from there they sent me to the war-widows' office. At the war-widows' office they wanted to see my marriage certificate. I told them I have never been married with a ring, but I have eight children from the same man and I am proud of it.

The girl behind the counter just said: Sorry, I can't help you.

Just like that, Suzan.

And then, Mama?

I was angry, full of regret and full of hate, all at the same time. Angry at myself because your father had asked me, not once but many times, to let us marry in front of the dominee. He always used to say: Just so we can show the children one day. To me it was just a piece of paper which some people frame and hang on the wall. But when I came out of that office I really wished I had that certificate, as she called it.

My heart was broken because I didn't have your father any more. In my eyes he did not go to fight for the King, he went so that my children and I could eat and live, because it was his duty as head of the family. If tears could've brought your father back to us, then they would've, because he was never out of my thoughts. And there were many times when I wished I was dead just to be able to be with him. I called the King the worst things I know. To think that he had the power to kill us whom he called his "subjects" and to teach our husbands to murder people they didn't even know and who they had never seen before. All in his name!

But at least Mama got letters and photos from that faraway place across the water where they had to go?

The letters, Suzan, were written by Oom Norman, as I said. The letters he wrote Ma Khumalo, she told me, were all about how much he missed her and what he hoped to do when he came home was to get married so that his mother would have someone to keep her company, and maybe the family would grow then. Ma Khumalo was very proud of his letters and the girls always came, after the postman had left, to ask if they could read them.

My letters were always about the new wonders that your father had seen. Naturally he said that he missed me very much. The one thing he said that he couldn't get used to was being without me.

There was a woman here in Vatmaar, her name was Moira Jacobs. She came from the Cape and her husband was also in the Cape Corps. Like Oom Norman, he also came home after the war, but was only here for a week when he said: Pack up, we're going back to the Boland. It was his house which Isaac Venter bought.

Now this Moira always read your father's letters to me. The next day the whole of Vatmaar knew what was in them, with a bit added on. Whenever I asked her why people are talking about things which are not in the letters, she always said she had to make them sound more interesting for these backward people of Vatmaar. And then she would cover her eyes with her hands.

Getting up slowly from the big piece of limestone where she had been sitting, Tant Vonnie said: We haven't done much work, Suzan, just talked, and already I feel tired and thirsty. Let's go home and when we come back we'll bring something to eat and drink.

Suzan picked up the spade.

Later, walking back alongside her mother, she said: I remember Oom Norman, Mama.

Yes, her mother said, it's possible. We buried him about six years ago.

Was his mother here for his funeral?

No, Suzan, Ma Khumalo was very old and she died. She was one of the few people who survived the Big Flu and her Norman was one of the last to return from the war. He had been on escort duty, he said, to take prisoners back to their countries.

Afterwards Ma Khumalo became bedridden and she said God had sent her a new friend. It was a girl whose parents had sent her away because she was pregnant. But Ma Khumalo said: I'll take you together with the child that is coming.

Ma Khumalo took her as her daughter and she kept the old woman clean and did the housework. She even got permission to fetch Oom Norman's monthly pay and deposit it in his post office savings book. Before she did anything else she had to do this, Ma Khumalo always said.

When Oom Norman came back home after he was discharged from the army, he stayed at home for the whole of the first week. And this must have been the happiest time of her life. Ma Khumalo, they said, did not get tired of saying: He was gone. Now he's back home. She had four paraffin tins of sorghum-beer made and out of her dress pocket she took money for a young ox. She said it was their birthday party because neither of them knew their birthdates.

The old woman gave Norman his post office savings book. You know, Suzan, she never called him my Son. It was always Norman.

Oom Flip was asked to fetch Norman's friends from Vatmaar for the birthday party. You went too, do you still remember?

Ja, Mama. And this Oom Norman loved talking to Kaaitjie.

Tant Vonnie tells Norman van der Westhuizen's war stories

This Norman van der Westhuizen was an ordinary Boer boy, these days called an Afrikaner. Short, just over five feet. Reddish-brown hair with a thick, golden moustache. Eyes the colour and appearance of the morning glory flower. Always in a hurry. He greeted by lifting his arm, pointing his forefinger, and without opening his mouth.

After he had come from the army, people could not understand

243

why he never came out of the house any more. Then one afternoon, while sitting at his mother's bedside, he called the girl – I've gone and forgotten her name now, Suzan, her child was a few months old by this time – and told her to go and call the elders and the minister of the Wesleyan Church to his mother's sickbed. That night, at about nine o'clock, Ma Khumalo took Norman's hand. He kissed her hand and she breathed her last breath.

Mama, Suzan asked, was Oom Norman there when Papa was buried?

When we get home and after we've had something to eat then maybe we can talk some more.

We must, Mama.

Yes, my child, we will and we must.

Poor child, Tant Vonnie thought, she doesn't remember much about her own father because she's the last born. He always called her Everything, and sometimes Everything-That's-Nice. But I don't think she remembers her pet names because I've never called her anything but Suzan.

After lunch Tant Vonnie said: I'm really getting old and I will have to look after myself a little better. I'm going to lie down a little and if I fall asleep don't wake me. And Suzan, keep yourself busy but don't go too far from the house.

Suzan collected some firewood and after filling the three-legged pot with water on the fireplace, she waited for her mother to wake up. She couldn't wait any more to hear how her father had died. And what was the meaning of the tent peg at the grave.

Every now and then she went to peep into the room to see if her mother was awake yet. Because she was ready for her, with the fire, the coffee and the water to wash. While sitting on the stone chair, Suzan thought: The last time I had such a nice chat was with Nellie Ndola. I wonder how life is treating her because to be black and a woman as well, is the lowest a person can be born, very close to a slave, sometimes worse.

When her mother eventually woke up, Suzan did everything she could to keep her in a good mood. After a while she said: Mama, remember your promise ...

What promise, my child?

Oom Norman at Papa's funeral.

Oh yes, as I was saying, their officer, Lieutenant Bob White, had already known Oom Norman before he went to school. Once when they were alone, he said to Norman: This Sergeant Müller is such a good soldier, it's a pity that he cannot read or write.

Lieutenant, Oom Norman said, that's why I'm here, to be close to my friend and to look after him. Please, Lieutenant, see to it that we don't get separated.

All right, Private van der Westhuizen, he said. The corporal and the lance-corporal have both been arrested for drunkenness. I shall have to have them both demoted and stripped of their stripes. So I'll need a corporal and a lance-corporal. I'll have a look at your army files, and if satisfactory, you'll be a full corporal. Now this is confidential, Private van der Westhuizen.

Yes, Sir, he said and saluted.

The next afternoon he was asked to report to the lieutenant's tent. The lieutenant said to him that the captain had looked at his file and approved the recommendation. So soon you will see your promotion to full corporal on the notice board and hear it read out on parade. Only one thing more. I order you to tell nobody that Sergeant Müller cannot read or write. You'll do his reading and writing. I see that his letters to his wife are also written by you. Is that so?

Ja, Lieutenant, Norman said, so happy that he actually saluted twice.

After the promotion he moved into the sergeant's, your father's, tent together with the new lance-corporal. They soon got used to this Lance-Corporal Joseph Naude. He was from an Apostolic church and was happy to do all their praying for them, all they had to say was Amen. He had a Bible which his church had given him when he was on embarkation leave. Lieutenant Bob White was very proud of his non-commissioned officers, his subordinates.

But just let me tell you about the day we lost Sergeant Müller, your Heinrich, Oom Norman said to me.

The Turks were lying in trenches and they picked us off like rats. We tried to break through their flank to rescue a platoon of English foot soldiers who were surrounded in a hollow between two hills. But they had us in their sights and since daybreak they had been picking us off just as they liked. It was about three o'clock, fifteen hundred hours, like they say, when we got the order to silence one of the cannons, no matter what it takes.

You see, Vonnie, he said, an order in the army must be obeyed, even if it is a stupid order, even if you know you could die. A soldier is trained to kill, and it seems that only the best are later killed themselves. On the map was this hill, called Square Hill, from where the cannon had been shooting. The cannon was beginning to fire nearer and nearer to us, and when a bomb fell right in front of us, Bob White ordered: Down, then up. Double up!

We jumped up and ran up the hill as fast as we could. Then we fell flat again and crept forward on our elbows and knees, with the rifles in front of us. We probably progressed about five hundred yards like this when the shells began falling between us.

Fewer and fewer of us were left. A few times a shell landed right on top of some of our men and blew them to pieces. A real nightmare with pieces of living human flesh falling all over.

Our artillery guns could not spot their cannon, you could only see it from where the platoon was, about a hundred and fifty yards from the cannon. I heard Lieutenant Bob swear: Why the hell did they not send us an artillery officer or mortars? Then he shouted: Charge!

I saw him jump up, revolver in the hand. Then a bullet went right through him.

You must remember, Vonnie, it was uphill, and the rifles with their bayonets were getting heavier. But we didn't even realise it. All we had in our heads was that order: Silence that gun.

Suzan, I asked him why he and my Heinrich didn't just turn around and leave the whole lot behind. No, Vonnie, he said, to obey orders had been drilled into us. If one of us had turned around he would've been shot in the back by one of our own men. And he would've been called a coward because he ran away in the face of the enemy.

Forward! Forward! I heard the sergeant's gruff voice. After Lieutenant Bob had fallen, he took over the command. Shoot the scum! he shouted. We ran, shooting from the hip.

So many things were happening all at once. The Turks were also now getting our rifle fire, and their firing was beginning to slow down. Up, forward, up we moved with bullets flying between us and into us.

Use the bayonets! Sergeant Heinrich shouted.

You'll be surprised how scared those people are of bayonets, Vonnie, Oom Norman said. We also took a few prisoners because only a lesser man would shoot another who has his hands in the air.

Our sergeant turned the cannon around and let it loose on the remaining Turks until all the ammunition was finished. The signalman had fallen so your husband ordered me to write a message to the company-commander: GUN SILENCED, I wrote in capital letters. SEND REINFORCEMENTS AND STRETCHER BEARERS. I signed it: *Sergeant H. Müller*.

We gave the message to one of our men to deliver as quickly as possible. There were many wounded who needed help. Your husband, my sergeant and friend, turned around to start helping. A sharpshooter's bullet entered his head in front and came out at the back. He died on the spot, Vonnie.

You see, Vonnie, whoever orders a bayonet charge also has to lead that charge. It all sounds very brave but if you've been through it once and came out on the other side without a scratch and you look back it looks so stupid to have men with long knives on their guns running through a rain of bullets.

It was my officer, Lieutenant Bob White, and your husband, Sergeant Müller, who led the charge. Neither of the two saw the sun come up the next day, or ever again afterwards.

This military medal that I wear belongs to all three of us: your Heinrich, Lieutenant Bob White and me.

That night we had, so to speak, no sleep. We were completely worn out and were beginning to feel the after-effects of the battle: a cold sweat, a thank-God feeling and a sensation of it-is-true-because-I'm-not-alone. Before your Heinrich was shot he had ordered that guard duty should be half an hour long. That was his last order. Lieutenant Bob White's order was: Up and charge!

The Cape Corps had saved the day, captured that gun and silenced it – with so many innocent souls silenced too. Circumstances had brought them together, most to die in this nightmare, others to remember the dream. For the "top brass", as they were called, it was just another order that had to be obeyed.

Before daybreak our relief party arrived. They threw the dead Turks out of their trenches and took up positions in those very same trenches. In the first light we allowed our Turkish prisoners to bury their dead. They also said a Moslem prayer. Some of them were in tears. Their grief was taken up in ours and there was a deep silence.

We of the Cape Corps who remained, took our lieutenant and sergeant and buried them under a tree. Lance-Corporal Joseph Naude, who had been wounded, said a prayer, and then I covered their faces with their steel helmets so that the stones and sand would not hurt them, and as I did this I thought of that wet morning in the concentration camp when I jumped into my mother's grave to cover her face with her bonnet.

The stretcher bearers were seeing to the wounded and some of the relief party were burying the dead. I called our men who were left and we helped the people who were not that badly injured down the hill. I will never forget how I reported to our company-commander: Sir, twenty-one men with arms, on roll call.

The captain said: Dismiss the men, Corporal, and take the day off. Report to me at six hours.

What did you do then, Normy? I asked. Because by this time he was the man nearest to me, now that your father was no longer there, and people thought I was his girlfriend.

Most of us got the cold shivers, as a result of the battle, he said. There was not a word said between us. We had to clean our bayonets, which were soaked in blood. This was another wordless experience because we knew the following day was inspection. I tried to write letters to you and my mother but I got just as far as my own name on the page. This is the first time that I've told someone how dearly the Cape Corps paid to silence that cannon on Square Hill. And I'll never tell the story again.

Where was I when Oom Normy told Mama all this? Suzan asked.

You were playing outside, my child. Kaaitjie sat and listened. And then she gave Oom Normy a cup of tea. She liked making him tea, sometimes up to three or four cups when he came to visit.

The people of Vatmaar were always asking me: Has that young man not asked you to marry him yet? I always thought: I'm fond of him, but I don't need a husband.

A few times Oom Norman said he was on a month's leave and after that he'd start a new life. I always wondered what he meant. Then on a very cold Friday afternoon he was suddenly looking all over for a tent peg. I don't know where he eventually found one, but he came to show us the peg. He was very happy, as if he found something very valuable. It began to get dark and I said to him: Why do you want to walk to the Pan? You can sleep here tonight. He just laughed so that his stomach bobbed up and down. Before he left Kaaitjie gave him another cup of tea.

It was late already, and cold and dark outside. He had never before stayed so late and he had also never before been so pleasant. We never dreamt that it would be the last time we saw him alive.

The Monday morning when the mounted policeman Prins was doing his inspection of Vatmaar, he spotted some dark thing in the Vatmaar cemetery. At first he didn't let it bother him because he thought it was an ox. But when he rode past the cemetery again on his way back he saw the thing still in the same place. He went nearer and saw that it was a man on one knee with a tent peg sticking through his military jacket and a hammer lying next to him on the ground.

Constable Prins immediately went to tell Oom Chai what he had seen and asked him to keep watch over the body and not to tell anybody anything. He said he would go to the siding to ask Mister O'Reilly to phone for a doctor, a man with a camera and the undertaker.

Some people saw the constable speaking to Oom Chai. Then they saw Oom Chai walk to the cemetery, something which nobody did so early in the morning. At first they thought he was looking for his livestock and one of the nosy big boys began following him.

When the youngster went nearer he saw the face of the dead man. He got such a fright that he ran back and told everybody that Oom Chai was busy burying someone. Before the doctor and the other two people who had been phoned could arrive, the whole of Vatmaar was already at the cemetery. It was a Monday and most of the workers had already left for work in the Pan, but everybody else was there.

When I got there – you stayed at home and Kaaitjie was looking after you – somebody had already fetched a blanket and covered the corpse. When I saw the piece of army jacket sticking out I knew, but I could not understand it.

You know, Suzan, said Tant Vonnie, the unexpected happens when you least expect it.

Eventually the doctor arrived with Mister May and a man with a camera in his Buick motor-car. I heard the doctor telling the policeman, who was standing ready with his pencil and his notebook: It's a heart failure case, caused by some prank or bet, for he hit the tent peg into the ground, and in doing so, he hit it through his great coat. When he got up the peg, or say spike, held him to the ground. That was when his heart failed and stopped beating, or he froze to death. He must have been dead for at least three days. I may as well draw up and sign the death certificate.

The blanket was taken off Oom Normy and everyone recognised him as the white man who always came to visit me. The man with the camera took a few photos saying he may as well, to make up for wasted time and so that he could put in a claim for his services.

Everyone looked at me, even the white strangers, Suzan. When I couldn't take it any more I walked away and went to cry my heart out, as they say. I was broken because I realised then that I did love Normy after all. My Heinrich, your father, was not there any more and I was sure he would've been happy if I'd taken this brave man in his place.

Norman van der Westhuizen would never grow old now. But now people who were not even good enough to tie his shoelaces were looking at his corpse and saying he was a fool.

But why did he die, Mama? Oom Normy was a soldier who used to kill the enemy's soldiers for the English King. If somebody had cornered him in our cemetery at midnight, surely he wouldn't have died from it?

My child, Tant Vonnie said, a soldier on the battlefield and a man after the war are not the same person. The man on the battlefield is a man under orders. In ordinary life that same man is a free man. He died of fright, my child. We are all scared, but not of the same things. And those so-called Europeans who came from Du

Toitspan that morning, despised without reason their brother who had abandoned his own kraal for another kraal. And our people again, will accept a white man with open arms but turn their backs on their own brother.

Tant Vonnie paused for a while to think. A tear rolled out of the eye which was alive but which could not see. When Suzan saw the tear she put her arms around her mother and began to cry too.

That's enough now, her mother said, what's past is past.

And then, Mama?

The doctor signed the paper and gave it to the policeman. The policeman told Oom Chai to see what was in Oom Normy's pockets. His pipe, tobacco and matches – I knew he had learnt to smoke in the army – a hanky which Kaaitjie had given him and the post office savings book in which Ma Khumalo had put half his army pay into every month.

These men from the Pan were very surprised at this and began passing the book from hand to hand.

He wasn't a poor man, I heard the doctor say.

Mister May was only interested in the savings book.

And then there was also his old army allowance book. The doctor looked through it and said: He even has a military medal for bravery. And then he said: Here it is. Here are his papers. His name was Norman van der Westhuizen. Age unknown. Corporal in the Cape Corps. His last will and testament states: All I have or ever will have belongs to my Ma Khumalo or her kin.

The doctor gave the two books to the policeman and asked him to write out a receipt for them. The man with the box camera also wanted to see the books. He then took a photo of the page of the army allowance book where it states that he had received a medal for bravery. He handed the book back to the policeman and said: This was no ordinary man.

I liked what he said, Suzan. The corpse was again covered with the blanket. And Mister May said with a very pleased look on his face he'd be back soon with a coffin and he'd also try and get in touch with the coloured dominee. And he'd also try and bring the next of kin.

Ja, you know, Oom Chai said to the corpse, your money's sitting in the bank. To Mister May, whose ancestors were slaves, something which one doesn't have to be shy about, he said: Slave-child, what about the digging of the grave?

I'll pay two pounds to the men who will dig the grave. I'll pay when they're finished, Mister May said.

Then we leave everything in May's hands, the doctor said. Agreed, Constable?

Yes, Doctor.

Then we might as well be off.

The doctor, the man with the box camera and Mister May got into the Buick and drove away. Then, my child, this stupid policeman who only knew how to ride a horse, said he needed more particulars. Firstly, did the deceased live in Du Toitspan. What was he doing here, and who were his friends.

Everyone pointed to me. I stepped forward and said: He was my husband's friend and mine.

And where did he get that tent peg?

I said: I don't know, we last saw him alive late on Friday evening. He was very happy and he said: I've found it and showed us the peg. My daughter Kaaitjie gave him a cup of tea because he liked tea very much. I asked him to sleep over because it was late, but he didn't want to. That's all I know and all I can tell you, Constable.

I take it the deceased was your friend?

Some people nodded their heads. He wrote it down in his book. I did not want to argue with this man who thought he was the law. So I just kept quiet.

Then he wanted to know about the tent peg. He held it up and said: Who has seen this thing before?

The oom wanted to buy a peg from us while we were sitting at the brazier to get warm, a boy said, pointing at two other boys. He said he would pay half a crown for a good peg. I knew where to get a tent peg so I went to pull it out of the ground. We used it to tie the dog's chain to it, but now that our dog is tame we don't use the peg any more. The oom gave me the two and six for the peg. Here it is.

He showed the money to the policeman.

Good boy, the policeman said and wrote down his name. Keep the half-crown, it's yours. And the peg belongs to this man, he pointed to the corpse. Anyone who takes this peg from the grave will be charged with theft. Do you hear? he shouted.

Yes, Konstabel! the people called back.

He didn't like being called Konstabel, he was Constable – to him a konstabel was a Kaffir policeman. He said: Charlie, I leave it to you to see that everything goes off smoothly.

Good, Meneer the Konstabel, Oom Chai said.

He gave Oom Chai an ugly stare and walked away. Oom Chai chose four men to dig the grave. The rest of Vatmaar went home to prepare their lunch. When I walked through the garden of what was still our old house, Kaaitjie called out to me: Is it Oom Norman?

Yes, I said.

She fell over right there, out like a light, as they say. Luckily Sis Bet saw what happened because Kaaitjie had given a loud scream. She dipped a piece of rag in water and kept it on her forehead.

Kaaitjie was out for a long time. I got worried and started crying and praying at the same time. You were standing there next to me, do you remember, Suzan?

Not really, Mama. Go on.

When Kaaitjie eventually opened her eyes I said: Thank you, Lord and ran to fetch the rooilaventel bottle and half a cup of water. But when I got back to the house she was out again.

Sis Bet prayed, most of the time in her Griqua language, but also in our language. I felt Kaaitjie's heart and it was still beating and it gave me hope. Then Sis Bet ran to fetch a rosemary branch. As she ran back she began crushing the leaves in her hands. I still had my hand on Kaaitjie's heart and all that I could say was: Please, Lord ... Over and over. Sis Bet put her hand with the crushed rosemary leaves under Kaaitjie's nose. Then the child opened her eyes and said: Is it true?

We didn't answer her. Sis Bet just said to her: Drink this first.

I lifted her head and she drank the rooilaventel very slowly. She couldn't get up, her whole body was lame. I fetched a blanket and a goatskin so that she could lie down a little and get her strength back. Sis Bet showed me with her finger on her lips that we shouldn't talk any more, and gave Kaaitjie the leftover rooilaventel to drink up.

I took her into the house because people were walking past on their way to the cemetery.

I heard that Mister May had brought the coffin, but he had to break poor Normy's legs to get him into the coffin. Then he closed the lid and waited for the Reverend Elias Cobb of the Congregational Church at the Pan.

This is one of his people, said Mister May.

Oom Chai did not like this. He said: You mean one of Norman's loved ones' people? Then he mumbled: Slave-child.

I couldn't go to the funeral, Tant Vonnie went on. I had to look after Kaaitjie. I heard that Oom Chai had knocked the tent peg back into its old hole.

After the funeral, Meneer Stoffel Jones brought the girl with the baby who stayed with Ma Khumalo, to see me. She wanted to come and say thank you.

She seemed like a very sensible young woman. I could see that life had not been kind to her and I immediately took a liking to her. She said she hardly knew him and she didn't know what to do now that the man of the house was gone. She cried bitterly. The only other thing she said was: He was always satisfied with everything. He liked playing with the baby and he always said: One day there will be a father for him.

What's her name, Mama? Suzan asked.

Mariam. But when she climbed into the Cape cart to go back to DuToitspan, she asked me to call her Mary.

Kaaitjie didn't want to see her and stayed in the bedroom. Poor Kaaitjie was sick for weeks. For the first three weeks she ate nothing. It was really hard for her to accept what had happened. Then, one morning, she woke up smiling and said: Mama, I had a dream.

Tell me your dream, my child, I said.

She smiled again. He came to tell me he's very happy where he is, and we must stop crying.

After that she was the old Kaaitjie again.

Then, one summer's day, a Monday, the mounted policeman came with papers for me to sign, saying it was about the investigation into the death of Norman van derWesthuizen. Not exactly his death but to track down his next of kin and to pay the outstanding debt. The clerk-of-the-court had received only one account, from Mister May. Some of us were told to be in court on Wednesday.

We were taken to the Pan in Oom Flip's trolley. It was the first time in my life that I was in a court case and I didn't like it at all, Suzan.

After a whole lot of talking the man on the platform said: The verdict is that Norman van der Westhuizen, not being of sound mind, was responsible for his heart attack. The next of kin, being Miss Mary Mohamed, is the sole heir. The belongings of the deceased can be collected at the office of the clerk-of-the-court, together with the certificate with the name of the heir. Mister Joseph May, who has submitted his account for the funeral, will be paid by the heir.

The man stood up and someone said: Silence in court. Everybody stood up and the man in the black coat walked out. Everything was over and the court was closed.

Suzan, now you know the story of the grave with the tent peg. Don't ever ask me about it again. Tomorrow is Sunday and Kaaitjie's day off. It will be nice for the three of us to be together again.

Oh yes, afterwards Mary invited us to her home and one day I'll tell you her story as she told it to us. That day she was wearing a concertina-skirt.

The story of Mariam, renamed Mary

This Mariam Mohamed's father chased her out of her mother's house when he saw that she was going to have a baby. At first he wouldn't believe it, but that's something that can't be hidden away, it gets bigger every day.

Screaming with anger he gave her a hiding with the sjambok and chased her away like a dog, shouting: Voetsek! Voetsek! Her mother's pleading did not help. In his anger he screamed that he had lost his mosgavie, his lobola.

The unborn child's father also denied her when she went knocking on his parents' door.

She told about how she walked and walked that night, her body black and blue from the sjambok, wishing that death would come and take her away.

At daybreak she had reached the old section of Du Toitspan. She walked past an old black woman who was feeding her fowls.

She saw me walking past in my torn dress, Mariam said, because my father had torn it from top to bottom and it was hanging loose like a jacket. The old woman saw me crying and called: Come here, my child, don't walk past my open door.

She gave me a blanket to cover me, heated some water and brought it to me with a piece of soap and a towel. After washing myself I went to sit in the corner of the room and soon I fell asleep. That was the deepest sleep I had ever had in my life, I was entirely gone. But when the old woman woke me I was back in the world of people and full of pain.

My heart was broken over what I had done, although I hadn't

done it alone. I got no mercy from my father, the father who had loved me so much and who called me his Flower-from-Heaven. I couldn't believe what had happened in just six months. My whole world had changed and I was alone. Allah, I said, you are merciful, please have mercy on this fallen girl.

I was only seventeen and I had lost everything that was worth having. Nobody loved me any more. When my father tore my dress he said my respect had been eaten up by the pigs. And now this old woman was calling me "my child", she had taken my hand and was pulling me up. She took the blanket off me and then she took off the dress like one would take off a jacket.

Bana! Men! she said, shaking her head. God gave Eve to Adam to be his doormat!

She put Zambuk ointment on the weals because by now they were very swollen and my whole body was sore. I started getting cold and my head felt dizzy. Then she took me to a room and said: Norman's bed.

I didn't know what Norman meant because I had never heard that word before.

She spread out the blankets for me and I got in. She came back with a mug of wilde-als and wynruit. Drink, she said, and sleep.

When I woke up it was already late in the afternoon. The pain was terrible. I cried and she said: Cry, my child. Then she brought me a mug of warm milk with garlic in it.

I drank it and she said: Forget all about it. Sleep.

I did what she said, because was it not Allah who had sent me to her?

It went on like this for about a week. When the sjambok marks began losing their blue colour, she gave me my dress to put on again. The front had been patched together and it had been washed and ironed.

You know, Tant Vonnie, this old black woman did all this for me without once asking me my name or what had happened. All she said was: If want to go, just tell me beforehand. I shook my head and cried. She closed the door and went to sit outside on her little bench. I couldn't stand it any more and I wrapped myself in a blanket and went to sit next to her with my hand on her knee. It was already late in the morning and after a while I told her what had happened and that my name is Mariam and that my family is Moslem.

A good man does not hide behind his religion, she said. We Tswanas were never without a God. It was the white man who said we were heathens, Kaffirs.

Then I said to her: Ma, I want to stay.

Then I will take you as my child, Mary, she said.

That is how I became Mary.

Thank you, Ma, I said, and kissed her hand.

When my baby was a few months old, Ma Khumalo tickled his chin and said: Lucas.

And I added: Lucas Khumalo. He was baptised thus because he is a real Khumalo.

His father came to see him only once. He came with his mother. You know that kind of young man who does everything with his mother, Tant Vonnie. I was lying on the bed with Lucas when Ma Khumalo let them in and called me. She went to sit back on her little bench as if it was none of her business.

I came out of the room and saw my child's father. His mother was sitting on a chair. Salaam, she said.

I greeted back: Wa alaikum, salaam, greetings to you too.

Then his mother said: We've come to see Taliep's child, my grandson. I want to raise him in our Moslem faith.

I didn't say a word because they had arrived unexpectedly. Then she said: I still remember the night you knocked on our door and asked Taliep to let you in.

Now it was my turn to say something. Yes, I said, I remember too. But Auntie did not talk to me. My father hit me with the sjambok, my dress was torn from top to bottom. That dark night I walked around in circles after I was chased away from my mother's house like a dog. Allah has sent me to this old black woman sitting outside on a bench and I can never repay her for what she has done for me.

I held up first one finger and said: My child has been baptised. His name is Lucas Khumalo. Two – and I held up two fingers – Taliep, Auntie's son, is not his father. My child's father is a married man with two children. I don't want to break up his happy family. He still comes and sees his child, I lied and held up three fingers. Three, I eat pork.

Ie blies! Satan! they both said and walked out without greeting. As they walked away they spat, keeping their eyes on the ground.

After another cup of tea we said goodbye to Mary, Tant Vonnie continued. Look after Lucas, I told her. I never saw her again, but I heard that she is married to a teacher and is very grand, as they say. May God bless her.

Mary was a Cape Malay girl. Some of her forefathers had been brought to the Cape from the East as slaves. She had eyes like two black buttons and her nose was thin with a slight bend. Her skin was the colour of oak furniture. Her shiny black hair hung down to her hips. It was cut in a straight line and it gave her the appearance of being thickset. She was of an average height. Sometimes, like the day in court, she plaited her hair and tied a red ribbon at the end, and hung earrings on her ears, also red.

That day she wore a pleated purple taffeta skirt and a crocheted white jersey. The purple taffeta showed through the white jersey. Her red shoes were the latest – high heels, as they called them. Oh yes, if you looked carefully you could see dark down on her upper lip. She stood out from the rest of us in that courtroom and the people of the law gave her a second look.

She was a Christian, she said, and a member of Ma Khumalo's church where she found her Jesus. Praise Him! she said, looking upwards.

You see, Suzan, Tant Vonnie said. There is always change in this world, whether for good or for bad. It happens to the seasons and to us people, and hope doesn't change anything.

Kaaitjie's day off

That Sunday Kaaitjie came and her mother told her to sleep over, she could go back the next morning with Oom Flip.

Now that we can afford the trolley money, my child, her mother said. There are very few men who can walk from the Pan and back in one day. You looked after us without thinking about yourself. You spent nothing on yourself. Look at your shoes, the heels are crooked from all the walking.

I walk most of the way without shoes. I only put them on when I see people or where the thorns are bad, Mama.

Remember, her mother said, God helps those who help themselves. He doesn't help fools. And in the same breath she said: Suzan and I are grateful.

But Kaaitjie's mother didn't know about the longing in her heart for the one who had held her hand every night and who had now just disappeared. My Kenny was all she had in her mind. My Kenny. Sometimes she would say the name out loud without thinking about it.

I'm going back to the Pan very soon because he'll be waiting there for me, she thought, but out loud she said: No, Mama. I have to go because I didn't tell Miesies Bosman I won't be home tonight. I've got the storeroom's key on me and maybe she'll want something from it tonight.

Kenny, my Kenny, Kenny, my Kenny, she kept thinking and she wasn't listening when her mother said: It could be nice if we could all three sleep under one blanket again.

Suzan made coffee and brought her mother and sister each a mugful. They sat outside on their stone chairs on hessian bags folded double to keep out the cold because a cold stone can give you piles.

Kaaitjie drank her coffee but to her nothing tasted as it should these days. Then the thought came again: Maybe Kenny is waiting for me.

I have to go now, Mama, she said. Why don't Mama and Suzan walk with me to the halfway-house. I've got nothing to carry and the walk back will be easy.

Kaaitjie, her mother said, of course we'll walk with you, won't we Suzan?

Suzan didn't like sitting at home. Quickly she pressed the lock down and said: Come, and to Kaaitjie: You see, now we've also got a key to look after.

I see, she said but the only thing in her thoughts was: Kenny, my Kenny.

Tant Vonnie began thinking that there must be something she didn't know. But either time or Suzan will tell me, she decided. I shouldn't try and control Kaaitjie because she has her own mind.

Kaaitjie walked in front in the path saying nothing but she was thinking: He must be waiting for me, Kenny, my Kenny.

Soon the three were at the big halfway-house. They said good-bye and from then on she began to pray from time to time: Lord, take care of Kenny Kleinhans. Please don't take him from me as you did with Normy.

In her anxiety she did not even see where she was going and when she looked next, she was in the alley behind the Bosmans' house. She looked out for bicycle tracks but there weren't any. Then she opened the double gate and unlocked her room and went on her knees. All that she could say was Kenny, my Kenny … Over and over.

When she woke up the next morning, she was still in the same position, ice cold and her knees completely stiff. She crept in under her only blanket and said to herself: Kenny, tomorrow is another day. Then she fell asleep again.

On the way back from the halfway-house Suzan told her mother everything she knew about Ouboet, as she called him. She was very excited and it made her mother happy that the Lord had given her daughter a man who loved her. But she still believed that there could be something wrong with her child, because that morning Kaaitjie complained that she had thrown up.

I gave her some coffee beans to chew to take away the nausea, and Suzan gave her a whole lot to take back with her. Ag, let it be, Tant Vonnie consoled herself, because she and Suzan had stopped talking.

How are things, Vonnie? asked Sis Bet when they walked past her house. You can tell me. You know we go back a long way.

Fine, Bet.

She walked over to Tant Vonnie, took both her hands in her own and kissed her on the forehead between her eyes and said: That's how we Griquas used to kiss in the days of Captain Waterboer's father.

Flip, look who's here! she called.

Oom Flip said: You two old women shouldn't stand and talk outside. Invite Vonnie inside.

They went inside.

You're not getting old at all, Vonnie.

What, not old? Look at this – and she pointed to the varicose veins on her legs.

Vonnie, Oom Flip said, there is a O.H.M.S. letter from the government for you. There were three letters. One was for a Müller, the post office said. It's probably not yours because I remember when I used to bring Heinrich's letters from the Pan for you, you've got a V. And this letter has one V with a tail – he made a V with his index and middle fingers and put a finger from his other hand underneath to show what the V with the tail looked like. But bring that letter, Buck, he said.

Sis Bet brought the letter and Tant Vonnie said: I was baptised Yvonne. It could be my letter. Let Suzan take it quickly to Teacher Elsa. She can read it and tell us what it says.

But let her first see if it is our letter, Tant Vonnie said to Suzan.

If it is, ask her to read it to you so that you can come and tell us what it says.

Why are you so scarce, Old Vonnie? Sis Bet asked while Suzan was away.

Bet, I'm busy tidying up that old grave where my children are buried so that it looks a little decent. I see you've got Star-of-Bethlehem plants. I'll be very glad if you could give me some.

Of course, just leave me some, about three or so, and take the rest. It is, after all, the poor people's garden plant.

That's true, Bet, it blooms almost throughout the year. Apparently it's also good for asthma if you make a tea with it. Talking about herbs, Bet, what can I use for a continuous headache? I've already tried all those funny things they sell in the Pan. Tommy Lewis brought me powders, but I still get this slight headache.

Vonnie, Sis Bet said, there's my peach tree. Pick a few leaves, make a tea and drink it three times a day. And then wait and see.

Suzan came back out of breath because she had run all the way. Mama, Teacher Elsa says it's Mama's pension money that Papa left for Mama. Mama has to fetch it every month from the post office. It's three pounds ten shillings a month, and Teacher Elsa says Mama must come to her because she kept the letter so that she can read it to Mama too.

It's very important, Vonnie, Sis Bet said. It's the best news I've heard in a long time.

A wild fowl in the pot is better than three on the vlei, Tant Vonnie said. I'll go and hear quickly. And Flip, I won't forget you, because you're the one who will be taking me to the Pan.

Ja, he laughed and Sis Bet said: Please come back here, Von, there's something I have to get off my chest.

Oom Flip always fetched Vatmaar's mail every Saturday. People paid him for what they thought it was worth to them. If it was good news he received a nice sum of money or a big favour. For bad news just about nothing, because then it was said he was the bearer of bad tidings. Tant Vonnie knew this. That is why he smiled when he heard there was money in the letter and said: That's the best news I've heard in a long time.

Elsa Lewis told the same story that Suzan had told her mother, only adding that Tant Vonnie should take all her papers with her and that pension would now be paid on the first Wednesday of every month, no longer on Saturday like in the old days.

Tant Vonnie went to tell Oom Flip that she had to be at the post office on Wednesday. Right, he said, slapping his hands on his knees. Then he got up and said to the two women: Excuse me, I have some gardening to do.

Sis Bet moved her chair right up against Tant Vonnie's and with her hand on Tant Vonnie's knee she said: Vonnie, have you heard what these wagging tongues are saying?

Bet, I'm busy fixing up the graves of the Big Flu where my children are lying. That is where, as I've told you, I want to put in those Star-of-Bethlehem plants.

There are also vygies that you can have. They can get by without water for a long time, Sis Bet said. Now, she said, after Tant Vonnie had thanked her for the vygies, lifted her hand and put it back on Tant Vonnie's knee, that woman who wants to be Miesies, you know who?

Who? asked Tant Vonnie.

That Miesies September. She told the people of Vatmaar, and you know how they like sticking their noses in other people's business ...

And, Tant Vonnie interrupted her, always adding a tail.

She said ... Sis Bet started again.

Ag, I don't have time for rubbish – and Tant Vonnie stood up.

No, Vonnie, sit. I'll make some tea.

Suzan went out because she knew she was not allowed to listen in when they spoke about grown ups' things.

When Tant Vonnie sat down again, Sis Bet said: That September woman said after that day you were in trouble ... But Vonnie, haven't you seen all those people going to her house?

No, I was at the cemetery as I've already told you.

I was also not there because it's got nothing to do with me and they all regard me as a leading woman, you know, Sis Bet said. So I waited for someone to pass while I worked in the garden. Then Nellie Spyker came past. I called her nearer and so she said: A person can't believe it. Then she said again it's all nonsense, she's sure Miesies September's own husband stole that ring. But the story that Miesies September is spreading is that the prosecutor spoke with her before she went into court. He said he believes her because he can see she's an honest person.

Sis Bet tells Settie September's side of the story

Even the magistrate called me Miesies September in a nice, friendly way, Settie September told everyone. She said when you came in, Vonnie, the policeman showed you the bench where you had to stand. The first thing you apparently did was to turn the Holy Bible upside down, which meant that our God was now supposed to look at you not from above but from below. And when you said: So help me God, apparently you smiled at the magistrate.

When she told this, Settie September stuck her finger in her mouth and pulled it out with a long m-m-m-uu (meaning that she was telling the truth).

She says you winked at him and that was when she saw something in your mouth – a witch's twig.

Jous know, people, Sis Bet mimicked Mevrou September.

She said it made the magistrate immediately take your side. Then somebody wanted to know what about Constable Prins then, she said: Ag, even he was scolded and she felt so sorry for him because he was only doing his duty. I tell you people, she's a witch, a witchdoctor don' stan' a chence agains' her, she said.

She says then the magistrate said you can go but you must come see him in his office. What happen dere is anybody's guess, she said. Jous know, I'm telling you she's dangerous and she got very strong witch metsin.

She begged them all to have nothing to do with you, Vonnie, and to keep you on your place. Because she's just our maid, like jous all know, she said.

The people wanted to leave, because they had heard enough, and they were burning to go and spread the story and add a tail.

Wait, wait, my sisters, Settie then said. I'm nort finish yet. Dere's more. Jous know, I'll never dig a grave for udder people.

We believe you, Settie, a few women said.

My poor husban' went to look for work in the Pan and he was so glad to see me dere. So he says: But how can det witch do such a t'ing?

Oh, I says, so you know she's called a witch?

Yes, says my Johnny, she what dey call a maloi.

When I ask him now what's dat he say: It's an old aunty who wear nutting excep' a necklace wit' der small bones of dead babies aroun' her waist. Dey rub a sort of white fat, or fat mixed wit' a white powder on deir bodies. Dey are ckshully grave robbers. Dey say when a baby dies, or somebody dies from a strange sickness, den dey open der grave and close it again before sun-up. Dey usually work in a team.

Den my husban' say to me: When I was a boy a white policeman caught a maloi. Der policeman was of the sort dat jus' believed what he saw. Der udder black policeman ran away dat night. Der white policeman said it was a old woman who was smelling like rotten meat. He couldn' hold her tight because she was as smood as soap. Dey all ran away and der nex' day dere was a half-open grave. People didn' want to believe it and said it could've been a wild dog dat dug der grave.

An' der white policeman? I asked, Settie said.

Oh, oh, my Johnny said, der sergeant told him: Go an' wash yourself, you stepped in shit.

Then my Johnny says to me: Don't let me talk about malois that rob graves, I'm scared of them.

Ja, an old woman said to Miesies September, there are such things.

Now my husban' did get work from an old baas who knew his farder before he died. This old baas gave Johnny a letter of recommendation to give to his son. But he only had to go see him the nex' Monday. He was so glad when he showed me the envelope, he even kissed me. Jous know, Settie said and looked around to see if anyone perhaps didn't believe her.

We walked home because Ol' Flip was already gorn, Settie went on with her story. But who comes upon us dere near der siding? Der grand lady in Ol' Stoffel Jones' cart dat nobody in Vatmaar can afford to ride in. Meneer Jones stopped like a gentleman should and say to me: Miesies, please climb in, Vatmaar is still very far away.

We climbed in. Johnny lifted me up like only a loving husband will do. When der cart pulled off, my sisters, I looked again because I couldn' believe my eyes. Johnny also pulled on my dress and showed me wit' der eyes. He still says: Good day, Tant Vonnie, and I hear her saying something back. It mus've been her witch's spell because suddenly I felt I'm flying, I tell you, flying t'rough der air right out of der cart!

Ol' Jones jus' rode on because he didn' know what happen. My firs' t'ought was: Where's my Johnny? But he got up on der udder side of der road, out of der dus' and said: Settie my lovie!

What happen? I asked.

I dunno, he said.

We walked der res' of der way to Vatmaar wit'out a word because we could hear our own hearts beating.

Dats der t'anks I got, my sisters, for being good to dat witch.

You shouldn't speak so loud, one woman told her. She can hear what you're saying.

God! Settie September shouted out. Now I won' talk any more, and slapped her hand against her mouth. I'm scared, my sisters. We mus' pray for dat woman.

Yes, said one, the Lord is stronger.

Bet, Tant Vonnie said, you can make of it what you like. Thank you for the tea, it was nice – and she got up from the chair.

Pleasure, Von. That tea is mashoekashanie tea, it grows near the halfway-house.

Yes, I've seen it and I know and use it too. But I didn't know sugar and milk gives it such a nice taste. Suzan! she called. Come. Sleep well, people, and Flip, I'll be here on Wednesday.

The pensioners

Tant Vonnie did not say it was all lies and gossip. She just got up as if she had not heard a word. Wednesday came and all Vatmaar's pensioners went to fetch their money, or like they said: That which is our due.

On the way back those old people who had had a few drinks under the belt would start getting talkative. Some would tell jokes from long ago, others began taunting those sitting next to them with things like: You don't know the days of the Rinderpest. Or: Why did you lie to the white man? Or: She rides with her feet hanging from the trolley. Or: You lied! Or: Look how young she is. And another one again said: The halfie sherry has gone to her legs because her brain is too old to get drunk.

Then everyone laughed and after a while everyone was quiet again. Some dozed off until someone again started with something to break the boredom.

Then there was Oom Houtstok who was forever sitting and twisting his moustache so that the points were sharp as matchsticks. His hat came from the time of King Arthur, he said, and he always swopped the feather for a nicer one whenever he came across one. In his young days he was a real womaniser, people said. Never married, but the father of enough children to fill a

Sunday school class. He loved smacking women on their behinds as he walked past saying: You lovely thing!

He never took strong drink but chewed tobacco. His knife was brown and sticky from the oil from cutting his roll tobacco into plugs. It was said that he could spit around corners and most people, if not everyone, believed this.

Oom Houtstok was often seen standing up behind Oom Flip on the trolley, busy chewing and shifting his little plug of tobacco from cheek to cheek and spitting between his teeth a thin yellow streak – over the heads of everyone on the trolley, with a few feet to spare. The yellow streak always landed in one spot on the ground.

Oom Houtstok was never short of something funny to say, and if it was to some old woman, she would say: You, old Houtstok, can do nothing any more!

To which he would reply: Me – throwing a hefty gob – I'm not scared of that little job …

Everybody would laugh and then one of the women would say: Old Houtstok, you're lying.

That's how they would carry on until the trolley stopped in Vatmaar.

Oom Flip went to drop Tant Vonnie in front of her door and helped her take her things off, something which he didn't do often. Tant Vonnie greased his palm well because for her the ride had been well worth it, and they were in a good mood. Her only disappointment was that there was not enough time to go and visit Kaaitjie. Because she was a new pensioner she had to wait at the back of the queue. They had argued about her identity because they thought she was a Boer woman. Luckily Oom Flip had been waiting outside the post office and they called him to tell the white man he knew her.

The other pensioners got off at what Oom Flip called his trolley stop. They all had to pay the usual sixpence before the horse and cart went back to Vatmaar.

Some, as usual, bought their little tot and on the way had a few sips so that when they finally got off they were happier than happy.

It was a good thing when a pensioner had someone to look after him, someone to whom the old person could say: You are going to bury me. Some people who adopted such an old person, would even take the day off from work to earn "my child's luck" – their bottle of sherry. The grandchildren too – and there were many of them – regularly sat and waited for the pasella sweets and to carry in Ouma's parcels.

So everyone looked forward to the first Wednesday of the month because it was a day to remember. And all you heard when the pensioners saw their children and greeted them, was: The Lord is good to me, my child.

The house and the cemetery

With her first pension money Tant Vonnie bought a lantern and a bottle of paraffin. When she saw Suzan she said: Tonight we're going on our knees with a stronger light. But remember, my child, there is no stronger light than the light of God.

Mama, Suzan said while looking at the packets of food in the lantern light, Mama, the Lord is good.

She never believed that such things could ever come their way.

When old Mrs Wingrove saw the light in the backroom, she came over. Good evening, she said, peeping into the open door. Tonight I've come to visit you. Because she had heard about the pension and had a plan. She knew there were no chairs but she looked around to make sure before she said: Suzan go and fetch your auntie a chair in the kitchen.

Miesies Wingrove must excuse me, Tant Vonnie said. On the way from the Pan I started thinking it would be a decent thing if I started paying rent for the roof over my head. It belongs to you and I thank you from the bottom of my heart.

Then she took out a candle and lit it and took the lantern, lifted up its glass and blew out the light and gave it to Mrs Wingrove: Please, accept it as my thanks.

It was as if the two women's hearts were one because their feelings were the same. I also thank you, Mrs Wingrove said.

To herself, Suzan thought: The Lord is good. But isn't my Mama giving away what He has given us?

Suzan, Mrs Wingrove said, please light the lamp for your auntie. When Suzan handed her the burning lantern, she said: Thank you, you have it, my child, also from the bottom of my heart.

Thank you, Auntie Wingrove, Suzan said and hooked the lantern back on the wire where it had been hanging. Then she snuffed out the candle with her fingers. Because the people said to blow a candle out with your mouth is to blow the light out of your home.

She embraced the old woman and lifted her up from the chair because she was a tiny woman and kissed her.

You're squeezing my breath out, Mrs Wingrove said, laughing.

Thank you so much, Auntie, Suzan said again. I shall take good care of it.

She went out and lit the fire. Mrs Wingrove knew she was going to make tea and said: Suzan, go and fetch another chair for your mother, and three cups and saucers.

It was the first time Mrs Wingrove had come to the back room since moving to Vatmaar. She was Tant Vonnie's landlady since she and her husband had bought Tant Vonnie's house. But she had always told her husband Erick whenever she saw mother and daughter going off to work for mahala – for free – or for someone else's leftovers: What was this woman's sin that she should suffer like this?

And he always replied: She is not of Vatmaar's kind. Her day will come.

Vonnie, she said now, my old man has been gone for three days now. He said he was going to visit our daughter Maggie in the Pan. Maggie has permission to draw my pension, and the next day the two always go and buy groceries. So he'll come back tomorrow with old Flip. I lie awake all night and can't sleep, especially when the old man is in Du Toitspan. Now I've been thinking, and I've told Erick too, I wish you could have your house back someday. He said he would be more than happy to go and live in the Pan and never come back to this dead Vatmaar again. You see, Vonnie, my daughter Maggie has an extra room which still has some of our furniture in it. Because when we bought your house we bought it with your house things. Some of it doesn't exist any more, but there are still a few things which were yours. The rest is mine.

When Erick comes back from Maggie, he always boasts about how nice it was to sleep in his honeymoon bed once again, and then he says he has to go and lie in poor old Vonnie's bed while she has to sleep on the floor. Then he looks at me and says: What kind of Christians are we?

Ja, Tant Vonnie said, we are all Christian people, each one with his own God – and thought: She is Marjorie Wingrove and I still call her Miesies Wingrove no matter how many times she says: No, I'm Marjorie

There are people in Du Toitspan who want to buy the house. But the problem is the two coffins. They say we have to take them with us but Maggie always says: Never! Over my dead body! Not in my house. I've been thinking about it and also told my old man about it before he went to away to Maggie: Now that I hear you've received your pension letter you can buy your house back for the same price we paid you. Erick says you can give us a little bit every month because we know you can't give everything at once. The only thing we want from you, Von, is … she paused and smiled – is that you look after our coffins for us.

Tant Vonnie sighed and held her hand on her heart. My God, she thought, now that I know where to find You. Thank you, she said, thinking at the same time about God and Marjorie. You say you and your husband will be happy if I bought the house back? she said again. I just have to take care of your coffins?

Ja, Vonnie, what do you say?

I'll do it, I give you my word. One: we just have to see how much of the pension money we need to live on. Your share I'll bring to you or you can come and fetch it from the post office on pension day. Just give me a receipt for it. Two: I'll keep the coffins in the house and fill them with khakibos to keep out the mice and insects. Every pension day I'll open the door and see if they're still like they were on the day you asked me to look after them.

Mrs Wingrove, smiling and nodding her head up and down, she said: Now you've really made me happy.

The tea was drunk and Suzan washed the cups. Then she said: Auntie, I'll take the cups back for you.

You know what, Von, I can't believe my eyes! said Mrs Wingrove.

Nor can I, Tant Vonnie said. She looked down at the smeared floor and thought that another door had opened up for her since the last one had shut, and who knew when the wind would blow through?

They got up and Suzan wanted to take the chairs back too. No, Mrs Wingrove stopped her. Keep them here because they used to belong to you and now they are yours again.

The two old women embraced each other and Ma Wingrove, as Suzan had decided to call her from now on, said: Von, please don't lift me up like Suzan did.

They laughed and said good night.

That night mother and daughter could not sleep. They were not used to the lantern and this was still burning when they woke up the next morning with the sun high in the sky.

We still have work we want to do at the cemetery, Tant Vonnie said. Suzan fetched the spade.

The two of them started stacking the limestone rocks in a straight line at the Flu-grave and at the Peg-grave, as they now called the graves. Two grown boys walking about in the veld, came nearer to see what they were doing. They knew that Tant Vonnie was among the poorest of the poor and one of the oldest in Vatmaar. And because Tant Vonnie always had to do what the rich ones said, one boy said to the other: Who gave them this horrible work to do? Nobody else will do it, Roman, the other said.

They came nearer and said together: Good day, Tante – and they smiled at Suzan because they were about her age.

Good afternoon, my children, Tant Vonnie said: You're Nicholas, aren't you?

Nick, Tante, he said.

What are you boys doing in the veld and where are the sheep and goats that you're supposed to be looking after?

Nick remembered that this old woman they were now standing and chatting to was the ouma his mother had called when he had almost died from a constipated stomach. For more than a week his stomach did not work from eating too many prickly pears. I wonder if she remembers me, he thought.

No, Tante, he said, we're going to shoot doves.

He put his hand on the fork of his cattie, turned around and said to Roman: Let's pick up the big ones for them – and pointed to the stones.

Which they did.

It's so nice to have boys in one's company who can behave themselves, not like those Venter boys, thought Suzan, smiling from ear to ear. Her cheerfulness was infectious and soon everyone was in a good mood.

The boys' complexions were soft and fine, not white or yellow. When they were born Vatmaar's midwife, Nurse-sister Gous, said they were true Griquas.

Nurse-sister Gous was known for keeping her patients in bed for ten days, not a day more, not a day less. In the mornings and afternoons she would regularly visit the new baby at home. She charged a labourer's wife two pounds, which could be paid off before the confinement. And five pounds for a well-off mother.

Tant Vonnie suddenly remembered what Nurse-sister Gous

had discussed with her the morning she delivered this strapping boy who was now standing in front of her. With a laugh she had said: If the Griquas have good food, their weight sits in their behinds, a black man's weight, on the other hand, sits at the back of the neck.

But back to the cemetery. The stones were packed in a neat row. When dark rain clouds began to gather, her mother said: Suzan, you go and make us some coffee, cut the bread and put on some jam. Ma and these two boys will gather up the stones on the inside and throw them out.

After they had made heaps of the stones they did not want, Tant Vonnie said: Come, boys, let us go before it rains.

They followed Tant Vonnie in silence. When they came to where the two paths crossed, she said: Oh no, you two big men are coming with me. Suzan is preparing something for us to eat.

This was her way of saying thank you for their help. The three of them reached the house just as the first raindrops began to fall.

Suzan brought the boiling water in from the fireplace outside and made the coffee and said: You're our guests, sit on the chairs.

When they had finished eating and drinking and were ready to leave, Roman said: Tante, tomorrow I'll bring our wheelbarrow to take those stones we don't need away from the graves.

What a good, no, what a wonderful idea, my child! Look, she said, I'll give you a penny for a load of manure from your father's kraal. And then while we're at it we can also carry in some sand with the wheelbarrow.

Nick, who also had something to say before he left, said: We must throw those stones away so that it doesn't look like another grave, Tante.

Suzan burst out laughing and the first rains of the season began to fall.

Away with you! Tant Vonnie said.

Thank you, Tante – and they were out of the door.

Mother and daughter had lived for so long from day to day, without knowing what the following day might bring, that the changes of the last few days were a complete surprise. After the boys had left, each sat on her chair in the light of the lantern. Then Suzan said: Mama, life is good.

What do you think it is that makes life good, my child?

I don't know, Mama.

Just think a bit, think.

After a while Suzan said: Money.

You hit the nail on the head. Yes, Suzan, money can buy almost anything, but not everything. And we must never forget the times when we had nothing. Because there was one thing we were never without.

What's that, Mama?

Our Father – and her mother placed her hand on her heart.

The Wingroves go away

The rain fell softly on the iron roof without a ceiling and gave those in the old outside room a feeling of contentment.

And who would it be standing in the door?

Good evening, you people, he said.

Good evening, Meneer Wingrove, the Müllers greeted him.

Sit, Tant Vonnie said, and Suzan stood up from the chair.

I'm not going to stay long. My old lady has told me about the plan to sell the house back to you, and that you'll keep the coffins ready for us until we need them. Because need them we surely will, he laughed.

Yes, Marjorie and I have reached an agreement, Tant Vonnie said.

Then I'll be going, that's all I wanted to know. I agree with my old lady. I've had a terrible day and I'm tired. Good night people.

Good night, Meneer.

The next day it rained again. Softly, and then it stopped and started again, as if the rain was not in a hurry. Roman came knocking on the door and said: Good morning, Tante. I've thrown four barrowloads on the Flu-grave and three on the Peg-grave.

What a sharp boy!

Suzan gave him two slices of bread and jam.

Roman, Tant Vonnie said, now that the ground is wet, it's easy to turn the soil. But the manure has to be mixed in with the sand, not with the clay. If you do good work I'll give you nine pennies.

Right, Tante – and as he walked away, she heard him say: Where does this ouma get all this money?

She laughed softly.

Mrs Wingrove knew that Suzan could not make a fire because their fireplace was wet and muddy. She went over to the old one-room and said to the two of them: Von, today I'm inviting you for tea, and then we can also talk business.

Good, said Tant Vonnie.

As they were drinking tea in the kitchen Mrs Wingrove said to her husband: We've already discussed things.

He stood up, took a piece of paper from his trunk and said: Here is the deed of sale that I want to take to the lawyer, Von, and we'll keep it at twenty pounds. Do you agree?

Tant Vonnie gave a thank-you chuckle.

Come, Mrs Wingrove said, come and see how neat I've kept your house. There isn't much of your furniture left, but we'll make a plan.

Show me the coffins, Marjorie, said Tant Vonnie, and when they went into the room: I'll keep them just as they are, Meneer Wingrove.

I'm sure you will, he said, closing the door again.

Erick Wingrove was a tall man who wanted his wife to agree with him even when he was in the wrong. He had a head like an egg, pointed at the back. He wore a cap and had hair only where the cap did not cover his head. Underneath the cap his head was the colour of very weak tea, and shiny and smooth like the porcelain teapot in which it was sometimes made. Ma Wingrove was short, with short-cropped, straight grey hair and a high-pitched laugh which changed the atmosphere in the place. From her black ancestors she had inherited a flat nose. Both Wingroves were coloured, only she was lighter from always being indoors. They were proud to be coloured and he often said: What the whites think of themselves is exactly what we think of ourselves, not so, Marge?

Yes, my husband, she would then reply, whether she had heard him or not.

One afternoon Pa Wingrove arrived home from the Pan a very angry man and he said to her: I joined the A.P.O.

What church is that? she asked.

It's not a church, it's a political party. It's called the African People's Organisation.

But now why, my comfort? – which was her little pet name for him.

Remember that dirty Englishman, Basil Green, who was forever visiting us, or should I say walking in whenever you were dishing up for supper? When we lived in the Pan?

Yes, I remember him very well.

Well, his son, the one called Raymond ...

I remember him too.

Well, today he says to me: Boy, come here!

And so what did you say, my comfort?

So I said to him: Up yours! Your family used to eat off my table. Frank du Plooy, the teacher, came past and I tell him what this gogga thinks of me, who am already a grandfather. So he said to me: Oom, Oom is the sort of man we need in the A.P.O. Come with me and join. Which I did. He said the A.P.O was started by Doctor Abdurahman.

Every time when Pa Wingrove came from his daughter Maggie in the Pan, he used to say: Vatmaar is too dead for me.

Ma Wingrove was always happy when he got back, but to put him in his place a bit she would say: You old boy, you can't do anything any more.

This usually shut him up.

Back in the kitchen Ma Wingrove said: Now we're quits, Von. We will also not take away the Welcome Dover stove because it's built in and to take it out would only spoil the kitchen. We don't need it in Du Toitspan, not so, my old man?

Ja, he said. Von, let it remind you of us.

Thank you very much, Tant Vonnie said, and said good night.

The next morning Ma Wingrove was up early and she came to ask Suzan to go and tell Oom Flip to pick her up at home because there were a few things she wanted to take to the Pan. She would pay extra.

Oom Flip came and she loaded her things and tied up bundles until he said: I can't load any more.

She just climbed on and said: The old boy can bring the rest of the stuff.

That was the Saturday. By the Monday the old man had had enough. Von, he said to Tant Vonnie, I can't stand it in this house alone any more. I don't know how my Marge could stand being alone in this house. Flip will just have to load what he can and what's left is yours. My daughter Maggie told me long ago anyway that she doesn't want our rubbish lying all over her house. Her husband is the sort who doesn't speak out in front of his in-laws, but at night he scolds himself to sleep.

Good morning, people, greeted Oom Flip and loaded up his trolley. Pa Wingrove climbed on, doffed his hat to Tant Vonnie and Suzan and said: Now it's all yours, I've left the keys in the doors. Take good care of those two … you know what …

It was not long after that when a man on a bicycle came to ask Oom Flip to take one of the coffins to the Pan. A while later and the same man arrived again. We knew why he had come, but we never heard who the first was to die. Without being told, we knew both had died and what had happened to the coffins.

Kaaitjie remembers

The two boys, Roman and Nick, were a big help to Tant Vonnie. She paid them and always made the price in advance. And what's nicer for a young boy than a piece of home-baked bread, or sometimes vetkoek and jam. This was Tant Vonnie's real appeal but they did not realise it.

The work in the cemetery was finally finished. The Star-of-Bethlehem plants and the vygies looked pretty because it seemed as if the rain had been waiting especially for them to be planted. The day after that the rain fell, and also just for that one day.

Roman and Nicholas were growing up and Suzan was forever joking and laughing with them and helped them with the work her mother gave them to do. Every now and then one of them would put his hand in his pocket. Suzan knew what he was holding, but she made as if she didn't see. They were cousins and both had the surname of Klipsteen. Their thighs were big and round and if they could have been placed naked among their ancestors in the Kalahari, they would have fitted in perfectly.

It was the Sunday before the first Wednesday of the month, the third pension day in Yvonne Müller's life. It was her eldest daughter Kaaitjie's day off. Her month off and day off were the same as that of a farm servant. She got one Sunday in the month off. On the other three Sundays she had to wait outside the church until the Bosmans came out of church. Then she had to take the children by the hand as if they would get lost. But actually it was so that the community could see the Bosmans' status. She had to open the car door for Miesies Ollie Bosman to climb in, and then only close it when she was seated, and then wait for the miesies to give her a nod. Then she had to open the back door, let the two children climb in, close the door and wait for the car to pull off. After that she had to walk back to her outside room and wait there until she was called to fetch her food on the windowsill.

The fourth Sunday was her day off. It began at daybreak and

ended at sunset. Her wages she received on Saturday already because the Bosmans believed that it was wrong to handle money on the day of the Lord. Only sometimes the last Sunday fell on the last day of the month.

On this Sunday she took the road later than usual and took nothing with her because her mother had said: Kaaitjie, my child, from now on you spend your wages on yourself.

First she waited to see if Kenny was not coming, hoping and waiting for his embrace. I wish, I wish, I wish, she kept thinking on and on. And then again: Let me just wait. She wished, she hoped, she yearned, she prayed that nothing had happened to her Kenny. Nothing was the same again since that damned afternoon when Suzan had turned up with the news about her mother. That was the last time she had seen her Kenny.

My whole body is beginning to change, my breasts are not like they used to be, she thought as she walked. Just because I let Kenny come into me. He didn't want to, it was I who felt so free, and who made him do that which made us one, and which gave me my first feeling of such deep enjoyment. When I thought back about it the next morning while I was looking after the children I was so happy, my spirit and heart were one with a big light. And I thought there would be many more such times. How long the next day was. Now the days are short, they fly, because the only thing in my head is: I wish, I wish, I wish … from daybreak until all the stars are in their places. Sleep, my love, sleep without dreams, even though you have left me in the lurch. Pray. I cannot pray any more, I always end with: Tomorrow is another day.

Kaaitjie was past the halfway-house. She came to a standstill in the path and turned around and said to herself: I'm going back. Maybe Kenny's waiting for me at the back gate with his bicycle. Then, without thinking, she turned around again and began to make her way to Vatmaar.

She felt how her mother embraced her when she got home, something she almost never did. And she heard her words: My child, my child. Her mother helped her to a chair saying: Look how swollen your feet are! Suzan, bring a dish of warm water for your sister and put in four spoons of salt.

Tant Vonnie could see what had happened to her daughter. But she thought: I won't ask her about it, I'll make as if I don't see it.

It was a big shame in Vatmaar to have a daughter who was going to have a child without having a husband. And the mother who didn't even know the father of her child!

To hell with them! Tant Vonnie said without meaning the words to come out loud.

I cannot remember if I have ever in my life been at the cemetery, Kaaitjie said. But I'll go with you, Suzan, just to be with you and to make you happy.

They walked on hand in hand, Kaaitjie in the path, because she was barefoot, and Suzan, who had shoes on, alongside through the thorns. They walked in the path made by the wheelbarrow and which brought them first to the Flu-grave. Suzan was very proud of what she, her mother and the two boys had achieved. The grave looked so lively under the mass of flowers that made it stand out against the drab surroundings.

Mama says we'll never know how many are sleeping here, Suzan said looking at her sister.

Ja, no names, forgotten, only the Big Flu that's remembered and that will also be forgotten with time. Kaaitjie walked over to a grave on the side which was also filled with flowers, pointed to it and said: And this one?

Oh, that's Mama's friend, Oom Norman.

What, Oom Norman? Did I hear you say Norman?

Yes, Norman, Sister.

Kaaitjie was pulled out of her present sadness and back to an old pain that had grown closed, but of which the hurt still lingered in her heart.

283

Just then her bare foot caught the hook of the peg and she almost fell. The hook had caught the top of her toe and blood began to ooze out. When she looked down, she caught her breath, but then she called out in a broken voice: Now I see you again, you murderer, and she swore at the tent peg.

She walked away, the tears streaming like water down her cheeks. With her bare feet she stepped onto the thorns without feeling any pain. Until she came to an anthill and went to sit on it.

Suzan wiped off her sister's cheeks with her dress.

I cannot cry any more, my little sister, Kaaitjie said.

Suzan knelt in front of her and put her head in her sister's lap. Kaaitjie let her hands rest on her sister's head. They remained sitting like this for a long time. Then Suzan turned around and sat down on the ground between her sister's feet and told her the story of Oom Norman as her mother had told it to her. She ended it with her mother's words: And don't ever ask me again.

After a while Kaaitjie was once again her old self. The little Windhoek-German blood in her which made it possible for her to take a lot from those who caused hurt, also made her say to herself now: Enough, no more, it's gone far enough.

It's true what our Mama has told you, but what I'm going to tell you now, Suzan, is also true. And after I've told it to you, you must forget it. Promise?

Suzan smiled and nodded her head.

Life is precious. If you lose it, what is it that you lose, yourself or life? Kaaitjie began.

Suzan kept quiet and Kaaitjie went on. It is I who caused Norman's death. Only I was too young to think of myself as the murderer. He was the first man to kiss me and to say: I love you, little kitten. I loved him too, but more in a childlike way. I always brought him tea because he said he had learnt to drink it in the army. I would always stand right in front of him so that Mama couldn't see him kissing my hand.

Did Mama like him? Suzan asked.

Yes, she did, but more like a big sister would. I think it was because he used to be Papa's friend. Then suddenly he couldn't keep away from us. Every day he came to Vatmaar and every day he brought something nice, for me, not for Mama. Then one cold winter's night, I will never forget it because in the morning everything was pure white outside. They said it was the worst frost we had had in years. That day Mama did the washing while I had to clean the house.

He came as usual and went to sit down on the chair. I walked past him and he put his arms around me and held me tight and said: Little kitten, I want to marry you. I can't keep it in any longer. I'm going to ask Vonnie because I want her for my mother.

No, wait, I said. And where I came across this I don't know but I said: A man must first go and knock a peg into my brothers and sisters' grave at midnight before he can have me.

Mama didn't know about our bet. We both lost. It was hard for me to forget Normy, but I soon grew out of it. That is what lies behind, and I know what it is, but what lies ahead I don't know. Now it's your Ouboet, as you call him, who has stolen my heart and broken the power which that peg had over me. But in that tent peg also lies a part of Kaaitjie Müller.

The two sister sat quietly next to each other, each one with her own thoughts. Then Kaaitjie said: What's happening now? Feel here, Suzan.

She felt and said: I feel nothing.

But then it came again, a jump or a kick in Kaaitjie's stomach. Ooh, you're alive! Kaaitjie said.

I also felt the kick.

It's the first time that I feel life, Kaaitjie said.

So you're going to have a baby?

Yes, came the soft reply.

I feel happy for your part, sister. Why don't you have the baby tonight here at home?

Kaaitjie gave a real Kaaitjie-laugh, the laugh she used to have long before she knew about someone like Kenneth Kleinhans. He'll come in his own time, she said.

Back at the house – because they were back in their own house again – their mother gave them a saucer of dried fruit and Kaaitjie said to her sister: Now the thorns are burning. Some must've broken off.

That's my work, Suzan replied. She put a bucket of water down by her sister's feet and went to kneel in front of her with a towel and a needle. Then she began to take out the thorns that had broken off. Suzan's Vatmaar brain could take only one thought at a time. When is the child coming? was all she could think about.

It was the small of the night, as the people of Vatmaar call the time soon after midnight, when Kaaitjie woke up suddenly and sat up straight in bed, her sleep disturbed by a dream. She said softly to herself: It was so real.

Normy sat on his favourite chair. He was clean shaven and she remembered once telling him she didn't like him with a beard. He smiled at her and said: My kitten, where I am there is just peace and compassion. Look after yourself. He smiled again. She woke up and looked at the outlines of the chairs in the darkness. It seemed as if the room was full of a different kind of light. She lay down again. What is lost you never get back again. I must make the best of it, she thought. And smiling she fell asleep again.

Oom Chai goes to the Free State with the family Bible

On the day before he would have been seventy, the three score years and ten which the Psalmist speaks about, Oom Chai had a young ox slaughtered. He was pleased with himself because he had reached the years granted to the offspring of Adam.

Wood from the witgat tree, which makes a red-hot coal when burned, was gathered and neatly stacked away. The thick grid lay ready on the stones for the braaiing of the meat. The Catholic Father was invited to say a prayer and a few words. But he sent word that he could not come as Oom Chai was not Catholic. That was the message that Tommy Lewis had brought from the Pan.

Oom Chai then said to Tommy: I'm not disabled. I can also pray. The Lord gave me a mouth too.

A week before, he had called some of the leading men together and told them he would be celebrating his seventieth birthday on Sunday. One wanted to know how he could be so sure that his birthday was on Sunday, 17 May. Oom Chai said he was very pleased his friends wanted him to be sure. Then he disappeared into his bedroom and came back with his family Bible. It was in a pillowcase plus wrapped in what looked like a piece of silk. The Bible was badly tattered because it was, as Oom Chai put it, the Word written in the first Afrikaans. By this he meant Dutch.

There were lots of names and marriages written in, and in some places the ink was completely faded. They are my ancestors, Oom Chai said. And then there were a few Terreblanches recorded, and then: *Steven Petrus, 11 December 1850.* And just underneath that: *Charles Hendrik, 17 May 1855.*

You see? he said to them, I am Charles. My older brother is Steven. I have decided to go to the Free State to take the family Bible to him. He has children, and as you all know, that wild horse that I shoed when the others were afraid to do it has weakened my breeding vein.

The big men all nodded their heads as if they knew and felt sorry for Oom Chai.

Walking to his kraal, he said: The wood is ready and that ox with the bald patch and the two sheep. And if it's not enough then take the ram too.

We'll slaughter the ram too, an old man said, because it's luckier to have meat over than to be short.

Ja, old Houtstok, you're also always so clever.

Oom Houtstok was apparently much older than Oom Chai and you would always find him among the oumas. All I ask, he said now, is that I don't have to lift a finger.

287

Just keep an eye on things for me, old Houtstok, Oom Chai said. Then he called Sis Bet and asked her to get together a few leading women and to see that there was enough roosterkoek, ginger-beer and khadie for the entire Vatmaar. And tell them to tell our people not to cook on Sunday, 17 May, he reminded her. Bet, you and I will go with your husband to the Pan and buy whatever you need. And I'll pay you extra for the khadie.

No, no, Chai, Sis Bet said, the khadie's on the house.

Then that's that, the old man said.

That was the Sunday when Kaaitjie's mother told her to sleep at home. It was a feast that Vatmaar still talks about to this day. And Oom Chai was in his element. After the toast he told us a little of his life story. But he had to cut it short because the old girls kept saying: Now tell us about your girlfriends.

There was laughter and everyone was happy.

Then we started eating. There was enough for everyone and some left over to be sneaked home. Everyone was glad to see Kaaitjie and as was the custom at Vatmaar, everyone wanted to shake her hand. And yet, that afternoon, when she and Suzan were walking home she said: I feel so unwanted and alone, as if I'm a disappointment.

Then all the young girls began to sing without shame: Mama, I want a man – with a champagne sparkle in the eye and each one dreaming of the man she wanted. And the big boys with their bare feet dreaming of white trousers when they sang: The white trousers they don't fit me, the white trousers have no crease, the white trousers are so tight.

Vatmaar had never known such merriment before and the people asked Oom Chai if he would throw another party the following year. He didn't answer, just giggled at a thought which didn't show on his face.

On the Tuesday he went to the Pan with Oom Flip to take the train to the Free State to go and give his family Bible to his brother, Oom Steven.

The feast gave us the feeling of being one big family without division and hate, Oom Houtstok said where we all gathered to say goodbye to Oom Chai.

The suffering of Katrina Müller

For Kaaitjie the winter had been long and monotonous. It was now October and the days began to get long and warm, but for her it was just another day, another night with nothing in between. She gave all her attention to the two children in her care.

It felt to her as if the two girls, one two and the other four years old, had become part of her. They accepted her too as if she was one of them. Their mother did not like the way they put their arms around her neck and the affectionate way in which they said her name.

Mevrou Ollie Bosman did not play or laugh with her children. It was Kaaitjie and their father, Meneer Willem Bosman, who gave them attention. He also once walked up to them and said something friendly to Kaaitjie that made her and the children laugh.

It was then that she thought: He's just like Kenny.

Meneer Bosman had heard from Kenny's boss what had happened to him and that a part of the building was still not finished because they were waiting for Kenny to come out of hospital. But he did not talk to her about this.

This Meneer Willem Bosman was a gentle man and his wife just the opposite – very crude and without feeling for anyone who was not "one of us". She eventually went so far as to tell him: That stomach of the nursemaid has got something to do with you.

That hurt him very much and he told her he would bring the poor girl to her: And if she says it's mine then I'll take her!

No, my husband, she said immediately, it's only a joke. I know it's that Hotnot's child who does white people's work.

Then she did what she always did whenever she had hurt him or said something nasty about his mother, she kissed him and pulled him by the hand into the bedroom to do that to him to which he could not say no. And when it was all over she knew she could ask him just what she liked, he almost never said no to her then.

Just the previous day Mr Andrew Burns, the man who was building the new Masonic Temple, had come to see her. It was the third time he had come to her house, but it was the second letter he had brought from his carpenter.

The first time Kenny had written to his boss asking him to go and see Kaaitjie at the Bosmans to tell her he has not forgotten her and never would. That he had had an accident but hoped to see her again soon.

Mevrou Bosman told Mr Burns he shouldn't bother, she would pass on the message. She is a pleasant, clean girl, she said. I'll tell her tonight when she comes in to eat or after she has had a bath.

She lied.

When Mr Burns brought the first letter, she said: Kaaitjie was very happy the first time to hear that her friend still thinks about her. She'll be very happy to get the letter. It's much better than just a message because she can read the letter over and over – just like I used to do when my husband and I were courting, she laughed.

Mr Burns said goodbye and left. She took the letter, tore it in half and threw it in the stove.

The second letter she found on the floor when she opened the front door. It had been slid under the door.

Aah, she said to herself, this letter I'm going to read.

She was surprised to learn that Kenny did not know that Kaaitjie was pregnant. How is it possible? she wondered. Now she was the one who was reading the letter over and over.

That night she couldn't sleep because she began believing her own suspicions. She said nothing to he husband, but thought: I'll keep my eyes open from now on.

The next day after work her husband came inside through the kitchen door, something he never did. She instructed her housemaid to see what the nursemaid did when the baas was near her.

Ja, my Miesies, the black woman said. The white man he like that kind. Because they never say no.

She had once heard what one baas had told another baas when she was still working for Baas Moses: They don't lie still.

Whether this humble maid had meant to stir up emotions in her Miesies with her answer, nobody will ever know. What is true though, is that Mevrou Bosman got a blinding headache. Her only thought was: It is him!

After all, did Oom Kallie, one of the church deacons, not have a child with one of his maids? It sent his wife to the grave. Then her thoughts shifted from her husband to her hatred for that which had caused Kaaitjie's stomach to swell like that. She began taking pills at night because she was going through hell, lying awake next to her sleeping husband.

Then, one morning, she went to sit with the children to speak to Kaaitjie in order to win her confidence. Kaaitjie was very respectful as usual. It was just: Ja, Miesies, and: Ja, Miesies.

Walking away, Ollie Bosman said to herself: As soon as her stomach's down I'll get rid of her.

The next day, at the church mothers' meeting, her friends were very concerned about how thin she was getting. You have to go to the doctor, an old school friend told her.

Marie, she replied, I can trust you. After the meeting I'll tell you everything.

What, your husband?

Yes, him.

Come, said Marie Koster. We can attend the meeting again next month. Your feelings are more important.

They went to sit in Marie Koster's Chevrolet car and she told her friend about her maid's stomach and who she believed was the father. She told her story in such a way that her friend said: I believe you, Ollie.

Then they sat quietly for a long time.

What are you thinking, Marie? Ollie Bosman asked.

There is only one way to get out of this. Chase her away and she'll bring the child to see its father.

Mevrou Bosman began to cry bitterly. Cry, cry, my friend, I feel it with you, Marie Koster said.

When, after a while, she asked again: What are you thinking about, Marie? her friend replied: As I said, there is only one solution. Let's go and see that Moslem woman, Motta Fatima.

Do you know her?

Yes, I know her quite well. That Moslem woman will take away that big stomach very quickly.

They drove through the old section of Du Toitspan and knocked on the door of one of the first homes to be built in the Pan by well-off people. A young girl opened and Marie Koster said: Good afternoon, is Motta here?

Nay, she said, but come and sit.

Ollie Bosman never knew that such places existed in the Pan. Expensive wallpaper and furniture, and two huge framed pictures on the wall with Arabic writing. What's this? she asked.

It's their language, her friend said softly.

Then a dark Indian man came in and greeted them: Goorafternoon, merrems.

Good afternoon, the two women returned the greeting.

The Motta's gone to town, she be here now, he said and went out. The girl again opened the inside door and another, slightly older girl came in with tea and biscuits on a tray.

They smiled at the two girls because they were white and dressed in long, old fashioned dresses and golden earrings. They can't be older than ten, twelve, thought Ollie Bosman.

They were busy drinking their tea when the Motta, as an older Malay woman is called, entered. They greeted and she said: Marie, what can I do for you?

The usual, Motta, Marie said.

The price has gone up. Two pounds for the hook and five pounds for the pump and Lysal. Payment in advance – she said.

Fine, Motta. It's a young girl. I'll tell her and come back to you.

That's good, the Motta said, my door is always open.

The two women said goodbye, climbed into the Chevrolet and drove off.

Ollie Bosman was confused. This Motta was also very dark. How do they come by those white girls? How can that be, Marie? she asked.

They have Moslem names, replied Marie Koster. The one is Khadija and the other is Aysha. They are brought up in the Moslem religion. They won't eat our food. They call our food geram and their food halaal. They batcha, pray, before they slaughter an animal. To them pork is worse than the devil himself. They are registered by their Moslem surnames at the births and deaths office, but I don't know what it is.

They look like our people but they are Coolies? Ollie Bosman asked again.

Do you know why they rear them? They get them while they are still babies. I don't know where, so don't ask me. Sometimes they pay the mother of the baby, usually young girls from another town who don't want their parents to know they have a child. A few years ago life was much harder than it is now, especially after the war. Many a poor girl who was put into trouble by soldiers, had their children adopted, usually at least by someone in the family. Some babies were given up out of poverty. My mother once told me: A mother who gives her baby away because she can't afford it, and because the child can have a better life with someone else, has a greater love for her child than a mother who allows her child to suffer without reason. Motta and them prefer baby girls.

Why? Ollie Bosman wanted to know.

When they become young girls, they are married off to the first man who can pay their price and who they're satisfied with. In most cases the man first sends his mother. They call the bride price mosgavie. And for these two innocent girls Motta and her husband Dulla could demand a high mosgavie.

And what if the girls don't like the man or don't want him? They don't have a choice, even if it is an old man. They call it "the faith". She is possibly the second or the fourth wife. All he has to do is see that he treats all his wives the same whether this is with love or with earthly goods. And it's very important that she's a virgin, a moekalaf. The morning after the nikka, the wedding, the Mottas, the old women come to inspect the bedsheets to make sure.

How do you know all these things, Marie? Ollie Bosman wanted to know.

My housemaid is a Moslem whose husband kicked her out just because she couldn't have children. She told me about Motta and about the faith.

Now if they find out after the nikka that this new wife cannot be moulded by her husband or her mother-in-law to their wishes, then he can divorce her. They call it talak. All he has to do is say he talaks her three times, sometimes in the presence of an Imam, a Moslem priest. Then she is sent back to her parents. If she is lucky she may marry again. But most men say that she has been spoilt because she is no longer a moekalaf. They call their God Allah.

Marie, tell me, Ollie Bosman wanted to know more, do these people love their daughters?

They are full of love. Of course they love them. Didn't you see how happy the two girls were, and what's more, how womanly? The Moslem woman is subservient to her husband. To them it is a man's world, and his religion determines when he should have his wife or wives – what I mean is sleep with them, you understand?

Ollie Bosman nodded.

To them it is about man marrying woman. With some of us Christians it is about men being in love with other men and women who live with other women.

It's true, Ollie Bosman said.

Adultery is their biggest crime.

What about murder? asked Ollie.

Yes, but adultery is worse than murder. But the man never gets blamed, it's always the poor woman who has to take the blame. And her punishment is very severe, too severe to talk about.

Marie, Ollie Bosman began again, what about a ngaka, a Kaffir doctor? Wouldn't it be easier to get the medicine and throw it in her food? One can then send her home and tell her she can have the week off. And then she can die at home.

No, no, Marie stopped her, it's dangerous and it will take time.

What d'you mean take time?

A Kaffir doctor and a Moslem doctor, a ngaka and a dukkum, are equally cunning. They'll give you medicine and tell you if it doesn't work you must come back because the medicine he has to give this specific person is finished and he will have to go to the bush soon to look for this special medicine. And they don't come cheap, Ollie. If you go to them in a car like this they'll charge you the ears off your head. They will milk you and there's nothing you can do about it. You, Ollie Bosman, for example can't tell your husband that you've been to see a dukkum or a ngaka to kill your nursemaid because she was going to have his child, right or wrong?

No, no, she cried and the tears began to roll.

Marie Koster put her arms around her friend and said: The hook's the thing.

I'll do what you think is the best to get this child of Satan on his trident to throw in the fire which he keeps specially for people like this nursemaid.

Marie looked at her watch with a start. It's late. The meeting's over, we have to go home.

She stopped at Ollie's car, which was parked just out of sight of the church. Look, she said, we've arranged everything with Motta Fatima. Pay the two pounds and let her use the hook. But first you have to get the maid to go with you and convince her that it's for her own good. Tell her this woman is a midwife and that you and most of the women in the Pan went to her because after she has treated you, the birth is so much easier, and that she'll never be sorry for following the advice of her miesies. Tell her you'll take her shopping and buy all her baby clothes and nappies after the Motta has worked on her. And that after the birth you'll take her back to the shop to buy a baptism gown. You can also just ask her what she would like, a boy or a girl. And the name – and Marie laughed. Tell her we'll call him Willem, your husband's firstborn son.

She teased her friend because they were two of a kind. Ollie's tears began to flow again. Wipe off your tears before you get out, old Ollie, Marie said, leaning over to open the door for her friend.

Mevrou Bosman arrived home late and found Kaaitjie in the bathroom washing the children. It was the only time she was allowed indoors. The housemaid was sitting on a bench near the door to try and hear something which she could tell her miesies.

Good afternoon, Lettie, Mevrou Bosman whispered. I see you've started playing spy.

Lettie laughed and winked, carrying the bench back to the kitchen. She sat on the bench, ready to be called.

It was the first time Mevrou Bosman ever helped dry her children. Kaaitjie wondered: What's come over her?

To her Ollie Bosman was one of the luckier ones on earth, she was her miesies and her employer, nothing more, nothing less. But when the children were in their nightclothes, she took Kaaitjie's hands and said: Come, I want to talk to you. I am fond of you and I hope you're fond of me too.

Kaaitjie laughed because it was unexpected.

Mevrou Bosman led her outside. Under the big tree where the children's swing hung, she said: I wanted to tell you before but there was no time. But now that we're alone I want to tell you from the bottom of my heart how much I care for you. Just the other day I told the baas what a good person you are. And he told me to talk to you and tell you because we would like to help you. He said if your child is born then he or she should play with our two daughters, then the baby doesn't have to lie and cry all alone in the storeroom.

Kaaitjie gave a sorrowful smile and said: Thank you, my Miesies, it's nice to know that I am not alone. Again I thank you.

Carefully and with much conviction Mevrou Bosman told her what she and Marie Koster had discussed. Kaaitjie again thanked her and Mevrou Bosman went to fetch her food from the kitchen. Come, my good little maid, she said, giving it to Kaaitjie, something which she had never done before. Remember, she said, tomorrow.

The next morning she asked her housemaid to look after the children because she and the nursemaid had something important to do. Keep your fingers crossed, my maid, she said. They both laughed and Mevrou Bosman called Kaaitjie and let her get into the car and drove off.

They say a person can sense when there's a snake in the grass, but this woman, this human-snake, buried her poison in her thoughts and hid it behind a smile. When Kaaitjie looked again, the car had stopped in front of a house with a red, curved corrugated iron verandah roof and brown wooden verandah pillars. On the whitewashed wall was painted a large number two.

Here we are. Get out.

Kaaitjie could feel that something was not right. Like many poor people she had developed a sixth sense. She climbed out and saw nothing because her thoughts were turned inwards. Master, she said in her thoughts. Her senses and that which is called the soul, were delicately quivering. She took a deep breath and repeated in her mind: Master.

The darkness of her sorrow at once lightened. I know You are with me, she heard herself say out loud.

Come, don't stand there like a block, I'm your miesies.

Mevrou Bosman had to take Kaaitjie by her arm to get through to her. She did not realise that this creature with her had just made contact with the greatest of all Madams, her Inner Master.

When they knocked a servant opened the door.

Is the Motta here? Mevrou Bosman asked.

Come inside, sit, the servant said.

Tell the merrem I'm coming, Fatima Motta called from somewhere in the backyard.

Here she is and here is the two pounds for the hook, Motta, the white woman said when Motta eventually appeared. She smiled and, touching the older woman's shoulder, said: You know what to do.

The Motta nodded. Don't worry, she said and left the room.

Then I'll say goodbye.

Mevrou Bosman opened the door and left, leaving Kaaitjie alone in a strange world.

The poor girl – no other word suited her better – stood alone in a world she knew nothing about. It all looked clean and expensive, but the atmosphere warned her.

Why are those sticks burning in a raw potato giving off a smoke that smells as if it had to clean the room of some or other unseen thing? Why did the Miesies give this woman, whom she called Motta, two pounds saying it was for the hook? And why has she left because I heard her car drive off? All these thoughts were going through Kaaitjie's head.

I can't leave, she said to herself. I must wait and see.

When the Motta came in she was still standing in the same place because nobody had said she could sit. The woman looked at Kaaitjie carefully as if to make sure she would recognise her if she saw her again. Then she locked the front door. Her servant carried in a long bench and newspaper. She also brought a jar of Vaseline and something wrapped in newspaper, and put it on the table.

The Motta spread the newspaper on the bench and looked Kaaitjie up and down. Then she went through an open door to the back and spoke to a man. Abdullah, she said, the Boer woman came to drop the bitch here. And she's left with her car.

Why don't you wait till she comes back with the money, Fatima?

Nay, Dulla, she paid, and she stays in the new town, more than a mile from here. This bitch will never make it if I use the hook.

Ask her, Fatima old girl. Maybe she wants to sell the baby. She can stay here until the time comes. We'll pay her well. If it's a girl we give her twice the sum.

He peeped through the open door.

To me she looks good. An' I'm sure it's a white man's child. Maybe we'll get a new daughter.

Kaaitjie heard everything although she did not know some of the words. The Motta came back all smiles, took her hand and led her to a chair. Sit, my child, she said. I'll fetch some tea for you and me.

She came back with two cups of tea and said: How much sugar?

Two, Kaaitjie replied. Please.

After they had drunk the tea, the Motta told her what she had just overheard. Kaaitjie could not understand what the woman wanted. Auntie, I don't understand, she said.

Then the Motta repeated everything, but more slowly, ending with: Such an offer you never get again in your life.

It's true, said Kaaitjie. Then she shook her head from side to side and put her hand on her breast and stammered: I will never, never sell Kenny's child.

Then we have to finish what you came for. I've already been paid for it.

She stood up, closed the door and locked it. Then she said to Kaaitjie: Pull off your bloomers and go lay on the bench. Just like when you did it. With your legs open. Then I take the hook.

When she took the hook from the newspaper Kaaitjie got a fright and thought to herself: Oh, so that's the hook.

It was a piece of fence wire, one end was straight, the other bent into a hook. Both points had been sharpened.

Then I'll rub on some Vesleen, the woman explained further. But it is still very cold! – and she walked to the door, opened it and shouted: Vela, come here!

The black woman who had brought in the bench came running.

Vela, take the hook and rub it warm.

At that moment Kaaitjie got up from the chair with the same fearlessness her father had when he had led the bayonet charge. This you will never do, she said to the Motta.

She unlocked the front door herself and turned around for the last time and gave the Moslem woman a fierce look. Then she walked out.

She walked back the way they had come, but somewhere she must've made a mistake because she ended up on the outskirts of Du Toitspan. She turned back and walked through old Du Toitspan seeing places and things which she never knew existed and which she could not understand: fences with the names of gangs painted on them, filthy backstreets where the mailers and the fahfee runners and dagga peddlers rose fully clothed, rubbing the sleep from their eyes with their knuckles instead of with water.

They looked at this girl walking past them on her own, and then looked again to make sure that she was pregnant. Nobody asked where she was going or where she had come from although they were all curious. Luckily the road led onto a neat gravel road, which she recognised because the church was on the next corner.

At the Bosmans' back gate she found the housemaid, leaning with her arms on the gate as if waiting for her.

Kaaitjie didn't say a word, just opened the gate and walked to the storeroom. She took off her servant's jacket, took the one blanket which was hers, packed into it the slate and other things which Kenny had given her, and tied the blanket's four corners together. She pushed her arm through it and walked out without closing the door.

Lettie ran to tell her miesies that Kaaitjie had come back and taken her things. It seemed to her that her stomach was flat.

I believe you, Mevrou Bosman said. That hook is powerful, my friend, Marie, told me.

She gave Lettie half a crown, saying: Look how good I am to you.

Thank you, my Miesies, Lettie replied.

Kaaitjie goes to jail

Mevrou Bosman immediately went to the police station to lay a charge against Kaaitjie for breaking her service contract.

The sergeant said: The police patrol for Vatmaar is not ready yet.

Vatmaar had been without its mounted policeman for four months when the first Harley-Davidson motor-bike with side-car, or side-bucket as the people of Vatmaar called it, arrived there. It was a new thing and the children of Vatmaar ran out of their houses to shout out their excitement, especially at the second man riding on one wheel only.

The whole thing began when someone on the farm Happy Dreams next to Vatmaar had stolen a sheep. Meneer Rudolph Kamies, the owner, went to report the theft in Du Toitspan, but there was no one to investigate the case. Kamies then took his complaint to the Member of Parliament for Du Toitspan. The result was that the magistrate was transferred to another town and three policemen from elsewhere were given instructions to serve Vatmaar.

The actual cause of these changes was the new horse with which Constable Prins once came to patrol Vatmaar. On the way back, passing the halfway-house, the horse suddenly bolted, sending its rider flying. People said the animal had seen the Boer freedom fighter hanging from the tree.

The constable fell, hitting the side of his head on a stone and lay there unconscious for almost half a day.

The workers who worked in Du Toitspan almost never walked alone, but all together because they said it shortened the road. In a bunch there is always someone who has something to say. On the day that Constable Prins fell off his horse, they stopped under the big camel thorn tree.

But that's the people catcher who rides the horse! Koos Vlermuis shouted to the others and went closer.

Let's go, said a man, I don't have time for his yes-and-no.

Their attitude was not one of hatred, but they regarded a police-man as someone who used the law against the poor people.

Just then Mr Tommy Lewis came by on his bicycle. He got off and laid his bicycle down in the path. He went to see what had happened and saw a face which reminded him of his father. It was he who went to report the constable's accident to Sergeant Piet Cronje.

The constable was taken to the Victoria Hospital in Du Toits-pan. He died there the next day, still unconscious. That's how it came about that Vatmaar was given three new men of the law.

Sergeant Piet Cronje, a white man. Detective-Sergeant Walter Kerns, one of the South Africans who was known as a coloured – or Cape-boys, as it was written on the cenotaph at Mafeking, erected for the fallen of this section who fought for the British against the Boers. The third policeman was Constable William Masibi, who wore a big helmet, shorts with leggings, a knobkierie and handcuffs. His race classification was Native, or "Naturel" in Afrikaans. He was so named, the joke went, because the first two came from God but poor old Masibi came from nature. Actually out of Africa, but because African and Afrikaner sounded so alike, they did not want to call him African.

Constable William Masibi was a friendly man and the children always shouted greetings to him when he came past in the motor-bike's side-car. Oom Masibi! they would shout. Then he would lift his hand up like a prince and sometimes take off his helmet and wave to them with that. Vatmaar used to say: He's one of us.

The coloured inspector would then give it stick, taking the corners on two wheels to the delight of the onlookers.

This Detective-Sergeant Kerns was the most hated man Vatmaar had ever known. They said Constable Prins carried out his duties like a man and always greeted before speaking to anybody, it didn't matter who it was. But this Kerns was more of a skollie than a man. That's how Boitjie Afrika judged him.

Sergeant Cronje never came to Vatmaar. He put Sergeant Kerns in charge and it went to his head. One day we heard that he had had an accident and that Oom Masibi was in hospital. Boitjie then said: It's I who bewitched Kerns – and everyone in Vatmaar believed him.

But now back to the police station in Du Toitspan. Sergeant Cronje told Mevrou Bosman that the patrol would only go back to Vatmaar the following morning, and added: But your maid won't be allowed to work for somebody else because she has broken the law. The usual punishment is one month's hard labour. And after she has served her sentence it's her choice whether she wants to work for you again or not.

I just want to teach her a lesson, Sergeant, and put her in her place. Thank you, Oom Piet. I'll see Oom Piet on Sunday at Holy Communion.

Thank you for your co-operation, Mevrou Bosman.

In the meantime, Kaaitjie had again taken the footpath to her mother's house. Eventually she stumbled into the house and collapsed on the floor. It was late afternoon and she had been on her feet since that morning, and with only one cup of tea at the Motta's house having passed her lips.

Luckily these things usually happen when there is somebody around to help. Sis Bet happened to be visiting Kaaitjie's mother and she said immediately: Von, bring the rooilaventel and some water. Suzan, you take off the shoes. See how swollen her feet are! Get some hot water going.

All Tant Vonnie could say was: My child, my child. What have they done to my Kaaitjie!

When she opened her eyes after a while, the two older women made her sit up and carried her onto a chair so that she could soak her feet in warm salt water. Then Tant Vonnie gave her a cup of mashoekashanie with milk and sugar, and a vetkock.

Eat, my child, she said, and to Sis Bet: I can see she's hungry. Kaaitjie, take your time, I'll get the bed ready. And Suzan, take the towel and dry your sister's feet when she's ready.

Before sunset Kaaitjie was fast asleep under the blankets, her first good sleep in months because thoughts about Kenny did not keep her awake now. The two older women went to sit outside. Suzan put a hand under the blanket and felt her sister's stomach. She wanted to know if that thing inside was still kicking and wished the time would come for it to come out. Kaaitjie slept on.

Outside Sis Bet was saying: She's completely run down, she needs a good rest and some herbs to give her back her strength.

You're right, Bet, Tant Vonnie said. I'll prepare some parsley and lucerne tea.

Yes, that will perk her up quickly.

I won't ask her what happened, Bet. Suzan told me about it, she calls the man Ouboet and she's fond of him. The worst is that he's just disappeared and the longing for him is killing my child. Kaaitjie never tells me her secrets, but I get everything from Suzan, without asking her.

Well, just be careful, said Sis Bet. They always add on something when they repeat things.

Suzan says she felt the thing inside give a kick.

Sis Bet laughed. You're on the way to becoming an ouma, Von.

I could use a son, Tant Vonnie laughed back.

After a week of home remedies, Kaaitjie was strong enough to help her mother around the house, something she hadn't done in years.

Now that she was on the way to becoming a mother herself, she took her mother into her confidence and told her everything, ending with: It wasn't Kenny who wanted to do it, it was me, Mama.

Mother embraced daughter and said: I know, I understand. I have a feeling your Kenny will come back, but when I don't know.

The day after Kaaitjie had arrived at her mother's house, Sergeant Cronje was off duty. His appendix had to be removed, they said. Detective-Sergeant Walter Kerns was now in charge of the charge-office in the Pan and Constable William Masibi had to go and do the rounds in Vatmaar on his bicycle, because he was not allowed to ride the motor-bike.

When he heard that he had to investigate a complaint of absconding from work against a servant by the name of Kaaitjie, he thought to himself: It's only poor people who are put in jail for absconding. And another thing, I'll either have to put her on the bicycle or let her walk to the Pan. I'll just tell Sergeant Kerns there is nobody by that name in Vatmaar.

And so it went on for three weeks. In the fourth week Sergeant Cronje was back in the charge-office, but he had forgotten the charge against the maid. When he bumped into Mevrou Bosman at the butcher, she asked him: Oom Piet, has Oom Piet caught the maid yet?

He had been off duty for three weeks, he told her, but promised to find out as soon as possible. The next day he ordered Sergeant Kerns to bring her in, and if he is too weak to carry out his duties, he, Cronje, would fetch her himself.

Because it was pension day, Tant Vonnie and Suzan had gone that morning with Oom Flip and the other pensioners. She planned to buy some calico, flannel and buttons for baby clothes and napkins. Mama, we mustn't forget to buy a big safety-pin and something nice for Sister, said Suzan.

Kaaitjie had to go and lie down again after she had cleaned the house, Tant Vonnie said, because she had to get as much rest as possible before her time came.

The two left home in a pleasant mood. And while they were in the Pan, Sergeant Kerns stopped at Sis Bet's house and asked her if she knew anyone called Kaaitjie. Sis Bet, thinking this had something to do with the father of the unborn child, showed him the house, saying: She stays in that house with the thorn tree.

The motor-bike with side-car stopped at the thorn tree and Sergeant Kerns shouted to a young woman sweeping the stoep: Are you Kaaitjie?

She stepped closer and said: Yes, Meneer.

Climb in.

Why? she asked.

You'll see, he said. Sit on the constable's lap.

Kaaitjie also thought this had something to do with Kenny and climbed in.

Is it about Kenny? she asked.

I said you'll see, he said again.

When they rode past Sis Bet, she waved to her. The motor-bike made a big noise and the wind burned her face. She could not get a word out before they stopped at the charge-office with her.

Get out, hurry up! Sergeant Kerns shouted.

The black constable just shook his head. What kind of law is this? he thought to himself. To do this, to one of your own people, what is more, to a pregnant girl? But that's the way it is. I, a black constable, am regarded as lower than a white convict.

Your name? asked Sergeant Cronje in the charge-office.

Kaaitjie Müller.

Did you work for Miesies Bosman?

Yes, Meneer.

Constable, he shouted, lock her up!

The constable took her to a cell, giving her an empty bucket and a bucket of water to take in with her.

This empty bucket is for your slops, he said, showing her with a finger to go in. He locked the barred door, leaving the outer door open.

After a while he returned with a convict carrying two blankets. He unlocked the cell door and threw in the blankets. Later the convict brought a tin plate with pap without salt and pushed it underneath the bars of the door as if it were meant for a dog.

Then the policeman locked the outer door too and everything became dark and still. In the charge-office the sergeant ordered the detective-sergeant to go and tell Mevrou Bosman at Number four O'Kiep Street to please be in court the following morning at nine o'clock.

306

When Oom Flip stopped in Vatmaar, Sis Bet was waiting to give Tant Vonnie what she thought was good news.

Thank you, Bet, Tant Vonnie said. We'll see what happens.

The doors of their house were all wide open and she said to Suzan: That's funny. I don't trust that coloured. When he does his rounds again here in Vatmaar, I'll stop him and ask him what he's done to Kaaitjie.

It was a very sad night for Tant Vonnie and Suzan. They did not have supper because without Kaaitjie they had no appetite.

In her cell Kaaitjie didn't cry because she could not understand why she had been locked up. Ag, she said to herself, I haven't stolen anything. She spread out the blankets and with her tired body went to lie down on them. The ride on the motor-bike had exhausted her because she was constantly scared that she would fall out of the side-car on Kenny's child. She soon fell asleep.

She woke up early and sat up. She felt rested, not at all caged in because it was still dark and she could not see the walls. She smiled inwardly because for the first time she had dreamt of Kenny.

She dreamt that she was sitting in a very big tree, on top of a very big mountain, and at the foot of the mountain was a path that wound up, up right to the top. Kenny began walking from the bottom. He called out her name and looked very heartbroken and sick. When he reached the top, he kneeled under the tree, folded his hands in prayer and said: Kaaitjie, Kaaitjie, without having seen her and without her letting him see her.

When the sunlight began to enter the cell, she opened her eyes and remembered where she was. She thought that it was worth the trouble to sleep in a cell, just to dream of Kenny. She now had something to think about. Her happy heart soon sent her back to sleep.

The rattling of the keys and the two doors opening, broke through her sleep. A cold wind cut through the open door. First she had to throw out the slop bucket, or as it was called, the shit-bucket. And after she had carried out the blankets, she had to throw the water in the other bucket on the cement floor and sweep it out.

It was six o'clock. Until eight o'clock she had to sit and wait in a passage with an icy draught. Then she was taken to the court building. She was asked to plead guilty or not guilty. She said she doesn't know. The magistrate said: We will record it as not guilty.

Then the prosecutor asked her. Did you work for Mevrou Bosman of four O'Kiep Street?

Yes, Meneer.

From where she sat Mevrou Bosman gave Kaaitjie a you-stole-my-husband look, a look that only a jealous wife can give, and sat there as if she had a share in the proceedings, in that this-is-our-inheritance manner.

Did you leave the job without Mevrou Bosman's permission?

Yes, Meneer.

Then the magistrate asked her: Married?

No, Meneer.

When she had stepped into the dock he could see that she was pregnant. He said that the minimum sentence was a month's hard labour, but taking her condition into account, sentenced her to fourteen days and a further fourteen days suspended for three years.

Take her away, the prosecutor said.

She was locked up in the court cells until she could be taken to jail. The side-car policemen, as they were called by this time, made their rounds in Vatmaar very late that day. Sergeant Kerns refused to speak to the family of a transgressor of the law, but the black constable said: She's going to court today.

The next day Tant Vonnie went to the Pan with Oom Flip. At the court they were directed to the jail where they were told that one Kaaitjie Müller had been sentenced to fourteen days hard labour without the option of a fine.

A tear came out of Tant Vonnie's eye, the one that was alive but could not see.

Fourteen days must come to an end. Let's go, Philipus, she said. Kaaitjie spent the days in prison on her feet, except Sundays. She had to wash the prisoners clothes in cold water while standing on a wet cement floor. She had to use Boersoap – animal fat and caustic soda mixed together, boiled, left to cool, then cut into pieces.

Her fourteen days came to an end on a Sunday, but she had to wait until the Monday to be discharged. After receiving her discharge papers, the door was opened for her to go out. She stood alone and lost in front of the prison gates turning her head from side to side. There was no one she knew and again she began the long walk to Vatmaar. Because the jail was located on the other side of the Pan, she had to walk a whole extra mile. Her hands were worn through and burning from the caustic soda. In a worse condition than ever, she finally reached her mother's house.

A sadness enveloped the household. Apart from a few comforting words, nobody spoke. Kaaitjie was helped to bed and she immediately fell fast asleep.

Tant Vonnie had thought that the fourteen days would only be over on the Tuesday and had asked Oom Flip to fetch her from jail.

Sis Bet was very sorry about the mistake that she had made. She apologised to Tant Vonnie. Bet, Tant Vonnie said, it's not your fault, don't take it to heart like that.

No medicine or home remedy could give Kaaitjie her strength back. She paid the price for one or other past misdeed – in this life or in one or other past life.

An unbearable physical pain now took over from the torture of hope and longing. And on the seventh day the pains of a new life began. In the early hours of the morning, Nurse-sister Gous, the midwife, was called.

Suzan had nearly finished making the baby's clothes. She was sewing by hand and she made small stitches because she wanted to do it well and was so excited.

Kaaitjie was weak and worn out, with blue rings under her eyes.

Along with the labour pains she began to bleed. The child was born bloodied and with the caul, a boy with a strong voice.

Sis Bet cut the navel cord. Tant Vonnie and the midwife did what they could to stop the bleeding, but in vain.

A loss of blood tapped Kaaitjie's last strength. Nurse-sister Gous said it was a haemorrhage. Sis Bet tried some of the old Griqua remedies which she could still remember.

In Vatmaar there was no doctor or priest. Tant Vonnie did what people do when nothing else helps – she went down on her knees, her elbows in the blood on the bed. I beg You, Father, she cried.

The blood-flow grew less and less.

Suzan began to cry because she could not understand or believe what she saw. She cried out of fear for so much blood and out of ignorance at what these oumas were doing to her sister. When she could bear it no longer, she went outside. All that she could get out was: Please, Lord … Over and over.

My child, my child, are you going to leave us? Tant Vonnie whispered in the room. When her child breathed out her last weak breath, she went to stand outside underneath the thorn tree. Her eyes were open, but she saw nothing, and out of tiredness she felt nothing. With her shoulders pressed up against the rough trunk, time was making way for eternity.

Only when she felt the setting sun cooling the air, the skin of her body aroused her senses to the reality that was around her, and that she was part of.

I must go in, she heard herself say.

It could have been an hour or four, she didn't know, but when she came back into the room everything was clean. The bucket and the blankets had been buried together with the afterbirth and Kaaitjie had been laid out on the sofa. The death bed stood outside, washed down.

Tant Vonnie threw one arm around Sis Bet and the other around Nurse-sister Gous and cried as she had never cried before. It was the first and last time that Suzan saw her mother cry.

I'm not crying over that which only God can do – give life, take life. I'm crying out of gratitude. I say thank you, Lord, for these two friends – and Tant Vonnie held onto them until Suzan came in with three cups of coffee.

While drinking their coffee, Nurse-sister Gous said to Suzan: Between life and death there is only time. Time belongs to no one and yet it is all we can say is really ours.

I'll take good care of our child, Nurse-sister, Suzan replied.

That night there was a vigil, and the whole of Vatmaar was once again one big family. A long, long day lay behind them. Kaaitjie was buried the next day and Vatmaar grieved in its genuine humbleness for the young mother, over her innocence and over the cruelty of death. The three old women, all three people with feelings but with different feelings, were the only ones who knew how to help bring people into the world. Vatmaar knew they had tried. But who can work against God? it was said.

Nailed to her coffin with four tacks was a sheet of drawing paper on which was written:

KATRINA
22 YEARS OLD

She was buried next to the Peg-grave. Suzan regularly brought water to the grave and it wasn't long before the Star-of-Bethlehem began to bloom over both graves making them one – a bit of life above the dead, no matter which way the wind blew.

It was the only time in her existence on earth that she had been called Katrina, her baptismal name. But in the years that followed it was Katrina who lived on. It was only Kaaitjie who had died.

Oom Chai's brother, Oupa Steven

Oupa Steven was a short man among tall people, a man who did not know what it meant to walk slowly. His voice was high-pitched yet manly. He had a full head of coarse red hair and an unruly red beard on his chin – the kind, as he himself said, which doesn't know when to stop growing. He still had all his teeth, even though they were golden yellow from chewing tobacco. His eyes were those of the small desert people, some of whose blood flowed through his veins. And it seemed as if he thought with his eyes. Those closest to him were at once afraid and fond of him. Others also found out quite soon that he was no ordinary man.

His friends and the dominee called him Stefaans, his war comrades called him Our Faan with pride or one of us with affection whenever they, real Burgers, met again and shook hands. Because after risking their lives for their beloved land which was taken from them by the strongest army at the time, they were not honoured with medals but with comradeship.

After the Three Year War, Oupa Steven was awarded Burger plot Number 193, registered in the name of Steven Petrus Terreblanche – a man amongst men, who fought a war on biltong and without socks.

After the Peace of Vereeniging the comradeship and the slogan remained: If you don't have, we share what we have. An outsider could never understand the brotherhood that existed between those on the Burger plots. There was no defiling by word or deed. The ground was worked, the well dug and every Friday morning the servants saw to it that the dung floor received its new layer of cow dung. Sunday was the Lord's day and everyone went to church. The dominee and the schoolteacher were respected and knew they also had to show respect.

In their simplicity these people knew what was right and what was wrong.

As a Boer War fighter, Oupa Steven was one of our heroes. But the heroes were not honoured with medals as the British soldiers were and the traitors who had helped them, who had won the war by burning down the Boers' mothers' farms and by putting their unprotected mothers, women, sisters and children in barbed wire jails. Just to break the morale and fighting spirit of their men.

The young Boer boys had no military training. But they were well mannered and had a deep respect for their elders and betters – even though they addressed their fellow fighters as Neef. Very few had ever seen the inside of a church.

The schoolmaster was friendly with Oupa Steven because he was one of the few who could read and write. And of the few who could read and write, Oupa Steven was the only one who had never seen the inside of a school. He learnt to count with stones in a calabash, which were exactly the same number as the sheep in his oom's kraal. We were never told the oom's name but it was apparently in the front in the old family Bible.

For every sheep that ran into the kraal, the oom would always call out a number and hand to Steven, his shepherd, a pebble from the calabash, who in turn had to put it into another calabash. If there were one or two stones left over after the sheep had been counted, the sheep were chased out and counted all over again. For every new-born lamb a stone was added to the calabash, and if a sheep was slaughtered or had died, a stone would be removed.

When the young Steven took the sheep out to graze, he took the calabash and stones along with him as they were his only playthings. He would make them into little heaps and like this he learnt to divide and multiply. This he could do long before he learnt or knew what the numbers looked like on a page. His pinkie he called One and so on up to his thumb which he called Thumb-for-five. Six was Thumb-plus-pinkie-of-the-second-hand, and so on.

He said the most wonderful thing of all was when he discovered that nothing is a nought, which he could make with his thumb and forefinger, and that ten had the same nought at the end.

In the church services he learnt to read the Bible by memorising the piece that had been read out and then trying to find the words in the Bible. No one ever taught him the alphabet and he could write words without being able to spell them. His slate was the bare ground and his forefinger was his writing implement. They spoke about him as one who knew the Bible and a reader of High Dutch in the days when it was only hoped that there would one day be an Afrikaans Bible.

Oom Steven was a concertina player and most of the time he played whatever came into his head. People who knew the tunes said that he almost never started a tune at the beginning. It was either at the end or in the middle. Actually he knew only the vastrap and everything he played he turned into a vastrap.

In the Three Year War for Freedom Oom Steven was apparently asked by the mother of one of the fighters to take a parcel to her son, because the next day it was his birthday. When he tracked down the commando and gave Pieter van der Merwe his parcel, he was so well received that he felt like one of them. After that he made about five or six such deliveries to the fighters in the veld, he couldn't remember exactly.

Two days later, approaching the same farm house from where he had fetched the parcel – because he wanted to give the mother news from the war front – all he saw were the burnt walls and an empty kraal. He had heard before that the Tommies burn down farm houses but he never believed it. Now he saw it with his own eyes.

He looked around and under the bed found a half-burnt wagon kist. It was full of bedsheets and clean clothes. Oom Steven and his black helper loaded the kist, and a box of Boer medicines which he had also scratched out, onto his two-horse cart and turned around to go and tell Pieter van der Merwe what they had seen and to ask him what he should do with his family's possessions which had not burnt out. From the horse tracks he could see that Pieter's mother had been taken away by the Tommies.

When he reached the Boer fighters, he found out that Pieter had been killed together with some of his comrades. So, instead, he told the veldkornet what he had seen. Veldkornet Jansen believed Oom Steven, because the proof was right there on his two-horse cart. He shook Oom Steven's hand and asked him not to breathe a word to the others. Because, said the veldkornet: I don't know how they'll take it.

Oom Steven took a spade and said to his helper: Come, we must help our people dig graves.

After they had placed the dead in their graves, he said the words that he used to hear the dominee say at funerals. After all the dead had been laid to rest the veldkornet just shook Oom Steven's hand, without saying a word, because it was a sombre occasion.

Years after Vereeniging the same Veldkornet Jansen said about Oom Steven: He made himself part of the struggle.

He remained with the commando. The sheets he tore up to use as bandages, and when the medicine in the box was all used up, he used honey, wild kopiefa leaves and other herbs for wounds. Later he said that he didn't know much about herbs. The most important was to remove a bullet from a wound. Afterwards he usually used paraffin and fresh, warm milk to clean the wound.

Oom Steven claimed to have a guaranteed cure for a headache: a tea-spoon of aloe juice – they called it a dirty stomach.

In the wagon kist was also a needle and cotton, as if it had been specially put in there. Whenever a soldier's trousers or anything else was torn, they would come and borrow the needle and cotton from him.

After many incidents and things, they said: Our Faan has become our Boer doctor.

Years later when England declared war against Germany, Oom Steven and the other Burgers of the Burger plots said: Not us. No more and no less.

That was the man Oom Chai had gone to in order to hand over their family Bible – his oldest brother.

Oom Chai returns with a wife and child

To cut a long story short: Oom Chai came back to Vatmaar with a pretty girl, Bettie, and an eighteen-month-old baby boy. Bettie was short but not stout. She had the body of a young girl, which she was too. She had a girl's voice, black hair and brown eyes, and a face full of fine freckles.

Later we heard that the child's father was one of Oom Steven's sons, a married man with children. Bettie was an orphan and she had worked for the wife in the kitchen.

We never learnt what had happened and how. Oom Chai had apparently just picked up the child and immediately the baby took to him, something which had never happened to him before. Because he did not have an heir, Oom Chai's family knew he was a well-off old bachelor from Vatmaar. They got together to discuss this unpleasantness that had befallen the family, and after they had talked a hole in his head, he agreed to take Bettie and the baby boy back to Vatmaar with him.

When they told Bettie the old boy is well-off and that he wants to take her with him and be a father to the baby boy, she said: Okay, but he must marry me first.

And she did not want to get married in church but with a special licence in the magistrate's court, so that she could show the people of Vatmaar the papers which says that she is the old man's lawful wife. Because she did not want to be a whore girl a second time.

And so they were married by a magistrate and she got her marriage certificate, which she had framed before they returned to Vatmaar.

When Oom Steven wished his brother good luck and everything of the best on his wedding day, he said: Brother, now your wings have been clipped.

Oom Chai returned with more parcels than he left with. After dropping the pensioners, Oom Flip had to go back to the station to pick him up. The news spread like a veld fire. Most of the old women made a bee-line for Oom Chai's house to greet him and to welcome him home.

When the cart stopped they called out: We're glad you're back, Old Chai! and: Why did you stay away so long?

He took the hands of the women and said: I can feel I'm at home.
When Bettie handed the child to Oom Chai from the cart, one
ouma asked her: And where is your husband, my child?

Another one said: Vatmaar's young men don't go for girls with
children. I hope her husband comes to fetch her soon.

Bettie opened her trunk, took out the framed marriage licence
and showed it to the onlookers. They all looked at the frame and
saw nothing strange because none of them could read. Some
asked: And what is this then?

This is my marriage certificate, do you hear! she said.

Then one pension ouma said to another: I've heard of such a
paper.

And this with a ready-made child, said Oom Houtstok.

Everybody was stunned – until Ouma Drieka shouted: He's
gone and married a child, the dirty swine!

They all turned around and walked away. That was one of the
biggest disappointments at Vatmaar, and as one old lady turned off
the path to go to her house, she said: And what's more, on our pension day!

The others walked on as if they hadn't heard her.

The stokvel

Tommy Lewis bought a gramophone and records with a picture
of a white dog on the covers. It was called His Master's Voice.
Vatmaar could not believe its ears when it saw this little black
record turning around and around and music coming out. And,
what's more, music which we had never heard before. The ma-
jority of us, oumas, oupas and children, could not remain seated
when this jazz music was playing. Each one did his own steps and
the big buttocks shook like jelly. The next day everyone was
whistling or humming the tune.

Then some or other fellow with a feel for music made a guitar
out of one of those long, thin tins. Oom Flip brought the strings

for him from the Pan. This fellow spent most of the day playing his self-made instrument, fixing it and tuning it.

Before people would sit in a circle, keeping the rhythm by clapping their hands while a couple sang and danced in the middle. But when Tommy Lewis got hold of a few records with concertina and vastrap dances it was wonderful to see how it changed Vatmaar's music world. Every boy and girl was going around singing "The white trousers don't sit properly" and the girls were singing "Mama, I want a man" from the bottom of their hearts.

All felt free to dance. Each one made his own steps and never tired of it, because it was not exercise or work, it was a novelty that had come to stay. Each one's unique movements came from the heart and the feeling, making the dancer feel good and everyone else happy. Most of the time the dancing only stopped at daybreak because nobody could get themselves to break away from such pleasures earlier.

Some parents would come and fetch their children, saying: Tomorrow you have to do this or that and it's late. Or: It's Sunday.

The dance was called the mabok and from that it turned into a party called the stokvel.

Before long Sis Bet began hiring musicians. It was that tin guitar, whose master had since learnt exactly how to tickle the thing, which made the sounds that Vatmaar wanted to hear. There was also always a drum and a regulation mouth organ – a boy who blew on a comb covered with tracing-paper. The drum was a piece of raw hide pulled tight over a three-legged pot. The instruments were very primitive, but they made a pleasant noise, especially when it was a vastrap. The drum's skin often lasted for only one stokvel.

One of the reasons for the stokvel was to sell Sis Bet's khadie. This is a Griqua drink made from honey and the mor root, which only she knew where to find. She would never say too much about the mor, because, she said, it would damage her business. The khadie cost a tickey for a jam tinful. It was enough for three people, who paid a penny each. But there were of course those who would buy a whole tickey's worth to drink alone.

Khadie is a very light, sweet drink but with a kick which made sure a greedy person made the mistake only once.

If at a stokvel things were moving too fast for the oupas and they wanted something which they knew the words to, they would shout: Give us Nearer my God to Thee with a quick tempo. Make it a vastrap!

Then they would stamp it out, about four or five times, until someone shouts out the name of one of the latest tunes: "Daar kom die wa" (Here comes the wagon) or "Jan Pierewiet" or "Ou ryperd, ons ry die pad tesame" (Old steed, we ride this road together). And in the small hours, when the moon was giving its final peep, they would sing the song "There is just one for me, there is just one for me, there is just one for me, and she breaks my heart so ..." with a one-two-and-three, one-two-and-three step. Some with the hand on the heart where he believes he is holding his love. Then one by one they would disappear with lazy kneecaps and an empty stomach crying out. Until the last few people said: We must go and sleep, tomorrow is Sunday, a day of rest.

This continued throughout summer and a few Saturdays into autumn. Then Settie September's brother came to visit his sister. She was all he had left after the death of their parents. He was a member of the Cape Coons.

Boitjie Afrika makes his appearance

Boitjie Afrika was a bachelor who lived with his mother and his brother Percy, his sister-in-law Frieda and her two children. His mother died and he could not get along with Frieda. It seemed to him that it was his brother who wanted her to drive him out of the house. Percy could just not get used to his happy-go-lucky way of life. He could never be bothered about tomorrow, because his mother's pension was always there.

Percy and Frieda belonged to the Apostolic Faith Mission and they used to say Boitjie had the devil in his heart. And they used to pray, sometimes loud so that Boitjie could hear, and ask God to get Boitjie to leave home because they knew He hears their prayers. Then Boitjie remembered he had a sister in a place called Vatmaar, near Du Toitspan. He didn't know the address and there was also nobody else who knew. So one pay-day, he packed his belongings into a suitcase, walked to the station and bought a single ticket to Du Toitspan – without telling his Cape Town family where he was going, because he had decided never to return.

In the suitcase he had packed his "something" – a parcel for when he needed courage – and a bottle of sherry for the road. On Du Toitspan station he was told to ask the driver of the Cape cart to take him to Vatmaar.

Boitjie was very pleased to learn that the driver knew his sister Settie and her husband Johnny September. I know them well! Stoffel Jones said, picking up the reins with a chuckle.

His sister was over the moon when she saw him again because when she and her first and much older husband Keppie, left the Boland, Boitjie was still at school. She married Johnny, as she always said, out of his mother's house. Keppie was well known in Du Toitspan and he had a good job. It was to him that Johnny always went to say what a big mistake he had made. And Settie always let him know how much she still loved her Keppie. As soon as Johnny began to talk about these things, Oom Keppie would take out his purse, give Johnny half a crown and say: Johnny, you saved my life. Here you go! Then, without another word, Oom Keppie would walk away.

Settie looked at her little brother with the thought: Who would say I used to change his nappy and clean his tail – and smiled to herself.

I'm-heppie-my-brudder took an instant liking to his brother-in-law because Johnny put his thumb into the palm of his other hand and twisted it. Boitjie knew that it meant: D'you have some tjarrie? – the sign and word for dagga because they never called it by its name.

He nodded and walked over to his suitcase and removed a piece of rolled-up brown paper as thick as a man's thumb, with the ends flattened and moistened. This was called a dagga-zol.

Johnny laughed and said: Not now, brother – because he knew he could not take Settie's brother away from her so soon. She made tea and did all the talking, and asked all the questions.

When the sun went down, Johnny said: We've got all night to talk. My brother and I are first going to take a little walk, my Set.

He kissed her. They left the house together and began talking about things which only those who smoked the weed were interested in.

When they got to what Johnny called his tree, Boitjie gave him half of the zol, saying: Share and share alike.

Johnny picked up a flat stone and said: Here's my waterpipe and look, there in the fork of the tree is a bottle of water.

I'll never leave this place, it's the heaven itself, Brother John, said Boitjie. My brother, you get the first pull, guests first.

When they had finished smoking the green tobacco called tjarrie, they began talking about things in which only the two of them were interested, things about another world because they were no longer of this world. They were zonked.

At home Settie was pleased because the two seemed to have taken to each other very well.

Boitjie Afrika was not built like his sister. The only things they had in common were their voices and their Boland way of speaking. He had coarse yellow hair with a forelock, freckles and a beard only on the chin and a moustache. His nose was not very flat and his eyes were light-brown. He was short and always busy whistling a tune, his cap lying skew on his head. When he was zonked his cap was even more skew. He walked by throwing first the one foot and then the other forward with a slight swing of the hips, and of course snapping his fingers. On one of his hands, between the thumb and index finger, he had a tattoo which looked like a mole, the sign of a smoker.

He was a sensible smoker because he never mixed the dagga – which was also known as the weed of knowledge – with wine. He was a member of the Dixie Boys Coons and he was more of a musician than a worker. It was at Sis Bet's stokvel the following Saturday that he heard what he called the unbelievable talent. But he did not listen for long because he bought a jam tinful for himself alone, and tried a second tinful. This one he only managed halfway and then went to sit against the wall in the shade. He just closed his eyes, and later he could not remember what had happened. The others left him just there where he had passed out for being so greedy. After that he had more respect for Vatmaar's khadie – because people believed it belonged to Vatmaar and not to Sis Bet.

The new Oom Chai grows old and Boitjie Afrika takes over

Either Bettie or Oom Chai changed his lifestyle. He was no longer the Oom Chai we had known before he went to his brother, Oom Steven. Before he wore braces and a belt, now just a belt was enough to keep up his pants. The handlebars of his moustache were gone and people laughed at his new appearance, some first turned away, others just laughed in his face.

The story that was doing the rounds was that Bettie had cut off the handlebars. Others again, said that she had told him: If you really love your son (who he really did regard as his own and his heir) you'll cut off those two thorns.

He now came to the stokvels with his wife and sat among the young merrymakers. Before he would sit under his pepper tree and condemn everything he saw happening at the stokvel. He never liked the dancing, but now he was one of the ringleaders. Whenever they had had one or two too many, the old ladies his age would say: The blarry fool, he's randy.

The young people made a new path past Oom Chai's back door to the halfway-house. Passing his door they would slow down to see if they can't see Bettie, or to greet her or exchange a few words. After a while the bicycle-riders also used the new path and Oom Chai began planting thorns in the middle of the road to puncture their tyres.

His biggest mistake was to buy a gramophone and records, because after that the lounge was filled with young people even before sunset. They were fond of playing with Job, the little one, and sometimes they would tell Bettie that he looked just like Oom Chai – which was true because the same blood flowed in their veins.

Oom Chai wanted to be a gentleman. He always held open the door for Bettie. When the tea was brought in he would take her cup from the tray first and hand it to her. But what she could not stand was that whenever she was sitting on a chair and there were young men around, he would pull down the hem of her dress as if he did not want them to see her knees. When he left the room the boys would then show her with their eyes that she should pull up the hem again.

Not before long, Oom Chai could no longer take the late nights. Because his body was once and for all an old body, and he wanted to dance every dance with his wife. He didn't like the boys dancing with her. All Oom Chai could manage was a sort of shuffle.

It was then that Boitjie Afrika took over the dancing. He taught the people the waltz and the foxtrot and to show them how, he liked to use Bettie as his dance partner.

Oom Chai didn't like this Kapenaar at all and he told Bettie this regularly. All she always said was: You're jealous, my old man.

The other young men also did not like Boitjie. They weren't smokers and they said: He's trying to be the main Boitjie around here.

We could never discover whether Boitjie put her up to making the old man dance every time he put on a fast record, so that she

323

could dance him into a faint. Because after that he could dance with her. They said Boitjie also gave her jalap to put in Oom Chai's food, saying that it would make him younger. But this of course only made his stomach run and made him run to the outhouse when the dancing was at its liveliest.

After a while Bettie got used to Boitjie. Maybe they even fell in love. They were in any case the same age and both were full of a zest for life and she began to prefer his company to Oom Chai's. Because Boitjie treated her like an ordinary person and she liked this better than Oom Chai's gentlemanly ways which she thought were unnecessary. As an orphan she also knew no better. And as it usually goes with women, she preferred an entertaining man – one without hands – to a quiet, hardworking one – a man with hands, as the old ladies said.

Quite soon none of Oom Chai's friends came around to visit any more, because, they said, they felt unwelcome. The only time they were together was on pension day when they went to the Pan together, but then Bettie was there too because Oom Chai had said to her: I don't trust that round-headed animal.

The oumas and oupas knew why he took her with him.

And as it is with old people, especially when they're together in a group, they sometimes said things without thinking. I say, Old Chai, someone would begin, you really do look after that wife of yours, don't you?

And with a wink to the others, he would add: And your child.

But can he still do the job? another would ask.

Ask his wife!

Bettie always just laughed as she thought: What a big mess have I put myself in! These pension days were for her a nightmare. She would begin to miss Boitjie because with him she didn't feel out of place because he always had something to say which made life bearable.

By now Oom Chai believed that he loved Bettie and thought of little Job as his own. While lying awake at night with all sorts of

324

body pains, he would think: Now I know where I've gone wrong. I should've adapted Bettie to my old style of living. I shouldn't have tried to live like a young man of her age.

He tried to change things, but it was too late. She had already found someone who was suited to her ways. So the first thing Oom Chai did when he was next alone at home was to take the gramophone, hold it above his head and let it fall to the floor, shattered into pieces. This made him feel better because in that thing lay all his dislike and hatred.

There was no more music making and dancing in his house. He liked it this way because this was how it had been before. But it was not enough.

The biggest problem in my life is that Kapenaar, he heard himself say one day when Boitjie simply walked in, sat down on a chair and had Bettie bring him a cup of tea on a tray. This was too much for the old man. He tried to twist his moustache as if the points were still there, and shouted: Out, you swine!

After this Bettie could not go anywhere without Oom Chai. She felt like a hen in a cage in her own house. But she did not have long to wait. The old body which wanted to be like a young body, finally paid its price. One morning, as it happens with oupas married to young girls, he did not wake up.

Mr May brought the coffin from Du Toitspan. He was also the one who registered the death in the Birth and Death Register Book which Oom Chai had always looked after.

After the doctor had signed the death certificate, he handed the O.H.M.S. book to Mr Tommy Lewis, saying to the onlookers: You are my witnesses. And just before leaving: The pleasure of healthy old men is that of old men nevertheless. Too much of a good thing stops the heart.

Nobody understood what he meant because these strange words went in one ear and out the other. But they understood Ouma Drieka when she said: He died on the nest.

Oom Chai had a big funeral. The whole of Vatmaar took off work and many other people came from Du Toitspan. It was the first funeral in Vatmaar with motor-cars in the procession behind Old Swing and the trolley with the coffin and Oom Flip on it, now himself an old man. The dominee from the big church in the Pan conducted the service.

Bettie stood there with little Job in her arms, a nothing. Every now and then she got a funny look from people who looked at the coffin and then at her.

Only Boitjie Afrika shared her grief and her loneliness with her. He took little Job from her and, kissing him, said: Don't worry, my darling.

They were the last to leave the graveside. Throughout all of it she had not shed a single tear. Now the tears begin to flow. She puts her head on Johnny's shoulder. He says: Cry it all out, my cheri. She lifts her head. He takes out his hanky and wipes away her tears, as gently as he can. Then she gave him a smile, her first Vatmaar-smile, the one that says it all. It sinks all the way into the marrow of his bones, his first taste of true love. They walked away with the words of Sis Bet ringing in their ears: Alone you are born and alone you die.

Bettie could no longer sleep in her and Oom Chai's bed. It was Boitjie who first went to lie in it and said: Bettie, my flower, come and lie here with me. Your loss is my gain.

She did not hear his words, but she jumped into the bed. Laughing, she became again the Bettie of the Free State.

Boitjie knew what Oom Chai had left Bettie. He went to the kraal often and every day he counted the livestock and in the name of Mevrou Terreblanche, as he now called her in front of other people, ordered the herder what to do. The framed marriage certificate he hung above the front door so that all could see it. And Bettie, who had no relations in Vatmaar and who was herself still a growing woman, became attached to Boitjie as if he had been sent from heaven.

After the first stokvel of the month, this Boitjie Afrika took her home and moved in with her permanently. She now carried his child and the old ladies said: He's landed with his backside in the butter.

An answer to the riddle

Kenneth Kleinhans lay motionless in hospital now that the pain had subsided, because he was more often under chloroform than without it. For three days his mother and father took it in turns to keep vigil at his bedside in the hospital in Graaff-Reinet. His thoughts and memories were only of that last moment before he had slipped off the dome.

His parents were Roman Catholic and he had been brought up with this religion. His mother told him that the priest, Father Lucas, had already given him the last rites and testament. Because we believed you were never going to make it, she said, holding his hand and crying.

If only she knew about the deep love of her only child for a girl who is different to them, Kenny thought to himself. And then: What does it matter? I know my poor mother would never understand.

Then the Apostolic pastor, a friend of the family, also came regularly to pray that Kenny would be healed. Now that Kenny had regained all his senses, the pastor boasted that it was he who had asked God to spare him and his prayers that had been answered.

Thank you, Pastor Vincent, Kenny said.

His eyes closed, Kenny thought: If you, all of you, knew what pain there is in my heart since regaining consciousness. The pain in the bottom part of my body I can withstand, but not this new longing in my heart. God, God, my God, please take care of my Kaaitjie. These people will not understand, my Lord.

He looked at the pastor as if seeing him but also not seeing him. If only he had known that death would be my best medicine, he thought. Now I am back in the world with all its pain and hatred. And his kind is pleased to have me among them!

Kaaitjie, my Kaaitjie, was all that kept swirling about in his head, day in, day out, until he could take it no more. It was then that he wrote the letters, but he received no replies. He asked the pastor to bring him the telephone book with Du Toitspan's numbers the next time he visited.

When, after weeks which felt like months, he felt strong enough to walk on crutches, he immediately struggled his way to the telephone. Mevrou Bosman answered. Oh, my nursemaid, she said, she left her job just like that, and after I'd been so good to her. That's the thanks you get from these people. But I've got a new maid now. If you'd like to come and visit her you have my permission.

She giggled and put the phone down.

That made the young man livid, but in a way it also helped him because now he had only one thing in his head: I must get better so that I can go to her. To lie here and worry is not going to help me one bit.

He began exercising his legs and it wasn't long before he could go to his parents' home. Immediately he phoned his boss and said he's ready to come back to work.

Kenneth, Mr Burns said, take some extra time. I'll come to fetch you in three weeks' time.

His mother had already begun to invite girls to come and visit her son. He is eligible and he can give a wife everything she needs, she told them. Some were teachers and others were nurses at the local hospital. He knew them all but had no affection for any of them nor did he enjoy their company.

After just over a week he phoned Mr Burns again. Come and fetch me, he said, or I'll take the Sunday night train.

Two days later Mr Burns pulled up at Number 18 Solomons Street. Mevrou Kleinhans was the first to see him. Please come inside, Mister Burns, she said when she opened the door for him.

He asked how it was going with Kenneth. Oh, it will still be a month or two before he can get out of the house again.

Mr Burns was sitting on a chair when Kenneth walked in with his suitcase and said: Ma, I'm saying goodbye. I'll ask Mister Burns to go around to the school so I can say goodbye to Dad too.

Before she could say anything, Mr Burns shook her hand. Next time I'll stay longer, he said and walked out behind Kenny.

With the suitcase on the back seat and him in front, Kenny sighed deeply saying: At least now I've got that weight off me.

He directed Mr Burns to the school. As he climbed slowly out of the car, right in front of his father's office, he said: My father and I live miles apart. He's always telling everyone what to do. But I love him because he's my father.

Kenny walked up to the door and, noticing his new walk, Mr Burns thought: I also love him like a father.

Meneer Michael Kleinhans knew his son better than the young man knew himself. He was not surprised when his son walked in and said: Dad, I'm off.

When he embraced his son, he said: I thank God that he has given you back to us. Standing back he said: Kenny, I want to ask you only one favour.

Yes, Dad, I'll do whatever you ask, if I'm able to.

Don't do any work in which you have to get onto some high place.

Good, Dad, I'll remember that.

Again he embraced his father. As he walked out the door his father put his hand on his shoulder and said: Look after yourself, my son.

Kenny smiled: I will, Dad.

Pa Kleinhans walked outside with him. Mr Burns got out of the car, shook his hand, and said of his own accord, I'll see that Kenny does no more climbing, Mister Kleinhans. I'm just so thankful that he's overcome his predicament. I'm delighted to have him back.

Pa Kleinhans thought to himself: Mister Burns, my son thinks more of you than of me. I would have preferred him to stay with us a little longer. It seems to me you're controlling his mind.

He didn't know that Mr Burns was the last person who controlled his son's mind, because he, a school principal, did not know about his son's deep love for a girl who had never seen the inside of a school.

Mr Burns started the car and Pa Kleinhans waved to them. When they turned into the main road Mr Burns smiled at Kenny.

Thank God that's over and that it went so smoothly, Kenny said.

They rode on in silence. Andrew Burns kept his eyes and attention on the road. He was a thickset man with a paunch and a bald head. The clump of hair that remained above his ears was going grey. His face was red and clean shaven, with jowls that hung over his collar. He always wore a tie, summer or winter. He was fond of whisky and proud to be a Scot, and everybody knew he came from Glasgow, because after a couple of tots of whisky he always broke into: I belong to geed ol' Glasgow toon.

Kenneth, Mr Burns said, I have the boarding house key in my satchel. I told the housekeeper I'm taking the key and if there are any of your things missing, I'll take it off the money you owe her. Please check and let me know. Also, your insurance has paid the hospital bills and you will be fully compensated for the time you were off work and the injury received.

Kenneth did not answer because all he had in his head was: Kaaitjie, I'm coming.

Did you hear what I was saying or are you asleep?

No, Sir, he said, I heard every word.

Well, if you want to sleep I'll leave you alone.

Mr Burns left Kenny to rest and he fell asleep. When they eventually pulled up at the La-Buona boarding house Mr Burns put his hand on Kenny's knee, saying: Here we are, my boy.

La Signora, as everyone called her, saw the car stopping. She looked and looked again. Oh, it's them, she thought. I was just planning to pack his things away because I wasn't sure if they were going to pay me. Oh! she said out loud. Now I remember, his boss, Mister Burns, took the key.

Mr Burns came in with Kenny. He unlocked Kenny's door and said: Just check if everything's there.

No, no, La Signora said, waving her forefinger at Mr Burns's nose. Nobody go inside. You have key. See window is close like you leave it.

Then she turned to Kenny and said: God was very good to you, I hear. First I clean. Room is nice. Ledia! she called in the same breath.

Kenny walked Mr Burns back to the car. I feel tired, he said.

See you tomorrow, it's Monday, a workday.

Both laughed because they understood each other.

You eat? La Signora came to ask at his door later after knocking lightly.

No thank you, I'm not hungry.

He went to lie on the bed. Kaaitjie, Kaaitjie, Kaaitjie ... It felt to him as if it was the only word and feeling he had ever known. I'll stick just this week out and see that the dome is finished by Saturday. Sunday I shall open my arms to you and say: Here I am!

His breath became heavy and quick. Kaaitjie, I love you, he said, swinging his head from side to side. That is how he fell asleep. He dreamt that there was a ten-foot high whitewashed wall with pieces of glass on top around the Bosmans' backyard in place of the wire fence. And a ten-foot high corrugated iron gate in place of the old wire gate. He knocked on the gate. When nothing happened, he picked up a stone and knocked on the iron. But no sound came out. Then he screamed, but he could not hear himself – and in the early hours of the morning he woke up from his own fist blows against his chest. Lying on his bed fully clothed.

This is the first dream I've ever had in which I'm so close to my Kaaitjie, he thought, and when he thought about the dream, he

331

said to himself: The high walls show that she is safe. I'll stick out just this week.

On Monday morning Mr Burns sat in his car waiting for Kenneth outside the La Buona boarding house. On the way from Graaff-Reinet they did not talk about the work that still had to be done on the Masonic Temple. But Mr Burns, who was the building contractor, had had a sleepless night because the work was behind. The consecration of the temple had been planned for the Easter weekend and the Grand Master had already been invited from the United Kingdom for the occasion. The only solution was to take Kenny into his confidence and tell him the truth.

Good morning, Kenny said as he walked out of the boarding house. Why are you waiting for me, Mister Burns? I'm used to walking to work.

Andrew Burns smiled, leaned across and opened the door for him. Morning, Kenny.

When they pulled up at the half-completed temple, Kenny wanted to get out, but Mr Burns put a hand on his knee and said: Wait, it's still early, there's nobody at work yet. Kenny, he said, I'm putting my cards on the table. Please listen to me and tell me what you think after I have spoken. As you know, the general foreman handed in his resignation the week that you had your accident.

Where is he working now, Mister Burns? Kenny asked.

At the public works department. As you know, these blokes get the best jobs because they are white, and think nothing of dropping their fellow white employer. I am through with that kind, Kenny. Two weeks ago the architect, old Tim MacDonald, died. Now it is only you and me that have to finish the job.

How much time do we have, Mister Burns?

Just over four weeks. I'll give you free rein.

Thank you, Mister Burns.

It was already ten minutes past starting time and they're all walking as if they're on their way to church.

Who's the timekeeper?

There he comes, he has the keys to the office and the store room, Mr Burns replied, about to get out of the car.

No, Mister Burns, stay here. I want you to call them all together and tell them what you've just told me.

What did I tell you?

About the free rein.

All, right, Mr Burns said, getting out. Samuel, he called.

The timekeeper ran up to him. Good morning, my crown, he said, doffing his cap.

Get all the men together at the office straightaway!

Samuel did as he was told and Mr Burns said: All of you, from this moment, Meneer Kleinhans is the general foreman, and as G.F. he will take my place if I'm not here. Did you all hear?

Ja, Baas! everyone shouted.

Okay, Kenny, they're all yours.

Give me the time-sheet, Kenny said.

Samuel went to unlock the office and fetched the previous week's time-sheet.

Who is in charge? he asked.

Me, Meneer Kenny, an old man said.

Your name?

Koos Blou, Meneer Kenny.

Every morning you will come and tell me what work is finished and what has to be done next. You will also beforehand give me a list of material that's needed, understand?

Yes, Meneer Kenny.

Kenny took the card and marked off the names of all those present. Anybody else? he asked. Well, all those who are not here are fired. You men have now wasted half an hour of the boss's time. It will be worked in tomorrow, understand?

Yes, Meneer Kenny, they all said.

Then he said to the timekeeper: See that you are here before starting time.

Then he went to inspect the office. The place was a mess. Where is the tea-boy? he asked. Let him come and clean here immediately.

Kenny's toolbox had been broken open and almost cleaned out by thieves. He went back to Mr Burns who had climbed back in his car.

Mister Burns, before you go, let us take a walk around the building and check on everything.

After they had checked, he said: We'll start on top, with the dome. You start where you want to start. I'm off to the shop first.

Mr Burns could see that the walking had exhausted Kenny. Sit if you feel tired, my boy, he said. Please don't push the body too hard.

Mr Burns came back with a piccanin carrying a riempie stool. Kenny! he called. Oh, there you are.

He said to the piccanin: Wherever the Baas goes, there you go.

It had been a punishing day for Kenny and that night he slept like a log. But when he woke up he again thought: Kaaitjie, my Kaaitjie, I'll see you on Sunday.

Kenny had the lightning conductor installed. The work on the dome was finished. The painters still had a few days' work left on the outside.

Now it can rain, Kenny told Mr Burns, because everyone will now be working inside.

That morning he called the timekeeper. Tell the men we'll be working a full day on Saturday and from today an hour extra. And come and tell me who doesn't like it.

When Kenny was not listening an old man in the team said: This work will never get done. I wonder if this cripple-arse knows it. Phew!

They've given him the dirty work to do, Oom Samuel said. The others ran away. And as soon as it's all going smoothly again, they'll kick his backside and put a white man in his place, you know how it goes.

334

On Saturday afternoon Mr Burns said to Kenny: Tomorrow I want to show you some plans for a new hotel that is to be built in Durban on the shoreline. It is a ten-storey building, using the new type of construction called reinforced concrete. I'm getting the tender ready.

No, no, Mister Burns, Kenny said throwing his hands into the air. Tomorrow, I have to … I have to go to my fiancée, my Kaaitjie. As far as I'm concerned everything can go to hell, even the Masonic Temple, but I have to go and see her. His eyes were glowing. Mr Burns had never seen Kenny like this before.

You said Kaaitjie, working for the Bosmans?

Yes, Mister Burns, my Kaaitjie.

Then I'll pick you up at about eight, Kenny, and take you to your Kaaitjie. By the way, where does she actually live?

In Vatmaar, Mister Burns.

Our best workmen come from that place.

When Kenny woke up that Saturday morning he felt as if he hadn't slept at all. But he wasn't tired, and after a shave and a shower he felt a new strength in him.

Kaaitjie, Kaaitjie, he said looking at his watch and seeing that it was five to eight. The time is drawing near when I will hold you in my arms. Your people will be my people. Kaaitjie, my love, our love is God's love.

Then he heard Mr Burns's hooter, grabbed the box of fruit and suurklontjie sweets that he had bought, slammed the door shut behind him and ran limping to the car.

Good morning, he called, out of breath.

Good day, my boy, Mr Burns said, switched on the engine and said: They say it's over the railway crossing, then over another one, and then we'll see the place.

I've never been there myself yet, Mister Burns.

Mr Burns thought to himself: You are madly in love, yet you don't know where she lives. Love in its purity can make a man a lunatic!

There it is! said Mr Burns when they rode over the second crossing. I'll turn in here.

They stopped alongside a child carrying a bottle of milk and Kenny asked: Son, do you know where Kaaitjie lives?

She is no more, Oom, but her mother, Tant Vonnie, lives in the last house – and he pointed to a house on the edge of the settlement.

Mr Burns could not fully understand what the boy had said, but he knew he meant the last house. Kenny was deep in thought because he could not understand the words: She is no more.

When Andrew Burns stopped, Kenny climbed out with the paper bag.

I'll pick you up after six, he said.

Suzan heard something droning and went out and saw a big, expensive motor-car pull off. Then she saw Kenny. Ouboet, she said, running closer. Ouboet, my Ouboet.

She flung her arms around his waist and began to cry bitterly. Where were you? she asked between the sobs. If you were here we would still have had Kaaitjie with us.

Kenny still did not understand. Where is Kaaitjie? he asked. Where is Kaaitjie?

He couldn't move because Suzan was holding him tight and she was a strong girl.

Tant Vonnie stood motionless in the doorway thinking: I've heard enough. Come inside, you two, she said.

But Suzan could not let him go or stop crying. Then Tant Vonnie walked over to them, loosened Suzan's arms and again invited him in.

Kenneth walked into Kaaitjie's mother's house with a crying Suzan holding on to his hand.

Sit, Tant Vonnie said, pushing a chair closer. Without a word she went to sit on the farthest chair, but stood up again and fetched Suzan a damp facecloth to wipe her face. Then she went to fetch the baby in the room next door and handed him to Suzan.

Kenny watched the young girl feeding the baby, looked at the old woman and thought: You two don't look like mothers who have just had a child. He felt something like the power of a magnet drawing him towards the child.

When she could no longer keep it in, Suzan began to tell Kenny about the birth of his son and the death of Kaaitjie. Her mother just sat and listened because it was the first time that she had seen this young man, the father of her grandchild and the cause of her daughter's death.

She could not understand why he had disappeared when Kaaitjie had needed him so much. Or was he simply the victim of unforeseen circumstances that befall the innocents? As if he had known her for a long time, he had begun to call her Mama from the moment he heard Suzan calling her this. Ever since he had come this morning in that big car with the well-dressed man behind the steering wheel who said: I'll pick you up at six o'clock, she had been watching him closely. I am Kenny Kleinhans, he said to her when she loosened Suzan from him. His clothes looked expensive. And she, Vonnie, could not get a word to pass her lips. He's got a funny walk, almost like the late Oom Chai ...

All these thoughts were going through Tant Vonnie's head where she sat in the farthest corner of the room.

Then suddenly the cup of Kenny's grief ran over. He pressed his hands against his ears, as hard as he could because he could take no more. His feelings took over and his body showed it. Openly and without shame he began to cry, fell onto his knees and touched Tant Vonnie's bare feet (because she did not wear sandals in the house) and said: God needs her more than we do. Angels are not meant to grow old in this dirt-smeared world of ours.

Then in his pain he stopped crying and with his handkerchief he wiped his tears off the feet of his beloved mother-in-law. He stood up and without a word made his way on his own to the cemetery. Without again looking at the child.

He saw the grave which the Star-of-Bethlehem had not yet completely covered up. He felt Kaaitjie and saw her slate and its little pencil stuck into the grave to show the head of the grave. These had been her only worldly possessions. He went to sit beside the slate, his eyes open but without seeing, his ears quiet. In and around him was peace. He felt so close to yet so far from that which had always been his.

Mr Burns arrived just before sunset. Kenny was not back yet. Tant Vonnie invited him in and asked Suzan to bring three cups of tea on a tray. She then told him that she was the grandmother of the child of the man he had brought that morning.

Mr Burns stood up and said: Excuse me, Madam, I am Andrew Burns.

Tant Vonnie stood up too and said: Yvonne Müller.

And then she told him about her daughter's death while giving birth and that it was the first time that she had met Kenny. My daughter, she said, and a tear trickled out of the eye which was alive but could not see, my daughter died from a broken heart, Mister Burns.

Without words they stood looking at each other. I'll leave Kenny to you, Yvonne, he said after a pause, and in the same breath: Call me Andrew.

After a few mouthfuls of tea, looking at Suzan, he said: It's a miracle that Kenny can walk, moreover that he did not fall to his death. His hip was broken and his pelvis fractured.

Suzan got up and took the empty cup from him and Tant Vonnie said: Tell, me how it happened, Andrew.

And he told them how, early on that ill-fated day, even before starting time, Kenny had come to see him in the hotel where he boarded. He asked to take the day off because he had something urgent to attend to. It was a cloudy day and they were expecting rain. So he asked Kenny if he couldn't go and fit the lightning conductor temporarily because the dome is the highest point in Du Toitspan. Kenny did so. When the copper band was in place he climbed down again. He must have slipped but nobody saw him fall. They found him lying on his side without moving, breathing very weakly. Mr Burns was ready to leave for his farm on the other side of Graaff-Reinet and luckily he decided to look in at the building to see if everything was in order.

When he pulled up someone called him to come and see, and there he saw Kenny, unconscious. He took him to the hospital immediately. Doctor Robert checked him and immediately sent him to the hospital in Kimberley where they took X-rays and put his leg in splints right up to his hip. But Kenny was still unconscious.

We then made Kenny comfortable in the back seat of my car. Doctor Robert gave him a strong dose of painkiller and without thinking I drove and did not stop until I reached the general hospital in Graaff-Reinet where we knew his mother worked.

Yvonne, Mr Burns said, God is great. Who should I see first when I stopped at the hospital? Kenny's mother who is a nursing sister coming off duty. He only regained consciousness three days later.

Suzan, who could not speak English, could understand what he was saying. Mama, she said, now I know what happened. Mama, Ouboet did not run away.

She started crying all over again, and went to lie down on her bed where she cried herself to sleep.

You keep him here with you, Yvonne, and let me know when I must come and fetch him. Tell one of the Vatmaar men working at the Masonic Temple to tell me.

He said goodbye and drove off, and decided that he would give Kenny a week to get over his grief. Then they could still finish the work in time.

That was Sunday night. The Monday morning Tant Vonnie said to Suzan: Leave him alone. By her voice Suzan could sense that she should not disagree. Tuesday morning at sunrise Tant Vonnie took a mug of water to where Kenny still sat by the grave. Without a word she put it down. That night mother and daughter went down on their knees and asked God to make Kenny understand that only He could do it – give life and take it away.

They went to bed without having eaten because their hearts were full of the things that cannot be changed and that must be accepted. They both slept with one hand on an ear and an arm around the other's waist.

The baby slept quietly on a pillow on two chairs facing each other.

Wednesday morning at daybreak Kenny walked into the house. Mother and daughter were up already and busy making coffee. They had not slept well. When he came in Tant Vonnie gave him her hand saying: Welcome to the family, my child.

He looked into her face and saw a teardrop on her cheek and kissing that cheek he said: Thank you, Mama.

Suzan, not used to a brother or a man in the house, had no words, neither in her head nor in her mouth. Kenny said that he had to go back to the Pan because his work on the Masonic Temple was not finished yet.

Oh no, Tant Vonnie said, not today. Today our son is going to spend the day with his new-found family.

It was a quiet day. Not much was said but the air was full of emotions of acceptance and being together that came from their hearts. Kenny kept feeling if the baby was not wet and kept patting his little chin. Little Heinrich, little Heinrich, is all that he could say. He did not know that this was the child's grandfather's name.

When Kenny got ready the next morning to go with Oom Flip to the Pan, he was a changed person. The people of Vatmaar came to the trolley to offer their condolences. Some shook his hand as if they would never leave it again. Others were happy just to touch him.

Kaaitjie's husband has come, they all said together.

Stay with us and become one of us, an oldish man said.

First the midwife, Nurse-sister Gous, and then Sis Bet took both his hands in both of theirs. Your loss is my loss, my child, Sis Bet said in tears, and again remembered the morning the police took Kaaitjie away in the side-car.

The feeling of belonging amongst these humble people drew Kenneth like a magnet. He stood on the trolley and cried openly when one of his own workers said: Meneer Kenny, I feel it with you.

The whole of Vatmaar stood around the trolley and looked into Kenny's eyes, because tears were streaming down his cheeks. Then they began to clap their hands together to express their compassion to him. As they clapped their hands their eyes made contact – invisible rays that flowed in a feeling of oneness. They clapped with a slow tempo without saying or singing a word. Suddenly, as if they had rehearsed this before, the clapping stopped. Old Swing knew it was time to pull off and everyone went their own way.

Kenny knew that he had been accepted into this poor, unrefined family of Vatmaar.

Clinic Katrina

On Saturday Kenny was brought back in the big motor car. He took out his suitcase and a building plan. After drinking a cup of tea and washing himself in a basin of water, he unrolled the plan and called Tant Vonnie.

What we need in Vatmaar, he said, is a clinic. I want Mama to get all the old ones together and tell them what I've got in mind.

No, my Son. For such a thing you have to get the whole of Vatmaar together. We believe Vatmaar belongs to all of us, by which I don't mean we don't respect our elders.

What does Mama think is the best way to start?

Let me see, she said thinking with a finger on her temple. Oh yes, tomorrow is Sunday and these days the church is full, now that we have that coloured teacher conducting the service. His name's Frans Kiewiet. As the name tells you, he's of Griqua origin, a straightforward young man who's very obliging. He's got all the

341

church papers which Boitjie Afrika gave him after going through Oom Chai's kist.

Good, Mama, Kenny said, then we'll go to church tomorrow and sommer ask him to baptise our baby.

Now you've spoken, my Son. (Tant Vonnie never called Kenny by his name, always: my Son.)

Sunday morning, just after the church-train whistle, Kenny with his new-found family stood waiting for the schoolteacher on the path leading to the church yard – as the erf was called.

Frans Kiewiet stopped, got off his bicycle and shook hands with Tant Vonnie and Suzan in greeting.

This is our schoolmaster, Frans Kiewiet, and this is my son, Kenneth Kleinhans, Tant Vonnie said.

The two shook hands and said to each other: Pleased to meet you.

Then Tant Vonnie began to talk about her grandchild's name. Good, Frans Kiewiet said, taking out his pocket-book, so the name then is Heinrich Kenneth Kleinhans. Then he opened his case and said: Oh, here it is, Tante, the Birth and Death Register Book.

This Frans Kiewiet was an ordained dominee in the mission church and a schoolteacher in the Pan. He preferred to have the teaching job, as he himself said, to look after himself.

Kenny said to him: I have a proposition, my friend. I would like to build a clinic here in Vatmaar, and I would be very grateful if you can tell the people if they could be at the church at four, or whatever whistle that is. Ask them to also let those know who are not at the service.

Don't worry, Dominee, Tant Vonnie cut in, today I want you to be my guest and have dinner with us so that the two of you can get to know each other better.

The train steamed nearer and blew its whistle. Some people began walking into the church while others still came running along.

After the service little Heinrich was baptised and the dominee told the people about the four o'clock meeting.

When they got home, Suzan changed the baby's nappy while her mother made his bottle. Suzan handed little Heinrich to his father saying: Ouboet, I have to help Mama.

The two learned young men were deep in conversation when mother, a towel draped over each arm, and daughter, with a bucket of fresh water, walked in. Suzan poured the water into two basins which stood on two chairs. Then, draping the towels over the backs of the chairs, she said: The table is laid.

At the dinner table, very little was said after grace because everyone was hungry and they were all big eaters. Kenny looked at Frans from the front and from the side. All faces usually have two sides, he thought, a good side and a side which was not so good, a bad side. But this man's eyes stayed innocent and clear, like those of a child.

It seemed as if you could look at Frans Kiewiet's tobacco-brown eyes but could not look into them. His coarse brown hair was brushed down well, and there was no beard on his cheeks because he was the kind of man who only got a beard at thirty and even then only on the chin and upper lip. Kenny judged him to be about thirty-six years old. He had a deep baritone voice even though he was a small man. But, Kenny remembered what Pa Kleinhans had once said: Great things are not measured in size.

Kenny, Frans Kiewiet began.

Here we go, Kenny thought. He's going to ask which church I belong to.

But he was wrong.

Kenny, I can always sense when people have a personal God. They are different to those who believe in a communal God.

Kenny laughed because he didn't know what to say.

Let us thank this household in the name of the Lord for this food, Frans Kiewiet said in his deep baritone voice.

Suzan threw the water out of the basins and poured in fresh water. There's the soap, she said, you'll have to share it.

Guests first, Kenny said, handing the bar of soap to Frans.

343

At four o'clock the whole of Vatmaar was at the church. Only Teacher Elsa and her brother Tommy, who were Catholic, had to be sent for and told that it was not a church occasion.

The church was too small and the dominee decided to address the people from the stoep of the church. When he introduced Kenny to them there was a murmuring of: I knew him before you. And when Kenny addressed the people as "my people" they mumbled louder: He's one of us.

Then Kenny said: People, I have loved deeply and have lost heavily.

Whenever he thought of Kaaitjie, his eyes filled with tears and he had to fight against it.

To keep the memory of my beloved alive I would like to build a clinic in memory of her. I stand before you today to ask your permission to build it. I will pin the building plan up against the church door – he held up the rolled-up plan – so that you can all see it. But I would first like to hear if there is anyone who is against the idea.

If a pin had dropped you would've heard it.

These poor, unrefined people had worn their Sunday best for the occasion. I thank you, Kenny said, without really seeing them.

The dominee, his hand held high, said in his deep voice: People of Vatmaar, receive the blessing of the Lord and go in peace. Amen.

Most said thank you and left.

After he had nailed the plan to the church door, Kenny walked back with the dominee. Frans Kiewiet pushed his bicycle along and when they walked past Elsa and Tommy Lewis, he introduced them to Kenny and said: See you again, it's getting late.

Tommy invited Kenny home for a cup of tea – after Elsa had tugged at his sleeve and indicated this with her eyes. Kenny found them very interesting and only left their place after dark.

Watching him disappear down the path, Elsa turned to her brother and said: That is the man for me. A man with a white man's job and who has standing here in Vatmaar. Think of it, Tommy, just imagine how happy Father would have been to give me away in marriage to a coloured man like that!

The Masonic Temple was finished three days before the consecration and the ground around it was cleaned up. A rose garden and lawn were planted. Mr Burns was in a jovial mood because he was himself a Freemason. Every time he walked past Kenny he would give his shoulder a squeeze and say: We've done it!

The next day he came to work looking very cheerful and with a new set of plans under his arm. Kenny, he said, come into this office.

He unrolled the plans on his desk and said: My boy, our tender has been successful. Here it is. Three police houses and a residence for the Standard Bank manager. I'll take you to the sites and ask the Du Toitspan Council to tell the works inspector to show you the pegs. Then you can shift our office and store room to the new site. And what we don't need you take to Vatmaar. Yes, I did say Vatmaar, Mr Burns said, and whatever else you need for the clinic, you just ask.

Who told Mr Burns about the clinic? Kenny gazed at his boss with a distant look in his eyes. Mister Burns, he said, the clinic will be built in memory of my Kaaitjie and it will come only from me. From the bottom of my heart I thank you but I must ask you to please understand.

So we'll keep the option open, Kenny? he said.

The material we don't need we can give to the workers from Vatmaar, do you agree, Mister Burns?

Yes, but they'll have to cart it away themselves.

Fair enough, Kenny said.

Kenny had the plan for the clinic approved by the Du Toitspan Town Council. He had the building pegged out and hired the men who had been laid off until Burns was ready to hire them again for the police houses. Oom Flip carted the material. At first he would not be paid because, he said, I am also a Vatmaar man.

But Kenny said: Oom Flip, either I pay you what I have to pay you or I get somebody else. Oom Flip could always donate some of the money to the church if you so wish.

Within a month the clinic was completed. The outside walls were of red face-brick, with a pitched roof. On two sides of the building there was a verandah, each with a garden bench on it. The inside walls had white tiles as in a proper clinic. There was a linen cupboard and a medicine cupboard both of which could lock, three chairs and a bed.

But what about someone who could be in charge of the clinic? This problem gave Kenny a sleepless night, but riding to work the next morning, it occurred to him to ask Mr Burns.

He cycled to work, from Vatmaar to Du Toitspan, because, he said, it's good exercise. And then he could give his boarding house money to Suzan. Right at the beginning Tant Vonnie said to him: I get a pension, Suzan is the one who looks after you and your child. And if you're not satisfied with something, you have to talk to her about it, not to me.

That very night he wrote Mr Burns a letter because Andrew Burns was an elected council member of Du Toitspan. He requested the following:

1. For a building inspector to approve the building as a clinic;
2. That the experienced local midwife be put in charge of the clinic as she can supervise, nurse minor ailments, and see to the cleaning of the place;
3. That a qualified nurse visit the clinic once or twice a week, as her work allows – if it suits the respected Town Council, she could be from the Du Toitspan hospital.
4. That a public telephone be installed next to the clinic – the nurse in charge must see to it that the kiosk is clean and that people are called to the telephone.

He concluded the letter with: Sir, I humbly beseech you to consider my application – and signed it: *Kenneth Kleinhans.*

The next morning he immediately handed the letter to Mr Burns who promised to present it to the next council meeting, which always took place on the first Tuesday of the month.

For Kenny there was still a long wait, but the riding to work and back helped – it gave him a good appetite and a good sleep.

Then, on the Wednesday after the meeting, Mr Burns said to Kenny in one of his pleasant moods (which you will get only from a fat-necked, greedy Scot): It went through just like that! – clapping his hands together. Only the telephone is a problem. The Council has to get in touch with the post office, but the one chap said they'll only need poles from the railway crossing. The Council will write you a letter after the building has been approved as a clinic, and then we can get the nurse on the Du Toitspan payroll.

Kenny took his boss's hand and looked him in the eye and said: Thank you, Sir.

I like him, Mr Burns thought, his face turning to its reddest ever.

Our soccer team

One Sunday afternoon Boitjie Afrika knocked on the door which was closed because of the strong wind. Suzan opened up.

Arfernoon, Miss, he said to her. He had a lot of respect for her because she would have nothing to do with him and kept his kind at a distance. He was what the Boers called a Capey and he was proud to be from the Boland, as he called his place of origin. When he first came he used to say that the people of Vatmaar were blind sheep and he put his hand in front of his face to show what he meant.

May I speak wit' der Meneer, please?

Certainly, come inside, Suzan said, and offered him a chair and went to call her Ouboet.

Kenny came in with the baby in his arms. Boitjie stood up, held out his hand and said: Boitjie Afrika.

Pleased to meet you, I am Kenneth Kleinhans.

I don' wanna waste Meneer's time.

Good, Kenny said, let's hear what's on your mind.

It's der football club. I started a soccer team. Der boys are very excited an' I'm sure we can put a good team onto der field. Der t'ing is der parents dey t'ink I'm keeping deir chirren from deir work but I always tell deir chirren to firs' finish deir work at home before dey come practise.

It's a good thing, said Kenny, but first try to get the parents onto your side.

Broer, der man who inherited Ta Vuurmaak's goats, has given us two goats for der stokvel. An' Sis Bet said she'll make der roosterkoek and der khadie if we jis get der money for all der ingredients. I got a lis' here.

He took a piece of paper from his pocket and handed it to Kenny. It's for donations to buy der ingredients, Meneer.

Kenny saw that there were only pennies and tickeys on the list. Altogether there were six shillings and six pennies.

How much did Sis Bet say it would cost?

She said two pound and two pound will make five pound but I must'n tell der people det.

Smiling, Kenny counted out one pound thirteen and six from his wallet. Good, he said, now you've got two pounds. I hope the stokvel's a success.

Yes, Meneer. I'm putting up posters all over. I'm running it der Cape way, you know. I hope Meneer won' mind' if I also put up one at der clinic.

Kenny laughed and gave a nod. He knew the Cape-boys well, as their English employers called them. But this man was trying to do something good for Vatmaar, he thought, and wasn't there both good and bad in all of us?

What are you going to do with the stokvel money? he asked.

Meneer, firs' der boys need football boots. If dey want to practise firs' dey have to fetch dem from me an' afterwards dey have to bring it back again. You see, Meneer, I have to control them jus' so a little. Some find der boots too heavy an' dey firs't have to get used to it. Most play barefoot but I can't let a team play wit'out boots.

Again Kenny just smiled.

And den dere's still der socks an' der jerseys dat have to be bought, Meneer. I t'ought maybe we mus' jus' play wit' long-sleeve vests because it will be der quickest way to get everyt'ing in order. An' I've also written to der Du Toitspan soccer club to register Vatmaar B. Dey wrote back inviting me as coach an' manager of der Vatmaar Sunbeam Soccer Club to attend a meeting dere on thirty October.

That's good news, Boitjie, said Kenneth.

But, good Lord, Meneer, I've gorn an' stuck my head in a bee's nest wit' dis problem of a football groun'. Der udder players will also have to come play on our groun's an' all we have is a bare piece of groun' dat isn' even as big as a normal soccer groun'. I'm goin' to have to do someting about it an' ask God to help us. But firs' der stokvel.

I'll tell you what I'll do, if you're happy with it of course. I'll write a letter to the Town Council, but then you have to rewrite it and sign it because it has to be in your handwriting.

I'll be more than happy, Boitjie said, standing up as if by standing the letter would carry more weight.

Kenny said to Suzan: Won't you please take Heinrich and fetch my satchel. Then he wrote the request for a football field for the Vatmaar Sunbeam Soccer Club asking that it be located: If possible preferably on the existing playing field. Signed – *Boitjie Afrika, Manager.*

After Boitjie had written everything very slowly, letter by letter, Kenny said to him: Now you sign it.

First Boitjie stood up and walked about, lifting his legs up as if his joy was making them itch. Then he went to sit down again and signed: *Boitjie Afrika, Manager.*

The spirit in Vatmaar had always been one of unity. Not of neighbours together but the entire community. And for every new undertaking, each and every one wanted to put his hand in his pocket, even if it was just to put a penny on the collection list, shown as a cross for a signature – as Boitjie's collection list showed.

Looking at the list, Kenny said: Bring me the correct measurements for the soccer field and the goalposts if they approve your request. I'll measure the field for you, but you have to see that the players pick up the stones and clean up the field. I'll donate the posts and a bag of lime to mark out the lines.

Boitjie stood up and said: Meneer, if I hear you right, then may God bless you. Take my hand – and he gave Kenny his hand.

He was already out the door when Kenny heard him say: Jissis, can this be true!

The Du Toitspan Town Council had difficulty in finding a suitable midwife, but on Mistress Elsa Lewis's recommendation they appointed Nurse-sister Gous.

Our Sister Gous was given the job – not because of her qualifications on paper or because she had written an exam, but because she had helped bring so many people into the world and always did her work with so much love and sacrifice. She never allowed herself to be bothered by the time, she was always ready and waiting to be called out.

The telephone poles were almost right up to the clinic and people said: Just another two weeks and Vatmaar will be connected to the Pan.

The soccer field was the first be inaugurated.

It was a proud Kenneth Kleinhans who that Saturday afternoon received the ball from Boitjie Afrika to go and place on the centre line – with the whole of Vatmaar watching from around the field. When he walked back Teacher Elsa let her handkerchief fall, something which very few people in Vatmaar carried. Kenny picked it up, shook out the dust and handed it to her.

Kenny, with his broken heart, gave it to her and said: Your handkerchief, lady. The words burned into her, she blushed. But this Elsa's desire, her deepest wish – this is the man for me – could not touch him.

The Vatmaar Sunbeams played against the Du Toitspan Wanderers' B-team and beat them one-nil. Vatmaar was never the same after that. By the time the final whistle blew the spectators were more tired that the players because most of them had been running up and down along the field together with their team and the ball. Some old timers kicked an imaginary ball every time the ball was kicked by their team.

After the match a whole lot of things were discussed, even how grand the whistle man was.

Suzan, who had also gone to watch, met Nellie Ndola in the path on her way home. She looked around quickly to see if she couldn't see Tommy Lewis. Nellie, she said, what happened? You're alone. Do you still live in the Pan?

Yes, with my ouma. Lukas has gone to the mines. And my mother is bringing up the children. Two boys. We call one Tom and the other one Lukas.

Nellie's twins were the spitting image of their mother, but they both had frizzy red hair that stood out around their heads.

Something else happened before the clinic was opened. Oom Flip donated two outhouses to the church. That Sunday after the church service Dominee Frans Kiewiet said: Congregation, please remain seated. Then he said: The congregation is very grateful to Oom Flip for the gift of two conveniences. Let us all stand up and look in gratitude to Oom Flip. We all say thank you, Oom. God bless you and Sis Bet.

The dominee had MEN and WOMEN painted on the doors, and the young people called one outhouse Oom Flip and the other Sis Bet.

Kenny went regularly with his new-found family to church because Tant Vonnie had said to him: God is God, my Son.

To that he did not have an answer.

The clinic is inaugurated

The Du Toitspan hospital wrote a letter to the town council in which they said that they could send a nurse to Vatmaar once or twice a week, on one condition: The town council had to pay for the transport, whether a Cape cart or a motor-car. Only for a bicycle or an ordinary horse and cart they did not have to pay.

The Town Council thanked the hospital-superintendent and accepted the conditions.

It was a cheerful Mr Burns who came to give Kenny the news: Here is the letter from the Town Council. The clinic will be opened, not this Saturday but the next. Get ready for the celebration, for there is a time to mourn and a time to be merry.

And so Kenny asked the dominee to put on his agenda of the service that the clinic would be declared open the following Saturday by the mayor of the Pan and his councillors, and that they would be pleased if the entire Vatmaar could attend the festivities.

Kenny gave Sis Bet money and asked her to make the best khadie she'd ever made. She said: On one condition, that the people of Vatmaar do not drink of the khadie. Let it just be for the people of the Pan.

Fair enough, said Kenny.

I expect you to stick to this promise, Sis Bet said.

The ginger-beer would be made by Nurse-sister Gous, and she had to see that she had enough four-gallon paraffin tins for the beer. Tant Vonnie was responsible for the roosterkoek and goat's milk. The money for all of this came out of Kenny's pocket. But the church donated an ox and Broer two goats – the ones which were too old to die, the people said.

The dominee arrived quite early because Kenny had told him that he doesn't have any experience in these matters. The hospital-superintendent and the matron came in the superintendent's car accompanied by a friend. The mayor and the councillors came in two motor-cars because Mr Burns had said at the council meeting: Please come, all of you, as I would not like to disappoint these people.

The councillors were shown to Vatmaar's best chairs and benches. When their watches said ten o'clock, the white elite began to whisper to each other that it was time for the proceedings to start. One councillor showed his watch to the dominee who was standing in front of the door on the verandah.

Wait, the dominee said with his hand.

Then, at about a quarter past ten, everyone heard KOOK, and then a longer K-O-O-K as the train crossed the crossing.

Ten o'clock! shouted the Vatmaar people.

The elite looked at their watches and laughed.

And only then did the dominee raise his arms and say: Peace be unto you, respected Mayor and Councillors of Du Toitspan – there was a short silence – and the beloved brethren of Vatmaar. We are gathered here for the opening of the Clinic Katrina.

Folding his hands to pray, he said: We ask, Almighty God, that Clinic Katrina be a place of healing and love.

Then he repeated everything in Afrikaans, the language of Vatmaar. He took the key out of his pocket. I now give this key to the Honourable Mayor of Du Toitspan to open Clinic Katrina.

The mayor opened the door and took off the paper covering the nameplate CLINIC KATRINA.

It was a very hot morning and everyone was thirsty. To keep the khadie and ginger-beer cool, the old ladies covered the tins with wet grain bags under the table. The roosterkoek was already on the hot coals and the meat was cut into strips and lay waiting in dishes. Some of the meat together with the liver was already in three iron pots cooking on the hot coals.

The bigshots then said they were all too familiar with ginger beer: We'd rather have some of that nice cool honey-beer.

To their grief they did not know the kick of Vatmaar's khadie when Sis Bet wanted to get someone drunk as quickly as possible. There were no goblets, only water glasses, and Sis Bet filled them to the brim.

The first to become talkative was an old fellow by the name of Oom Faan, the only Afrikaner among the bunch of English. They called him Oom Fun. Tant Vonnie tried to make herself invisible to him because she remembered him from the day of the court case, when she was with his sister, Juffrou Bonnie Pienaar, at the rectory in the Pan.

Bring that bench and come sit over here, my Hotnot, he said to an old man. Your oubaas likes a Hotnot better than a raw Englishman. So they call this honey-beer but I know it's khadie – and he drained the rest of his glass. The Kaffir makes sorghum-beer, you Hotnots khadie and we Afrikaners, who put the Zulu in his place, we make mampoer.

The old man sitting next to him kept saying: What's that? – because he was stone deaf. Every time Oom Faan said: My Hotnot, he put his hand behind his ear and said: What's that?

And that's how it went on and on.

When Oom Faan again said: My Hotnot, another glass appeared in front of him. Drink, my Oubaas, said the old man next to him on the bench.

Oom Faan gulped down half the glass and said: You know, my Hotnot …

Yes, my Baas.

God made the Hotnot to be, as the Englishman says, "my boy". Actually I don't have time for a Hotnot.

The people of Vatmaar heard what he was saying, but they didn't take any notice of him because they knew where they stood with him. They didn't call him the Boer for nothing. But it was at that moment that a man with black hair appeared from nowhere, making his way between the people up to the old man on the bench. He stood in front of the old man and, tears streaming from eyes, he shook his head without saying a word.

He's my Hotnot, Oom Faan said, taking the old man by the shoulder.

The afflicted black-haired man grabbed the oupa by the hand, pulled him up from the bench, took his own jacket off and helped the old man put it on.

All the oupa could say was: Thank you, my Baas – and he was not seen again that night.

A councillor with a red tie and a pair of very big buttocks came to stand and chat near Oom Faan. Oom Faan let rip and slapped him on the haunch and said: He's more woman than man.

Bloody Dutchman, the councillor said and walked away.

Then an old councillor with a hooked nose came to sit next to Oom Faan. Suzan gave him a glass of khadie too, and after he had swallowed it, he stepped over to the roosterkoek and goats' milk cheese. He stuffed his pockets full of roosterkoek and cheese and with roosterkoek in each hand he walked past Oom Faan, saying: I'm taking this home to my Sophia, it's a new kind of bread.

Now what does a Jew-boy know about roosterkoek and goat's milk, my Hotnot? Oom Faan asked the empty bench next to him – he never noticed that the oupa was gone.

Suzan and the other young girls had a wonderful time teasing the councillors. Some of the girls went to sit on the benches near these old councillors and the old ladies of Vatmaar began saying things like: They can't do it any more, and: Look how that old fellow's pulling his mouth.

In their drunkenness some of the old timers could not keep their hands to themselves and tried shamelessly to fondle the young girls' breasts. A councillor with a big bald head said to one of them: To be sure, my girl, take my watch, my darling ... to be sure that you are at the café corner at eight o'clock ...

The poor old fool did not even realise that the girl didn't even know where this café was he was dreaming about in his khadie stupor. She took the watch and was also not seen again that night. Kenny, who himself did not drink alcohol, did not like this spectacle. He tracked down his Mr Burns where he was chatting to the driver of the motor-car which had brought the doctor and the matron. They were the only ones who were sober. The driver said: I don't drink poison like these bigshots from the Pan. They think their behaviour makes no difference because these people are backward and don't know any better. But they don't realise the shame is on themselves and that these people never forget and may have lost their respect for them.

What he did not know was that Vatmaar would lay the blame on the khadie and not on the people.

Kenny shook this man's hand and said: Kenneth Kleinhans.

Joe Cappelli, the man said. I'm glad I didn't take any of that drink, I'm used to taking my tot *after* sunset.

The cake with the cheese is wonderful, Mr Burns said as he walked away.

Some of the councillors were lying asleep in the motor-cars. Oom Faan tipped over with his head on the hooter and the driver had to push him away. Then a woman got in to the back. She leaned over, pressed the hooter and giggled: K-O-O-K, K-O-O-K, ten o'clock! Until she too fell over.

A thickset woman with a blood-red face who was apparently born in Germany and was a nurse at the Du Toitspan hospital, walked around feeling and rubbing the tummies of all the pregnant women.

I'll see that it will be delivered, she kept saying.

Long after the inauguration of the clinic people still said, whenever they saw a pregnant woman: She is delivered.

Dominee Frans Kiewiet drinks khadie
and breaks into song

Because Dominee Frans Kiewiet came from the Pan, he was entitled to drink khadie at the inauguration of the clinic. And to the surprise of the audience, as the night dragged on, he suddenly stood up, held his hands in the air (he was still wearing his black cloak) and in his deep baritone began to sing: I only have eyes for you ...

Then he went back to sit with the man who had been keeping him company the whole time since the clinic was opened.

What a wonderful song, Mister Doolie, the man said, and again the dominee stood up, held his hands up and sang: I only have eyes for you ...

It seemed as if he knew only this one line, because every time his friend said: What lovely words, Mister Doolie, he stood up, looked at the people to make sure they were listening, and sang with hands giving a blessing: I only have eyes for you ...

Eventually Kenny walked over, and took his arm to take him to Tant Vonnie's house. But after a couple of steps the dominee turned around and sang: I only have eyes for you ... His one hand was still out of the cloak.

He had such a powerful voice that they could still hear him long after he had disappeared into the house. Kenny came back and told Cappelli what the dominee's last words were: This is a bed! And, Kenny thought to himself: In his drunkenness he had expression in his eyes for the first time.

When he woke up the following morning, Dominee Frans Kiewiet could not believe what was being said about him. And wherever he went that Sunday morning people laughed at him. There was no church service that morning. He told Kenny that he had been drinking khadie ever since he had known himself, because it's a Griqua drink. Something else must've been thrown into the khadie. Afterwards we heard that someone had in fact thrown in a couple of bottles of Lennon's witdulsies. But Vatmaar never found out who the culprit was. From that day on Frans Kiewiet's nickname was old I-hef-ownly-ice-for-you.

Now back to the festivities. The councillor with the red tie and big buttocks went to sit next to Mistress Elsa. Where she had got the lipstick from nobody knows, but she started calling him Rosie and began to smear his lips and cheeks red. He had on one of the ladies' headscarves.

Rosie does not wear a jacket, he said, took off his jacket and handed it to a man who was standing and watching the whole business with his mouth open.

The man folded the jacket absent-mindedly over his arm. You, Sir, do you have a sausage or a cut? he asked with a frown between his eyes and showed the "cut" with the side of his hand.

I wish I had a cunt, sighed the councillor. And then he said to everyone: I wish I had a cunt. Vatmaar's people didn't take any notice because, in their language, Afrikaans, the word for "side" is "kant" and they were not sure which side he was talking about.

By the time the khadie was finished most of the bigshots were in the motor-cars, some in the wrong car and fast asleep. Joe Cappelli, who had been sitting in his car while the matron napped on the back seat, was the only one laughing and feeling sorry for them. Mr Burns just kept saying to himself, over and over again: What a shame, what a shame.

Joe was waiting for the doctor and kept telling him they have to go home now. But every time there was another person the doctor had to examine. Sis Bet poured out the dregs of the khadie for him from the paraffin tin. Afterwards people just got tired of showing him their tongues.

Come and see me in a week's time, he said to them, or: You should've been in bed.

Strangely, some people believed him. Even though he was not the big doctor from the big hospital in the Pan.

The khadie dregs which Sis Bet had given him were what finally did the trick. He walked to the car, lifting his legs like a circus horse and putting them down as if he was walking on eggs. Joe Cappelli put him onto the back seat with the matron, lights out, and drove off.

Mr Burns also left with a full load, all fast asleep. Never again, he said when Kenny lifted his hand to say goodbye.

The wife of one of the dignitaries went to answer the call of nature and bolted the lavatory door on the inside. The men also went to pee and stood outside waiting. When the need became unbearable one of them knocked on the door. There was not a sound from inside. Another councillor picked up a stone and knocked on the door. Dead silence. There is nobody inside, he said.

Where is my wife? the man with the paunch wanted to know and also knocked on the door.

She fell into the hole. (It was a pit toilet that got moved every time it filled up.)

What? he said. Did you say my Connie fell into that shit hole?

He fetched a bench, stood on it and peeped through the opening above the door. Oh, there you are, my darling. Sleep, my Connie, sleep.

He went to the car where he himself fell asleep too.

The mayor, who was also jumping around in front of the closed door, stuck his hand from the top into his pants. (He had on braces.) To hell with it, he said, went to stand behind the lavatory, pulled down his braces and peed against the wall.

What a relief, he sighed. His gold mayoral chain hung behind his back. When he was finished he shook off his forefinger because this was what he was holding, having stuck it from the top of his pants through his fly, blissfully under the impression that it was his thing. Then he took his hand out of his pants and walked over to his car, without feeling or seeing the wet patches on his trousers.

Suddenly the lavatory door flew open. The councillor's wife stormed out. She fell and grazed the skin off her knees. She managed to stand up and kicked off the panties around her ankles. She went charging down on Oom Flip, grabbed him around the neck and as they both went tumbling, she said to him: How I love you, my darling.

Hey, that's my husband that! called Sis Bet who had seen what happened from the side.

But the woman only tightened her arm around Oom Flip's neck, and with the other hand she began caressing his paunch. How I love this stomach, she said over and over.

She's looking at the paunch, not the face! someone shouted. Her husband's got exactly the same stomach.

Oom Flip helped her to the car but she wouldn't get in. You get in first, my darling, she kept saying. Eventually he pushed her in next to the mayor where she fell asleep immediately. Her bloomers were clean gone.

What a spectacle! Tommy Lewis said.

Is this really happening? one oupa asked another.

I don't know. They say a man with sense gets drunk quicker than a man without sense.

What a lovely place this Fatma is, said another councillor, his face shiny with animal fat, on his way to the car. Just before he fell over.

Vatmaar's people could not laugh any more, they were past laughing, their mouths just opened and only their stomachs made a noise.

People are people, Sis Bet said. Whether he wears a gold chain or holds his balls with his hand in his pockets.

Mr Burns came back in his motor-car and told Kenny that he dropped the whole lot at the Jewish councillor's house because there was a motor gate in the side street and his wife had not come with him. Also this man was not as asleep as the others as he had eaten more than he had drunk.

He got out with his pockets full of "Fatma cake". His wife Sophia was very upset. First she asked me if the others were dead,

Mr Burns said. She was so happy to see her husband walking into the house. What a job we had getting them out of the car, Kenny! Me, Joe and the garden-boy had to carry them into the house. Sophia got very hysterical, looking at her watch and saying: What will the neighbours say? It's a quarter past one and they're all dead drunk! Where have they been? Just as well I did not go to Fatma.

Only then did Mr Burns remember the other car which was still in Fatma. Not the people who were here, Kenny, he said, but what a royal time *The Du Toitspan Chronicle* newspaper-men will have on Monday! You take my car and come to work with it. I'll take this lot still asleep in this car back to Sophia's backyard and leave them there. I'll just walk to my hotel from there.

The woman sleeping in front had in the meantime taken up the entire front seat for herself and Mr Burns had to push her aside. And then he couldn't find the key anywhere. In the end Kenny had to loosen the wires and hot-wire the car. That got it started.

On Monday morning Kenny loaded his boss's car with workers. For these people it was their first ever ride in a motor-car.

In the office Kenny and his boss had a good laugh over the sport that Du Toitspan's honoured guests had put on for Vatmaar.

I don't know why I did not partake of that honey-beer, Mr Burns said. The ginger-beer took my thirst away and I enjoyed the meal of liver and your Fatma cake. So I suppose it's because the doctor told me to lay off sweets and sugars.

He again started laughing. I think the one who stole the show was your priest. But I must say the Fatma people are like the Russians with their vodka – they do not get drunk.

Now it was Kenny's turn to laugh.

Kenny becomes a carpenter once more

On Friday, after they got paid, Mr Burns told Kenny that Mr Davidson, the previous general foreman, had come to see him the day before about his old job. He was prepared to work for less than he had earned before he left. He said that an inspector at the Public Works Department in Pretoria had been rude to him and that eventually he could not take it any more. Then one day he hit him, giving him a blue eye and almost killing him. In the end he was dismissed for fighting with a senior official.

I told him to start work on Monday. I need you as a carpenter, Kenny, said Mr Burns.

Kenny was stunned and he didn't say a word. That afternoon, riding home on his bicycle, he remembered his father's parting words. Don't climb again, my son. And then what Oom Samuel, the timekeeper had said when he, Kenny, had to take over as foreman and he made as if he hadn't heard. He's just doing the dirty work, then they'll give him a kick on his backside.

That Monday Kenny started work as a carpenter. The boss told him to wait a while. The first house was ready to have its roof put on, and the wood for the roof was already on the site.

I'll get the trusses ready on the ground, after all that's work too, Kenny decided. But I'm not getting onto that wall.

That week he got a visitor, Joe Cappelli. He brought him a Coleman's pressure lamp, a box of Coleman's pressure lamp bags and a four gallon tin of paraffin. Take this, he said to Kenny, I have no use for it. You'll need it at the clinic.

He thanked Joe (at the inauguration of the clinic he had asked Kenny to call him Joe). It's funny how everything comes right on its own, he said.

Kenny still did good work for his boss, but the trust he had had in him was gone. And Andrew Burns took little notice of Kenny. He was no longer as he had been before.

Let it be, Kenny told himself. I'm tired of him too.

Tant Vonnie is no more and the baby calls its parents

One Saturday night Tant Vonnie went to bed hale and hearty after she and Suzan and Kenny had held hands and prayed together.

Kenny, with all his learning, never realised how important something as simple as sitting with a bowed head between a mother and a daughter could be.

The following morning little Heinrich was up to his tricks and his father had a good time laughing with the boy. Suzan made some coffee.

Mama, here is your coffee, she said putting the cup on the chair next to her mother's bed.

Suzan! Kenny called, let Mama sleep, it's Sunday, a day of rest.

When the sun was high in the sky Suzan decided that she should at least go and see if her mother was awake and ask her if there is anything she could do for her.

Mama, she said and gave her shoulder a shake. When her mother did not stir at all she said: Sleep on, Mama — and walked away.

Kenny took the baby for a walk in the veld. At work he always looked forward to this because he enjoyed being alone with his child and his thoughts.

Sunday lunch was soon ready because they had not gone to church that morning. When Kenny came back, he said to Suzan: Ask Mama what's wrong.

Again Suzan went to give her mother's shoulder a shake, first gently and then more and more firmly because she was beginning to get anxious. Mama, Mama, Mama! she called. She rolled her mother over because she had been lying on her side. When her mother was lying on her back, she got a fright. Mama, Mama! she shrieked. Kenny! Mama, Kenny!

Kenny came running and told her to go and call Sis Bet and Nurse-sister Gous.

The two old women could also not wake Tant Vonnie. After trying a few remedies they just turned around. Kenny went to Oom Flip to tell him what had happened. By now the old man had become familiar with Kenny. When they got back to the house they found Sis Bet, Nurse-sister Gous and Suzan in tears.

Without greeting, Oom Flip asked: Is it so?

Both oumas nodded.

You women know what to do, he said softly and took Kenny by the hand: Bring the child.

After the two oumas had laid out the body and washed it, ready for the coffin and the grave, Kenny took his tape measure and took measurements for the coffin. He said to Oom Flip he would go and make the coffin himself at his workplace in the Pan. He arranged with Oom Flip to bring Old Swing and the trolley around to his workplace to fetch the coffin. But first he had to phone the doctor.

Tell the people, Kenny said and rode off on his bicycle, preoccupied with his thoughts – which were many. The path to the Pan gets used, no matter what happens to man, he thought.

First Kenny went to Dominee Frans Kiewiet to give him the sad news. The dominee promised to come before sunset for the vigil of the beloved sister of Vatmaar. He had actually only just got back home after the afternoon service.

Monday morning after the vigil the body lay in the coffin, ready for the funeral that afternoon. Kenny and Suzan took the baby and went to see how the gravediggers were doing.

No! No! Not here! Suzan said at the cemetery. She took a spade from one of the men and began closing the hole. Come, she said and took them to the Peg-grave.

Right next to this grave, nowhere else. Throw the topsoil onto a heap so that it can be put back on top afterwards, she ordered.

She stood still and closed her eyes a while out of respect. Then she bent down to pack new stones around the peg. Kenny could not understand why she was doing this, but he never asked her why.

That Monday the entire Vatmaar stayed off work because the memories of Tant Vonnie could not easily be forgotten.

A sadness descended over Vatmaar, and in their grief little was said. There were only thoughts of what was and what would be forgotten as time goes by.

Because among the poor there exists a certain dignity, the love for one's equally poor neighbour.

Tant Vonnie was buried next to the Peg-grave and the topsoil was put back so that the Star-of-Bethlehem flowers could grow over her too. With the help of some soccer players Kenny made a cross out of an old piece of iron which was lying there. This was the only cross in the whole of Vatmaar and the only grave with a name on it. Simply:

TANT VONNIE

14 JUNE 1929

The people said Tant Vonnie never died. She just went to bed leaving her earthly sleep and body to us. That she was now in the Love that surpasses all understanding.

At the funeral service Dominee Frans Kiewiet said: Tant Vonnie died like only those die who used their time on earth without squandering it. Her end came without a sick bed. She lived a full life. Our Tante knew her God.

After the funeral, walking back home along the path with the baby looking over Suzan's shoulder at Kenny walking behind, Heinrich said his first words: Mama, Papa – as if nothing had happened.

Before they went into the house, little Heinrich looked once more at Kenny and, smiling, said: Papa. Then, laughing, he tugged at Suzan's plait with a laugh and said: Mama. Kenny took him from her, put him on the ground and flung his arms around Suzan, who did the same without realising it.

Kenny looked into her face as if he was really seeing her for the first time. Her still, peaceful eyes made his heart beat faster. She opened her mouth and he kissed her open mouth. An electrical contact which sealed their hearts in a way that an ordinary marriage ceremony could never do. The virgin and the man stood still. Time went its way.

Up to now Suzan and Kenny had not yet cried, but when she

365

put her foot over the threshold, she broke down. She put the baby down on the sofa while the tears rolled down her cheeks.

Kenny saw her pain and put his arms around her to console her, but then he too began to cry. She put her arms around him too, her only comfort and refuge. Kenny kissed her, tasting the salt on her lips. Then she kissed him too. He held his hand behind her head, holding the kiss on his mouth. Again he put his arms around her and whispered: Suzan. He breathed in deeply and said again: Suzan.

The closer he held her the more he felt it was Kaaitjie he was holding in his arms.

Ouboet, she said, as if the word had come from her stomach.

Their heartbeat was in divine harmony. The tears of grief and sadness rolled away and became tears of joy, which later transformed into tears of love – the kind of tears which flow when a child is born. The kind of love we all long for.

The unexpected

After the funeral Kenny and Suzan continued to sleep under the same roof. The gossips wagged their tongues, but Kenny did not hear them. Suzan heard about it from Sis Bet because Sis Bet wanted to know if it was true. I was your mother's friend and now I want to be your friend, she said.

No, Sis Bet, Suzan said and took her by the hand and led her to the bedroom. This is where Ouboet sleeps, she said. Then she took her to the room where the coffins had once been stored. And this is where I sleep with little Heinrich. Satisfied? Let me make us some tea and please don't tell me what these poison tongues are saying. Kenny would not like to hear such things because he thinks the world of Vatmaar.

There will always be love and hate among the same people, Sis Bet said.

When Kenny came home from work he picked up his child and

kissed him. Then he put him down on the floor because little Heinrich could sit on his own. Then he took Suzan in his arms and they kissed and every time it was hard to pull themselves away.

The time will come for us to marry, but until that time we will go only this far, he said to her. Because he was once again in the clutches of the time which made him think: As long as I have you in my arms I am happy.

The days began to grow longer. At work it seemed as if time was standing still, but when he was with Suzan the time went by quickly. He had finished the timber work on the roof. The purlins, eaves and rafters had been planed and nailed together and the timber for the wall was ready to be erected.

Next week, Kenny told himself, I start on the woodwork for the bank manager's house, but I'm not getting onto that wall. He couldn't understand what was going on because that morning Uncle Lesley, the previous carpenter, arrived on the site and Mr Davidson, the foreman, told him to wait. After a while Uncle Lesley came over to Kenny and told him he was tired of waiting, he would rather go and work for Mr May, even if the pay was less, because then at least he'd be able to look after his family.

I'm not getting onto any wall, they can do what they like, Kenny told him.

Mr Davidson refused to replace Kenny's stolen tools and so Kenny went to tell Mr Burns about it.

How do you expect me to work without tools, Mister Burns? he wanted to know.

Burns asked for a list of the stolen tools and had them replaced. But not with a good heart. It was as if he had changed completely since Mr Davidson had come back.

But haven't you heard that Mister Burns is courting your foreman's sister? Uncle Lesley asked Kenny.

No, said Kenny, nor am I interested because it's got nothing to do with me.

Old pal, Uncle Lesley said, if it were not for you that temple would still not have been finished – and the old man got onto his bicycle and rode away.

To ride back to Vatmaar by bicycle took a while. Riding back this Saturday Kenny had a long time to think: Suzan has agreed to let me ask the dominee to announce our marriage – tomorrow after the church service.

Because then, Kenny had told her, we can sleep together.

I can't wait any longer, she had said.

And you are the only mother whom Heinrich will ever know – but then he had made the mistake of calling her Kaaitjie.

No, no, Ouboet, she had said, let us leave Kaaitjie's name on the clinic where it belongs, and let me be Suzan.

All right, he had said, but the Ouboet should become Kenny.

God, my God, he sat and thought now on his bicycle, I thank you for putting love back into my heart. Please let me accept this girl as she is, let me not try to change her. Because she is innocent and pure in word and deed. Please let me never be the cause of anything that might hurt her. She is mine and I belong to her. And may we worship You in our togetherness, my Lord.

That afternoon before sunset, he said: Suzan we have to go and hang that lamp at the clinic. I'll carry Heinrich, you can carry the satchel with the lamp bags and the *Instructions*.

They first stopped over at Nurse-sister Gous. Yes, she said, I was beginning to wonder when the two of you were coming because the people tell me there should be a little bag in the lamp and you've never given me such a thing.

Here they are, Sister, Kenny said tapping on the bag.

As they neared the clinic the midwife suddenly looked around and said: I smell smoke, a huge veld fire that the August wind is blowing this way.

It never entered her mind that it was the first building in the history of Vatmaar that was going up in flames.

At the clinic Kenny asked: How are things going here, Sister?

Very well, she said. Some people come around simply to sit on the benches and to forget about the world. Others, again, want to be the first to hear the telephone ring, so when you're in the Pan please phone us, she laughed.

It was Saturday afternoon and all of Vatmaar was at the "grouns", as they called the football field. After showing the clinic sister how to light the Coleman lamp, Kenny and Suzan took the shortest path home.

Suddenly a girl came running towards them, out of breath. Oom, Oom, we're looking for you, she called. Tant Vonnie's house has burnt down.

It can't be, said Suzan and began to run, with Kenny, the child in his arms, behind her.

As they neared the house all they could see was a smouldering ruin and smoke.

It's true! Suzan shouted running faster.

Around the burnt-out house stood only old people and children because everyone else was at the soccer. Broer was busy at the well, bringing up bucket after bucket of water to pour into any bucket, mug, tin or anything hollow to pour onto the coals. Everything was ash, only the iron frame of the bed, the bicycle and the Welcome Dover stove were still recognisable.

There's nothing left, Kenny, cried Suzan. Nothing! Nothing! Nothing, Kenny.

Still holding the child in one arm, he put his other arm around her waist. He led her to a flat stone against the wall of the outside storeroom so that she could sit down.

Not here, not here, not me again! she cried pointing at the flat stone.

He did not understand what she meant but walked on further to where Broer was.

Broer, he said, who was the first to see the fire?

Me, said Broer pointing to himself.

Tell me a little what you saw, my friend.

Broer said that he saw huge lights in the window. Then the

curtains caught fire, then the front door began to burn and fell in. Then the wind blew in through the door and windows and the flames rose up to the roof. The fire only abated after the roof had caved in.

Now all we have left are black walls, Suzan cried with her head on Kenny's shoulder. She asked Broer again what had happened, as if she could not believe her ears and eyes.

The wind came up, blowing stronger and stronger, Broer said. By the time he was near Tant Vonnie's house there were no clouds in the sky and the sun was just beginning to set. But there was lightning in the house jumping all over the place. Then it stopped and there was a big fire in the lounge. And then the whole house was one big ball of fire. Then he remembered what Ta Vuurmaak had told him about fire-spitting ghosts, one night when they were sitting around the fire. After seeing Tant Vonnie's house burn he now believed in such ghosts.

Oom Flip came to call Broer to fetch more water from the well to kill the fire.

People, bring your buckets! Sis Bet called. Because she and Oom Flip were the oldest people in Vatmaar, they could not run with the full buckets of water and at the start Broer had to take the buckets into the burning house himself. The flames were very hot then, he now told Kenny, but it was nice for him to see what the other people had not seen.

At least you still have the storeroom, said a woman as they stood looking at the ruins.

Suzan just stared at her saying: Not me again, not me again.

At that moment Boitjie Afrika came running with the whole soccer team in tow. When he saw what had happened he shook his head and walked over to Kenny and held him around his waist. His eyes shiny with tears he kissed him on the cheek saying: Jus' talk, Meneer, jus' talk, the Sunbeams are waiting on your word.

The sun had gone down, the darkness had crept nearer and a stillness descended as if a curtain had been pulled down over everything. Then suddenly there appeared a massive red ball, the colour of the blacksmith's iron at the moment it is pulled out of the fire. And just as it reached Vatmaar it rose into the sky. As it climbed into the sky this heavenly ball gave all the earthly things their own shadows, and there was light without heat. It was a full moon.

At least you still have the storeroom, someone said again.

Suzan stood one side. She did not move and just bit her lower lip because the memories that were flashing through her mind were painful. In the moonlight she looked at the stone chairs, shook her head from side to side saying to herself: Only I know. Those who also knew are no more – Ma and Pa Wingrove, Kaaitjie and Mama.

But she didn't cry again. She just kept biting on her lower lip, took the baby from Kenny and gave Kenny the satchel. Heinrich put his little arms around her and said: Mama.

Come, she said taking the path to the halfway-house. For a moment Kenny did not move, but then he began to follow his new-found love and his child. He walked behind her, not saying a word. She led the way as if she knew where she was going. But in her simplicity she had only one thought – never again to sit on those stone seats.

Some of Vatmaar followed them, walking behind them like a weaning calf follows its mother. At the halfway-house she stopped so that Kenny could piggy-back the baby and she could take the satchel from him. They turned around and held their hands high in the air. And in this way, without a word, they said goodbye.

Boitjie Afrika and his soccer team remained standing behind in the path and did not return their greeting. Before turning back towards Vatmaar, he said: I loved him more den my own brudder, even dough I'd only known him for such a short time.

That was the last time ever Vatmaar saw or heard of Kenny Kleinhans, Suzan and little Heinrich. And Vatmaar was never again the same.

Suzan's first train journey

It was Suzan's first ever train journey. Kenny spent almost all his money to buy themselves and "our child", as they called Heinrich, third-class tickets and to pay to have his tools put in the guard-van.

She had said: Take everything otherwise we'll have to come back here again.

Kenny had only one thought in his head and this thought he tried to dismiss: What will Dad and Ma say? Take us or leave us, he heard himself reply.

When the baby fell asleep, Suzan gazed out of the window not thinking about what tomorrow would bring, her hand on Kenny's knee. He was her first love, and just as he thought about her she thought about him: I want to be near you always. I have found love and I am going to hold tight on to it.

Ouboet, she said, because she had not learnt to stop saying it, remember when we went to the clinic, I lit the lantern as always so that it wouldn't be dark when we got back home? I was so proud of that lantern because it was the very first ever thing that was really mine. I had left the top door open and I didn't want to go back to close it again, do you remember? And so when the wind came up so suddenly it naturally began first to swing the lantern about from the nail and then it swung it off. The paraffin caused the fire to spread. That is what happened and that's what Broer saw. That lamp and the wind caused us to lose everything.

And here I was racking my brains trying to work out what happened, Kenny said. Thank you for solving the riddle of our accident, my All. But at least we did not lose everything, we still have each other, my All – and holding her head in both his hands he gave her a long kiss.

Beneath them the train wheels thundered over the rails. Outside a grey world passed by.

My All, he said. She looked into his eyes, thinking. Then her mother's words came to her: Your Papa always called you my

All, my All-that-is-nice, do you remember, Suzan? No, Mama, she had said, I don't remember.

Tribute

Vatmaar is a reality. The people who live in this book are all dead now because what lives is never without death, or should we rather say: without change.

So, if things were said which should not have been said, please don't wake them up. Let them rest in peace.

Thank you, Reader.

We will remember them.

Years later a doctor came, a woman doctor. This was the time of the radio. A Doctor (Miss) van der Merwe. It is she who stole the hearts of these backward, inside-out people and put their story in a school exercise book.

The end

Glossary

aia – servant
boer – farmer or white Afrikaans-speaker
bogadi – bride price
braai – barbecue
chaila – knock off from work
dagga-zol – joint (marijuana)
Kapenaar – resident of the Cape Colony
kaross – blanket made of soft skins
kaya – house
koppie – small hill
kraal – fold, enclosure for stock
mageu – a drink made of slightly fermented mealie-meal porridge
magoepelas – entrails
meneer – Mr, sir
mevrou – Mrs, madam
oom – uncle
ouma – grandmother
oupa – grandfather
pap – stiff mealie-meal porridge
pasella – free gift
riempie(s) – leather thong(s)
rooilaventel – folk medicine
roosterkoek – dough cakes baked on a grid over an open fire
skelm – rascal, villain
skollie – hoodlum, thug
sommer – just like that
stat – traditional village
stokvel – fundraising party
taal – language
tante/ tant – aunt
tjarrie – dagga, marijuana
vastrap – fox-trot

velskoen – handmade hide shoes
vetkoek – fried dough cake
vlei – wetland
voetsek – go away! (rude)
wilde-als – wormwood
witdulsies – folk medicine, drops for shock
witgat – tree with white trunk
wynruit – rue, herb of grace